THE SCARRED MAGE OF ROSEWARD

BOOK ONE: THIEF

SYLVIA MERCEDES

*This book is humbly dedicated to
The School Librarian and Grandmother Approved
Fairy Tale Ladies
with many thanks for all the inspiration.*

(Now I'm officially one of you!)

PROLOGUE

HE WOULDN'T GO MAD. NOT YET. NOT TONIGHT.

His feet heavy, his shoulders bowed, the hooded man climbed the tower's winding stair. Each step was a battle to be fought and won before he could attempt the next. A flickering candle held high created a small sphere of light around him, but darkness pressed in on all sides, ready to overcome him should it go out. Sliding his other hand along the curving stone wall to his right, he breathed in a slow, steady rhythm.

With every breath, he whispered the promise again: "Not yet. Not tonight. Not yet. Not tonight."

He'd made the same promise every night for . . . he couldn't say how long. It felt like years. Like centuries.

A grim smile twisted his lips within the deep shadow of his hood. He pressed on, taking the treads a little faster. No guardrail stood between him and the empty space down the tower's center. One false step would send him plummeting to a gruesome end. But he couldn't deny the unmistakable lure of that drop, that darkness. It was like the lure of insanity itself—a sense of inevitability waiting to be fully embraced.

"Not yet," he whispered again through grinding teeth. "Not yet."

Of course, he might be mad already and simply not realize it.

At last he reached the landing at the top of the stair and stood before the door. Open, but only a crack. He pushed it wide and passed into a circular chamber built around a central stone basin filled with slick dark oil waiting to be lit. Tall, wide windows, many with broken panes, ringed the room.

Once upon a time, this lighthouse had stood watch above the cliffs of Roseward Isle, guiding ships safely through the treacherous channel between the island and the mainland. But many years had passed since any ship dared to brave the channel and sail near these haunted shores. The basin remained unlit and cold.

A salty breeze wafted through one of the broken windowpanes. The candle he held sputtered and threatened to go out. Carefully the mage shielded its glow with his free hand and carried it to a desk against the one windowless wall on the north side of the tower. A candle nub in the bottom of a clay bowl had sunk deep into a puddle of its own wax. He pried it out and stuck the fresh candle in its place.

Books, pages, and scrolls littered the floor around the desk, stacked in baskets, tucked between the desk's legs, or lining the walls in haphazard array amid bottles of ink, quills, and trimming knives—an assortment of mage's implements. On the desk itself lay only a single book, a lovely volume worked in tooled red leather and bound with straps. Gold leaf embellished the delicate petals of a rose on its cover, and an aroma of crushed roses seemed to mingle with the musty scent of parchment.

The hooded man drew a long breath through his nostrils. His candle flickered gently, and the rose on the book cover seemed to dance and move in its light as though stirred by a breeze. His gut twisted painfully, and a weight of stone bowed his shoulders.

He pulled back the chair and took a seat. For a moment he could only sit there, his face immobile, his hands still. Working up the will to do what must be done.

Time to begin.

Like a soldier on the frontlines leaping suddenly into action, he flipped the front cover open. A cloud of rose perfume filled the atmosphere, clogging his nose and lungs. He choked, eyes watering. With a savage shake of his head, he leaned in, focusing his vision through the pink-hued miasma, concentrating on that first page, on the spell written there with painstaking precision in bold red lettering.

He began to read. His lips moved silently, forming the shapes of the words, but he dared not speak them aloud. Sweat broke out across his brow, and his heart raced by the time he reached the end of the first line of script. Methodically he kept going, refusing to skim or skip over the more dangerous, more powerful words.

By the time he reached the end of the page, a pulsing throb of energy radiated up into his face, thrumming a frequency that struck the very core of his soul. He paused to catch his breath, and the energy immediately died back. That was no good. He must maintain the spell, the entire spell. If he let it break, he would have to start over from the beginning.

His hand trembled, its fingers awkward as they gripped the badly worn corner of the page and turned it. New words, new precise lines of written magic glared up at him. These were both harsher and more confident than the first page. The spell's power grew with every line he read.

Hours or minutes or mere seconds passed. It hardly mattered. He fell into a rhythm almost like a dance. A dance of magic whirling in his soul. He gathered the energies to himself and sent them out again, and with every beat, every give and take, his heart stuttered, and he wondered if tonight would be the night his mortal body finally broke under the strain.

Shadows deepened along the edges of the room, pooling together. They gathered in a mass, crept across the floor, and crawled over the basin, trailing through the pool of oil, causing ripples where there should be stillness. They closed in on the mage at his desk and mounded together before shooting out tendrils to climb his chair, to snake up his legs and wind around his waist.

He gasped. Knifelike protrusions cut through the thick fabric of his robe, slicing into his skin. But he could not be distracted, he could not be swayed from his purpose. Grimacing, he bowed closer to the book and read on. Shadow thorns wound around his neck, crawled through his beard, his hair, and pulled at his hood until it fell back across his shoulders. The perfume of roses intensified.

She was there. Standing just at his back. Her hands gripped his shoulders, fingers digging through flesh down to the bone.

Let me visit you tonight, my love.

Her voice was sweet, poisonous. His skin prickled at her breath against his ear, at the warmth of soft rose-petal lips teasing gently at his earlobe. The sensation was almost enough to distract him from the thorns biting into his flesh.

You are lonely. I can feel it. Let me come to you. Let me care for you, satisfy you. What am I but your most perfect dream come true?

Her hands moved from his shoulders, sliding down to pull at the front laces of his shirt, parting the fabric. Her fingers reached inside, tearing his skin, lacing his body with pain. But through the pain he felt the delight she promised, and his body responded with a pulse of need that shamed him.

Quickly he focused on the spell and continued his reading. Now he gave voice to the words, speaking them aloud. The power of the spell intensified.

She uttered a ferocious hiss. The soft petal-lips gave way to biting teeth that grabbed and savaged his ear. The dangerous fingers playing across his skin tore deep into his flesh, and blood flowed, soaking through his shirt and robe, pouring in rivulets down his body to pool on the floor.

Why do you fight me? Why do you resist? Was I not created for you and your pleasure? Why do you refuse all that I can give?

He read on, his voice louder than before. With each word, the spell strengthened and her hold on him faded. The shadows retreated, dissipated, and vanished. Only a soft flutter in his ear remained, a ghostly echo.

You will understand in the end. You will be mine . . . mine . . .

His candle in its bowl burned down. When at last it guttered out, the golden light of dawn streaked through the east window and bathed his desk in its glow. By that light he read the last of the spell, the final words. The Binding.

With a tremulous sigh, he shut the book fast and sagged back in the chair. Sweat soaked his matted hair. He touched his ear, wincing, and drew back his fingers to find them red with blood. More blood soaked through his shirt and robes. Not as much as he'd believed, however. Most of the attack had been a dream. Only a dream.

But she was getting stronger. Her reach into the physical world strengthened with every passing night.

The mage rose from his seat, his legs shivering. He stripped off his outer robes and let them drop in a pile on the floor. Then he staggered to the narrow, rickety bed on the far side of the basin and collapsed across it, little caring how many bloodstains he left on its threadbare blanket. He lay for some time neither sleeping nor awake, simply existing.

Her voice whispered at the back of his mind like a wind wafting through an aromatic garden, tickling his senses: *You will be mine. Mine for eternity . . . mine . . . mine . . . mine . . .*

At last he fell into a dreamless sleep.

CHAPTER 1

THIS WAS EITHER THE BRAVEST THING SHE'D EVER DONE or the stupidest. Possibly both.

Nelle scowled as she pushed open the window. Its diamond panes swung silently outward, and only a cold night breeze blowing through her hair and whistling down the hall behind her betrayed any change in the atmosphere. Even so, she froze in place and held her breath. Every hair on her arms and neck lifted, every sense prickled with unease.

One . . . two . . . three . . . She silently counted to twenty, just as Mother had taught her. It never paid to move too quickly, especially when nerves were jumping.

Multiple doors lined the passage at her back. Behind each door lay a small dormitory bedroom, and in each room slept a young student mage, a disciple of the illustrious Miphates Order. At any moment one of them might stumble out into the moonlit hall, candle in hand, on his way to the kitchen for a late-night snack. Or, more likely, a tryst with one of the friendlier scullery maids.

She could deal with a student. She was prepared. Her lips burned with the Sweet Dreams stain she'd applied before setting out tonight. But she'd prefer to make it through the night *without* kissing some spotty-faced boy, gods help her!

Nelle finished her silent count, then let out a long steady breath. The wind tickled her face again, but the passage remained still and quiet. It was well after midnight—the distant cathedral bells had tolled twelve dolorous strokes some time ago now. If she were quick, she could be out of here before they sounded again.

Better careful than quick, she reminded herself and pushed the window a little wider. It wasn't difficult to hoist her slim figure up onto the sill. Clad in a pair of loose trousers, she swung her legs out over the drop below. Then, drawing another steadying breath, she made herself look. Down between her feet, down six stories to the shadowy ground below.

This was another of Mother's tricks impressed on Nelle from the time she was eight years old and first trailing after her mother on little . . . excursions. "Look once," Mother had said. "Only once, no more. Accept the height, accept the distance between you and a bone-shattering death. And, once you've accepted it, don't look

14

again."

Nelle looked. And she nodded slowly. Six stories should be nothing. Certainly not enough to make her head spin, except . . . well, she was out of practice.

A slight movement along the wall drew her eye, and she gratefully redirected her attention. She could just discern Sam's silhouette in the deepest shadows behind a flowering privet tree. The Miphates posted guards at night to protect their many secrets. Sam was to watch until the change of the guard, then signal to her. Any moment now . . . any moment . . .

Suddenly, there he was, standing in plain sight, the moon gleaming bright on his upturned face. He waved his left arm in a single sharp motion.

Not yet.

Nelle huddled back into the window, watching as Sam vanished into the shadows. The guards were a good several minutes behind their usual schedule. She couldn't risk climbing out onto the side of the building where she'd be totally exposed to view from below. If there were time, she would have waited for another night, a night when the moon had reduced to a thin slip, or better yet, was entirely obscured by clouds.

But there was no time. It had to be tonight, or else . . .

She closed her eyes, lifted her chin. When she opened her eyes, her gaze reached beyond the university wall and across the rooftops of Wimborne City spread below her. From this window she could see all five of the startlingly clean streets of Northon

District that surrounded the mage's tower in concentric rings. Within those rings, elegant sprawling buildings with arcades and tiled courtyards displayed sumptuous gardens and silvery fountains.

A far cry from Draggs Street. Like a different world.

Her lip twisted bitterly. She'd never attempted a snatch from Northon before. She'd ventured into Estward and climbed through the windows of the great lords' and ladies' houses, eluding jowly guard dogs and sleepy footmen, leaping from gabled rooftop to gabled rooftop, nimble as a cat. She'd once perched on the back of the oldest, ugliest gargoyle on the ridgepole of the mayor's palace, keeping watch while Mother slipped through an attic window. They'd made off that night with Mayor Quindove's finest silver cutlery. An excellent snatch.

But Northon belonged to the Miphates. Anyone who tried stealing from the Miphates must have a death wish, according to her mother.

"Sorry, Mother," Nelle whispered. "I've got to try. For Papa . . ."

She looked down into the paved yard below, searching for Sam in the shadows. To her relief, he reappeared within moments, this time waving first his left arm then his right in two broad circles. That was the signal. The guard was changing, distracted.

Time to move.

Nelle swung out of the window. As her hands found grips on its decorative stonework frame, she feared for a heart-stopping moment that she'd forgotten too much of her training. Had two

16

years of orderly civic life eroded away her hard-won skills? A tremble raced down her spine, but it vanished almost at once. Her muscles remembered. Her calloused fingers gripped stone and her bare feet found purchase. She climbed.

How many times since she'd taken this job as a scullery maid in the kitchens of the Miphates University had she eyed these fancy moldings? How many times had she caught herself visualizing the best route to the roof above, where she would place her feet, where she would best find a grip?

Each time, she'd shoved such notions aside and concentrated on scouring a burn-crusted pot, her knuckles chafed, her skin stinging with lye. She'd abandoned that life of crime. She'd gone legitimate and taken honest, back-breaking, soul-crushing work. She was making her way in the world, out of Mother's shadow, and she wasn't going back.

But old habits die hard.

Her fingers gripped the sharp edge of the gutter. With one last heave, she sprawled onto the nearly flat rooftop of the dormitory. For a moment she rested and simply breathed. Then she peered over the edge, searching for Sam in the darkness. She could just see him, not quite hidden behind the privet tree, watching her progress. She waved and saw him wave back.

Pushing loose strands of hair out of her face, she rose onto her knees, then her feet, and turned to face the next obstacle. The Evenspire loomed tall in the night.

Tradition said the mage's tower was built by the fae long ago—

before the Pledge, even before the War. Its spire was imposingly tall, rising thirty stories at least to a needle-sharp point that seemed ready to pierce the night sky above. Masons had carved the stones to fit together so perfectly, it was almost impossible to find a seam or a crack.

The Evenspire had stood on this outcropping above the ocean since time immemorial. Only in the last century had the Miphates built their square university building around its base. The tower itself, so full of magic, drew magic-users like moths to a candle, but only the most exalted members of the mage's society were permitted to ascend the spiral stair and delve into the secrets contained within those lofty chambers.

Nelle didn't give a pile of dragon scat for mages or their secrets. So long as the Miphates paid her wages, they could do what they liked with their arcane arts and their dark divinations. Only . . . after tonight, she wouldn't be able to return to the hot stinking kitchen down below. She wouldn't dare risk it. *Never return to the scene of a snatch*—the number one rule Mother had pounded into her skull since childhood.

"Bullspit," Nelle hissed. She would never forgive Cloven for this, for interfering in her life. She'd thought she was free of him and his ruffians after Mother died. But now he had Papa. And if she didn't make this snatch . . .

Nelle shook her head fiercely. No good in dwelling on such thoughts. She'd do the job, make the snatch. She would get Papa back, gods help her.

Her hand fished into her trouser pockets and pulled out ten small silvery trinkets. With practiced ease, she slipped them over the knuckles of each finger and thumb. A sharp flick of her wrists unsheathed the cat-claws, making a bright, dangerous *tsing!* in the silence. The sound set her teeth on edge.

Stepping to the base of the tower, she gazed up at her goal. The twelfth window. Cloven was sure about that. The twelfth window on the south side. Nelle shook her head. Cloven's source had better be right! If things went wrong, she would take the blame.

She clicked the ends of her claws together in unconscious anticipation. Then, placing her hands against the stone, she flexed her fingers slightly and drove the claw-tips deep. The ancient masonry seemed to shiver in response to the touch of *nilarium*—faerie silver, as it was called in these parts. The claws, of fae craft, were far more valuable than any other trinket Nelle's mother had acquired over the years. Worth a king's ransom at least. If Papa knew she still had these, he would have sold them ages ago, no doubt, and already lost the money in one of his idiotic ventures. Nelle had let him assume they'd been confiscated when the authorities arrived to collect the body after . . . after that last job. She never told him she'd managed to slip in, slide them off her mother's fingers, and scuttle away before the Green Caps arrived.

"Good thing," she muttered as she reached up, snagged a second handful of Evenspire stone, and began her climb. Without the cat-claws she could never climb this sheer expanse of white stone.

It was painstaking work. Her bare feet offered balance but no leverage—her entire weight hung from her arms. But the faerie silver held magic of some kind. Not only did the claws sink into the stone as if it were warm butter, they seemed almost to pull her along behind them. For the thousandth time she wondered how her mother had come by such miraculous treasures. But that line of thought was useless. Everything about Mother was a mystery. And now that she was dead, only her mystery, inscrutable and unsolvable, lived on.

Nelle concentrated on her goal, climbing as swiftly as she could, eager to put this job behind her. Halfway up, she was obliged to stop and simply hang for a moment, catching her breath. Did Sam watch her from below? She could almost feel his eyes following her from his hidden place in the shadows. She was half tempted to look down and search for him. Instead, she turned to one side, gazing out to the ocean.

A pinpoint of light out in the darkness caught her eye. It wasn't much. Just a little glow, like a distant yellow star fallen to the sea. But something about that light disturbed her. She knew what lay out there in the darkness, a mile off the coast of Wimborne.

Roseward. The Haunted Island.

No one lived on Roseward anymore. Everyone knew that. The palatial manor house built on its highest crest stood empty, the little villages along the coast abandoned. The lighthouse tower listed dangerously, waiting for one great storm to send it tumbling into the sea. No one was there to set a light in the tower window.

It ain't nothing, she told herself. *Just a trick of the eye, moonlight glinting off a bit of broken glass.*

If so, why did her heart respond to the sight of that distant gleam? Why did she suddenly yearn to follow that light, like a traveler smitten with a will-o-the-wisp and lured to his death? No. No, this feeling was different, more profound. She felt like . . . like a sailor after a long journey, eager to turn her vessel to safe harbor.

Nelle gave her head a little shake and refocused on her goal. No time for diversions. Her limbs trembled with cold and exhaustion by the time she finally reached the twelfth story and hauled herself onto the narrow window ledge.

Gripping the frame with the claws on her left hand, she peered through the leaded glass. As best she could tell, the dark chamber was empty. After deftly using her claws to cut through the glass, she reached in and undid the latch. The window swung outward, but she was prepared for that. Angled carefully, she sprang inside and landed in a crouch.

After the brilliant moonlight on the white stones of the Evenspire, the interior shadows seemed much darker. Her ears were alert for any sound out of place while her nose filled with the scents of parchment and ink, quills and pumice. Cloven's source had been right: The window let her directly into a quillary. As her vision adjusted, she saw the tall desk in the center of the room, nearly buckling beneath the weight of heavy grimoires.

Nelle rose slowly and steadied her breathing. Walking on the balls of her bare feet, she approached the desk with some trepidation. She may have served in the Miphates University these last two years, but scullery wenches rarely saw the mages themselves. She'd never been this close to actual magic before. A strange sense of power, tremendous power, emanated from between those silver-fastened leather covers. The air held a tempting sweetness that wasn't quite pleasant and a tantalizing vibration of sound just beyond hearing range. Her feet took one step, then another . . .

She stopped short. "Get ahold of yourself, girl." Her voice sounded like her mother's in that moment. "You've not come here for the books."

Turning away sharply, she redirected her attention toward shelves built into the curved wall of the tower, absolutely crammed with implements of a mage's craft. Bottles and boxes. Strange contraptions with weird angles and sharp edges. Jars containing floating things she didn't want to look at too closely.

But on one wall, the wall opposite the window she'd left ajar, dozens of quills of all different sizes and colors were displayed, including eagle, owl, heron, turkey, and hawk feathers. There was even a large fluffy red plume that must have come from some exotic bird.

Nelle held her breath as she leaned in closer, studying the selection before her. Unlike the grimoires, the quills emitted no sense of power or portent. They hung there in neat array, oddly tame. She didn't trust that quiet docility. Mages' quills were well known to be the most powerful source of magic in the human world. Even the fae longed to possess them, though they could never hope to wield them. And a Draggs Street girl like her? She had no business even looking at them.

Her mouth quirked at that thought as she tapped one claw-tipped finger against her lower lip, considering the options before her. Cloven had been very specific: His client wanted the black swan's quill. Color was difficult to discern in this gloom, but one feather was definitely darker than the rest. It had better be the right one.

She hesitated a moment before pocketing the cat-claws. It wouldn't do to risk tearing the quill with their sharp nilarium points. Ever so gently, she reached for the black plume. Though the muscles in her arm tensed, there was no sudden shock of magic when she lifted it from its stand. If any magical alarm had been tripped, she couldn't sense it.

Releasing a long breath, she hastily tucked the quill inside her shirt front. It tickled against her bare skin, but for all she could tell it was nothing more than a feather. Was it really worth that dangerous climb? Worth her father's life? Or her own?

Too late now, she thought. Besides, it wasn't as though Cloven had given her a choice.

She secured the ties on her shirt and turned to the window. But she hadn't taken three steps before she heard it: the creak of the door latch.

Bullspit! The quills must have had a protection ward after all, and a mighty effective one if someone was already at the door. She had less than seconds to decide: Could she spring for the window and get over the sill and down the wall before she was seen?

No. There was no time. No choice.

Nelle dove for the door itself, slipped into the shadows behind it just as it swung open, and pressed her back against the wall. Her heart raced, her blood pounded, and her throat tightened until she couldn't breathe.

Let him be alone. Whoever it is, let him be alone. If more than one man came through that door, she was in trouble. But if only one, then maybe, maybe . . .

Nelle heard the rustle of long robes dragging on the ground. She watched the candlelight's shifting glow beneath the door. Her next move must be perfectly timed. The Miphato's next step brought him far enough into the room for her to gauge his height and breadth.

She didn't wait to see what other details the candlelight might reveal.

With the silence of a panther, she sprang from her hiding place, caught the man by the shoulder, and pivoted him on his heel. In the split second that followed, she saw the whites of his eyes flash in the candlelight, saw his mouth open to cry out, "What in the—"

Then she caught him by the back of his head and pressed her lips to his. It was a violent act, hardly a kiss. Her teeth clashed against his, and she tasted blood on her tongue.

The Miphato uttered a guttural cry and dropped his candle. As the brass candleholder struck the floor, the room plunged back into darkness. A hand grasped Nelle's shoulder and shoved her brutally away. "You little vixen!"

A backhanded blow staggered her, and the grip on her shoulder hauled her back into place so that she couldn't avoid the second blow, equally hard. Pain exploded in her head. She swallowed a cry; she couldn't risk alerting others. His body was weakening. She felt it already. The fingers pinching into the bone of her shoulder trembled.

"What have you . . . what . . . You've . . . poisoned me!" The Miphato's voice slurred more with each word he uttered. He fell to his knees before her, and his hand slid from her shoulder, blindly pawing at the front of her shirt, trying to catch his balance. He pulled hard enough that a few of the front ties came undone, and the quill nearly fell free.

Nelle leapt back and smacked his hand away. He sprawled on the floor, jerked, then lay still. The Sweet Dreams had done its work.

For the space of three breaths, Nelle simply stood there and rubbed her stinging cheeks, grimacing at the pain. Then, with a growl in her throat, she gripped the man under his arms and dragged him far enough into the room that she could softly close the door.

Her lips burned. She wiped them with the back of her hand without thinking, then realized what she'd done. She'd better not

25

need to give any more kisses tonight! Without bothering to check the Miphato's pulse, she hastily retied her shirt strings, slipped the cat-claws back on her fingers, and hastened to the window. After pushing the sash back open, she climbed onto the sill.

And paused.

That gleam of light. Shining from the dark blot on the ocean that was Roseward. It seemed brighter than before.

Once again she sensed that it was shining for her.

"Bullspit," she growled, swung herself out the window into the night, and descended the Evenspire.

CHAPTER 2

HER HEART HAD NOT YET STOPPED ITS FRANTIC BEATING when she stepped through the kitchen door, shut it softly, and stood still, holding her breath and listening to make certain she hadn't been followed along the passage. No sound met her ear, yet instinct roared in the back of her head, warning her.

It wasn't a clean snatch. That Miphato lying drugged on the floor of his quillary would cause trouble. Somehow. She knew it.

Grinding a curse between her teeth, Nelle whirled and hastened on through the kitchens. The multiple chambers connected beneath heavy arched ceilings felt cavernous as she wove her way between the long preparation tables. The silence felt almost otherworldly. She was used to the bustle, shouts, clatter, and scrapes that filled each working day with raucous cacophony. Low light simmered in the pits of the great brick ovens, ready to be stoked to life in just a few hours. Otherwise, all was still as a tomb.

Her pulse throbbing furiously in her ears, Nelle skirted the last table and made for the back door. She'd descended the Evenspire as fast as a spider on silk, then waited on the rooftop for Sam to signal the all-clear below. He'd appeared shortly, waved an arm, and she'd darted back down the front of the building and through the open window in the dormitory hall below, meeting no one either coming or going.

Nelle pushed the scullery door open just far enough to peer out. From this angle she could see one long stretch of the university wall. No sign of watchmen above. She pushed the door wider and stepped out onto the stone porch.

"Welcome back, Ginger. Have fun?"

A chill spiked up Nelle's spine. "*Hsssssst!*" she gasped and pivoted on her heel to see Sam leaning casually against the wall, chewing a blade of sugar-grass. Her eyes, usually so keen in the darkness, had passed directly over him without recognition. But then, Sam was fae-gifted. Mother had always said so.

Nelle made an aggressive shushing motion with one hand and pulled the door softly shut behind her. It was the work of a moment to secure the lock with the key she'd stolen off a baker boy the previous morning. This accomplished, she turned on Sam.

"Idiot," she snarled. "You want to call the guards down on us, do you? Bullspitting boggart-brain!"

He laughed, making no effort to lower his voice as she grabbed his arm and dragged him along the back path leading from the scullery. "Relax. The last of the guards are already in their cups down at the east watchtower. I heard 'em discuss a dice match, and I've kept me eyes open this last quarter hour at least. Not a flash of moonlight on a single breastplate in sight, and those breastplates are *shiny*, let me tell you! They'd have flashed plenty if they was around to do it."

Throughout this speech Nelle made vain attempts to hush him, but she finally rolled her eyes and simply hurried. Sam was likely to get louder the more she urged him to silence. The wonder was that he'd not been caught on a snatch night long before now.

"There's no use fighting it, girl," Mother told her one night after they'd teamed up with Sam. Nelle had been certain his loud voice and devil-may-care attitude would bring all the watchmen of Wimborne down on their hiding place, yet they'd made it through the night without incident. "Sam's been fae-touched. He can feel trouble in his bones a mile off. You can trust that sense as sure as you can trust a compass at sea."

Mother had a point. Sam seemed to possess a preternatural ability to detect impending threats. He would go as silent as a cat on a winter night when need arose. But when he was convinced no threat was at hand, nothing anyone could say or do would make him shut his spitting mouth.

Mother had always liked pairing with Sam, particularly for big snatches. She told him he was good luck, ruffled his hair, and made him blush. Nelle didn't like it. If he *was* fae-touched, truly fae-touched, well . . . fae gifts were fickle things. One of these days, he would be wrong. He would fall into the trap of his own overconfidence and drag everyone close to him down as well. One of these days . . .

"Shut your prattle and spare my poor ears," Nelle snarled, which only made Sam chuckle again. He shook her hand off his arm but then immediately reached out to capture her fingers, interlacing them with his. Startled, Nelle tried to pull away, but he held on, swinging her arm companionably, as if they were a couple of children. Once upon a time, they had walked like this frequently. Once upon a time, she'd even let him steal a kiss or two—a quick peck, nothing more. Just enough to make her flush and dream and smile into her pillow at night.

That was a long time ago now. Before Mother fell.

Nelle tugged, but when Sam didn't release his hold, she growled and pulled him along faster. At the low gate that was the servants' entrance, they didn't bother fiddling with the lock. A tree stood close to the wall, and though its lowest branches were several feet over Nelle's head, it would serve well enough as a ladder.

"Need a boost?" Sam asked. Before she could respond, he yanked her arm, making her pivot toward him. His other hand slid around her waist and pulled her in so that she hit his chest hard. He grinned down at her, his eyes twinkling in the moonlight.

Nelle glared up at him. "What do you think this is, Sam?" she said, working her free hand high enough to plant against his chest. "What do you think we're doing tonight?"

His grip on her waist tightened, and he ducked his head a little lower so that a dark lock of hair fell across his forehead. "I should think that was obvious." The blade of sugar-grass dangled from one corner of his mouth, sweet-smelling in the darkness. He rolled it around to the other corner, giving her a droll smile as his gaze drifted down to her lips. "You. Me. Working together again. Just like old times."

"Is that so?" She shoved her fingers into the front of his shirt, digging her nails through the fabric into his skin.

He gasped in surprise, dropping the sugar-grass, and loosened his hold enough to let her escape his arms and back away. "Boggarts, Nelle!" He shook his head and rubbed at his crinkled shirtfront, grimacing. "What was that for?"

"We ain't friends, Sam." Nelle braced her feet, her arms loose at her sides, her fingers curled into fists. This was not the place to have this conversation. Seven gods, couldn't he at least have waited until they were over the wall? "We ain't *working together*. There ain't no *together* here."

Sam cursed. "Don't go all lofty lady at me! You know our best snatches were always as a team. It's been two years, and I ain't had a take like I used to in all that time. I've hardly so much as caught sight of you. You pretend not to see me when we pass on the street. It ain't right, Nelle. You belong to this life. You belong to—"

"I don't belong to no one." Nelle drew a long breath through her nose, forcing her voice to be steady, forcing back any trace of the tears threatening to clog her throat. "Not to you. Not to Mother. And not to your boss neither. Do you understand me, Samton Rallenford?"

Sam had the grace to look ashamed at her mention of his employer. "Come on, Nelle," he said, rubbing a hand along the back of his neck. "Cloven's not so bad. He's in a rough spot same as the rest of us, and—"

She didn't wait to hear his glib excuses. She'd had enough of Sam's glibness to last her a lifetime. She spun in place and took three running strides toward the tree. Using her own momentum, she scrambled up the limbless trunk until she reached the lowest branches, then swung up even faster. It was dark among the branches, but darkness never bothered Nelle. Her eyes seemed to absorb whatever light the moon had to offer, intensifying her vision. Maybe she was fae-blessed in her own way.

She swiftly gained the upper wall and dropped into the street on the far side. Sounds of grunting and rattling branches told her Sam was close behind, but she didn't wait for him. Let him scramble to catch up. It wasn't as if she needed an escort.

The streets of Northon were far too clean for comfort, and too broad, and too well lit. But she managed to find shadows deep enough to hide her and deftly avoided any Green Caps on patrol.

Sam caught up before she left the wealthy district behind, falling in step beside her as she plunged into the tangled streets of lower Wimborne. He seemed at least somewhat cowed after their exchange and didn't try to take her hand. Better still, he let her pick their route through back ways and alleys, far off the main roads. Anywhere the Green Caps weren't likely to be. It took her more than two hours to guide them back to their own fetid quarter of the city, down by the river.

The stench of Draggs Street rose up to hit her like a blow. Her quick pace slowed, and Sam took several strides ahead before pausing to look back. "Somethin' off, Nelle?" he asked.

She didn't answer. Her gaze fixed on the row of six houses leaning heavily against one another near the slowly eroding banks of the River Wim. A candle gleamed in the attic window of the third house from the left. Nelle swallowed hard as a shadow passed in front of that candle, momentarily blotting out the light. She knew who was pacing back and forth, his shoulders hunched, his head bent so as not to hit the low-hanging rafters.

Cloven had been specific in his demands. She was to be back by dawn or else . . .

Sam put out a hand, almost rested it on her shoulder, but thought better of it. "Don't worry," he said, his voice almost somber. "Cloven'll keep his side of the bargain. He's a man of the code."

Nelle spat bitterly. Without a word to Sam, she hastened into the alley behind the row of houses. There was no key to the back door. Why bother? No one was desperate enough to steal from the poor families crowded into these rooms. Like a rat scurrying home, she slipped inside and tried to reach the back stair undetected by her landlady. A forlorn wish.

"'Ere now, what's this slatternly wench up to?"

As though summoned from the pit, the ugly, toothless visage of Mistress Dirgin appeared at the base of the back staircase, her gums chomping on the end of a foul cigar. The smoldering light on the end of the cigar flickered in her beady little eyes. "Tryin' to sneak young men up to yer rooms? Be this 'ow ye pay yer way now, girl? A pretty face doth hide a lyin', lustin' 'eart, so me old mum always warned me!"

Nelle paused, one foot on the lowest tread, and felt Sam approach through the shadows behind her. She didn't have time for this.

"Not that it's none of your business," she growled, "but this fellow's here to see Papa. That's all."

"Oh, is he now?" Mistress Dirgin popped the cigar from her mouth and gave Sam a once-over, then a more lingering second-over that didn't quite suit a woman so deeply concerned with maidenly virtue. "Well, pretty boy, maybe yer'd be wantin' to sit a spell by the fire? It's much warmer in me kitchen than up in that drafty old garret. Besides, the wench 'ere's already got men aplenty waitin' for her upstairs. Yer'd have to wait yer turn."

Sam cleared his throat, nonplussed perhaps for the first time in his life. "Well, um, mistress, I'm much obliged for the offer . . ."

Nelle didn't wait for more. With a curse she pushed past the distracted landlady and hastened up the creaky steps as fast as she could go. She and Papa had rented the pokey attic room of this house for the past two years, ever since Mother's death. Sometimes it was hard to remember life before Draggs Street, hard to remember the snug little house they'd enjoyed together in humble but respectable Westbend. They could have afforded much better on Mother's takings, but she liked to maintain the appearance of a simple tradesman's family of comfortable means. Nothing elaborate, nothing to draw undue attention their way.

Nelle hadn't realized just how comfortable they were until it was all gone.

She reached the top of the stair and hastily pulled herself together. The next few minutes would be . . . tricky. Downstairs, she heard Sam still caught in Mistress Dirgin's clutches. He wouldn't be up anytime soon, wouldn't be at her back. Not that she could trust him to truly have her back anyway.

She put her ear to the door, listening carefully. Heavy breathing inside, shifting weight, the creak of floorboards, the rustle of fabric. Unless she missed her guess, five men were in there with Papa.

"Five," she whispered, and bit back a curse. With a little shake of her wrist, she loosened the knife tucked in its sheath up her sleeve. It was no longer than her middle finger but razor sharp. It would serve her in a pinch.

Forcing a brazen expression onto her face, she put her hand to the latch and threw the door open with a bang. "Hullo, lads!" She beamed a huge smile. "Miss me?"

Six faces whipped around, six pairs of eyes fixing on her. She took them in, one after another. Cloven stood by the window, one arm upraised, his hand gripping a rafter beam. Two of his men sat cross-legged on her own pallet bed, playing a game of dice. Another two sat on overturned boxes, one on either side of Papa, hunched like vultures.

And Papa was bound to his chair like a criminal.

He raised his bleary eyes, his face so swollen, so purple and red that she almost couldn't recognize him. He managed a gruesome grin, revealing a gap where one of his teeth had been knocked out. Nelle's heart twisted with pain. But she allowed no change to her mask-like smile, sparing her father no more than a brief glance before setting her attention solely on Cloven.

He was a huge man. Another few years and his muscle would soften to fatness, but for now he was still physically impressive. A trim goatee framed his jaw, and narrow clever eyes peered out from beneath a brow so deep that his eyebrows seemed to round a curve. He'd always been her mother's . . . friend. Whatever else he'd been, Nelle didn't like to speculate. Mother was the only person who'd ever dared laugh in Cloven's face. He had been more than a little in love with her, Nelle knew. He had always hoped that one day she would abandon Papa for him, so he let her get away with it.

But Mother wasn't here now.

"Well, if it ain't little Lady Peronelle back from the ball," Cloven said, his voice strangely high and reedy for a man his size. He released his hold on the rafter and squared his great bulk in front of her, his head hanging slightly forward to keep from hitting the ceiling. "Cutting it a bit fine, aren't we, m'lady? Another hour and . . ." He nodded her father's way and made a slicing movement across his throat.

Although a shudder raced down Nelle's spine, her mother's training held her steady. She stepped lightly into the room, still beaming that brilliant smile. "Well, la! Master Cloven," she trilled. "I was just so caught up with the dancin' and the music, I quite lost track of time!"

The hand with the hidden dagger hung casually at her side. With the other hand, she undid the top tie of her shirt . . . and regretted it immediately when Cloven's eyes fastened on that part of her anatomy. For a moment she felt her vulnerability. Mother always knew how to use her womanly attributes as weapons. She could drop men with a look, keep them slavering and hungering without ever giving more than she wished. But in her eighteen years, Nelle had not yet mastered those tricks. She had to be careful.

Her smile still firmly in place, she drew the quill from inside her shirt. It was slightly rumpled but undamaged. Holding it high, she gave it a twirl, successfully distracting Cloven's gaze from places she didn't want it going. "A feather for your cap, m'lord," she said. "Though I'm sure the milliner would recommend something with a bit more plume—"

Before she could finish, Cloven took two strides and snatched the quill from her hand. He turned it over in his fingers, looking at it with deep intensity as though trying to discern something just out of sight. "This is it?" he said doubtfully. His eyes flicked to meet hers. "You're sure?"

"The black swan's quill." Nelle nodded. "It was the only black one there, so I'd imagine—"

His hand shot out and closed around her throat before she could react. Cloven's face hovered so close that she could see every enlarged pore of his hawk-like nose with painful clarity. "My client will know the difference," he snarled. "If you've played me for a fool, girl, I'll be back to teach you a lesson." His teeth flashed large and yellow. "You may have *her* pretty face, but it won't save you."

"Now, now, m'lord," Nelle wheezed out the words through those clenching fingers. "No need to get angry. Give us a kiss, and let's be friends again."

"A kiss, eh?" His gaze dropped to her lips. When he leaned in, the stink of fish and strong liquor on his breath made her shudder, but still she refused to drop her smile, even when his fingers ever so slightly tightened their grip. "I know about your kisses, girl, and the sweet dreams they bring. You are your mother's mongrel, aren't you? But I learned long ago to put a muzzle on that bitch, and don't think I can't muzzle you just as easily. She came to like me well enough, and maybe you will—"

His voice broke off as he felt the prick of her knife jutting into his gut. A fraction more and she'd pierce something important. Blood trickled down the blade and across her hand. His grip on her neck loosened.

Nelle twinkled up at him and batted her lashes. "You never touched my mother," she said through grinning teeth.

"Nelle!"

Sam's voice broke into the room. From the edge of her eye she saw him appear in the doorway and stop dead in his tracks. "Nelle, don't be a fool!"

Was he afraid? Nelle almost laughed. She'd never heard fear in Sam's voice before, not in all the years she'd known him. But did he fear for her or for his boss? She didn't break Cloven's gaze.

Slowly Cloven drew his hand away and took a step back. She gave a last little dig with the knife before springing away, putting distance between the two of them. Her awareness exploded with the movements of the other four men, all of whom had risen and drawn toward her.

Papa, battered almost senseless, seemed to become vaguely aware of what took place in his home. "Come, Cloven," he slurred, lifting his head and rolling it onto one shoulder. "We're all old friends here!"

"Friends. Yes, friends," Cloven growled, his brow drawing into a tight knot above his glittering eyes. Nelle waited, poised. Ready for him to bark a command. She knew she couldn't take down five men. Bullspit, she'd be lucky if she managed one! Mother had taught her self-defense, but not for all-out brawls. She was supposed to be swift enough on her feet to get away instead.

And she could get away. She could see exactly where to place her knife, her foot, her elbow, her knee, all in a quick succession that would leave her with a clear path to the door. Sam stood there still, but he wouldn't stop her. He wasn't so thoroughly crushed under Cloven's thumb yet.

But she couldn't leave Papa. She couldn't.

Cloven pulled his hand away from the wound in his side and studied the blood on his fingers, tilting his hand to catch the candlelight. Nelle held her breath. He was an unpredictable man; she never could guess which way his mood would swing. These next few moments could easily be her last, or maybe . . . just maybe . . .

With a suddenness that made her start, Cloven tossed his head and bellowed a laugh, twirling the quill in his fingers. A final flourish, and he tucked it out of sight inside his vest. "Scatting dragons, girl, but you take me back!" he chortled, shaking his head. "I could almost believe I was a wet-eared youth again, trailing along in Seroline's shadow. Ah, but she was a grand one! Mixael, old boy, you must be proud. Somehow your weak water didn't dilute this fine wine."

These last words he cast over his shoulder to her father. Papa lifted his head and offered another grisly smile, as though sharing in the joke. Nelle's teeth clenched harder, her lips twisting into a grimace rather than a grin.

She maintained a defensive stance even when Cloven

motioned to his men. One by one, they filed out the door, ducking their heads under the lintel. Sam backed away to let them pass but continued to hover there. Nelle felt his gaze upon her, felt the desperation emanating from him, the silent helplessness. She wondered if she hated him for it.

Last of all, Cloven paused in the doorway and looked back. "I'll let you know if my client is satisfied, girl," he said. "If you've been good, there may be more work for you. Your old man's debt ain't paid off yet."

Bile rose in her throat. *Swallow it back,* she mentally snarled. *Don't let him see he's got to you.* But Cloven saw the look in her eye. He laughed again and left, stomping loudly down the stairs. Only Sam remained. He cast her a final look, an expression she couldn't fully read. At a bellowed command from his master, he caught the door and pulled it shut.

Nelle stood still, listening to the footsteps descend and retreat through the back door. She waited until she was certain all six men had left the house. Then she sprang across the room to her father's chair. Using her knife, she sliced through the bindings holding him in place. Immediately he slumped and fell, and she was only just in time to keep him from hitting his head on the floor.

"Papa? Papa!" she cried. He was so thin and bony these days, it wasn't difficult to roll him over. His head lolled in her lap, and tears pricked her eyes as she looked into his battered face. "Papa, what were you thinking?" she whispered, her throat suddenly

SYLVIA MERCEDES

thick. "Why'd you ever take a loan from Cloven? You should've known better!"

"Ah, my Nellie, my sweet Nellie girl." Papa lifted a trembling hand, traced the line of her cheek and jaw. "It was a good venture. Foolproof, they said! Sure to make us triple back in profit. But they needed more . . . they needed more . . ."

She didn't bother to question him. This had always been Papa's way. Some new idea would take his fancy, some investment or speculation. Mother always supported him, even egged him on. When each new venture inevitably failed, she laughed it off like it was a grand joke and went on to pay the creditors with her snatches. And Nelle had been too young, too ignorant to recognize the precariousness of their lifestyle. Not until it was much too late.

"Poor Papa," she whispered, cradling his head and choking back her tears. "Poor, stupid Papa. We've got to get you cleaned up. Cleaned up and into bed, and then . . ."

"Don't fret, sweet girl." Papa coughed. Then, his voice quavering, he tried to sing through the blood in his mouth, *"Hush-a-bye, don't you cry . . . Sleepy now, my . . . my . . ."*

His voice trailed away in an anguished groan. His head slumped against her shoulder. Nelle blinked, and tears fell fast, spattering on his bloodied cheek. She rocked him gently, just as he used to rock her when she was a child and woke up screaming from some bad dream. As she rocked him, she sang in a rough, cracking voice:

42

"Hush-a-bye, don't you cry
Sleepy now, my little love
When you wake, I'll give to you
A sparrow and a soft gray dove
A lark, a linnet, and a jay
To sing for you throughout the day."

She felt the tension leave his body as he fell asleep there on the floor. For a long while she sat holding him as the sky outside the dirty window lightened and the sun began to climb. She had to make a plan. Somehow, she had to get them out of Wimborne. Away from Cloven, away from Sam, away from the Miphates.

Away to . . . somewhere. Anywhere.

CHAPTER 3

"IT AIN'T ENOUGH, GEL." THE FERRYMAN SHOOK HIS HEAD, showing crooked yellow teeth in a sneer. "Do you know what it's worth if the toll men catch stowaways in my boat? Lot more than you've got there, I tell you."

Nelle drew a breath through her teeth. *Don't show weakness. Don't show fear.* She forced her determined grin to grow until it strained the edges of her mouth. Mother would have had a man like this eating out of her hand by now.

She wasn't Mother. She never had been. But confidence could be faked, couldn't it?

"What, sir?" she said brightly, giving her head a coquettish toss. "That's three months' wages, that is! Help a girl out, won't you? I know you ran for Rowly last winter when he had need, and he spoke highly of your work."

The ferryman looked her up and down slowly. Lingeringly. Her skin crawled, and half of her smile drooped despite her best efforts. "I think we might find a way to reach an agreement," he said and put out a hand to touch a stray coil of bright-colored hair close to her cheek. "What'cha think, gel?"

Nelle turned her head sharply, whipping the hair out of his reach. "I think you're dangerously close to losing a finger." She batted her eyelashes.

The next moment her little knife flashed and cut right along the length of his index finger. It was so sharp and swift, he didn't at first feel any pain. Then his eyes widened as blood welled, and he howled, "Why, you little—"

She was too quick for his grabbing hands. Her elbow caught him in the chin, her knee in the groin. He doubled up and fell to his knees, choking for breath.

Heavy-set figures stomped up the ramp from the ferry boat, ruddy faces scowling at her ominously, while other figures closed in on either side. Nelle raised her knife and whirled lightly in place, flashing another deadly smile. "Anyone else want a taste?" she asked. "I got plenty more where that came from!"

The men cast each other glances, then looked down at their moaning captain. *Go on, fellas,* she silently urged them, giving her knife a twirling flourish. *You don't want to join him gasping on the ground. You ain't that loyal, are you?*

The moment passed. They shrugged and stepped back. Taking the opportunity to slink away before they changed their minds, Nelle vanished into the crowds along the river quay.

"Bullspit," she cursed as she wiped her dagger on her skirts and slid it back into its hidden sheath. That was the third ferryman she'd spoken to and the third rejection. The safest way out of Wimborne was by river; the guards at the toll bridges were laxer than those at the city gates. She'd hoped she and Papa could smuggle their way out before the day's end, but if she couldn't find a ferryman willing to take the risk . . .

She put her hand in her pocket and weighed the little sack of coins tucked away inside. Half her meager savings from the last two years. It wasn't much, but she couldn't afford more. They'd need something to live on once they got out of Wimborne, something to see them safely to some new town or village.

A shadow seemed to grip her heart as she shouldered her way through the crowd. The idea of leaving was terrifying. Not once in her life had she set foot beyond the city limits. But Cloven was too dangerous. If they stayed, he'd be back with more jobs he wanted her to take. Now that she'd successfully stolen from the Evenspire—a feat previously considered impossible even among the most talented snatchers of Draggs—her reputation would spread. She'd never be able to outrun it. No, it was best if she and Papa got out. But she wasn't willing to give what the ferrymen were asking in exchange for her freedom. She wasn't that desperate. Yet.

There's always the nilarium.

The thought plucked at the back of her mind, and she grimaced. With her snatcher's satchel hanging at her hip, it was easy to imagine she heard the silvery nilarium rings clinking inside. She'd always promised herself she wouldn't sell them. To exchange such treasures for a few measly copper sprells somehow seemed dis-honoring to her mother's memory.

But that was stupid. Mother wouldn't care what price she got for her trinkets. She had only ever wanted Papa safe and provided for. She'd never cared for anything else, not really. Not even her own safety . . . or her daughter's . . .

Nelle sighed and focused her attention on a ferry docked close by. She'd try one more time before attempting to sell the claws. Maybe she could manage to—

She paused.

That face.

It had flashed past so quickly in the tail of her eye, she'd almost missed it. But something clicked in her brain and set alarm bells ringing. That face with the wart on the cheek and the pale, lazy eye under that drooping lid—one of Cloven's men.

Mother's training jumped in her veins. Nelle whirled and, without taking time to confirm what she saw, before her eyes had adjusted enough to recognize the ugly face looming just a step behind, her hand darted out, driving her fingers straight into the man's throat. He choked. His eyes bugged behind their drooping lids, and he fell hard to his knees.

Nelle planted her hand on his shoulder, leapfrogged over his back, and ran. The crowd parted before her, but that was no good. She needed the crowd. If Cloven had sent his goons after her, she needed to disappear.

When a narrow alley mouth offered itself, she ducked inside, her thin shoes slapping on the hard-packed dirt. Squirrel-like, she sprang up on a broken crate, pushed off lightly with one foot, landed atop a stack of barrels, and whipped around to catch the edge of the sloping roof above her. She could *feel* pursuit at her back, though she couldn't yet hear or see anyone. She hauled up onto the roof and, using her hands and knees, crawled to the ridgepole and over the other side, scraping skin as she slid down. There was no time to be careful; she could pick out splinters later.

Why? Why? Why? her brain screamed silently as she swung down from the roof and landed in a crouch in a dark side street. Why had Cloven sent men after her now? He could easily have killed her last night. Or, if it was more work he wanted from her, he could have leveraged the situation and forced her to comply. Had he simply changed his mind? Or had something happened with his client? Had the quill been a fake?

She reached the end of the street and skidded to a stop. The milling crowd at the fish market awaited her, but among the dirty heads of her fellow Draggs Street denizens she saw flashes of Green Caps, which never came into Draggs unless sent on a mission. She couldn't assume they'd come for her, but . . .

She recoiled into the shadows, her back to the wall, breathing hard. Cloven wouldn't put the Green Caps onto her. *Oh, wouldn't he?* she mentally snapped. But no, that would go against his code. If he wanted her dealt with, he'd do it himself. He had the men for it and plenty of connections throughout lower Wimborne.

It must be a coincidence. The Green Caps could be at the market for all sorts of reasons, but better cautious than caught. She retreated. This street would let her out on Taystone Way, and there she could climb through an upper window and make her way through the conjoined attics. Years ago, her mother had cut secret doorways between attic walls up and down Taystone. She could crawl all the way to the end and emerge on Horvard near the brothel. From there she could . . .

Nelle stopped short. Green Caps trotted down the street from the far end, heading her way. She glanced to each side, but the street was empty other than a lame old beggar and an ancient woman toting a basket of apples.

They're coming for you, Nelle. You know they are.

There was no time to think. No time to try to reason away this fear.

She whirled and leapt for the low-slung roof. Her hands gripped hard, and she pulled herself up in a flash of skirts and exposed bare legs. A shout rang through the air behind her, but she didn't understand the words through the roaring in her ears. She scrambled to the crest of the roof.

Then she was off across the rooftops like a rat fleeing a pack of rabid terriers. She knew the different textures of wood and thatch beneath the thin soles of her shoes and deftly avoided the weakest spots. Rounding chimney pots and springing over walls, she made her way to the narrowest gaps where it was easy to leap from one house to the next without ever touching the ground. Distantly she heard commotion and clamor, but she knew they wouldn't catch her. The Green Caps didn't know the world of roofs, not like she did. But in the daytime she was conspicuous. Onlookers would be only too happy to point out where she'd gone. She must be quick, quicker than quick, to lose her pursuers.

Papa . . .

He was alone. Alone and unable to move from his bed for pain from his beating. Had the Green Caps gone after him too? Had Cloven betrayed their home to the lawmen? But *why?* If word got out that he'd betrayed a snatcher, he'd be hunted down. The rough law of Draggs Street was harsh and swift. Not even Cloven was powerful enough to circumvent the rules of his filthy kind.

She raced lightly along the ridgepole of a stable, then scrambled up to the higher roof of a nearby inn, rounded the large chimney pot . . . and stopped short. The wind caught at her hair and skirts, knifing through the thin fabric. But it wasn't cold that sent the prickles racing up her arms and the back of her neck.

"Sam."

He stood at the far end of the roof, poised like a dancer with perfect grace. His long hair tossed like a pennant behind him. "Well met, Ginger." He grinned.

He knew her routes. Years ago, she'd taken him on nighttime excursions across her favorite rooftop paths, revealing the safest, surest ways. She should have known better. A snatcher's secrets were worth more than any snatch. But surely Sam was safe. He was Sam! Her Sam!

Only, he belonged to Cloven now.

"It'll be better if you come quietly," he said, lifting both hands in a nonthreatening gesture, his smile too bright, too friendly. "No one wants you hurt. You know that, right? You know *I* would never hurt you?" He took another step, and another.

She didn't wait for him to take a third.

With a wordless cry she turned and skidded down the roof's steep slope, its shingles scraping right through her shoes and bloodying her feet. She didn't care. She reached for the gutter and hung out over the four-story drop.

Her snatcher's satchel swung wildly and almost fell free, but she managed to hook it on her elbow and slide it back to her shoulder. Sam's voice bellowed behind her, but she ignored him, sidling along the gutter until she reached a pipe. Could it hold her weight? Maybe. It definitely wouldn't hold his!

She grabbed the pipe and immediately felt its weakness. With a creak and a groan, it pulled away from the wall. No time to correct her decision now. She shimmied down as fast as she could go, her feet balanced against the wall. The pipe gave, buckling as she caught hold of a second-story window and hung there. Sam shouted at her from above, and more shouts joined his voice from the street below. She was making quite the spectacle of herself, with her skirts flying and bare legs kicking.

But she wasn't about to give up.

She looked down. The drop was too great; she would break an ankle at least. The window was open, however, so with a surge of pure will she hauled herself up onto her elbows, pulled her stomach over the sill, and tumbled into the room beyond. The room wasn't empty—she heard shuffling feet, heard floorboards creak. Gathering her limbs beneath her body, she pushed into a crouch . . . and looked up into Cloven's smiling face.

"Well now, Lady Peronelle," he growled. "Fancy meeting you here."

Someone struck her from behind. She fell into darkness.

She woke to the stink of mold, rot, and rat feces. The pungent miasma was so overwhelming, Nelle almost wished she'd died already just to avoid this moment. But no. She was decidedly, painfully alive. And aching in every bone and joint.

With a groan, she cracked her eyes open. It didn't help. It was utterly dark, as dark as pure blindness. Wherever she was, there were no windows to the outside world. Could this be the Tower of Correction in central Wimborne? Nelle shuddered. Mother had always told her it was better to die than to land in one of these cells.

"Bullspit!" Nelle growled and tried to move. But she couldn't.

Iron shackles bolted to the wall gripped her wrists above her head. Her legs felt cold, exposed to the knee, and her feet were bare. Someone had taken her shoes. And what about her other belongings? What about her satchel and the nilarium claws?

She scrabbled in the straw and managed to get her legs tucked up under her skirt, sitting on her feet. She couldn't begin to guess how long she'd sat unconscious in the dark. The last thing she recalled with any clarity was Cloven's face leering down at her.

Papa? What's happened to Papa?

Was he still waiting for her back home? Had Cloven gone after him too? Her teeth clenched in a snarl. *If I ever get out of this, I'm going to find that man and—*

A screech of protesting metal startled her. Nelle jerked in place, knocking her head against the wall. Pain pounded in her skull as a gleam of light silhouetted the bars on the window of her cell door. A face peered in at her, eyes glinting maliciously. Then the lantern lifted and shone into her face, blinding her.

"Yup," a brutish voice said. "This is the one right enough. Can't mistake that pretty face."

The lantern lowered. Another horrendous squeal of metal followed as the heavy door to her cell swung open. Nelle tucked her chin in close, squeezing her eyes tight as the light dazzled her vision.

"Very good," a cold, deep voice intoned from the doorway. "Leave the lantern and go."

"But, Your Learnedness—"

"The creature is bound, as you see. I am in no danger. Go."

The echo of pounding feet retreating up the passage followed this command, and the raucous sound of a distant door shutting. Then stillness. And quiet, rhythmic breathing.

Nelle risked opening her eyes and squinted, blinking, into the glare of the lantern. Slowly, painfully, her vision adjusted until she could discern the shadowy form of a tall man standing in the doorway. He seemed strangely . . . familiar. She shook her head and looked again, studying the weird shadows and orange highlights cast on his face by the lantern's glow.

Her heart stopped.

It's him.

The man she'd encountered in the Evenspire last night. The Miphato she'd kissed. She'd caught only the briefest of glimpses before his candle fell and went out. But it was enough. She recognized that dark, heavy brow, those poison-green eyes, and full red lips framed by a neatly trimmed dark beard. Last night his only expression was pure surprise. Now his mouth pursed in a contemplative pout and one brow arched with sardonic interest. The lantern light glinted red in the depths of his black pupils.

"So," that dark voice spoke again, deadly with calm. "You are as beautiful in reality as in memory. When I woke on the floor late this morning, I thought I must have dreamed your face. I thought whatever drug you'd slipped me had conjured something in my subconscious that couldn't possibly be real." He stepped into the cell, kicking musty straw, and crouched before her. "But here you are. In the flesh."

He reached out as though to touch her cheek. An animal growl rumbled in Nelle's throat, and her teeth closed with a snap. The Miphato jerked his hand away just in time, then chuckled mirthlessly. "No fear, dear lady. *That* isn't what I have in mind."

He stood again and looked around the cell. His gaze fixed on something in the corner, and with a few brisk movements he fetched a three-legged stool from the shadows, placed it in front of Nelle, and settled down on the seat with a graceful flourish of embroidered silk.

He's young for a Miphato, Nelle thought. Most of the Evenspire mages she'd glimpsed during her time in the kitchens were much older men with long gray beards and long gray faces, their shoulders stooped from years of bowing over desks, their fingers so ink-stained they would never be clean again. This man, by contrast, could be only thirty-five or thereabouts. He was undeniably impressive in figure and form. Even seated on the stool he towered over her, his shoulders broad and straining slightly at the seams of his fine robes. His face had an unreal quality in the lantern glow, but under other circumstances it might be considered handsome. Beautiful, even.

Nelle shuddered and squeezed her hands into fists, straining at the shackles over her head. The mage's mouth twisted into a knowing smile. "I am Dusaro Gaspard," he said, "Learned Spellmaster and Conjurer of the Faowind Ranks, Miphato of Evenspire. And whom do I have the pleasure of addressing?"

She squeezed her fists even tighter, driving her nails into her palms. "Don't you know?" Her voice scraped rough and ugly from her fear-thickened throat. "I'm the bullspittin' Queen of Seryth. Set me free, and maybe I'll tell my chief bone crusher to go easy on you."

"My, my! You are a brazen one, aren't you?" Mage Gaspard shook his head, still smiling. Then his expression hardened. "I have come to inform you, *Miss Peronelle Beck*, that your case has already been presented to the low court and your sentence passed. An easy conviction, especially with so reliable and esteemed a witness to take the stand." He waved a hand to indicate himself.

Her heart—and whatever was left of her bravado—dropped. *Sentence?* There could be only one sentence for a crime like hers, for a snatcher who dared steal from the Evenspire.

The Miphato picked disinterestedly at a loose thread on his sleeve. "Tomorrow at dawn you'll be taken to the Square of Correction, where Master Shard—known familiarly to the populace as Old Razor-Clean Shard—will carry out the mayor's judgment. You will be summarily parted from both your hands. But not to worry! You'll then be released to the care of your family, who I am sure will provide you with ample medical attention. With proper treatment, you'll make a full recovery and may go on to whatever life a no-handed young lady may expect to enjoy." He flashed her a winning smile. "There are always men of *unusual* interests. You'll have lost nothing of real importance. I'm sure you'll thrive."

His words struck her ears, each one a physical blow harder than the slaps he'd given her in the quillary the night before. Nelle bowed her head, nausea whirling in her gut. She feared she would be sick then and there, right down the front of her dress. But she couldn't do that. What would Mother say? A snatcher always knew that her path might eventually cross with Master Shard's. Would she disgrace her mother's memory with cowardice and quivering?

If only they'd hang me. If only they'd kill me outright . . .

"I sense that my news has moved you." Mage Gaspard shifted on his stool, leaning closer to her. "Don't lose heart just yet, Miss Beck. I may be able to offer another solution to your current situation. A solution of interest to you."

Despite herself, Nelle's gaze flicked up sharply to meet his eyes. *Don't show weakness. Don't show fear.*

But it was too late. He knew he had her in the palm of his hand.

The Miphato smiled again and rested his elbows on his knees, his fingers laced lightly together. "Tell me, my dear lady, are you familiar with the Isle of Roseward?"

She blinked. She felt dull. Stupid. Unable to comprehend the question. How did . . . how did Roseward relate to the horrors of her immediate future? Belatedly she remembered to nod.

"I know the rumors say the island is abandoned," Gaspard continued. "Haunted, even. But it's not true, or not wholly true. There is a man there, one Soran Silveri, formerly of Evenspire. A Miphato, like myself, though fallen from the ranks. Are you

58

following me thus far, Miss Beck?"

Nelle nodded again slowly. Blood thudded in her temples.

"Silveri has in his possession a certain spellbook. The Rose Book it's called, for the distinctive rose mark on its binding. Impossible to miss." The Miphato's teeth flashed suddenly, his smile knife-like in the lantern light. "I want it. I want that book."

She stared at him, hardly believing what she heard. Did he expect her to . . .? Was he . . . was he trying to *hire* her?

"During the past fifteen years," Gaspard continued, leaning back on his stool, "many have tried to infiltrate Roseward and pillage the treasures of Dornrise Hall, the once great home of the Silveri family. Thieves like you have been commissioned and lost. Three years back, pirate sails were spied on the horizon. The ship docked on the far side of the island and has since rotted away in the harbor. No one knows what became of the crew. Such a sorry waste! And no spellbook to show for it."

He did. He really did intend to make her the offer. It was ridiculous, but it was real; Nelle could see it in his eyes. "And you think I would have better luck?" she rasped, desperately trying to disguise the tremble in her voice.

"I do, yes. We've never tried sending a snatcher of your particular . . . talents." Gaspard's eyes traveled up and down her figure, which must have been singularly bedraggled and disgusting by then. But his expression was far from disgusted. "I know Silveri from years ago, back in our student days. He always had an eye for a fair face and form. And he's been fifteen years now on Roseward, alone. Something tells me you won't meet the same fate as the others. Something tells me you—and that venomous kiss of yours—may stand a chance where others have failed."

His gaze fixed on her mouth. Something in his eyes filled her with more dread than the prospect of meeting Master Shard in the Square of Correction. Something like lust and loathing mingled into one nameless emotion.

Don't show weakness. Don't show fear. She set her jaw and refused to let her gaze drop, refused to shrink before this man.

Gaspard chuckled and rubbed his chin with one hand. "Our mutual friend, Cloven, claims you are the most skilled snatcher working the streets of Wimborne these days. He says that you—"

"What?" Shock burst in her head and coursed through every vein of her body. "Cloven? *You* are Cloven's client? *You* commissioned him to steal from the Evenspire?" Her mouth dropped open, and for a moment she felt as though her brain had simply stopped working. Then the last word burst from her lips: "Why?"

"Reasons that don't concern you," Gaspard replied coolly. "Needless to say, I was *not* expecting our little encounter last night when I stepped into the quillary to see if the job had been done. You took me quite by surprise. But I must commend your methods. And how you managed to scale the Evenspire is beyond my reckoning! If I didn't know better, I'd think you had magic of your own."

"But . . . but it's your quillary." Nelle shook her head, and coils of unbound hair fell in her face. "If you wanted a quill, couldn't you just take it?"

"That's not how it works." The Miphato smiled condescendingly. "Don't trouble your head about it, girl. You did your job rather well. Well enough to impress me. Thus, I asked Cloven to arrange our introduction. He told me you might be difficult to persuade for the job I have in mind for you. But you're not so inflexible, are you, Miss Beck?"

She drew a long careful breath. The ground on which she trod was deadly. Scatting dragons, she'd rather be face to face with Cloven right now! But she had a few small advantages she might still leverage if she were careful.

"Let me be sure I've got this right," she said slowly. "You're proposing a trade: The spellbook for my hands. I'm to go to Roseward, snatch this book off some mage fellow who lives there, and bring it back to you." She narrowed her eyes. "What sort of assurance do I have that you'll let me go again when I return?"

"None at all," Gaspard replied with a smile. Then he laughed. "Oh, don't look at me like that! You may trust my word or not. It makes no difference to me."

"And what if I were to just disappear? Like those pirates. What if I never return?"

"Then I'll see to it that your beloved father pays the penalty for your crime."

Her heart stopped. For a moment she couldn't make herself believe she had truly heard that threat spoken so softly, so gently.

She tried to cling to the belief that she would somehow wriggle out of this, that she could find her mother's strength and simply brazen her way through.

But whatever hope remaining to her fled as Gaspard's words echoed in the darkness of that cell: "What do you think, sweet lady? Would good Mixael Beck enjoy an introduction to Master Shard?"

CHAPTER 4

IT WAS IMPOSSIBLE TO GUESS HOW MANY HOURS PASSED before her cell door opened again. Exhaustion descended on her spirit like a smothering hand, but Nelle couldn't fall asleep no matter how her head bowed or her eyes drooped. Her arms were numb from being held over her head for so long, and she couldn't feel her fingers anymore. She shifted her legs beneath her, trying to find a more comfortable position on the cold floor. But it was no use.

She was trapped not only in body, but also in spirit. She couldn't get Gaspard's voice out of her head. Again and again she heard that insidious confidence breathing through his threats. Threats he was more than capable of carrying out.

He'd not even waited for her to agree to his terms. Her face must have told him everything he needed to know. Still chuckling to himself, he had risen from his stool, plucked up his lantern, and left, pulling the cell door shut.

That was who-knew-how-many hours ago now.

Nelle shifted again, her bare feet scrabbling in the straw. The iron shackles chafed her blistered wrists. "Bullspit," she hissed. Then louder, more vehemently, "Bullspit. *Bullspit!*"

Just as the last word escaped her lips, she heard the ear-splitting creak of a door being opened somewhere beyond her cell. Tensing, she struggled to pull herself together, to appear less broken and vulnerable. A vain attempt, and she knew it, but she had to try.

Footsteps pounded on stone. Then another, louder shriek as her own cell door was pulled open. Light flared painfully, forcing her to turn away. Once her eyes adjusted, she blinked and squinted toward the doorway, where an austere woman with deep frown lines around her thin-lipped mouth stood like an apparition, gazing down at Nelle with obvious distaste.

"Unshackle her," she said in a tone so imperious, the guard didn't dare hesitate.

The relief of having her wrists released, of letting her numb arms fall and simply rest in her lap, was so great that Nelle could think about nothing else for some while. Once her senses finally returned, she found herself perched on the three-legged stool with a lump of bread clutched in her prickling hands. The strange woman was hard at work combing and arranging her hair.

Suddenly ravenous, Nelle stuffed bread into her mouth. It was dry and hard, but she somehow managed to swallow without choking. Only after taking a second, smaller mouthful and forcing it down after the first did she bother asking, "What are you doing?" Her voice creaked from her throat.

"Making you presentable," that authoritative voice answered at her back.

Nelle shivered. "Presentable for what?"

The woman did not reply, so Nelle returned to munching the crusty bread while half her hair was tied into a knot at the back of her skull and fixed in place with pins. The rest was left to fall down her back and shoulders, its tangles somewhat tamer than usual. Perhaps the woman was an enchantress.

"May I . . ." Nelle hesitated, then shrugged. No use in being timid. "Is there a . . . bucket?"

The woman sniffed. "In the corner."

While Nelle answered the call of nature—which had become more urgent as the hours passed—the woman opened a bundle she'd brought along and produced a dusty-blue gown so much finer than Nelle's own ragged garment that she almost hated to touch it. *Too fine for a Draggs wench,* she thought as the matron pulled out a pair of shoes and a creamy muslin chemise to go with the overgown.

"Don't dawdle, girl," the woman snapped. "Get over here."

Nelle obeyed and let the woman strip her down and clothe her again. *What about my snatcher's bag?* she wondered. *My picks, my knife, the claws? And the Sweet Dreams?* She wouldn't be able to do much snatchery without the proper tools of her trade. But questioning the woman, who was hard at work tightening the blue gown's laces until Nelle couldn't draw breath, seemed pointless. So, she held her tongue.

At last the matron stepped back, surveying her work by the lantern's glow, and gave her head a shake—whether with satisfaction or disapproval, Nelle couldn't begin to guess. The expression on her face could go either way. "This way," she said, picked up her lantern, and turned to the door.

Nelle blinked. *Is that it? I just walk out of the Tower of Correction?* Was it possible her agreement with Mage Gaspard was legally binding and approved by the court? She doubted it. *He probably paid off the guards. Or threatened to ensorcell them, more like.*

Whatever the reason, no guards were in sight on their way out. In fact, Nelle began to wonder if she was truly in the Tower after all. While it was certainly a tall stone building, it was terribly dilapidated and seemed nowhere near large enough to be the prison structure she'd always regarded with such dread.

After following the matron down a narrow stair and out a side door, Nelle realized they were not even within Wimborne's city limits. A thick sea mist dampened her face, and a salt-laden breeze tugged at her tied-up hair. Gaping, she realized they stood at the base of the old Tyrane Fortress, a ruin many hundreds of years old. Few of its walls still stood against the elements, and three of its four towers had long since crumbled in on themselves. Only part of the main keep and one tower remained standing, defying the decay of centuries.

Just as Nelle opened her mouth to ask what in the bullspitting blazes they were doing all the way out here, the woman motioned with one hand. Two figures materialized through the swirling mist on either side of Nelle, grasping her arms. They were hooded, and she couldn't see their faces, but she knew at once that the one on her right was Sam. She'd know him anywhere by the way he carried himself, by the way he breathed. The other man must also be one of Cloven's mongrels.

"What?" she snapped. "No 'Good morning, Ginger'? A girl could start to think we never was friends."

Sam's grip on her arm tensed, but he said nothing. He and his companion led her down to the strip of cold rocky beach below the Tyrane Fortress. The tide was going out, so they skirted several tide pools while making for the water's edge. The fog was so thick that when the dark beautiful visage of Mage Gaspard seemed to manifest before her like a phantom, Nelle barely stifled a scream.

"Ah, there she is." The mage looked her over, taking in the way her new gown clung to her skinny frame, gathered just beneath her bust to make her look fuller and rounder than she was. "Well, well, Mistress Lidgeon. You've made a success of your work."

The matron grunted and crossed her arms, though something in the set of her head indicated pleasure in the compliment. Not even a stone-faced woman like her could be entirely immune to the handsome Miphato.

Gaspard motioned to the men on either side of Nelle. "Unhand her. She's not going anywhere."

Nelle hated that he was right, hated that the moment her arms were released she could only stand and glare daggers at this man. *But he has Papa,* she reminded herself ferociously. *Don't forget he has Papa.*

"The fog will lift soon," Gaspard said. He reached to take Nelle's hand, but when she turned sharply away from him, he shrugged and indicated she should walk beside him along the beach. Sam fell into step behind them. She felt his stare on the back of her head, but she refused to look around at him, not even once.

"Your boat is at the ready," Gaspard said. "You know how to row, I trust?"

"Well enough." Mother had thought a little sea-craft worth knowing if one intended to be a snatcher in a coastal city.

"Excellent. Roseward is a good mile off the coast, and the waters can be rough. You'll have the tide in your favor at least." He led Nelle to a little one-man craft moored in the sand, a lantern gleaming at its prow. Her stomach clenched. This was truly happening. She was truly going to climb into that tiny boat and set off into the ocean alone, making for the Haunted Island.

Gaspard plucked something out of the boat and tossed it to her. She caught it on reflex and was both surprised and relieved to

BOOK I: THIEF

discover that she held her own snatcher's satchel. Hastily she undid the flap and put her hand inside, touching the lock picks, the jar of Sweet Dreams ointment, her knife and sheath. But . . .

"Where are they?" she snarled, her gaze snapping to Gaspard's face.

He raised an eyebrow. "Where are what, Miss Beck?"

"You know what." She closed the flap and slung the satchel over her shoulder. Her hands clenched into fists. "I had them on me when . . . when . . ."

Realization dawned. While she lay unconscious, Cloven would have searched her thoroughly and immediately recognized the nilarium claws. He'd coveted them for years and, since Mother's death, he'd several times offered to buy them from Papa, if Papa had known where to find them.

Her heart sank to the pit of her stomach. Losing the claws was like losing one more piece of Mother. She would almost have preferred to let them chop off her hands. Almost.

Gaspard watched her closely, his brow still upraised. "Nothing more was in that satchel when it came to me. I trust you have all that you need to accomplish the mission before you?"

Nelle nodded and wiped a hand across her face, turning her gaze out to sea. "I'll make do." Even as she spoke, the mist parted like a curtain before her eyes, opening a clear line of sight straight to Roseward Isle. The island reared high above the water; its shore appeared to be sheer cliffs. Where would she beach her little boat? She'd have to travel around the island to find a landing place. Her arms ached at the thought.

"Remember, Miss Beck." Gaspard took a step toward her, suddenly standing very close indeed. As close as he'd stood two nights ago when she'd leapt from behind the door and pressed her mouth violently against his. His gaze dropped ever so briefly to her lips, and she saw the flash of a sharp canine as he smiled a predator's smile. "Remember our agreement. I will allow you three weeks, no more. Bring me that book, or your father will suffer for your failure."

Nelle nodded slowly, holding his gaze. "I remember," she said, an edge to her voice. "I never forget."

For an instant, his right eyelid quivered. Then he grinned again. "Good."

Her back was to the island as she pulled hard at the oars and watched the figures on the beach get smaller and smaller. It was a relief when they finally faded into the mist. Sam's face had remained hooded, but she'd felt the intensity of his eyes watching her and didn't like it. She wanted no concern or sympathy from him. Whatever friendship they'd once shared was gone. If they ever met again, it would be as enemies. And she would make him pay. She would make them all pay.

Nelle dropped her gaze and concentrated on the push and pull, the pitch of her boat, the cold spray forming droplets on her skin and damp patches on her gown. The muscles across her chest already ached. She would be in agony tomorrow. If she made it to tomorrow . . .

What exactly had become of those others who'd ventured out to the Haunted Island? Why had they disappeared, those snatchers and pirates seeking to loot the abandoned hall? Was this Mage Silveri so dangerous? Although fallen from the Miphates ranks, he must have retained at least some of his magical abilities. Did he take delight in blasting trespassers with curses?

And why the rumors of haunting that surrounded every whispered tale of the island itself?

"Bullspit, bullspit, bullspit," Nelle growled in rhythm with her strokes. Damp hair clung to her face and lay in limp strands over her shoulders—all the matron's hard work undone long before she reached the shore. If Gaspard expected her to snatch this spellbook of his by using her seductive wiles, he was going to be sorely disappointed.

But she'd get it. And she wouldn't take three weeks about it either. She had wiles at her disposal more effective than seduction.

Every so often she peered over her shoulder to make certain she was still aimed at the island and not simply rowing out into open sea. The rising sun spilled a fiery path across the water and rendered the lantern in the prow of Nelle's boat useless. She turned around to douse the light, glad to give her sore muscles a chance to recover. Best to save the oil; she might need the lantern tonight.

This thought made her stop to check what other supplies Gaspard had thought to send with her. Tucked beneath the rowing bench she found an oilcloth sack containing a water jar, a lump of bread, a wedge of cheese. And nothing else.

"Does he think I'd try to escape if he gave me more?" she muttered and closed the sack, fastening the ties securely. With a groan she settled back on her seat, her stomach twisting as the boat bobbed gently on the waves. She was more than halfway across the channel now. Roseward and its imposing cliff walls cast a shadow on the sea behind her. A shadow she would soon enter.

She wiped salty spray from her cheek and realized that some of that dampness might be from tears. She swallowed painfully, her teeth gritting. No time to fall to pieces now. She had a job to do— get the book, get out, get back to Papa.

"Now move!" she growled and took up the oars again. The mist had mostly cleared, offering her a fresh view of Wimborne sprawled languidly across the coast. Imagining she could still see Gaspard on the beach, his robes billowing in the ocean breeze, she made the time pass by inventing interesting curses for him with each pull of the oars.

Suddenly a shiver ran through her body as though she'd just passed through a curtain of ice. She blinked and almost believed she saw an iridescent shimmer in the air, a ripple of light dancing then gone. The sensation was brief, but the effect it left behind remained. Cold, yet not cold. More like an emotion than a sensation, yet not wholly like either.

She closed her eyes, shook her head. Then she looked up again and . . . and . . .

Her jaw dropped.

Wimborne, which had been less than a mile away only a moment before, was now a distant smudge on the horizon. The Evenspire's point caught the sunlight, clear and crisp, but everything else had faded to a faint impression, a shadow. As though it were miles away and seen through a darkened glass.

She shook her head, looked again. And again. Something wasn't right. Something was playing with her mind. Could it be seasickness? Or the stress of the last several days coming down on her all at once?

Panic whipped through her veins. She scrambled in her seat, dropped one oar, caught it up again, tipped the boat wildly to one side, and nearly fell into the water. This was bad. This was wrong. She had to get out of here, had to turn back. Surely if she turned the boat around now, she could push through whatever barrier she'd just penetrated, make for the far shore, and get away before . . . before the island caught her.

Then what?

Gaspard would be waiting and only too happy to carry out his threats.

Would she meekly offer up her hands to Master Shard?

"Nothing's happened to you yet, girl," she growled, forcing herself to sit properly on the bench, her hands gripping the gunwales. "No monsters. No ghosts. So, let's put your back into it and get this over with!"

Though her arms trembled, she picked up the oars and set to work, faster than before. Her boat cut through the waves, and she twisted in her seat every few strokes to look where she was going.

A weird chortling sound caught her ear, and a shadow flicked across the boat, momentarily blocking out the sun. Nelle glanced at the sky and winced. Frowning, she settled one oar in its holder, lifted a hand, and shaded her eyes. A winged creature wheeled overhead. Was it a bird? A seagull? No. A cormorant, maybe. The shape seemed odd though. More of them appeared. Five, ten . . . She lost count. More chortling filled the air, strange yet tuneful in a way.

Nelle set her jaw and continued rowing, all the while aware of the circling birds, aware that more of them were gathering. By the time she entered the island's long shadow, she couldn't bring herself to look up again for fear of how dense that flock had become.

Without warning, one of the birds swooped down from among the rest, so close that Nelle had to duck or be hit in the head. Hearing a thump and a rustle of wings behind her, she whipped around to see it perched on the prow of her boat, causing the unlit lantern to swing wildly from its hook.

It wasn't a bird.

"Bullspitting boggarts!" Nelle cried and dropped her hold on both oars as she jumped and fell over, nearly overturning the boat.

The creature clinging to the prow uttered an irritable bray. Its wings outspread for balance, at least as broad as a cormorant's but leathery, veined, and bright emerald green. A long head ending in a blunt nose with enormous ridged nostrils turned and regarded Nelle with a pair of brilliant ruby eyes.

It opened its mouth and brayed again, sounding more like a donkey than a bird.

Nelle clutched the gunwales, her fingers white-knuckled, her chest heaving with every gasping breath. "You're a dragon. A spittin' *dragon!*" She choked on the word, and her head whirled, black spots dancing at the outskirts of her vision.

The creature tilted its head sharply to one side, peering at her. A crest rose along the top of its head and down its back, translucent skin flapping in the sea wind. Then, as though deciding it disliked the looks of her, it craned its neck at a bizarre angle, hunched its shoulders, and shot up into the air again. The downward force of its launch made the boat rock wildly, and a wave washed over the bow and soaked through Nelle's skirts. She tipped her head back, squinting into the morning sky at all those shapes wheeling overhead.

"Gods have mercy," she whispered. She wasn't much of a one for prayer, but her hand moved, unconsciously tracing a circle of protection in the air before her heart. She hadn't bargained on something like this. None of the rumors surrounding Roseward had breathed a word about . . . dragons. They were creatures out of faerie tales. *Real* insofar as possibly existing somewhere in some world. But certainly not in this world.

This world isn't your world anymore, she grimly reminded herself, looking back toward Wimborne in search of that shimmering, near-invisible veil she had passed through. She couldn't see it, of course. She couldn't even see Wimborne now. Only the very tip of the Evenspire was still visible, piercing the sky like a thorn.

Had she crossed the boundary into Faerieland? Was it possible?

Even as Nelle pressed a hand over her frantically racing heart, she knew she couldn't sit here in the boat all day, letting the currents carry her out into the open ocean.

"You don't have a choice," she whispered. "You have no choice, so get to it, girl."

She crawled through sloshing water back to the rowing bench and resumed her place. Bracing her feet, she took up the oars and fell into a rhythm of strokes. The dragons overhead kept whirling and chortling and sometimes uttering those raucous brays. Thankfully, no others swooped down at her.

Finding a place to land took some doing. Though she searched all along the Wimborne-side coast of the island, she found nothing but high, rocky cliffs. She could only continue on around the island, certain her arms would drop off from sheer exhaustion by the time this journey ended.

Just when she was ready to give up, she spied a little stretch of pebbly beach. Beyond it the cliffs rose imposingly, but she glimpsed a path that might lead to the top. Above, the lighthouse tower stood at its perilous tilt.

"That'll do." Nelle angled her craft toward the beach. When trickling sweat stung her eyes, she paused to mop her forehead, then glanced again at her destination.

Someone stood on the beach. Someone who hadn't been there before

CHAPTER 5

THE MAN WOKE WITH A GROAN AND REACHED FOR HIS head. His fingers touched sticky, clumped hair, and he pulled them back tipped with blood. He grimaced. Some of the cuts he'd received in the night were deeper than he'd realized. But he never bothered to stitch them up. They healed in their own time, regardless.

With another groan he rolled onto his side, then hauled himself upright, his feet planted on the cold stone floor. The rickety bedframe creaked beneath him, threatening to collapse. A breeze blew through the open windows, whistling playfully from one to the next and sending ripples across the slick surface of oil in the central basin.

He raised his head, dully watching the effect. Business demanded his attention, tasks that must be accomplished well before the hour of sunset. The ward stones all had to be double-checked, the Hinter currents tested, the snares examined.

But for that one moment, he couldn't will himself to move. Every limb ached, and the place in his chest where his heart ought to be felt simultaneously hollow and heavy.

Another day. Another year, another hour. What difference would it make? In the long run—

He frowned suddenly. A searing sensation shot across his awareness, bypassing mortal senses to cut straight to the quick. He stood abruptly, swayed on his feet, then stepped around the oil basin to his desk and the many boxes of books, scrolls, and folios scattered around it. Kneeling, he reached into one box and extracted a worn leather folio. His brow tightened in a frown.

The sensation came again: a plaintive cry, full of fear. And pain. Imperceptible to the ears, yet unmistakable.

He thumbed hastily through pages in the folio, his eyes scanning and dismissing each in turn until he discovered a small page at the very back. He pulled it free of the others and drew a sharp breath between his clenched teeth. The parchment was torn, a ragged rip right up the center, almost to the middle of the page.

"No," the man breathed and hastily folded the page to protect it from further damage. Tucking it within his shirt, he shut the folio and stood upright. For the space of several breaths, he did not move. His eyes were wide, his breathing uneven.

Then he heard the cry again. Desperate and distant. Fading fast.

Spitting curses through the tangle of his beard, the man gathered up the thick robes he'd discarded on the floor last night and hastily shrugged into them. He pulled the hood over his head and, ignoring the continued throb from the cut across his forehead, hastened down the stair.

The wind whistled around the tower, hissing through chinks in the stones as he raced down the curving steps. He passed through an opening into a square stone chamber that had once served as the lighthouse keeper's home at the base of the tower. The remains of a fire smoldered on a hearth, and sparse furnishings broke the open space into a few room-like sections.

With long strides he hastened to the largest piece of furniture, a tall armoire on the wall opposite the stair. Flinging the doors open, he fumbled about in its contents until his hands found what he sought. He pulled out a leather sling, threw it over his shoulder, and was out the door the next moment.

Midmorning sunlight momentarily blinded him as he stood on the threshold. Shading his eyes, he gazed out across the ocean. Many colorful shapes darted and danced in the air above the waves, their bright wings glinting like jewels, a sight that usually sent a stab of delight through even his stone-cold heart.

Today he could only mutter, "Where is it?" and wait with

anxious impatience.

It sounded again—a sad, songlike moan touching the edge of his mind. He mentally reached out for it, trying to grasp it like a thread. The faintest tug came from below the ocean cliffs.

At once he hastened to the path leading from the lighthouse to the beach below, obliged to keep his eyes on the narrow strip of ground, for one misstep would send him plunging. If he were lucky, the fall would kill him . . . but he knew full well his luck had long ago run out. Most likely he would only break a limb or two and be unable to climb back up to the tower. Such a fate would be worse than outright death. Far worse. He would be obliged to wait in agony, watching the sun descend and the night deepen. Watching and counting the hours until . . . until . . .

It didn't bear contemplation. He would find that broken spell. Quickly, before more damage was done.

He had scarcely reached the end of the path and stepped onto the shore's uneven stones when he heard the sad mewling cry. This time it was audible, a sound heard with his mortal ears that shot like an arrow straight to his heart. Turning toward the sound, he saw a flutter of creamy parchment covered in red-ink script.

Two steps, however, and that paper-like translucence was no longer creamy but bright blue, and the red ink was no longer an elegant script but instead delicate veins. A crested head with a blunt nose rose from between the rocks, bright yellow eyes pleading and pained. Those eyes turned to the man, and the blunt snout opened, revealing rows of sharp teeth and a rattling tongue.

It hissed like a snake.

"Now, now, little friend," the man said, crouching beside the creature. Its long sinewy body was caught between two stones, one wing fluttering helplessly, the other extended at an unnatural angle. A long rip marred that wing—a piece missing, the edge ragged. Patches of scales along the haunch were torn away as well. Bright silver blood spattered the rocks around.

"What did this to you?" the man muttered, studying the tear. He raised an eyebrow at the creature, which blinked sorrowfully back at him. But though its expression was intelligent—or at least not wholly stupid—it could offer no answer beyond another mewling whimper. "Don't worry," the man said, his voice low and soothing. "It's not as bad as I feared. I might even be able to repair you, given time."

The creature seemed to have tucked its body between the stones while attempting to escape whatever had attacked it. A useless endeavor that had served only to wedge it awkwardly in place. Why the attacker had not finished off its prey while it was pinned down, the man could not guess. He glanced at the other shapes whirling in the sky above. Perhaps some of them, seeing their brother in distress, had chased off the foe.

The man reached out to grasp the upper body beneath the wings and gently pry it free. He heard a hiss just as the creature's long neck propelled its razor teeth toward his hand and recoiled, quick as a viper.

A metallic *clang* sounded, and the man didn't so much as

flinch. Shaking its snout, the creature chortled in mingled surprise and frustration.

"I wouldn't try that again if I were you," the man said with the faintest hint of a chuckle in his voice. He braced himself to push one of the stones with his foot, creating just enough space to pull the beast free. Its lithe body wrapped around his arm, the long tail flailed, and the healthy wing flapped. The torn wing, however, remained limp and useless. The creature uttered a series of pathetic mewls.

Shrugging the leather sling from his shoulder, the man spread it on the flat surface of a sea-smoothed stone. Then he folded the creature inside, careful to pry each individual claw free from the thick fabric of his sleeve. The beast, exhausted from its vicious display, let its head droop, and the man scooped it up and slung it around his shoulder, onto his back.

"I'll find whatever did this," he said, rising and brushing sand from his robes. "The currents have carried us near to Aurelian shores. Something must have gotten through the wards."

Whatever it was, now that it had reached the island, it wouldn't soon wish to leave again. The air here had an addictive influence on creatures of Aurelis and the other Eledrian realms. If once they tasted it, they craved more. If he didn't defend it ruthlessly, the island would soon be overwhelmed by faerie beasts.

But such vigilance required power. Power he could ill afford to spare.

Shaking his head, the man adjusted the set of the sling at his back. The creature mewled again, more irritable than pathetic now that it was free of the rocks. "All right, little friend," the man said gently. Turning back toward the cliff path, he faced out across the open water. "I hate to take you from your brethren, but I hope it won't be for long. With any luck we'll get you flying again . . ."

His voice trailed off. His heart lurched, and he took a step back in surprise.

There was a boat. A small sturdy craft. No sail, just a single set of oars and one industrious rower pulling hard toward this very shore. He blinked hard and looked again, certain his eyes must deceive him.

The rower was a woman. Slender but strong, with a shock of red hair that glowed like fire in the sunlight, as bright as the dozens of brilliant wings circling in the air above her. Was she fae? Even as the question washed over him, the woman turned on her rowing bench to look back at the shore. She was still too far off for him to clearly view her face, but he knew at once that she was mortal. Young and mortal.

And beautiful.

Nelle caught her breath. Her blistered hands tightened on the oars. She blinked hard and looked again. Yes, someone really did stand on the shore. Someone quite tall. Long pale hair streamed out from under a hood, ghostly and strange even in bright morning sunlight.

It was most certainly a man. A large imposing man wearing a heavy brown cloak with its hood pulled over his face.

"Silveri," she whispered. Unless it was the ghost of a dead pirate, it had to be the mage. No one else lived on Roseward.

Why was he just standing there?

She shivered, and her stomach twisted as the boat bobbed on the waves. He must have seen her coming. There was nothing else on the ocean for miles, and the flock of dragons overhead would draw attention her way. Had he come down to greet her? Or did he hide some deadly spell within the folds of that thick robe, ready to pull out and hurl at her the moment she beached her boat?

Nelle drew a steadying breath. She hadn't planned to arrive this way . . . not that she'd had opportunity to actually *plan* anything about this whole insane venture. But she'd hoped she might manage to come and go from Roseward without encountering the renegade Miphato at all. Gaspard hadn't exactly said the man was dangerous, but he was Miphates trained. Unlikely to be the friendly type.

"A shipload of vanished pirates don't say much for your hospitality, eh?" she muttered. With a shudder in her spine, she faced the open sea again and pulled at the oars. Turning her back to that forbidding figure wouldn't be her first choice . . . but she had no option, so she gritted her teeth and rowed hard, trying not to think about dead pirates. Every so often she looked around again. The man didn't move. Only the wind in his cloak let her know he wasn't carved out of driftwood and propped on the beach like a scarecrow to warn off unwelcome visitors.

With a last roll of waves, the boat's prow crunched into sand and pebbles. Nelle heaved the oars inside, then jumped into the water, soaking her already damp skirts to the knee. Grabbing the gunwale, she awkwardly hauled the boat up the shore. She would have to drag it much farther to keep it safe from the tide, but for now she rubbed her aching, blistered hands on her hips and faced the figure on the shore.

He still hadn't moved a muscle.

Maybe she ought to climb back into the boat and search for some other harbor. But what would be the point? He already knew she was here. Perhaps sneak-snatching wasn't the way to go about something like this anyway. Gaspard certainly had other ideas in mind when he sent her.

She eyed her sopping satchel in the bottom of the boat. Could she apply a smear of Sweet Dreams to her lips without being too conspicuous? One quick glance back at the man on the beach, and she decided against it. There was no way she'd have the courage to try landing a kiss somewhere inside that shadowed hood anyway. Who knew what her lips might find? Tusks?

"Seven gods," she whispered, and made a tiny circle in the air with two fingers. Then she hiked her water-logged skirts halfway up her shins and stepped lightly across the pebbly strand. She felt every rock, shell, and sharp edge through her shoes' thin soles, and several times she staggered and cursed.

Through it all, the robed man simply stood there. Watching her. He was already tall, nearly a head taller than her, and he'd taken a position on a pile of stones, which made him tower over her like a giant, a great beast of a man. Every instinct told Nelle to stop, or at least to hesitate. But she couldn't. Any pause would reveal her uncertainty, her weakness, and that she couldn't afford.

So she approached the man, squared her shoulders, and widened her stance. In a clear, crisp voice, she said, "Are you Mage Silveri?"

No answer.

Nelle waited, pushing wind-blown hair out of her eyes. "Oi! Did you hear me? I'm looking for a Mage Soran Silveri. Are you him?"

Another silence. Then, so slight that she almost missed it, a nod. She thought she saw a glint of eyes beneath the hood, but mostly it was just shadow. And hair. A lot of hair.

She set her chin. Then, moving swiftly, she swung up a hand and poked him hard in the upper arm. He started and turned, and she jumped back two steps, nearly tripping on the stones. "Good!" she said, a bit breathless. "You ain't a statue then. That's something." She crossed her arms. Her sleeves were rolled up to the elbows, and she felt gooseflesh rise along her forearms. "I'm come from Wimborne. My name is Peronelle Beck. Pleased to meet you." Uncertain what else to do, she lifted her heavy skirts again and offered a rather soggy curtsy.

Was that a sense of . . . *surprise* she felt emanating from under that hood? Amusement?

No. No, it was just silence. And more silence.

"Well," Nelle said through salt-gritted teeth, "not a lively sort, are you? I don't suppose you get much company out here. No matter. I'll get to the point. I'm really just here for—"

A rough, angry bray interrupted her, so loud and so sudden it made her jump. "Bullspit!" she cried, pressing a hand to her racing heart. For a moment she thought the sound had come from the man himself. Movement drew her eye to his shoulder. A blunt face with ridged nostrils emerged from behind the hooded head, and bright topaz eyes glared at her from beneath scaly brows. A wing spread behind the man's head like a bizarre headdress. Another wing, sporting a long bloody tear, fluttered pitifully in the breeze.

Nelle gaped stupidly. "Dragon!" She pointed a trembling hand, shaking her head. "Sir, you . . . you've got a dragon on your back!"

The creature opened its mouth again and, rather than a bray, issued a terrifying, snake-like hiss, its tongue waggling in the air. The man said nothing. One robed arm lifted, and Nelle saw a flash of silver—gauntlets? gloves?—as he pushed that ugly little head back down behind his shoulder.

Then he turned abruptly on his heel and, with long-legged strides, set out across the pebbly beach, his robes billowing behind him. Nelle had a clear view of his broad back, over which he carried a leather sling. The winged creature nestled comfortably there, like a baby on its mother's back. It brayed at her, its head bobbing in time to the man's gait.

Nelle was too dumbstruck for a moment to move. But she couldn't let him just walk away. Giving herself a shake, she gathered her skirts and set out at a trot, stumbling over the rough stones while growling curses. "What are you going to do with it?" she called to that broad back. "With the dragon? Are they . . . Do you eat them? Mind you, looks like he'd be a bit on the tough side, but I suppose anything stewed long enough—"

The man stopped. The creature hissed again, then uttered a strangled little gargle as the man whipped around fast, facing Nelle. She got another impression of flashing eyes and mounds of white hair, but otherwise no sense of a face.

Every instinct told her to shrink back. But she stood her ground and met that shadowed gaze as squarely as she could. Another of Mother's tricks—the honest, open gaze. Unafraid, unabashed, unsuspicious. It worked for Mother every time. But holding the gaze of those strange eyes was almost more than Nelle could manage. She had to steel her spine and squeeze her fists in the folds of her skirts.

Though she couldn't tell for certain, she thought the man eyed her up and down. Taking the measure of her. At long last, a deep, abrupt voice spoke from the depths of that hood: "Wyvern."

Nelle blinked up at him. The word was strange to her. Was he speaking another language? Or had she imagined the voice entirely? "What was that?"

"Wyvern. Not dragon."

She raised her eyebrows, and her mouth opened in a silent, "Ah," but without comprehension. Maybe it was a Miphates term. Or maybe he was just cracked. She hesitated, her lashes fluttering against the sting of the salty air. "So . . . are they?"

"Are they what?"

"Good eating."

Another long pause. Another stillness offering nary a hint of expression or reaction. Then: "No."

"What're you doing with that one then? Thing's wounded, bleeding. Do you hunt them for sorcery experiments? Are . . . are wyvern parts good for spells?" She swallowed hard, her throat painfully dry. "That's awful, you know. Poor beast."

The creature poked its head up from behind the man's shoulder again, and this time it showed its cage of teeth in what might pass for a smile on any other creature. Its beady eyes rolled unpleasantly, and it gave a sing-song chortle that was probably meant to be winsome.

Once again, the man pushed the head back down. Nelle saw another flash of silver. She jutted her chin, indicating his hand. "Why're you wearing gauntlets?" she demanded, then quickly added, "I suppose wyverns bite. Or maybe they breathe fire. Come to think of it, I wouldn't want to touch one without something to—"

"You must go."

There it was. A reaction. Something she could grasp hold of. Sure, the words were unfriendly, forbidding even. But she might yet manage to take charge of the situation.

She offered a blisteringly bright smile. "Go, sir? But I just got here. I need a place to rest a while." She tossed her head, took another step toward him, and tried a trick she'd seen Mother perform more times than she could count, fluttering a gaze up into that shadowed face from beneath her lashes. "I've had a run of bad luck lately," she said with perfect honesty. She made her eyes limpid, vulnerable. "If it's all the same to you, I should like—"

"You must go. Now." The man took a step back, widening the space between them. He swung a robed arm. "Get back in your boat and get out of here. While you still can."

Shadows flicked suddenly on the ground around her feet. Nelle started back several paces. She looked up and saw many draconian silhouettes gathering in the air overhead. Their sweetly chortling voices melted into a whole storm of ugly brays. Flashing, jewel-like eyes glared down at her.

"Get out," the man said.

And the wyverns swarmed.

There was no time to think. No time to plan or react with anything but a gut-wrenching scream. Nelle turned and fled along the beach, hardly feeling the sharp things tearing into her feet. Wings pounded the air behind her, and nasty, raspy voices bellowed at her heels. Claws lashed her hair and skirts, and her mind told her that wings pounded her head and teeth savaged her body.

She reached her boat and nearly fell into it, but she managed to brace herself, grip the side, and push it out into the water. The waves caught and tried to yank it out of her grasp, and she only just managed to tumble inside. She tried to rise, fell over her own skirts, pulled upright again, scrambled onto the seat, and took up the oars.

Only then did she realize the wyverns had withdrawn. They flocked in a cloud along the beach but didn't approach her boat. Through that storm of brightly colored wings, she saw the ominous figure standing solemn and straight and silent.

Her arms shaking so hard she could barely hold the oars, Nelle pulled and pushed out into the deeper water, putting distance between herself and that beach. The wyverns didn't follow.

CHAPTER 6

THE MAN WATCHED THE LITTLE BOAT PULL AWAY FROM the shore. He watched until the pursuing wyverns dispersed in spreading rays of brilliant color, catching updrafts and soaring higher and higher, returning to their lilting dance high above the waves. He watched until that red hair vanished into the haze of the Hinter Sea.

And still he stood there, watching.

Had it been a dream? It must have been. A face like hers, so lovely, so fine featured, so otherworldly in its beauty, could hardly be real. A face like hers must have been born from the fever of his isolation, his loneliness as he tipped ever closer to madness.

Except . . . would he dream such a conversation? By the seven holy names, she'd interrogated him on his eating habits!

So perhaps it was no dream. It wasn't altogether unusual for mortals to wash up on this shore, especially at this turn of the cycle when the currents of the Hinter Sea drew the island close to mortal shores. He had upon occasion seen fishermen drift close to his beach before realizing their error and correcting course in a scramble of sails and oars. And over the years there had been . . . visitors.

All of them had met terrible ends. The same end that awaited this girl if she stayed.

He drew a sharp breath as a sudden cold wind blew in his face, knocked his hood back, and twisted through his hair. The wounded wyvern dug hooked claws into his shoulder to put its head up close to his ear and snuffle dolefully.

"It was for her own good," the man said, pushing the creature back down into the sling and turning away from the sea. "Whatever her story, she cannot remain here. It was a kindness to drive her from these shores. We must hope your brethren frightened her enough to banish all thought of return."

The wyvern grumbled as though in answer as the man carried him up the cliff path.

"I don't care if you liked her." The man gathered his robe's hem to avoid tripping on it as he climbed. "I'm not intending to eat you. I never was intending to eat you. All her sympathy is wasted. Don't go sighing after her, fool beast."

The wyvern hissed and continued to mutter all the way to the top of the cliff. There the man turned again to gaze out across the ocean, his eyes peeled for any last glimpse of that small craft. He saw nothing. Perhaps it had already passed through the Veil, returned to mortal seas.

Soran Silveri . . .

That name. He knew that name. Didn't he?

Was it his own?

Heaving a sigh, he wrenched away from the view, trudged to the lighthouse door, and ducked to enter. The large square chamber was dreary after the brightness of the day. When he closed his eyes against the gloom, dazzling images of sunlight glinting on strands of brilliant red hair played behind his eyelids.

With a sharp shake of his head, he pulled the sling off his back. The wyvern squawked in protest as he gently lowered it to the table in the center of the room. Struggling to get free of the sling, it scrabbled with the clawed tips of its bat-like wings, kicked with its hindquarters. When it finally plopped in a heap on the table, all scales and tail and oddly jointed limbs, it cast a baleful look up at the man.

"Wait there," he said and moved to the staircase. He climbed fast, passing through the hole in the ceiling up into the dark and empty tower with its support beams and slit windows. The shadows felt almost as deep as night.

But there was no living, slithering sensation in those deeps.

Not yet. Not until nightfall.

Trailing his hand along the wall, he climbed around and up to the chamber above, where the air was cool and clear, and his many tools waited in their crates around his desk. He selected a fresh sheet of parchment, a quill, a trimming knife, ink, and a pumice stone, then turned back to the stair.

At the last moment he paused, his gaze drawn irresistibly toward the window overlooking the sea cliffs and the shore. For a few breaths he hesitated, at war with himself.

Against all inner protests, he moved to the window and looked out. From this higher vantage, the view spread much farther out across the Hinter Sea, even to the shimmering impression of the Veil that parted this world from the other. But all was hazy to his vision even when he narrowed his eyes and tried to force clarity. He could see the tip of the Evenspire in the distance, but everything between was obscured. Not with mist or fog—the day was crisp and clear enough, a bright blue sky arched overhead with white clouds lacing the blue. But the obscurity was undeniable.

No matter how he searched, he saw no sign of the girl or her boat.

One would think, after all these years of breathing Hinter air, he would begin to develop something akin to fae senses. No such luck. He remained as limited in his mortality as ever. Still, despite these limitations, he didn't doubt the *feeling*, the sensation like an instinct plucking at the edge of his awareness.

The girl was still close. She had not gone from the island.

He clenched his teeth until his jaw ached. He'd warned her, after all. He'd been clear. It wasn't his business if she chose to ignore him, if she chose to throw her life away. He should not interfere. And yet . . .

Setting the instruments of his craft aside, he returned to the desk, knelt before one of the crates, and opened the same folio he had searched through less than an hour before. He took the topmost sheet from inside, clutched it carefully in both hands, and returned to the window. Swiftly he began to read the words written in careful, elegant, close-lined script, his mouth moving silently to shape each sentence.

A flash of brilliant color drew his eye up from the page. Great red wings spread wide against the blue sky, spiraling down toward the tower. A large wyvern tilted, ducked its head, and passed through the window to land on the man's upraised forearm, its great hind claws gripping the thick fabric of his sleeve. With its exquisite feathery crest, and wings that at first seemed as red as the rest of its body but which, when they caught the light just so, flashed with iridescent luminosity, it was a far more elegant creature than the blue beast downstairs on his table.

It bowed a tapered face, its emerald eyes meeting the man's gaze.

"I must beg a favor, my friend," the man said, gently stroking the beautiful creature along its long neck. "A mortal came to the island. You saw her, I believe. I want you to fly out, search the boundaries and the wards. Make certain she has gone, truly gone. Return as soon as you may and take care you are not out past sunset."

The wyvern blinked its jewel-like eyes in acknowledgement. Turning its head and body, it launched from the man's arm with enough force to send him staggering back several paces. It drew its wings close to its body as it shot through the window, then spread them wide to catch air currents as it wheeled out into the open sky.

The man turned away with a bitter scowl and a pang in his breast. "That's done," he muttered, gathering his tools and tramping down the long dark stair. "Best to know for sure," he continued, speaking the words aloud as though by the sheer act of enunciation he could make himself believe what he said. "That's all I require. Confirmation. The rest is out of my hands."

Something in the darkness listened. Something unseen, unheard, but present.

The man cast an uneasy glance behind him, then faced resolutely down the steps and quickened his pace.

To Nelle's surprise, by the time she stopped frantically rowing long enough to investigate the wounds she fully expected to lacerate every inch of her body, she discovered no bites or scratches. Only her poor feet bled into her slippers, having taken the worst of that rough beach. But that flock of monsters—those not-dragons, according to the hooded man—though terrifying, had caused no damage other than a few small rips in the blue gown. She was winded, frightened, bedraggled, but unharmed.

She pulled out into the open water, away from the beach. The hooded man and his flock of wyverns shrank into the distance. The man seemed to watch her for some while before he turned and made for the cliffs, where he took some upward path she couldn't see. She shipped her oars and waited but didn't see him reappear at the top of the cliff. The not-dragons scattered, some soaring high above, others tucking away into crags and crevices along the cliff wall. Before long, the beach looked peaceful and abandoned once more.

But she didn't dare land again. Not there, anyway.

"Boggarts and brags," she growled, setting to with the oars. When she glanced over her shoulder, she couldn't see the Evenspire anymore. If she tried to set out for Wimborne, she'd likely end up twisted around by these strange currents and meet her end on the shores of Faerieland. Or worse. She must find another place on the island to land.

After nearly an hour of hard rowing, she rounded a bend that brought her in view of Roseward's far side. There she paused to drink the water and eat the food Gaspard had provided. While munching on pungent cheese, she studied this new coastline. On a hill high above appeared the impressive rooftops of a once fine manor house. Dornrise Hall, if she remembered correctly, where the lords of Roseward had dwelt in luxury for generations. From this distance it still looked mighty impressive, with its many chimneys and gables.

If she were a betting woman, she'd put money on Gaspard's spellbook being somewhere up there. No doubt a house that size boasted an entire library among its other lost treasures.

"That's where the ghosts'll be too," Nelle muttered, brushing crumbs from her skirt before picking up her oars again.

Within another quarter-hour she came in sight of the harbor. It was tucked away between cliffs but large enough to accommodate several tall ships. Three long quays stretched out from the shore, the perfect place for expensive goods to be brought in for the Lord of Roseward's enjoyment. There was only one ship in the harbor, moored to the middle quay. Rotten, partially sunk into the water, its sails full of holes and sagging like broken wings. The prow yet remained above the waterline, so she could just read the name painted in elegant script—*Queen's Disgrace.*

The pirate ship. It must be.

But not a single pirate in sight.

Where had they gone? Did the dragon creatures kill them? "Bullspit," Nelle snarled. Mother had always said an imagination was *not* a snatcher's best asset. It was far too easy to start seeing all the worst ways a snatch could end, resulting in fear-induced paralysis.

Nelle shut down her mind as firmly as she could and guided

her little boat along one of the quays to the shore, where she dragged it up onto a much softer, sandier beach than the one on the other side of the island. A small blessing, but her battered feet were grateful.

Slinging the snatcher's satchel over her shoulder, she made her way up the beach to a paved road sloping gently toward the high cliffs above. Numerous houses stood close to the docks, but the harsh ocean wind and waves had worked a destructive influence, tearing off doors and rooftops and battering in windows. In another few decades, with no one to shore up and make repairs, the whole village would collapse. Ultimately, all traces of its former life and bustle would be wiped from the face of Roseward Isle.

Those gaping doors and empty windows made it much too easy to believe in hauntings. Averting her gaze, Nelle adjusted the set of her satchel, hoisted her sodden skirts, and hastened up the road, which was ruinous too, but serviceable. After hours in that hateful little boat, getting used to solid ground again took some doing, but she continued doggedly. The sun was already high overhead. If she wanted to snatch this book and get off the island before nightfall, she must hurry.

Keeping a wary eye on the sky for draconian silhouettes, she gained the top of the cliff. Here she had to watch every step. Not many years ago a carefully tended and ornate garden must have lined this stretch, but the once shapely trees were now overgrown and ungainly. Briars and thorns mounded over

103

crumbled walls and tore into the paving stones of the road itself.

At the end of the road waited Dornrise Hall.

From a distance it had looked grand and imposing, but the closer Nelle came, the more hideous she realized it was. Once it must have been gloriously festooned in climbing roses that bloomed throughout the year. After years of neglect, the briars had multiplied, spread, snarled, struggled, and died, burying the graceful lines of the house in their death throes. Yellow leaves and black spots marred the few patches of green growth remaining. It was all so ugly. And so sad.

The wrought-iron gate, torn half off its hinges by more of the destructive briars, sagged open before her, far from welcoming. Nelle stopped at that gate and peered down the drive to the once magnificent double doors. She could hardly see them through the snarl of thorns.

"Now'd be a good time to have those claws," she whispered. The nilarium silver would have torn through those briars easily enough. Still, no good in sighing over what she didn't have. She'd have to make do. At least there was no sign of little dragons roosting among the chimney pots.

Finding a way through proved complicated. Within an hour she was scratched and bleeding, hot and frustrated, and so horribly exhausted, her knees shook. After all, it wasn't as if she'd had restful nights or nutritious meals leading up to the day's events, and that jar of water and the morsels of bread and cheese she'd almost inhaled in the boat were faint memories. By the time she found a path through the thorny canes, she was swearing and sweating and disheveled enough to frighten off any ghosts.

It was a narrow, partially overgrown walkway that led to a back door. Maybe the pirates had cut their way through here, and the briar simply hadn't had time to grow back completely? Speculation aside, her hands were scratched and shivering by the time she fought through to the door and tried the handle. It gave at the slightest pressure. This surprised Nelle so much, she gave a little cry of delight as she slid her skinny self through, emerging into cool darkness on the other side.

She paused to let her eyes adjust after the noontime brilliance outside, gradually recognizing large brick and clay ovens, long worktables, hanging utensils, pots, and pails, all familiar after her labors in the Miphates University scullery. A grin pulled at the corners of her mouth. If this was the kitchen, then . . .

She sprang into motion and flung open doors and cupboards. Her nose tingled, and she followed it until she discovered a larder full of crates and goods. "Don't get excited," she whispered harshly. "It's been fifteen years. Nothing here's going to be edible."

But she couldn't resist stepping inside for closer inspection. Just enough light filtered through one of the windows to reveal sealed jars of fruits and vegetables. Further exploration led to flour and sugar, barley and molasses, and various spices, including cinnamon and cloves. When tentatively sampled, everything tasted surprisingly unspoiled.

Best of all, she found a loaf of bread in a basket under a cloth. While she knew that by all rights it should have long since molded away to dust, it appeared as fresh as if it had been baked that morning. When she poked it, the crust was hard but tempting. When she tore it in half, it revealed a soft, delectable interior.

She made short work of the entire loaf, little caring that it was impossible, little caring that it was probably enchanted. When she'd finished, she found a handful of dates in a basket and stuffed them into her satchel for later. Temporarily satisfied, she wiped sticky fingers on her skirts and ventured out from the larder. She'd return for a more thorough search later. For now, her appetite sated, she had a job to do.

A stair led from the kitchens to the main floor of the house above. From that stairway Nelle stepped into a passage rich with ornate moldings and a carpet soft beneath her poor tired feet. She breathed in a scent of wealth and . . . emptiness.

"Find the book," she whispered. "That's all you need. Find the book and get out."

She proceeded with caution, walking on her toes. Every sense was sharp, every muscle tensed. Every door she passed stood open, as though someone had come along before her and peered into every room by turn. She peered into a few rooms stuffed with ornate furnishings and decorations that stank of mildew. Many of the windows were broken, and briars climbed through the cracks and spread along walls or ceilings.

In places, she saw strange . . . gashes. As though someone had taken a sword to this table or that wall, tearing long, deep grooves. She tried not to look too closely at these.

At the end of one passage, another door stood partially open, revealing bright daylight. Nelle frowned. It was easy to get turned around in a house this large. Had she somehow made her way to the front entrance? Approaching the door on tiptoe, she peered through the opening.

She stood on the threshold of an enormous dining hall. Light poured in from a domed glass ceiling overhead and fully illuminated a bountiful banquet table laid as though for a feast. She saw cut-crystal wine decanters and silver ewers, silver and gold chalices and place settings, jewel-studded knives, and a tablecloth of rare purple silk embroidered in a pattern of gold-threaded roses. There were footed bowls piled high with the shriveled remains of fruit, and the ugly skeletons of a boar and an enormous bird, one on each end of the table, still perched on huge silver platters.

Guests sat at the table. Slumped over in their seats, heads down on their plates. As though they'd fallen asleep mid-feast.

They weren't as rotten and ruinous as everything else in that room. There was still flesh on their bones, hair on their skulls, clothes on their limbs. Nelle noticed the clothing right away. It wasn't the rich doublets and hose of lords, or the corsets and jewels of ladies. The bodies wore slouchy rough cloth, stained and worn, and the men themselves, what was left of them, were equally rough and unsavory. Their emaciated hands grasped the goblets and place-settings with a covetousness that lasted beyond death.

So. This was where the crew of the *Queen's Disgrace* had met their end. Their throats cut and their clothing slashed. Their limbs sliced to ribbons while they took their ease at a dead lord's feast.

CHAPTER 7

His hands wouldn't obey him.

Fingers aching with tension, the man tried yet again to hold the quill steadily in place above the creamy sheet of parchment. He rested the nib softly on the surface and applied a trace more pressure as he began to form a long, careful, flowing line. He felt at once that the pressure was off; the line was too thick, and when he attempted to adjust, it nearly vanished altogether. The trace of shimmering energy that had flared for the briefest of instants dissipated into nothing.

He would've liked to blame it on the quill. Or possibly on the thickness of the ink. But he knew better. The fault was entirely his.

The blue wyvern sprawled on the table before him, its blunt nose resting between the claw-tipped points of its arm-wings. It rolled a baleful eye his way and muttered. When he threw down the quill in frustration, the creature lifted its head sharply and showed its teeth in a snarl of pain. It pulled its broken wing close to its side, the torn, translucent skin bunching in ugly folds. The piece of parchment with its little scrawl of uneven lettering whipped out from under the man's hand and fluttered to the ground.

He sat back in his chair, shaking his head. His temples throbbed and his shoulders ached. How long had he sat here, intent upon his work? He'd lost track of time. Hours, perhaps. Crumpled and discarded pages littered the floor around his chair, all marred by his poor writing. Here and there a strand of shimmering energy pulsed, but it would soon fade to nothing, too feeble to be of any use.

"Sorry, little friend," he muttered as the wyvern sat up on its haunches and drew its wings around its body, wrapping itself up like a scaly sausage. When it glared at him, he could offer only an apologetic shake of his head. "Forgive me. My hands . . ." He lifted them helplessly, then, with a grimace, pressed his palms against his bleary eyes. Shaking his head, he pulled at the rough skin of his face and ran his fingers up through the tangled mats of his hair.

His thick outer robes draped across the back of a chair across the table. He wore only his trousers and the same loose, torn shirt he'd worn the night before. It was still brown with bloodstains, but when he idly pulled the fabric back to inspect the flesh beneath, he found that the cuts had healed over into ugly, puckered scars. One of the advantages of breathing the air of this world: His wounds, though severe, healed swiftly. His body was always hale and whole for the next night, the next round of lacerations.

The wyvern, sensing his distress, unwrapped its body and sank to its belly, sliding across the table to stretch out its long neck.

He met its blinking yellow eyes. "You'll have to stay here, little friend. Until I can figure out some way to help. You'll be too vulnerable, flightless after dark. I can protect you well enough so long as you remain within these walls."

A shudder rippled along the wyvern's spine. It continued to blink at the man, tilting its blunt-nosed head slightly to one side. When an inquiring expression lit its eyes, the man stood abruptly, overturning his chair. Locks of matted hair fell in his face as he crossed the dim room to the door. He hardly knew what he was doing until his hand was on the latch and he'd flung the door open. Stepping over the threshold into open air, he closed his eyes and drew a long breath as though tasting freedom after the long stagnation of a prison cell.

The sound of beating wings caught his attention. He opened his eyes, shaded his face, and peered up to where a lithe, elegant shape on wide wings danced through the bright sky. He extended one arm at the last moment to provide a perch for the beautiful crimson wyvern. Its claws wrapped entirely around his forearm, and he braced to balance its weight.

The wyvern opened its mouth and uttered a songlike string of sounds.

"You were fast, my beauty." The man lifted his free hand to a run a finger gently along the creature's extended, saffron-hued throat. "What news do you bring? Is . . ." He hesitated. He didn't quite want to ask the question. Something in the wyvern's eye told him he wouldn't like the answer. But he needed to know. "Is the mortal girl gone from our shores?"

The wyvern bowed its head, its crest unfurling along its neck. Then it turned both head and neck in a twining motion and looked to the north of the island.

The man's heart sank as his gaze followed the wyvern's. From this vantage he could see all the way to the far end, nearly a mile distant, where the rooftops and chimneys of the great hall jutted in silhouette against the sky.

He clenched his jaw, stifling a curse. So. She'd chosen to ignore his warnings and head straight to the corrupt heart of Roseward.

It wasn't his fault. And it wasn't his business. He'd warned her. If she chose not to take heed, her fate was on her own head.

The man faced the wyvern again, nodding. "You've done well. Now go and stay hidden tonight. *Her* attention will be elsewhere, but best not to take unnecessary risks. Warn the others."

The wyvern flared its crest and sang an acknowledgement. The muscles in its powerful haunches coiling, it launched into the air, circled once, twice, gaining altitude, and flitted off and away from the cliff's edge to rejoin its brethren in their aerial dances until the day's end.

The man idly watched, not really seeing the wyvern. Instead, he saw—if only for a flashing moment—a pale face peering up at him through a veil of wet, windswept hair.

He turned back to the door. Though he'd been eager to leave behind that dark, close space, now he sought it again like a refuge and slammed the door hard, making the wyvern squawk and dive off the table. It scuttled away to the fireplace, up the stones, and onto the mantel, where it hunched and hissed menacingly.

The man ignored it. He set to work, picking up the various discarded pages and refusing to look at the mess he'd made on every single one. He smoothed each sheet and stacked them all neatly on the table, but though his face was set and his actions were purposeful, he worked in a fog.

When the floor was clear, he looked stupidly at the stack of pages, uncertain why he'd taken such care. It wasn't as though he could reuse them. Besides, no matter how much paper he took from his meager store of supplies upstairs, it never dwindled. One of the many blessings—or curses—of Roseward. One he had long since ceased to appreciate. But now that he'd gathered the pages, he might as well take another look. Perhaps there was more in those scrawled lines than had first appeared. Perhaps something like life or power could be coaxed out of them if he just . . .

He leaned heavily on the table, his shoulders hunched, one hand resting on the pile of pages, the other clenched in a fist and pressed hard into the wooden surface. Who was he fooling? He could pretend all he liked, but his mind wouldn't focus on this work. Every thought strained toward the far side of the island. Every nerve tensed, waiting for the hours of darkness fast approaching.

"Why didn't she listen?" he whispered. "Why didn't she go?"

A scrape of claws on stone, scurrying across the floor. The next moment, the wyvern hooked its wing-arms over the edge of the table and pulled its long body up. It slid toward him on its belly and laid its head on his hand atop the stack of pages. Blinking up at him, it whined softly.

The man glared back. "Don't look at me like that. I'm not one to be so easily manipulated."

Indignant, the wyvern hissed at him, rattling its tongue. The man sneered back, jerked his hand from under the creature's chin, righted his overturned chair, and sat. He tried to ignore the persistent gaze of the little beast, but it slithered further across the table, extended its long neck until its nose was mere inches from his, and emitted an incessant, high-pitched whine.

"Enough!" The man sprang up again. "Enough of this. It's

foolish and will certainly mean the end of all of us. When *she* tears through your flesh and scatters your essence to the twelve winds, don't go blaming me!"

The wyvern opened its mouth in a toothy snarl that might have been a grin, watching as the man snagged his robes from the other chair and hauled them across his shoulders, then strode to the armoire, poked around inside, and withdrew a little moleskin book. Thumbing through its pages, he noted the various spells inscribed within, none of them great spells, but all potent enough. They would have to do.

"You'll see," the man muttered, tucking the volume away in his robe. He shot another accusatory glare the wyvern's way. "You'll regret this. We all will."

With those words, he turned and hastened out the door, leaving the wyvern seated upright on the table, its one good wing flared triumphantly.

"Get ahold of yourself. Breathe, girl. Breathe."

Nelle clutched her head in both hands, her back pressed against a wall as far down the passage as she'd managed to stumble before her knees gave out. Her body was all a-shudder. Which was ridiculous. It wasn't as though she'd grown up in a sheltered garden all her life. She'd seen more than her fair share of bodies, more than her fair share of horrors.

But this was different.

Those men . . . they were so relaxed. Yet they'd died so grue-somely! How could anyone suffer wounds like that while simply dozing over a table? Why had they not tried to escape? Why had they not tried to fight back? Why were their faces not contorted in the agony they must surely have experienced?

Maybe she'd misread the scene. Yes. That must be it. She'd had only a quick look before terror chilled her veins and she retreated into the shadowy passage. If she'd looked more closely, she would have seen, would have realized . . .

Nelle gripped the hair at her temples, pulling hard enough to hurt, hard enough to force her thoughts back into order. She couldn't let her mind shut down. "They died a long time ago," she whispered. "Years ago. Whatever did *that* to them, it's long gone now."

Did she believe herself?

Did it matter?

"Get up and find that book, Nelle." Her voice growled, deep and dangerous in her throat. "Get up and find it. Papa's waiting for you. He's counting on you. You've got to do this. For him."

Using the wall for support, she pushed back up onto unsteady feet. With both hands braced against the molded plaster at her back, she drew long, careful breaths until her heart rate slowed. She wasn't a coward. She'd had a shock, but she wasn't undone. Not yet, anyway.

Thrusting a tremulous hand into her satchel, she withdrew her knife and sheath. Her fingers were almost too stupid to get it properly attached to her wrist and hidden under her sleeve, but the moment she felt that familiar pressure along her forearm, she felt better.

Not that her tiny blade would do much good against whatever had sliced those men to ribbons . . .

Nelle squared her shoulders, took the first turn out of the passage, away from that dining hall, and passed several open doors without peering inside. Mother had once spread detailed house plans of Mayor Quindove's house in Wimborne across their table and, although she'd never let Nelle venture inside, ordered her to memorize every room, stairway, window, and attic before they paid the mayor a late-night visit. Quindove's city palace was nothing compared with the sprawling magnificence of this ruin, but Nelle suspected its layout would be similar. Which meant the library ought to be on the second floor.

After a few more turns, she discovered a grand staircase that led up to a landing and split in two. A large window adorned the wall above it, and although briars obscured its bottom half, sunlight poured through the upper panes, casting a path of gold down the center of the stairs.

Nelle approached, then hesitated. The decorative newel posts were shaped like dragons—no, *wyverns*. Their jaws gaped grotesquely, and they seemed to vomit carved briars adorned with perfectly shaped roses, which wound up the banister rails.

Avoiding this unsettling blend of the hideous and the lovely, Nelle ascended the very center of the staircase, in the middle of the sunlit strip. On the landing she paused a moment, then turned right. At the top, facing another dark passage lined with cracked-open doors, she felt prickles down her spine as if someone might be watching her, peering through those cracks. Just waiting for her to pass.

She twitched her wrist to feel the comforting presence of her knife, then boldly strode down the hall and stopped at each door to kick it open wider and look fully into the room beyond.

The third door on the left yielded the result she sought. "At last!" she breathed, entered, and stopped short. Her eyes slowly widened.

The room was so shadowed and dark that she hadn't immediately grasped the vastness of the space. Inset bookshelves stretched from the floor all the way to the crown molding just beneath the arched ceiling, two-and-a-half stories above. Spiral staircases led to landings and walkways, and sliding ladders tempted anyone more daringly bookish to pluck a volume from the topmost shelves. A cavernous fireplace grounded the space, its huge scrolled mantel crowded with decorative tomes. Ornate yet comfortable-looking chairs—the size of thrones, Nelle thought— were drawn up close to the hearth.

For a moment she forgot her fear. It was a wonder simply to stand in that doorway, to breathe the atmosphere of knowledge and beauty and mystery caught in paper and parchment through- out centuries past. She'd always loved books, though there never had been much time to indulge in the pleasure they gave her.

But . . . she was here for a reason.

Memory of her mission crashed down on her, and her shoulders bowed. "Bullspit," she said. Her voice bounced and echoed back at her before that solemn silence swallowed it. How was she ever supposed to find one book out of all these hundreds, thousands?

Unless she was lucky—unreasonably lucky—she would not be out of here by sundown.

CHAPTER 8

THE MAN PUT HIS HEAD DOWN, FOLDED HIS ARMS DEEP into his robe, and strode along the cliffside path heading north. He watched his feet rather than look toward his destination, unable to quite believe he was doing this, venturing out of the lighthouse this close to sunset.

But, one after another, his footsteps carried him across the island. The sky darkened. The sun dipped toward the ocean, casting a fiery trail across the waves. In another hour it would set completely. And he would be out after dark.

He felt inside the front of his robes, touched the little moleskin book hidden there. He may not be what he once was. He may never reclaim true power again. But he wasn't without weapons. Though his hands would no longer serve him, his mind was as sharp as ever. Or at least he thought it was.

He might actually be insane, in which case he was doomed anyway.

The sharp wind billowed his robes and penetrated the snarls of his beard to chap his lips and freeze his skin. The day had been mild, but this change in the air promised a storm. Perhaps not tonight, perhaps not even tomorrow. But soon. He smelled the threat of rain in the atmosphere.

When he raised his head and saw the hall before him, his heart constricted in his chest.

Dornrise.

The name flitted through his mind so subtly that he almost wasn't aware of it. His mouth moved, his lips trying to form the word, which at first seemed wholly strange, wholly foreign. "Dorn . . . rise . . ."

The mere speaking of it worked a powerful influence. He closed his eyes. Memories washed over him in a relentless torrent—memories he had long worked to shut out of his brain, memories he had thought lost forever. But they could never be truly lost, not so long as he lived.

He stood before the broken, battered gates, but with his eyes closed he saw them as they had once been, tall and graceful, always open to the travelers who passed to and from Roseward Isle in a steady stream. He saw the long avenue of carefully tended elms casting their thin shadows across the drive. He saw the house, massive and majestic, at the far end. In the green lawn before the door, he saw a pair of young lads race together after a red ball, laughing carelessly as they tripped and fell over one another in their efforts, staining their fine white trousers. Their golden hair streamed behind them like horse tails.

And the roses. He smelled them. Even now as he breathed in, their vibrant aroma filled his head. How he had once loved them with a deep but unconscious sort of love, a feeling he hadn't been aware of though it pulsed through his veins. Roses were the life and soul of Dornrise, of the whole island. He'd breathed their perfume from the moment of his birth, drawn it into his soul.

The roses were long dead. Withered on their stems. A few blackened husks still clung to the dry and brittle branches that choked the once magnificent hall and its grounds. Their former glory was long gone, leaving behind only skeletal, thorn-ridden remains.

But the perfume . . . it lingered. Lingered in every stone, every stump. As rank as poison.

If the mortal girl possessed any sense whatsoever, she would have taken one look at Dornrise as it now stood, turned on her heel, and fled. But she hadn't. He felt it. She was there, inside. Somehow she'd forced her way through that mad tangle of briars and offered herself up to the house. A stupid little lamb skipping merrily into the slaughterhouse.

Clutching his robes with both hands, the man passed through

the gates. As he strode along the drive, more scenes erupted in his mind: scenes of carriages arriving on torchlit drives, scenes of ladies in low-cut gowns, servants hastening behind them with canopies to shade their delicate skin, scenes of young men in tall boots and plumed hats astride high-strung colts. Scenes of life as it once had been.

Soran Silveri.

It was his name, though he had long striven to forget it, along with every other detail about who he had once been. Now this girl had come and forced him back into environs he had long avoided, driven his mind down paths best left untrod. Perhaps he had gone more than a little mad over the course of the Hinter cycles. But madness was better than the torturous sanity now settling into that dark space behind his eyes.

Soran Silveri. The second son of Lord Sothale Silveri of Roseward. His mother's darling, his brother's bane. The scourge of all he once knew and loved.

Teeth clenched, he plunged into the snarl of thorns concealing the once proud front entrance of the mighty hall. He tore into the briars, his hands grasping and ripping, and little cared how they lashed back at him. Few of the thorns were sharp enough to penetrate the thick fabric of his robes, and his exposed hands felt no pain.

At last he made his way through to the massive front door and tried the latch. It was, as he expected, unlocked, and the door swung silently open on its hinges. He stepped through into the cavernous space of the front foyer.

Another wave of remembrance swept over him, and he was momentarily unable to move, unable to breathe. As though reliving it all, he saw the crush of lordly men and lovely dames in their silks and velvets at the base of the stair. And on the landing, poised with her hand just resting on the rail, clad in her bridal white and as yet unaware of his presence . . .

"Helenia." Almost against his will, his mouth moved, forming her name.

Did she hear him? It seemed as though she did, the way her vision-self flinched, turning her head so sharply that a cascade of black curls tumbled over one shoulder. Her eyes flicked back and forth, searching through the crowd, searching for him.

He ducked his head, grinding a bitter curse through his teeth. The illusion vanished, the lords and ladies, the lights, the music, and that moment. He turned sharply to yank the door fast behind him, plunging the foyer into blessed darkness that blocked out the past, pulling him back into the shadows and gloom of the present. Helenia was gone. Long, long gone. As were they all. No one remained on Roseward Isle except the monsters he himself had brought here.

He straightened, his ears pricked, listening for some telltale creak of a floorboard or click of a shutting door. Something that might betray the location of the mortal girl. It would be an interesting game of cat and mouse through these many halls and passages. The girl might have ended up anywhere.

125

His skin prickled along the back of his neck. He slid back his hood, letting it fall across his shoulders, and peered into the deepest shadows beyond the stair and banister rails. They were empty—empty shadows, empty darkness.

But he knew better.

She wasn't far away. She was never far away.

A growl rumbling in his throat, he set off down the nearest passage on his right, leading toward the banquet hall, as good a place to begin his search as any. Creeping movement followed him, just beyond the edges of his vision, and though he ignored it with firm nonchalance, he kept one hand on the booklet inside his robes, just in case. Silently he passed through this tomb that was once his home, every muscle tensed, eyes wide and staring. If only he dared strike a light! But that would draw unwanted attention his way. Just now *she* seemed to be distracted. Better to let her remain that way.

Most of the rooms he passed without pause, but faint vibrations in the air, like the subtle dance of dust motes, alerted him to the few doors that had recently been opened. He peered into those rooms with interest. All were empty. The house was silent and still. No sign of the mortal girl.

He came to the end of one passage and saw the doors leading to the banquet hall slightly open. The hall where a lush wedding feast, never eaten, was left to rot and spoil over the years.

Would the girl have ventured in there?

He approached the doors and peered inside—and his heart

leapt to his throat at the sight of the gruesome slaughter within.

He'd known they were dead, of course, those foolish men who had come to this shore seeking the lost treasures of Dornrise. He'd never seen them, but he'd watched their ship sail into the harbor, and he'd known when they disembarked like an infestation swarming his shores, eager to begin destruction.

They'd never even gotten started. He'd heard their screams in the night. And when *she* visited him later, stained with their blood, she had smiled and preened.

I wish you could have attended my little party, she'd murmured into his ear. *How you would have enjoyed yourself!*

He could feel her now, her arms draped round him from behind. When he breathed, he inhaled her perfume, her miasma of sweet rottenness. The poison of her silken lips tickled his ear, turning his blood to water.

Oh, gods above, why had he left the tower? He knew better. After all this time, he knew better!

A rustle disturbed the air at his back. He whirled in place and almost caught a glimpse of . . . something. Something sinuous and snakelike. His fingers tightened around the book hidden in the front of his shirt. He hated to draw it, hated to use power that, once used, could never be reclaimed. He was so vulnerable as it was. Every day, every hour saw his once incomparable strength depleted.

A scream split the air. Faint, far away. Echoing from some distant quarter of the house. Overhead?

He stood paralyzed, his soul frozen in a moment of decision, a moment for which he felt entirely unprepared. Reason told him to abandon this mission, leave the girl to her fate. She had been warned, after all. It wasn't his fault. It wasn't his fault. It . . . wasn't . . .

With a snarl, Soran Silveri sprang into motion. He whipped the book from the front of his shirt, opening it in front of him as he ran in pursuit of that scream.

Nelle rubbed bleary eyes with the heel of one hand. If she rubbed hard enough, perhaps she could rub sense back into her head. Or rub away the deepening shadows of the library. But when she pulled her hand away, her head was just as thick and stupid with exhaustion, and the light fading in the briar-clogged windows had dimmed dramatically.

Perched high on one of the bookshelf ladders, her elbow looped through a rung for balance, she sighed and looked down to the ground beneath the ladder, which was littered with books she'd pulled from the shelves and set aside for closer inspection. She'd found candles and matches stashed in drawers and lit a dozen or so, scattering them on various tables. One candle flickered on the shelf in front of her, making a golden sphere of light.

But all the candles in the world couldn't disguise the truth: The sun had set. She would be spending the night in Dornrise Hall.

"Bullspit," she muttered. Leaving the candle to sputter and die in its holder, she climbed down the ladder, sat cross-legged in the circle of her skirt amid the various stacks of books, and studied their covers, trying to determine whether any of them might be the book Gaspard sought.

There were a few possible candidates, leather bindings edged with floral tracings, maybe roses, maybe not. When she cracked the covers and studied the words inside, they didn't *look* particularly spell-like. One was filled with painfully small typeset print depicting the lives and times of the kings and queens of Seryth in stultifying detail. Another boasted curling script and saccharine poetry that made her teeth ache.

But there were roses—or what might be roses—on the covers. And how was she to know if they were proper spellbooks or not? Those lines might hold some magic she couldn't sense.

Then again, she'd felt the power emanating from the grimoires in Gaspard's quillary. If Gaspard coveted this Rose Book so intensely, it must be at least as powerful.

Nelle picked up one book, turned it over, and set it aside. When she rolled her neck and shoulders, they crackled in protest. She'd climbed up and down for what must be hours by now, pulling out books, shoving them back again, absorbed in her work. And she'd scarcely scratched the surface.

Her knees shook as she staggered between candles and books toward her satchel, which she'd dropped on one of the throne-like armchairs. From it she plucked the handful of dates she'd tucked away earlier. Suddenly ravenous, she plopped down in the chair and ate every date, tearing through the firm flesh and savoring the delicate sweetness. They were gone far too soon, and she sagged back into the chair.

"What now?" Her voice sounded strange in that echoing space. For the last few hours, she'd carefully not let herself think of the dead pirates. But now, as darkness settled in around her, memory of their shredded corpses intruded.

She shivered. Most definitely, she didn't want to stay the night in this place. Could she set up a camp of sorts in one of those abandoned buildings down by the quays? Surely one of them would be sturdy enough just for one night.

Who was she fooling? *One* night?

She lifted her gaze to the shelves and shelves of books towering around her, and her stomach clenched. "Good thing Gaspard gave me three weeks," she whispered. Shaking her head, she looked down at her hands folded limp in her lap.

An image flashed through her brain: a misty shore and three figures disappearing in the distance as she pulled further out on the water. Two of the figures melted away to mere smudges of shadow in her memory while the third stood out with distressing clarity.

Sam. Sam, standing there beside that Miphato monster. His face full of regret, shame. And fear. Sam, who had betrayed her, chased her down, trapped her, and handed her over to Cloven like the tithe from a fine night's snatching. Her Sam.

How stupid was that? He wasn't *her* Sam. He never had been, not really. At best he was Mother's little pet, and whatever foolish fancies Nelle had once indulged, she'd long ago given up. Why should it surprise her that he would, in turn, give her up to his boss so easily? Why should it surprise her that, for all his guilt, for all his regret, he would simply stand there and let her be sent out into cursed waters without uttering a word of protest?

She was on her own. She'd been on her own since Mother's fall. She had Papa, of course, but Papa must be cared for, incapable as he was of caring for himself.

"Papa," she whispered and closed her eyes against the threatening sting of tears. What would he do without her? Mistress Dirgin would turn him out of the attic in a heartbeat if he couldn't produce coin enough to cover rent. How could he, with his pretty face and his gentle voice and his soft hands, manage to scrounge up even half the sum from the dirt and squalor of Draggs?

If he hadn't died already from the shock of the beating Cloven had given him . . .

This thought was so sharp, so distressing that Nelle jolted in her seat. She shook herself and blinked several times. Had she nodded off? Maybe a little. The shadows in the room had deepened, and several of her candles had gone out.

No, wait . . .

She sat up straight in the armchair, looking round the room. All the candles were dead, every last one smoking softly as though just blown out by a single breath. But the room was not as dark as she would have expected. She could see everything clearly enough. There were the piles of books around the base of the ladder. There was her snatcher's satchel on the floor by her feet. She could even make out the pattern of embroidery on the elegant armchair standing opposite hers. Every thread was distinct and clear but parched, as though all the color had been drained away. All the life.

Nelle let out a breath. It streamed before her face in white clouds that shimmered, almost luminous. How very cold the room had grown. But of course, the sun was set, and she hadn't bothered to build a fire.

Why, then, did she feel as though this cold wasn't exactly . . . *cold,* as such? It was more like a creeping sensation. An emotion of . . . she didn't like to name it. Not even in the privacy of her mind. But the thought was there now and couldn't be denied.

Dread.

She sucked in a breath and stood up. A crawling shiver slid down the back of her neck, and she turned sharply. But nothing was there except the high back of the chair itself and, beyond it, the tall walls of books. The elegant plaster moldings along the baseboards were sharp and clear to her vision despite the lack of any light source.

Nelle wrapped her arms around her body. Panic swelled in her throat, but she clenched her teeth against it. Had the ghosts come out to play? Was this all part and parcel of the famous haunting she'd heard tales about?

"Ghosts are just dead folk," she whispered. "Dead folk can't hurt you. They're dead." Her voice sounded hollow and faraway, echoing as though from another world.

A flickering gleam caught the tail of her eye. Nelle turned toward it, her heart jumping, and saw a little flame in the doorway of the library. Ghost light? No . . . it was a golden flame, a warm flame, not ghostly at all. It called to her in this cold place like a lighthouse beacon breaking through heavy fog. Before she knew it, she had taken several steps toward it. But she stopped once she could see what it was that burned.

Not a candle. A rose.

A brilliant red rose, sprung from a briar that had crawled along the interior wall of the passage outside and now clung to the doorpost. The blossom bobbed gently on its stem, stirred by no discernible breeze. Its petals crumbled into ash as the fire consumed it, but somehow it continuously renewed itself, unfurling new bounteous petals even as the old ones blackened.

The sight was bizarre, unsettling, unnatural. But at least it was a living thing. Or a *dying* thing, still alive but enduring excruciating pain as it succumbed to those flames again and again. Dying was not the same as dead, however, and Nelle moved toward it, drawn by the warmth of its torment.

Before she knew it, she stood in the doorway with her back to the library. Another bright flicker of light down the passage caught her eye: a second burning rose sprung from another

133

section of briars crawling up the paneled wall. Had they already penetrated inside the house when she came this way earlier? She couldn't remember.

The rose close beside her extinguished suddenly, its flame doused like her blown candles. The smoke carried a trace of sweet perfume mingled with a distinct stench of sulfur, which turned her stomach. Nelle quickly moved on down the passage toward that second rose, drawn to its light like a moth. Anything was better than remaining in darkness that wasn't truly darkness.

Somewhere in the back of her head, a warning voice tried to protest. She was being lured—lured like a fish after a worm. And she was stupidly going along with it. Why? Why didn't she stop?

Yet she continued until the perfume of the second rose filled her nostrils and she stepped closer to observe again the phenomenon of crumbling petals self-renewing only to feed the fire. The canes never caught, nor the rest of the briar. Only the rose itself.

Nelle reached one hand toward the flickering flames, entranced. Her fingers flinched at the heat, yet still she reached, suddenly eager to catch and hold that rose, to claim it.

Abruptly this fire went out. Her fingers closed around cold, crumbling ashes. The world plunged into total darkness, and she stood blinking and blind for several breaths before her vision adjusted to the strange, shadowed clarity of the night around her. She'd nearly reached the end of the passage near the gallery rail overlooking the foyer.

On the gallery railing on the far side, across that open space, glowed a third light, as tempting as the previous two had been.

Without a thought, she set out after it, her feet stumbling in her eagerness. She'd taken no more than a few paces when her ears caught an unexpected sound. The silence had been so pervasive and deep that she'd almost forgotten what sound was like until this lovely, lilting voice broke through. It was a woman's voice, low and husky. Singing.

The moving flames of the third burning rose seemed to dance in time to the song. Nelle hastened along the upper gallery, following the rail round to the far side, pursuing the light and the voice, eager to catch up to both. Her footsteps were light, and her heart thrilled with a sensation she couldn't name. It couldn't be fear. How could she fear a voice so beautiful, so enchanting?

She began to discern words in the song:

> *"Red blooms the rose in my heart tonight,*
> *Fair as the dawn, new as the spring*
> *Dark flows the tide, yet the stars they shine bright*
> *And summon my soul now to sing."*

Nelle hastened through the shadows as the third burning rose went out and another burst into flame, and then another, leading her deeper into that wing of the great house, toward that voice.

The walls writhed on either side of her, creeping with darkness that her peripheral vision discerned as living branches and cruel

135

thorns tearing into the wood and plaster. Behind her she felt briars closing in, blocking off the way she'd just come, twining together in an impassable, choking tangle.

She couldn't be afraid. The voice was close now. Nothing mattered except finding its source.

She arrived at a wide, stately hall lined with doors on either side, all of which stood partly opened. She didn't care to peer into those rooms, however, for a final burning rose gleamed over the doorway six doors down. It must be the room she sought. The voice, the lovely, lovely voice, poured out from inside.

> *"Come down to the water, my love, my love,*
> *Come down to the banks of the sea.*
> *Come down to the boat, set sail in the night,*
> *And your true love forever I'll be."*

Nelle hastened to that doorway, and though the rose overhead snuffed out just as the others had done, it didn't matter. The room inside was aglow with light. Dozens of roses filled the space, suspended from clinging briars that climbed the walls, wound up the posts of a large canopied bed, and crawled along the ceiling. A large bouquet hung from the center of the ceiling like a chandelier, and the effect was dazzling, glorious.

But Nelle's attention fixed on the figure across the room, seated at an elegant vanity. Five roses climbed the mirror frame, and their light illuminated the glass to such perfection, Nelle could see the face and form reflected there as clearly as daylight.

It was a woman—a young woman, hardly any older than Nelle herself, but so different from her in every respect. Her skin was like dusky cream, soft and supple, the result of beauty treatments only the wealthiest could afford. Her hair was long and black and almost perfectly straight, falling down her back and across her shoulders in waves that caught the firelight in a glossy sheen. An exquisite face set with compelling dark eyes, fine cheekbones, and a pointed chin tilted at a slight angle from her long, elegant neck. She wore only a dressing gown, which fell away from her shapely shoulders. Everything about her bespoke years of breeding and refinement, as though generations had labored long to produce this one exquisite specimen of womanhood.

A gold chain gleamed at her throat, and a delicate oval charm rested on her breastbone above the swell of her ample bosom. She held a lock of hair in one hand while the other worked a comb through it in careful, even strokes, moving in time to the song she sang. The whole vision was so arresting, Nelle froze in the doorway and simply stared. For a moment she couldn't even feel the shame welling up inside her—shame at her own ragged, rumpled, sea-stained appearance, her Draggs-wench ungainliness.

The song broke off suddenly. The dark eyes in the glass shifted from self-contemplation to fix on Nelle in the doorway. Those straight brows drew together in a stern line of surprise. One by one, the roses around the room snuffed out, leaving behind the heady stench of perfume and sulfur mingled.

"Who are you?" the woman demanded in a deep voice.

Nelle gaped, unable to answer. Her mind clamored suddenly with warnings she had been unwilling to heed for some moments now. She opened her mouth, trying to think of an excuse.

Instead, she screamed, "Watch out!"

Her voice was small. Distant. Too far away to hear, as though coming through a thick wall.

It was too late anyway.

Briars swarmed around the base of the woman's chair, crawled up the vanity, and closed around the woman herself. She jerked and tried to rise, but briars wrapped around her legs, binding her to her seat, and clawed up her dressing gown to encircle her arms. A thick branch wrapped around her shoulders, her neck, its thorns tearing into her flesh. Blood streamed in brilliant rivulets down her smooth skin. The woman's mouth dropped open in a scream, but no sound emerged from her throat—only leaves, thorns, and a huge blooming rose. Her jaw broke as they exploded from inside her and overwhelmed her face.

That womanly body was still there, still visible. Only now it was made, not of supple flesh, but of twining rose canes interlaced and molded into a feminine shape. The long dark hair was a cascade of leaves and rotten rose petals, and the face was a bizarre conglomerate of blossoms and thorns. Petals blinked like eyelids over two black holes where the eyes ought to be.

Those holes fastened on Nelle's face in the glass.

She had one moment to decide. One moment only. She could

succumb to the fear quaking through the very marrow of her soul. She could give in to the swarming briars crawling along the ceiling, walls, and floor, reaching out from that figure seated before the mirror. She could cast herself into that inevitable embrace, let her flesh be torn from her bones, let her blood splatter the red blossoms and feed this ravenous vision. Or . . .

Turning on her heel, Nelle leapt from the doorway out into the hall.

CHAPTER 9

JUST PAST THIS VEIL OF REALITY, POWER PULSED.

Soran stopped at the foot of the great front staircase to examine the landing and shadowy spaces above. All looked clear, but he knew better than to trust his mortal vision.

He lifted the spellbook, turned to a certain page, and read the strange characters written there in his own hand, years ago—ages ago—back in the early days of his training. It was not a strong spell compared to the powerful workings he'd created in later years. But it would have to do.

As he read, the characters brightened, burning in ribbons of energy from the page, scalding his eyes. Refusing to blink, he read on in a steady, calm voice: "*Ilrune petmenor. Mythanar prey sarl-*

enna sior . . ."

When he reached the end of the page, he slowly let his eyelids drop and stepped out of the waking world into the other.

The shadows here were just as dark, just as deep, but they no longer obscured his vision. He saw everything as clear as daylight, clearer even, for no color or life distracted his gaze from the cold reality of this warped world shared by every mind in every existence and every realm known and unknown.

The Realm of Nightmares.

Briars clung to the banisters, gouging the decorative wyvern newels. They ripped into the polished wooden treads and tore at the woven runners. Here and there, blossoms unfurled their petals among the thorns but swiftly burst into flame, burning away to ashes even as they bloomed. The fumes left behind filled his senses with the stink of death.

He dared not hesitate no matter how reluctant he might be to climb into that snarling nest of infestation. The scream still echoed in his head, but no second scream had followed. The girl might already be dead, but if there was still a chance she breathed . . .

He sprang forward, opening his physical eyes to block out the realism of those choking briars. It might be a mistake to plunge into the deeper Nightmare without watching his step, but if he saw the materiality of that world all around him, he would never have the courage to continue.

Turning right at the landing, Soran hastened to the floor

above. He was almost certain the scream had come from that direction. If he was wrong, well, it was probably too late for the girl anyway.

The other world closed in around him. He felt thorns snag his sleeves, grab at his feet, and clutch at his soul, eager to drag him out of this actuality and into the Nightmare. He resisted. The longer he held his ground, the longer he could delay using his spells. He only had two left, and he must make each one count.

He followed his own sixth sense down the passage. Suddenly, the pressure of dark power around him became so intense, it blocked his way. He closed his eyes again, using his spell's remaining magic to step back into that Nightmare.

A wall of thorns loomed before him. Roses bobbed from the ends of their stems, flaming bright before his dazzled vision. Briars coiled and tightened into an unpassable boundary.

Soran took a step back, teeth clenched. He knew this was the library door. Was the girl inside? She must be, and she must still be alive if the Thorn Maiden was so determined to keep him from her. If she were dead already, what difference would it make?

He opened his eyes again, returning to the waking world. But now the power of the Nightmare was so strong, he could see it on the edges of his vision even while fully awake. He opened the little spellbook again, turning through pages of already-used spells, and found the fresh spell he sought. He read it out in a clear voice, and again the words burned bright on the page: "*Venrel farkatra atra, yesmenor atra.*"

When he closed his eyes again, he held a sword, its razor edges pulsing with light in that strange darkness.

"Let me pass," he ordered the briar, bracing his feet and readying his weapon. "Let me pass, or it will go the worse for you."

The roses burned, died, bloomed, and burned again. The vine-like canes coiled tighter than before, and his head whirled with the stink of perfume. A low, throaty voice whispered through the shadows:

Leave her to me. You have no need of her.

"She's just a child." He took a step nearer and raised the sword threateningly. "She's lost, innocent. I'm taking her with me."

Why? Why will you take her? Will you keep her? Love her? Will you forget about me?

"I'll send her away. She'll be gone from Roseward by sunset tomorrow."

You lie. You want her. You want her for yourself. Her soft, smooth flesh. You crave her.

Argument was useless. Who could reason with a nightmare?

Soran swung his sword—swung the spell—and hacked straight to the heart of the briar wall. The spell was well wrought, one of his better efforts from early days of training. It burst and disintegrated against the dark power of those twined canes in a fountain of brilliant white sparks. The roses exploded in showers of petals, the thorns crumbled, and the Nightmare drew back her arms with a piercing shriek that sliced across the spirit like shards of glass.

The afterglow dazzled Soran's eyes. He staggered back, turning his face away. When he could bear to look again, this time with waking eyes, the doorway was clear. He gazed into the library—a beautiful, spacious chamber that once had been his favorite sanctuary. Stacks of books pulled down from the shelves littered the floor around a ladder.

And in the depths of one huge armchair curled a little figure.

Seconds later, his hand pressed beneath her jaw and found the quick throb of her pulse. She was alive. Miraculously, impossibly still alive. Her sleep was troubled, however. Her breath came in short, tight gasps, and beads of sweat dotted her brow.

Her soul was deep inside a nightmare. Too deep to return?

Soran tucked his spellbook away and slid both hands under the girl's arms, hauling her upright on the chair. Then, with a single heave, he hoisted her over his shoulders. She wasn't heavy, bony little thing that she was, hardly more weight than a wyvern. Her head bumped against his shoulder, and he adjusted his grip and his stance, consciously trying not to touch her in any inappropriate place, though why he should bother about niceties at such a moment he couldn't begin to explain. Once he was certain his grip on her was secure, he turned to the open doorway.

He stopped and bit out a curse through his teeth.

She was there. He knew she was there. The seeing spell had worn off, but it didn't matter. He could feel her presence as clearly as though she had manifested in the waking world. Tall, womanly, her face sculpted from leaves and petals. So strange and yet hauntingly familiar, her graceful limbs shaped of twining stems and briars. She was naked and sensual, desirable and horrifying.

Soran drew a breath, then squared his shoulders. "Let me pass," he said again, firmly. "I don't want to hurt you."

Hurt me?

She stepped into the room, dragging briars behind her. They crawled along the wall, swarmed across the floor, tearing and gouging as they came.

You hurt me even now. You wound me more deeply than any sword may pierce.

He shook his head. One hand steadying the girl, he used the other to pull out the spellbook and fumbled to a fresh page. He'd already used two spells—he hated to use the third and final one. If only there were another way . . .

He knew what he must say, but the words burned like poison in his throat. He moistened his dry lips and swallowed painfully.

"Helenia." He whispered the name like a last desperate prayer. "Helenia, you have to trust me. You must believe in me, in the bond we share."

He felt her studying him, tilting her strange head to one side. A curtain of leaves and petals like hair moved across her thorny shoulder. The gesture was familiar, agonizingly familiar. His heart jolted in his breast.

Why should I trust you? You say you love me. What is love? I know the love of a man! At its core, it is only betrayal.

"I could never betray you." He took a careful step toward her.

146

"We are one—one soul, united. You are me and I am you. How could I possibly betray my own self?"

If what you say is true, you will leave the girl.

She took another step into the room. He breathed her perfume, the sweetness of roses and burning and rot.

Leave her as proof of your love.

"I won't do that, Helenia," he whispered.

And then he unleashed the spell.

It lashed out in a scything arc, a brilliant burst of magic that cut through waking world and Nightmare alike. His aim was true. It sliced at a diagonal through the woman's neck, down across her torso, cleaving her in half. She screamed and crumbled in a burst of flaming roses, and Soran did not wait even to draw breath. He sprang into action with the mortal girl across his shoulders, breaking through the quaking tangle of briars, which writhed away from him in fear of yet another blasting spell.

But he didn't have another spell. The book was empty now, useless. He had only his own determination to live, to escape, the need for survival that pulsed through his being.

He raced down the passage with echoes of the Thorn Maiden's shrieks in pursuit, then descended the staircase at a full run. If he fell, all would be over. In the darkness behind him, he felt the briars amassing as the Thorn Maiden rebuilt herself piece by piece.

He reached the bottom of the stair and bolted across the foyer to the door. Why had he shut it behind him? Such a fool, such a fool! He had to stop, yank on the latch, and pull it wide, all without dropping the mortal girl, all the while knowing the Thorn Maiden could hurtle down the stairs after him at any moment.

The door swung inward. A gust of cold night air filled his lungs, driving out the funk of burned roses. He took a lunging step forward but stopped. Though every instinct urged him to run, he turned and looked back into the foyer, up the grand staircase.

The girl. He carried her body, but her soul was loose, wandering the Nightmare somewhere. Saving the physical shell was not enough, not if the soul was lost.

"If you're there," he called, his voice resounding in that huge open space, "come with me. Now. It's your only chance."

Unable to know whether or not he was heard, Soran turned and raced out into the night. With every step he expected thorny arms to catch him from behind, drag him back into the Nightmare, and flay his flesh to the bone.

CHAPTER 10

TERROR VIBRATED THROUGH NELLE'S SPIRIT, DRIVING HER to flee, to survive. She ducked, dodged, and sprinted for the end of the hall even as thorns clutched at her gown and her hair. One wrong step and she would fall and be overwhelmed in briars.

But she didn't step wrong. She reached the end of the hall, turned down a passage, and, seeing the open gallery ahead of her, she ran for it. On every side, briars swarmed to claim her, and the floor moved in violent snake-like undulations beneath her feet.

Only she didn't have feet, not here. She was like a wind, a being of air and spirit darting between the intertwining branches, uncatchable so long as she was immaterial. She sensed her material body heavy and far away somewhere . . . but that wasn't *her*. She was here, and she was unbound.

She reached the gallery rail and without hesitation launched out into the empty space above the stairway. For a terrifying instant she felt the weight of her mortal body surround her again, felt gravity poised to drag her down to bone-shattering death. For an eternal weightless moment, she hovered.

The moment passed. Then another moment, and another after that. She floated in midair, immaterial, light as gossamer. Thorns and branches lashed at her from the gallery rails like angry tongues seeking to lap up her essence. But they were too heavy. They could not reach her.

Was she dead? The thought whirled through her, a rush of feeling within her formlessness. Had she simply forgotten the moment of her death, of stepping out of her lifeless mortal body? Was she now a ghost bound to this house, bound to this darkness?

The door down below opened.

Nelle saw a gleam like moonlight fall through the opening and spread across the foyer's marble-inlaid floor. It was so bright compared to the darkless gloom surrounding her that her eyes would have been dazzled . . . had she possessed eyes.

A shadowy column stood framed by that light, a featureless smear that somehow struck her as not truly part of this reality. She could barely see it, yet she felt its presence, and it felt . . . familiar.

The shadow turned, and she almost thought she glimpsed hooded robes and a tangle of white hair.

If you're there . . .

Startled, Nelle twisted in on her formless self. Was that a voice? A mortal voice? It reached out to her from across what felt like an incredible distance, and she strained her strange, inhuman senses to catch it.

If you're there . . . come with me. Now.

It's your only chance.

The shadow at the door turned and vanished out into the gently pulsing glow.

A thorny cane whipped out from the rail, striking at her. It lashed through the center of her essence, and Nelle twisted and tumbled, fully expecting blood to gush from a wound that did not exist. She recovered herself quickly, pulling her airy nothingness together.

She couldn't stay here.

With a determined flick, she flew down to the door. The brightness beyond was uncomfortable for her non-eyes, but she pushed out into the openness. For a thrilling moment she felt cold night air around her and tried to breathe it in, forgetting she had no nostrils, no lungs.

The shadowy form was ahead of her, moving fast. The world around him coalesced into the outer yard of Dornrise, much as Nelle had seen it earlier that day but overlaid by the un-dark strangeness that warped everything into an aberrant, disturbing veneer. Yet the moon shining high above cast a silvery light even into this realm. The sight gave her courage.

A growl sounded behind her. Nelle looked back and saw thorny branches reaching from the doorway, clawing down the porch steps. It was enough to galvanize her into action.

Flitting after the shadow, Nelle passed through the tangling briars and on to the clearer road ahead. Along the way she slowly merged back into a shape rather like her mortal body. She even seemed to be wearing the dirty dress again, and her hair floated behind her in a cloud. Every step she took sent her floating several yards before her foot touched the ground again.

She caught up with the shadowy form, which now more closely resembled the shape of a man. It was like seeing him through several layers of hazy veils, indistinct yet solid on the other side. Hearing him puff and pant as he walked, she thought perhaps he carried a weight across his shoulders.

She looked back to see Dornrise already receding in the distance. Would the thorn-woman pursue them out from the house? Nelle shuddered and hovered near the shadow, which provided scant comfort, for the closer she drew to him, the more unreal he felt.

I know you're there.

The echoing, distant voice reached her again. Startled, Nelle looked at the shadowy figure, certain it was he who spoke.

It would be best for you to wake if you can. Once you're awake, you will be safe. Will you try?

Awake? Was she asleep? The thought was comforting. If she wasn't dead, maybe she could escape this dark realm simply by opening her eyes. But where would she be when she woke? Back in Dornrise? Not a pleasant thought. The last thing she wanted was to find herself back within those haunted walls, waking or otherwise.

Still, what choice did she have? She didn't want to stay ghostlike and floating forever.

"All right," she said at last, uncertain whether the shadowy man would hear her. "How do I do it? How do I go about waking up?"

He didn't answer. He couldn't hear her.

Nelle took several more long floating steps, then concentrated, trying to get a feel for her physical body. Was it . . . close? She almost thought she could sense it, the heaviness of bone and flesh and tissue. Draped in a most uncomfortable position too, with a terrible crick in the neck.

She frowned, and the sensation vanished. She was back to her ghostly, weightless self again. Even her imagined body partially disintegrated, and she had to concentrate to bring it back into shape around her.

Never mind, came the distant voice of the man. The shadowy figure shifted as if rolling his neck and adjusting the set of his shoulders. Nelle saw that he did in fact carry something heavy that bowed him down. *Stay close to me. We'll have you awake soon enough.*

Since she had no better ideas, Nelle obeyed. She even placed an immaterial hand on what she thought might be the shadow-man's arm. He seemed to flinch under her touch, though she

153

might have imagined that. He didn't speak again, and she floated along at his side, only occasionally shooting glances back for telltale signs of creeping briars. Once or twice she thought she saw unsettling movement in the deeper shadows but hoped it was her imagination.

They followed a path along the edge of the seaside cliffs high above the ocean. She could see the effect of a brisk wind billowing through the shadowy man like a cloak. It didn't touch her, however; nor did it stir the still, darkless world around her. Even the ocean seemed to be emptiness, a black void. It was too upsetting, so she looked away, focusing ahead.

The lighthouse tower appeared ahead of them. Was this their destination? The shadowy man seemed intent upon it. Would they be safe there? Would he be able to wake her? And when he did, what then? The questions were too many, too unanswerable.

But her questions fled when a terrible moan rolled through the darkness. The sound sent a shock through Nelle's being, and she flinched back into formlessness and wrapped her airy substance around the shadowy man like a child flinging her arms around a parent's leg. He staggered two steps but righted himself quickly and continued, faster than before.

The moan sounded again, low, wordless. Almost animal.

Then came the words:

My love.

My love!

Why have you betrayed me?

Why, why, why?

The sound was so chilling, Nelle couldn't bear it. Peering around the shadowy man, she saw the ground behind them creeping, writhing. The thorns were coming fast now. Terror thrilled through her core.

You are mine. I am yours.

Leave the girl. Leave her to me. Leave her to me, my love.

Three thorned arms rose from the mass like snake heads ready to strike. Nelle screamed, her voice distant and yet so near.

Hold on, the shadow man whispered. He surged forward just as the thorns lashed out. Nelle ducked down into the man, into herself, and screamed again.

There was a thud like a door slamming open and a following crash as it slammed shut again. Three sharp, terrible cracks battered at Nelle's senses, and a distant, agonized, prolonged shriek.

Then silence.

Had she died? No, she couldn't have. If she were dead, wouldn't she know it? Fighting against her own trembling essence, she forced her awareness upright and looked around.

She seemed to be in a large, square chamber filled with the same un-dark gloom as the rest of the world outside. The shadowy man was there too, stepping to an alcove in one corner of the room, where he seemed to lay something down. Then he moved to a large, cold fireplace near the alcove and set to work building a fire. She heard the crack of flint and almost thought she saw a flickering glow as the spark caught. But it was too far away, through too many veils to be quite real to her. There was certainly no light or warmth in her present world.

Uncertain what else to do, she floated listlessly over to the alcove, trying to see what the man had laid down. She discovered a pile of fur rugs that she guessed must be a bed. And was that another shadowy form? Smaller than the shadowy man, but just as featureless and distant.

Why did she feel so . . . drawn to it?

The shadow-man, his fire lit, returned to the alcove, stepping right through Nelle. She wafted away from him with an indignant snort. Rude! He knelt beside the pile of rugs and seemed to lift the other shadowy figure in his arms.

Wake up.

An appalling, burning stench seared through her head.

Nelle jerked, shocked, surprised at the sensation of having a head, of having the ability to feel that burn. She choked, gagged . . . and felt the heaviness of mortal limbs all around her. She wasn't weightless anymore, and she wasn't in the un-dark world. She was in utter darkness, and something was searing her nostrils.

Her limbs spasmed, uncertain of themselves, and her hands clawed wildly for something to catch hold of, something real. She found a fistful of cloth and gripped it hard. Her eyelids fluttered, heavier than she'd ever felt them, and when she managed to pry them open just a slit, the brightness of fire glow nearly blinded her. The darkless realm pulled at her mind, trying to draw her back, and she almost let herself sink back into it.

"Wake up. Come, I know you can hear me."

With a supreme effort of will she managed to part her eyelashes again. A haze of white like a cloud filled her foggy vision. Slowly the image solidified, and she found herself gazing up into a pair of silvery eyes framed by hideous puckering scars and a wild mane of white hair and beard.

"Ah. There you are," a voice growled through that tangle of hair. An arm shifted beneath her, an arm that was looped behind her shoulders, cradling her close to a broad, robed chest. "It's all right. You can let go of me now."

CHAPTER 11

NELLE'S BODY REACTED IN A SERIES OF JOLTING MOTIONS.

She bucked, her back arching, her legs scrambling in a tangle of skirts. Her hand still gripped a fistful of fabric, and she couldn't quite make her fingers let go, but the rest of her pushed away violently.

She tumbled to the floor, sprawled out flat, and pulled the wild-haired stranger down with her. His face was close to hers, his eyes so wide, she saw her own reflection in his dilated pupils. Long hair fell over his shoulders, mingling with the beard and tickling her cheeks.

"Let go, girl." That deep voice rumbled through the thicket of white. She felt something hard and cold pry her fingers free of the rough fabric in her grasp. The next moment the stranger rose and backed away, holding up both hands in a nonthreatening gesture. Firelight gleamed off cold metal encasing each finger. "I won't hurt you—"

A guttural wordless bleat erupted from Nelle's lips. She popped up onto her elbows and tried to propel herself back, but her feet caught in her own skirts, pinning her. She rolled, fell on her face, pushed up again, and somehow managed to get upright.

Where in the nine hells was she? The whole room tilted. The whole strange room, which she couldn't remember seeing before, with a low fire burning in a dome-shaped fireplace, an alcove in one wall, and crisscrossed beams supporting the high ceiling. But she couldn't take it in. Her eyes fixed on one thing only: the door.

She leapt for it.

"Stop!"

A hand closed on her upper arm, pinching painfully into flesh. Instincts and training kicked in: Nelle drove her elbow into a gut, heard a surprised "*Oof!*" and the grip on her arm relaxed enough for her to twist free. She dove at the door, caught the latch, and pulled inward. Night air whistled through the narrow opening, whipped across her face, and howled up the chimney.

Then two hands planted heavily, one on either side of her, and slammed the door shut.

"Don't be a fool!" a rough voice growled close to her ear. "The Thorn Maiden is still out there."

160

Nelle stood caged between two muscular arms, bare to the elbow and covered with innumerable puckered scars. Ugly though they were, she scarcely noticed. Instead, her gaze fixed on those hands just inches from her nose. For the space of ten frantic heartbeats, her mind tried to tell her they were wearing gauntlets. It wasn't true.

They were encased in nilarium—faerie-silver poured in liquid form covered each finger, running down the palm and across the veins on the back of the hand, all the way to the wrists. It was dried and hardened, yet she could still see each individual run and drip, like the spill of wax dribbling down a candlestick.

She stood frozen in place, unable to move, unable to turn, scarcely able to think.

"You're safe in here," the rough voice spoke again, as though squeezing between gritted teeth. "But if you cross that threshold—gods help me, girl—I won't be responsible for what happens. Do you understand?"

She drew a breath. Then she nodded.

"Good."

One of the hands shifted. She felt the weight of the powerful body at her back turning. The other hand remained firmly in place as the stranger stepped to one side, giving her room to move. "Go on. You're cold. Back to the fire."

She glanced sideways and met that silvery gaze peering down at her through the tangle of hair. Once more she saw the ugly scars framing those eyes and quickly looked away. Too unsteady to do anything but obey, she backed into the room, returning to the hearth. There was a small stool overturned on the hearthstone. She picked it up, set it right, and sat. Her gaze fixed on the dancing flames, but she didn't see them.

Every sense in her body fixated on the movements of the stranger behind her. Although she didn't turn to look at him, she felt when he crossed the small chamber. A series of clunks followed, then the sound of liquid pouring. A moment later those two nilarium-covered hands appeared before her vision again, awkwardly holding a wooden cup.

"Drink this."

Nelle flicked a glance up, not quite meeting those intense eyes. "Wh-what is it?"

"Water."

She wasn't sure she believed him. At the same time, she was so parched, she would probably have accepted it if he'd said poison. Her trembling hands sloshed more than a little as she took the cup, lifted it to her lips, and downed the contents in a few desperate gulps.

"May I have more?" she whispered.

He took the cup and returned it a few moments later. She drank again as deeply; then, after drawing a quivering hand across her mouth, she murmured, "Thank you," and clutched the cup in her lap.

He grunted. With a noisy scrape he dragged a chair across the floor, placed it across from her at the hearth, and sat. Firelight played on the folds of his robes and gleamed on the fisted hand resting on the chair's arm. She tried to look at his face, but he'd pulled his hood up. Which was probably just as well.

Nelle stared down at the cup in her lap, trying to order her frantic mind. Where was she, and how had she come to be here? Vague images played in the back of her mind. A dark walk along an ocean cliff. Winding halls and passages clogged with living briars.

It all felt like a distant dream.

She shifted her gaze to the room around her. It was much larger than she'd first taken it to be. Roughly used chairs, a table, and other furnishings seemed to be scattered at random, and a stair with no rail ran up one wall, disappeared into the ceiling, and presumably continued higher still.

"Is . . . This is . . ." She glanced her host's way. "Are we inside the lighthouse?"

The hood moved as he nodded. "Do you remember how you came here?"

Rubbing one hand across her face, she remembered searching through the books in the library. She remembered taking a seat in one of the big reading chairs. After that, it all went shadowy in her head. There was an impression of thorns. Of darkness that wasn't dark. Of herself disembodied and desperate. Of roses burning.

When she tried too hard to concentrate on any one of those impressions, they scattered, leaving her with only confusion. Nelle scowled, pinching the bridge of her nose.

When she looked up, the strange man was watching her. His eyes gleamed in the depths of his hood.

"Are you . . . are you Mage Soran Silveri?" she asked softly.

He didn't answer at first. Then his voice rumbled from the hood. "I am Soran Silveri. But I am no mage. Not anymore."

She swallowed, her throat tight. "Why have you brought me here?"

"To keep you safe."

Another trace of dream flashed across her mind, the image of a woman made of twining branches covered in thorns, an unreal, beautiful, ghastly face. Nelle squeezed her eyes tight and shook her head. The vision scattered as the others had, leaving her to grasp at nothing. She shuddered, feeling suddenly small and terribly vulnerable. Had the mage drugged her? Put a spell on her? Was that why she didn't remember anything after the moment she sat down in the library armchair? If he had . . . why?

Her gaze flicked briefly to that bed in the alcove, but she wouldn't let it rest there. She lifted her chin, squared her shoulders, and faced the mage, meeting his gaze firmly.

The mage shifted in his seat, leaning his elbows on his knees, his heavy hands limp at the wrists. Nelle started at the movement but stopped short of leaping up from the stool. Her fingers gripped her cup so tightly, she felt it straining to crack.

"I would suggest," the deep voice rumbled from the hood's shadow, "you remain here tonight. Come dawn, you must leave Roseward. You will return to wherever you came from and think of this place no more."

Nelle stared across that little space between them. Was that it? He wanted her to go? No, it couldn't be that simple. If he'd really drugged and carried her here, he must have shadier intentions. She knew what Gaspard expected of him. After fifteen years alone on the island, any man would be hungry for a little company of one sort or another.

With a sudden twist in her gut, she realized she'd left her snatcher's satchel back in the library, with the Sweet Dreams poison tucked safely inside. If the mage . . . if he tried to . . .

He stood.

Nelle caught her breath, sprang upright, staggered around the stool, and backed toward the wall. But the mage again held up his strange hands and simply stepped away. He paused at the fireplace to light a candle, then made for the stairs. "You are safe tonight," he said. The light of his candle illuminated the white tangle of beard covering his lower jaw and gleamed in his pale eyes. "I promise you that. But I promise no more."

With those words, he turned and climbed the stair. She watched until he passed through the hole in the ceiling, then listened until she could no longer hear his footsteps. In the distance, a door shut.

Then silence.

Exhaling a shuddering breath, Nelle sank back down onto the stool. All strength seemed to have drained from her limbs. Nevertheless, she looked back over her shoulder at the door.

Oughtn't she to flee? Now, while she could? After all, she'd be vulnerable if she stayed here. If he chose to creep back down those stairs in the middle of the night while she slept, what defenses did she have?

She felt for her little dagger, but though she found the sheath, a comforting weight against her wrist, the dagger itself was gone. When and how she'd lost it, she couldn't recall, but it was certainly gone. She wouldn't be wise to stay here, unarmed, at the mercy of this man, this stranger, this . . . Her eyes closed, and she saw again the disfiguring scars, the hands covered in dripping nilarium.

"Monster," she whispered.

Wrenching her eyes open, she rose from the stool and stood a moment in shivering indecision. Then she turned toward the door and, straightening her shoulders, took three firm steps.

Before she took a fourth, a strange sound vibrated from the other side: *Tip-tap. Tip-tap. Tip-tap.*

Too perfectly timed. Too precise to be a branch blown by the wind.

Tip-tap. Tip-tap. Tip-tap. Tip-tap.

Boom!

Nelle flinched back. Her heart leapt to her throat, beating so hard she nearly choked. The door rattled in its frame. The whole tower shook. Plaster and dust crumbled and fell in one corner of the room.

There was no twisted woman made of briars and blossoms and thorns.

It was only the wind. And a branch. Nothing more. Just the wind and a branch and her own exhausted imagination.

It didn't matter. Under no circumstances was Nelle leaving this tower tonight.

She picked her way to the pile of furs in the alcove and laid herself down on top. Finding a thin blanket folded at one end, she pulled it up to her shoulders. Even then, even with the fire glowing on the hearth, she couldn't stop shivering. She simply lay there, too exhausted to think or move, too terrified to invent a plan, and watched the glow of firelight on the wall slowly die away.

That incessant *tip-tap, tip-tap, tip-tap* continued deep into the night.

CHAPTER 12

HOW DID SHE SURVIVE?

For the first time in memory, Soran mounted the stairs to his tower chamber swiftly, with no trace of hesitation. He dared not hesitate, not with the night already well underway and the reassertion of his spell not yet begun.

He felt her just outside the tower, just outside the powerful wards that kept her at bay. Her hands were everywhere, her fingers tensing, testing, eager to find some crack in his defenses. He must reassert the spell. Now.

But as he climbed, a question pressed upon him, impossible to ignore: How did that girl survive? Her dreaming soul had been separated from her body, at the mercy of all the terrors of

Roseward after dark. No mere mortal could have endured it. The Thorn Maiden should have caught her, slashed her mind to pieces, and, in so doing, destroyed her physical body as well.

Yet somehow the girl had eluded the Nightmare's grasp to follow him out of Dornrise and across the island, ready to reunite with her body the moment he plied her with pungent vapors. He might expect a talented Miphato with many years of training to accomplish such a feat. But a young girl like her? Without a trace of discernible magic?

Something strange was going on here. He didn't like it. He didn't like any of this, being pulled out of his day-to-day work and thrown into memories of the past he'd long battled to forget.

And now pushed into terrible danger as night darkened and the Thorn Maiden remained unrepressed.

He reached the top chamber and set to work, first arranging his candles in their bowls, then taking his seat at the desk. He unfastened the straps binding the red book lying there. The energy contained within the covers mounted, quivering against his silver-encased hands.

He braced himself. There was no time to prepare, no time to mentally arm for the battle ahead. He must simply dive in and trust that the instinct of many years' practice would serve him. Setting his jaw, he flung back the cover and began to read the spell.

The magic force struck him like a blow, almost sent him reeling from his chair. He clutched the edges of his desk, holding his place, and read on, forming the words with careful precision. His heart thundered in his breast as another wave of magic struck him, but this time he was ready for it and took the blow with scarcely a flinch. By the time he reached the end of the page, the spell had settled into a thrum of energy, steady and bearable, radiating from the book into his soul and out into the realities of air and ether around him.

He turned the page and read on, his voice now rhythmic and even. He was in control, the master of this moment. The initial brunt of the battle was over. Whatever else the night had in store for him, he could endure. He must endure.

She was there.

He felt her closing in on the edges of his mind, both enticed and repulsed by the spell he worked. He heard her voice sobbing in the darkness, the very sound enough to break his heart. But she did not try to speak, and she did not try to come to him. Not yet.

He read on and on, deep into the darkest hours of the night, lighting candle after candle as they guttered out. The physical strain of calling such magic to life made him lightheaded, and the three smaller spells he'd used earlier in the evening had already taken a toll. His vision swam, and sparks danced on the edges of his vision, but he never let the flow of the spell break. As dawn tinged the edges of the sky and he neared the end of the spell, his spirits revived. Only two pages to go. He spoke the words with more confidence, his voice firm and hard.

Just as he turned to the final page, the Thorn Maiden

manifested behind him.

He felt her there even before she spoke, even before she touched him. Her presence was unmistakable, a miasma of perfume and death. She stepped toward him, her briars crawling across the floor, and wrapped her arms around his shoulders from behind. Her petal-soft lips played at his ear, and a thrill of desire shot through him despite his exhaustion, despite every determined effort of self-control. It was the roses. The scent was intoxicating.

I will get her in the end, you know.

Her voice was softer than moonlight, more vicious than venom.

I will get her. I will break her. One bone at a time. Then I will peel the skin from her still-living body and wear it as a cloak, and you will see how frail, how loathsome is this mortal flesh.

She kissed him. Her tongue played with the shell of his ear and her teeth nibbled on its lobe. Then, with a violent hiss, she raked her thorns across his face, tearing through his beard, across his skin, cutting his cheek and brow.

The next moment she was gone.

He read the final words just as the sun rose. The spell was complete. He bent over the open book, his shoulders bowed, his spirit all but broken. When blood droplets splattered the page, he cried out and hastily mopped them up with the edge of his sleeve. The stains remained, not deep enough to obscure the spell-script, but marring it.

Hastily he closed the book and fastened the straps. Blowing out the last candle, he tried to rise. His knees quaked so hard, he almost dropped to the floor, so he sat down heavily again, bowed his head, and hid his face in the cold palms of his silver hands.

The Thorn Maiden would return tomorrow night. In her rage she would be more terrible than ever. And he would be hard-pressed to keep her at bay.

It didn't matter. The girl would be gone long before then. He would drive her away himself. Because, of course, he couldn't let her stay. He couldn't risk it, not even to seek the source of the power that had enabled her to elude the Thorn Maiden. It wouldn't be right. It wouldn't be fair.

He wouldn't risk another life.

Resolve firming in his heart, he pushed up from his chair and this time managed to keep his balance. He straightened his robes, pulled his hood up over his head, and made for the door. The tower stair spiraled down below him, a dizzying distance in his foggy, exhausted state. He braced a hand on the wall and began his descent.

A piercing scream echoed from below, resounding off the stone and shooting through his ears like bolts of ice.

The girl! Soran froze, his heart thudding in his throat. Had the Thorn Maiden gotten through? Had he made a mistake in the spell-reading, left a binding unloosed? Had he—

Another scream, louder than the first.

His exhaustion momentarily forgotten, Soran lunged down the

stairs, praying he wouldn't be too late.

CHAPTER 13

AN ACHING HOLLOWNESS IN HER MIDSECTION WOKE
Nelle from uneasy sleep. Groaning, she rolled over and buried her
nose in something musty. A deep inhale brought on an abrupt
sneeze, which shocked her awake. Bleary and rubbing her nose
with the back of one hand, she sat up. The blanket slipped from
her shoulders, leaving her shivering as she stared down at her
other hand, very pale against a backdrop of dense fur.

Where am I?

For several panicked moments, her brain couldn't form a clear
answer. She remembered iron shackles pinning her arms over her
head while she crouched in a fetid prison cell, but that memory
twisted into remembrance of sinking into a soft armchair in a

glorious library.

Then it all came back. She knew where she was.

Nelle slumped, half tempted to curl over and try to go back to sleep. Her body felt wilted; her arms and chest ached from the hours she'd spent rowing. And she was bullspitting hungry! The blaze in the stone fireplace had burned down to embers, but when she peered up through a high slit window, she saw pink and blue sky. Dawn was well advanced.

She turned a quick glance toward the stair. No sign nor sound of Mage Silveri. But he could come stomping down at any moment with more of his dire warnings, determined to drive her from Roseward.

Well, he could send her away all he liked. He couldn't stop her from turning around and coming back again. Next time, she'd be more careful too. She'd make certain he never saw her, and she'd find that book and . . .

"How did he do it?" she whispered, her voice soft in that close musky air. How had he found her and transported her back to this tower without her being aware? Did he have some drug like the Sweet Dreams? She hadn't eaten or drunk anything from his hand, so he couldn't have slipped it into her food. Was it magic?

She shivered and pulled the blanket back over her shoulders, huddling into it like a cape. Her stomach groaned, achingly empty. Mage Silveri had given her water last night, but she hadn't properly eaten since the dates stolen from the Dornrise larder. She peered from her alcove again, searching through the dim shadows for anything edible. Surely the mage wouldn't begrudge her a bite before he sent her back out to sea.

Spying a basket of what looked like eggs tucked away in one corner, Nelle crawled out of the alcove, trailing the blanket behind her. A copper pan hung beside the fireplace. While she did not consider herself a particularly inspired chef, she knew how to fry an egg.

She moved quickly for fear the mage would come down and kick her out of the tower before she had a chance to eat. After stoking the fire until it blazed bright again, she settled the pan over the coals to heat, then reached for the eggs. Her lip curled. These certainly weren't chicken eggs. They were a lot bigger and gray and speckled. She'd never seen any quite like them.

Still, an egg was an egg, right? She reached into the basket.

An ugly bray startled her out of her skin. The next moment, something fell from the rafters above and landed with a thunk beside the egg basket. Nelle sprang back, stepped on her skirts, and fell over a stool, landing with a crash. With another ugly bray, the something scuttled up from the floor and draped itself over the basket of eggs. One leathery wing arched in the air while the other draped limply over the clutch like a blanket. A pair of large nostrils turned toward Nelle, with beady eyes peering out from behind them.

"Oi!" Nelle yelped. "You trying to scare the skin off me?" She pushed upright, dashing a lock of hair out of her face.

The dragon creature showed its teeth and rattled its tongue at her, filling the room with another raucous bray. Then it abandoned the clutch to crawl straight toward her. "Oi!" Nelle sprang to her feet and grabbed the nearest weapon, which proved to be the copper pan. Its handle was warm from the fire but not yet too warm to touch, and she whipped it around, swinging for the creature's head. It ducked, flattening itself impossibly to the floor, then popped up again and feinted a snap. Nelle swung again, and this time it caught the pan in its jaws and began to worry it like a dog with a bone, still uttering a series of choking, growling brays.

"Get off, you bullspittin' lizard!" Nelle shrieked. She lifted the pan with both hands, and the creature came up with it, back legs waggling, good wing flapping, bad wing dragging on the floor. She kicked, planting a foot in the middle of its pale soft underbelly. Rather than loosen its hold on the pan, the beast latched on harder and, worse, spiraled its long sinuous tail around her ankle and up her shin. "Get off!" Nelle screamed again and hopped in a circle, balancing on one foot and shaking the other. "Get off, get off, get off, get—!"

"*What* is going on?"

A startled jolt shot through her heart. Nelle overbalanced and fell, landing with the frying pan on her chest, the creature still firmly attached. It beat at her with its one good wing, leathery skin slapping against her face, and she screamed and cursed, trying to roll free.

A flash of silver. Then the beast's weight lifted from her chest. Nelle shook hair from her face in time to see the creature drop hold of her frying pan and display teeth and tongue in a hideous sneer as Mage Silveri tucked it under his arm. Its tail was still wrapped around her leg, pulling it up awkwardly and displaying rather more calf and knee than was entirely proper even for a Draggs girl.

"Oi!" she protested. Her quick kick nearly jerked the creature out of the mage's grasp, but it didn't let her go. Its tail constricted, scales biting into her skin. "Oi, get it off me!"

"What did you do to upset the wyvern?"

"What did *I* do? I didn't even know it was there! The vicious little spitter launched itself at me, all MREAAAH!" She gave her best rendition of a bray, flapping one hand over her head like a crest, which startled the creature into unwinding its tail. Its crest lowered, and it tilted its head, chortling piteously.

Nelle couldn't see Silveri's face under his hood, but there was an odd tightness to his voice when he said, "My wyverns are many things. Impulsive, impudent. Strangely lacking in self-preservation instinct. But vicious, they are not. You must have provoked it."

"*Provoked* it? I was trying to make breakfast!" She indicated the basket of eggs with a wave of her hand. "What, are you going to tell me that's its nest or something? Are those—whaddaya call 'em—wyvern eggs?"

"Wyvern eggs? No." She didn't care for the distinctly condescending tone of his voice. "That's not how wyverns are born. It's merely protecting my property. It thinks you're a thief."

Nelle glared at the creature, which chortled back. Lifting its crest again, it showed its teeth and rattled its tongue. She snarled right back at it. The wyvern flapped its good wing and scrambled up onto Silveri's shoulder, where it chattered and chortled and nuzzled into the shadows of his hood. Judging by the way the mage stroked the loathsome beast's head, he probably didn't intend to use it for spell parts.

"Nasty little spitter," Nelle muttered and got to her feet. She used a fold of her skirt to wipe off the copper pan, which, considering the state of her gown, probably wasn't sanitary. Oh well. "Better than wyvern spit," she growled, and raised the pan to inspect the impressions the monster's teeth had left behind. Shaking her head, she crouched to put the pan back on the fire. "So, what are they?" she tossed back over her shoulder.

"What are what?"

"The eggs. If they ain't wyvern eggs, what are they?"

"Seagull."

"Oh." Nelle sat back on her heels and regarded the clutch of spotted eggs in the basket. "Good eating?"

"Sufficient."

A pause followed. Nelle looked around just in time to see the wyvern pull the hood back from the mage's face, granting her another eyeful of his wild hair and the ugly scars ringing his eyes. They looked even worse by this light, raw and painful, some of them quite fresh. Blood streaked his cheek and forehead, matting in a clump of hair. How had he come by that new gash in the middle of the night?

His pale eyes watched her through the thicket of hair, his expression impossible to read. Angry, perhaps. But also curious. Nelle repressed a shudder and forced a smile. "Want some then?"

Thick brows drew together. "Are you offering me my own eggs?"

She shrugged and nodded at his hands, one of which he was using to steady the wyvern. The other hung immobile at his side. "I figure you can't do much cooking with those. Don't look terribly nimble."

Another pause. The wyvern climbed onto his head, claws pulling at his hair. He was surprisingly stoic amid these attentions, his considering gaze never leaving Nelle's face. Slowly and precisely, he said, "They are not."

"Shouldn't think so." Nelle reached for the basket but hesitated, hand poised over the topmost speckled egg, and glanced at the wyvern. It turned sharply her way and hissed again, its one good wing flaring up until the mage looked as though he wore a somewhat-the-worse-for-wear carnival hat. "May I?"

Silveri covered the wyvern's face with his hand and gently pushed it from his head back to his shoulder. "You can cook?" Did his colorless voice hold a hint of interest?

Nelle grinned and shrugged. "I don't burn things, at any rate. Fried or scrambled?"

"Your choice."

With that, the mage pulled the wyvern from his shoulder,

taking care to unhook its hind-leg claws from the rough fabric of his robes, and hoisted the creature back into the rafters, where it perched, vulture-like, over the fireplace, watching Nelle closely. Nelle stuck her tongue out at it and helped herself to the basket of eggs. The wyvern merely chattered and hissed in return.

After a brief search, Nelle found fat to add to her heated pan then set about cracking eggs. All the while she watched Silveri from the corner of her eye. He took a seat in the same chair as the night before, arms folded into the deep sleeves of his robe. He'd pulled his hood back into place, and she felt his gaze watching her every move. It was disconcerting.

"My name is Nelle," she said to fill the silence. "Peronelle Beck. If you care to know it."

He obviously didn't. Not a word did he say in response. For all his posh manner of speaking, he was a rude fellow. Then again, fifteen years of isolation had probably eroded most of his manners.

At least he wasn't kicking her out the door before she'd had a chance to eat. She should count her blessings. He was probably glad to have a guest who could manage a little egg-cracking and frying. How did he usually prepare eggs for himself? She couldn't imagine those hands of his successfully cracking eggs without leaving plenty of shell behind. Did he boil them? He'd still have to remove the peel, which would be a painstaking process with metal fingers. Maybe he ate them raw.

An idea bubbled up in the back of her mind.

"You know," she said, speaking above the sizzle of eggs, "I saw supplies in the kitchen larder up at the great house. Spices, flour. Salt." She flicked him a quick glance, then forced herself to look again and maintain the gaze. "It didn't seem as though anything had spoiled."

"No."

It was too short an answer to be particularly informative. Was he agreeing with her? Disagreeing? Did it matter?

Nelle carefully wrapped a fold of skirt around her hand and turned the pan on the coals to better disperse the heat. "I'm just saying," she continued, "a little salt would go a long way. I don't see much by way of dining choices in here, but with everything I saw up at the house, you could be eating rather well."

She looked his way again, trying to gauge a reaction beneath that shadowy hood. Nothing. Just a glint of what might be firelight reflected in his eyes.

"Well?" she pressed.

"Well what, Miss Beck?"

"You're all alone here, ain't you? There's no one else wanting those things. Why haven't you fetched them for yourself?"

"I was not placed here for my comfort."

Nelle frowned and turned her attention back to the eggs. They were done and on the verge of overcooking. After her boast about not burning things, she'd better not spoil this batch. She quickly removed the pan from the fire, gripped in both cloth-wrapped hands, and faced the mage. "Plates?"

The mage stood, moved to a cupboard propped up against one wall, rummaged inside, and returned with two battered but serviceable wooden plates. Without a utensil for serving, Nelle simply tilted the pan and slid eggs out one at a time, which worked well enough. Silveri set the plates at the table, then, after a moment's consideration, returned to the cupboard and produced a somewhat bent and battered two-pronged fork. He offered it to Nelle with all the solemnity of a page offering a knight his sword.

Nelle raised an eyebrow. "What about you?"

"I have only one," Silveri responded. "Besides—"

"Not much good with fancy ware like this?" Nelle finished for him, nodded, and shrugged one shoulder. "Well, I'm just a girl from Draggs. We don't fuss overmuch about table manners anyway."

This said, she sat at one end of the table and immediately dug into her egg, so hungry by this point that she scarcely took time to cut her serving into bites. Hunched low over her plate, she used the fork to transport large sections of egg to her mouth, chewing quickly. The seagull eggs were larger than she was used to, but even so, she wished she'd thought to make herself an extra two or three.

She scraped the plate clean with the side of her fork, and only when every trace of yolk was gone did she look up. Mage Silveri was just popping a last bite into his mouth, pinched delicately between thumb and forefinger. The hood prevented her from seeing how he managed with all that beard, but she got the impression he was more mannerly eating with his hands than she had been with her fork.

Her mouth twisting ruefully, she pushed the plate away, rested her elbows on the table, and propped her chin in her hands. "You know," she said, watching Silveri produce a napkin as though from nowhere and fastidiously wipe his silvery fingers, "it wouldn't be much bother."

He paused, napkin poised. "What is that, Miss Beck?"

"Me. Fetching the salt. And a few other things. From the great house, I'm saying. I'm sure you've got . . . magely duties to attend to." She lifted her chin enough to wave a vague hand, then offered another winsome smile. "I can't promise much, but I worked in a big kitchen for two years, and I do know a bit more than eggs. I can do flapcakes and porridge, and if there's leavening, I can manage a bit of—"

"You are leaving Roseward." Silveri stood, setting his napkin neatly to one side of his plate. "Now."

She blinked up at him. Did he actually mean *now?* As in . . . this very moment? When he swung an arm, indicating the door, she couldn't mistake his intention.

Nelle pushed back her seat and stood up, wiping her hands on her skirts. She cast a look around the room, but she had nothing, no satchel, no supplies. Nothing to stall over. So she followed the mage to the tower door, which he pulled open. A beam of golden morning light spilled through, momentarily blinding her. Hearing the mage step out over the threshold, she stumbled after his shadowed silhouette.

The morning was clear and crisp with a sharp chill in the air. They stood on the cliff above the strip of beach she'd tried to land on yesterday. From this vantage, Nelle gazed out across a sweeping view of the ocean and could just see the top of the Evenspire shining in the distance. Wyverns coasted in air currents overhead, chortling cheerfully to one another.

"My boat's on the other side of the island," Nelle said, wrapping her arms around her middle. The wind played with her hair, blowing it back from her face in long streamers.

"Yes." Silveri turned and pulled the door fast, then squared off in front of it.

She tried a last appealing grin. It felt feeble on her face. "I can clean too, you know. It might not be so bad to—"

"It's a full mile from here to the harbor, Miss Beck. I suggest you set out at once." He took a step toward her, out of the doorway. He was so tall, she craned her neck to look into his hooded face, met his glittering eyes, and held his gaze, her chin set in determination.

"Be off with you," he said. "And warn any who ask that death awaits those who dare set foot on Roseward Isle."

"Oh, I'll just mention the bullspittin' wyverns. That'll be enough to scare anybody off."

He blinked. The puckered, scarred skin around his eyes crinkled suddenly so that she almost thought—but no. He ducked his head before she could be certain. It couldn't have been a smile twisting his mouth beneath the mess of white beard.

He crossed his arms over his chest and nodded to one side. "It's that way."

"I know, I know." Nelle heaved a sigh. With a shrug she turned and set off down the narrow footpath winding its way along the cliff. In the distance she could see the chimney pots and rooftops of Dornrise. She didn't look back.

But she knew Mage Silveri watched her until she was out of sight.

CHAPTER 14

A STRANGE ACHE SETTLED IN SORAN'S CHEST AS THE GIRL disappeared behind a stand of pine trees.

Dared he be honest with himself? Dared he admit the truth? It had been pleasant. Pleasant to exchange words with another human being. More than pleasant, it had been like cooling his lips for the briefest moment in an oasis spring after crawling on his belly across blistering sand.

But the oasis was an illusion. The parched and dying had better face facts than cling to unreality.

She must go, and the sooner the better. He had saved her once, risked everything to fetch her out of that Nightmare. He wouldn't be responsible for her life. Not again.

Soran entered the lighthouse, slamming the door behind him. The wyvern, which was licking egg remnants from the copper pan with loud scrapes of its tongue, looked up, startled, and slowly raised its crest at him. Soran scowled in return but didn't have the energy to scold the beast. Or even to care. Not about eggs. Not about wyvern-slobbered cookware. Not about anything.

Lacking the will to climb the tower stair to his chamber and bed, he stumbled instead to the alcove and collapsed on the pile of furs. His eyes dropped shut with the force of a slamming portcullis, and the sweet oblivion of sleep reached out to claim him. His body relaxed as though sinking down through the furs, the stones, the rocky soil of the cliffs, and into the ocean water far below. It was good to surrender to the darkness, to the silence, to the dreamless, timeless nothing.

And when he awoke, if he were lucky, his memories would have seeped out of him again. He would have forgotten the faces of those who once lived and died in Dornrise Hall. He would no longer recall the love, the hatred, the betrayal, the pain he had both inspired and endured. He would remember neither his own name nor the place he had once boasted in the world of men. He would return to a cold, hard, single-purposed existence.

But as he lay there, his eyes fast shut, he couldn't fully deny the images playing in the darkness of his mind—images of vibrant untamed hair, a pinched, anxious, yet extraordinarily beautiful face. He couldn't forget the feel of a lithe feminine body cradled in his arms . . .

Soon enough, sleep overwhelmed him.

A mile-long trek provided plenty of time to think through her next maneuvers.

"Obviously, I can't set out for Wimborne again," Nelle muttered as she walked along the winding cliff-edge path. Every now and then she looked out across the water, checking for some sign of the city. It remained stubbornly invisible, though there was no mist to obscure it from view. Only the Evenspire was visible, its sharp point shimmering in the morning light but distant.

There could be no room for doubt: She wasn't in her own world anymore.

The knowledge was less unsettling today than the suspicion of it had been yesterday. After all, she'd battled a wyvern over a basket of eggs this morning. The very idea would have been unfathomable just the morning before, but now . . . all those strange stories of faerie beasts and enchantments and other worlds floating just beyond the edge of perceptible actuality were suddenly no longer stories but fact. She might as well make the best of it.

But this decision failed to address the instinct burning in the back of her head—the instinct to heed the mage's warning, hurry to her boat, push it out into the waves, and row for the Evenspire as hard as she could, hoping and praying to find her way through that veil of reality back into proper mortal waters and proper mortal air.

That instinct must be quenched. At least for the time being.

"What are my options?" she asked herself, marching on with long, determined strides. "Find a place to hide out on the other side of the island?" There was always that abandoned village by the docks. She could scrounge supplies from the Dornrise kitchens and set up a little camp for herself. Then she could continue hunting through that vast library at her leisure.

Why did that thought bring her up short?

Nelle held still but for the salty wind battering her skirts and hair, her gaze focused ahead toward the not-so-distant great house. Dornrise seemed to lie in wait for her. Shadows played on the edges of her mind, almost-memories from which she flinched away, unwilling to look too closely. Memories of . . . thorns.

"The Thorn Maiden," she whispered.

Wasn't that the name Mage Silveri used last night when she, in a blind panic, tried to run from the lighthouse into the night? *The Thorn Maiden is still out there,* he'd said. Could this mysterious entity be the monster that had torn apart the pirates while they slept in the banquet hall?

Or was the monster Silveri himself?

Another shudder rippled down her spine. Nelle tucked her chin, wrapping her arms around her body. She couldn't really believe the man who'd sat across from her that morning, primly eating his egg with dainty bites pinched between finger and thumb, would do something like *that*. No. With a fierce headshake, she forced her legs back into motion, continuing down the path. It was a bright, beautiful morning. She wasn't about to let herself fall into gloomy imaginings. And all those half-mad muttered warnings about a Thorn Maiden and certain death? Nothing but tricks to make her leave. Or he was insane. Or both.

"One way or another, you won't be able to hide without his knowing," she informed herself, kicking a stone out of her path. "He knows every inch of this island better than you ever will."

He hadn't followed her this morning, which meant he must possess some magical means to watch her movements, to know her comings and goings. Hiding out wouldn't work. He'd found her last night easily enough and somehow rendered her unconscious. No doubt he could do it again.

Nelle paused and glanced back to the crooked lighthouse standing on the brink of its cliff. Her brow knotted, and she chewed unconsciously at the inside of her cheek. Everyone knew mages were strange sorts, particularly the Miphates. Stories said they were power-hungry, ravenous for more magic. Nelle believed it. In her two years as a university drudge, she'd seen her fair share of Miphates. A funk of megalomania followed them everywhere like perfume. Gaspard fairly reeked of it.

This Rose Book, then, must be extremely powerful. More powerful than those grimoires in the quillary. Something utterly unique. Could Mage Silveri have chosen this exile of his? Had he isolated himself here on Roseward, cut off from the rest of mankind, so that he need not share his spellbook with others?

But what about that offhand comment he'd made this morning: "*I was not placed here for my comfort.*"

Nelle puffed a frustrated breath between her lips, spun on her heel, and continued marching toward the great house. There were too many unknowns, but of one thing she was almost certain: The Rose Book would be in the lighthouse, not Dornrise. Which meant she'd have to get back inside the tower without alerting the mage. Or his wretched attack-wyvern, for that matter.

"One problem at a time," she whispered. "Before anything else, you must get your satchel."

The walk passed swiftly. Before she was quite ready, the ruined gates and the long drive leading to the great house lay before her. At the top of the cliff she paused to look down at the harbor below and the remains of the *Queen's Disgrace* rotting by the dock. She could just see her own little boat where she'd left it, pulled up above the high-tide line.

With a heavy sigh she turned and faced forward again. Setting her heart and jaw in determination, she hastened on, her skirts billowing behind her like sails.

She made her way to the kitchen door far more easily this time. The briars around the door weren't as thick as she remembered, and with little effort she reentered the cool dimness of Dornrise's kitchen. Pausing on the threshold, she took three slow, measured breaths. "See?" she whispered. Then, clearing her throat, she spoke out loud, filling the silence. "There's nothing to fear. It's only an old empty house."

Her voice echoed away. Vanished. And still she stood there, ears straining for . . . something. Something she couldn't name. Something like an echo of laughter deep in the shadows. A sensation of mockery and dark mirth.

No. There was nothing. Just silence and dust.

Nelle hastened to the larder and peered inside. It was something of a jolt to discover a loaf of bread nestled inside the same breadbasket she'd snatched one from the day before. Was it the same loaf? Hardly. She'd devoured that one. Had some invisible baker been hard at work the night before? "Magic," she muttered. How quickly she was becoming inured to the idea.

Since yesterday's loaf hadn't caused her any harm, she went ahead and took this one, stuffing it into a cloth sack she found folded on a shelf. While she was at it, she claimed a few more choice items and tucked them away as well, including a fancy little cut-glass bottle containing some clear liquid and bearing the strange word *qeise* in elegant script. It looked expensive . . . but, after all, she was a snatcher, wasn't she? And she didn't know of any other food sources on the island, unless she wanted to go hunting for seagull eggs.

Her sack filled, Nelle swung it over her shoulder and hurried on through the kitchens and up the servants' stair, on into the broad passage above. She saw the tall double doors leading to the banquet hall at the end of the passage. They were shut. Strange. She could have sworn she'd left them open yesterday. Startled so much by the sight of the dead bodies inside, she'd backed away at once and hadn't dared return close enough to pull the doors . . .

She shook her head firmly. "You're misremembering," she muttered. "That's all." Yesterday was something of a blur in her mind.

She took a quick turn, then another, and soon approached the huge stairway with the ugly wyvern newel posts. It was darker this morning than it had been yesterday, for the sun had not yet progressed far enough across the sky to shine through the big landing window. Nelle had never minded darkness before. "And I don't mind it now," she reminded herself firmly and trotted toward the stair.

A gleam of gold caught her eye.

She stopped short and slowly turned. Her lips parted in a sharp inhalation of breath.

A single ray of sunlight fell through one of the briar-veiled windows and shone on a gilded picture frame. She hadn't noticed it yesterday, for in the afternoon that part of the hall would be deeply shadowed. Now, however, she couldn't help seeing a life-sized portrait. It so completely arrested her attention that she forgot everything else.

It was those eyes. Those startling eyes. The sun hit them just so, and though the rest of the image had faded, the eyes were brilliant. Intense.

Nelle turned from the stair and approached the portrait. Why was her breath suddenly tight in her chest? Why were her feet hesitant and yet unable to resist? The frame hung high on the wall, but she continued until she stood directly beneath it, her chin lifted, her eyes raptly studying the image.

It was a young, proud face with a thin, sarcastic mouth, one corner of which quirked just enough to reveal a deep dimple. Long, pale-gold hair framed strong cheekbones and fell to the shoulders, curling at the ends in almost feminine elegance. But there was nothing womanly about the breadth of those shoulders, about the strength of that jaw and brow.

Nelle narrowed her eyes. Frowning, she reached up, placed one hand to hide the nose and lower half of the face, the other over the brow, framing the eyes so that they stared fiercely out at her. Daring her to recognize them. Daring her to realize upon whose face she gazed.

"Well now, Mage Silveri," she murmured. "You're missing your scars, ain't you?"

She took a step back, letting her hands fall away. Only then did she notice the second portrait just to the right of the first. The light was too dim to get a clear impression of the face depicted, but it appeared to be much like the first one. How odd. Why would two portraits of the same subject be hung side by side in this place of prominence?

Her brow puckered and she frowned, feeling as if she ought to understand something here. As though this moment of revelation should explain the mystery of the fallen Miphato and his spellbook. He must have been part of the household, the Lord of

Roseward's son perhaps. But why was he here now, alone? Why had Dornrise been left to fall into ruin and the harbor town abandoned? Why did he remain here when all others fled and Roseward itself drifted away from the mortal world?

"I wasn't placed here for my comfort."

She shook her head. She ought to continue, of course. The library waited for her. She had to find her satchel and make proper plans for her next move. But for some moments she couldn't bear to look away. She couldn't bear to have those eyes on the back of her head, watching her go . . . just as the living Silveri had watched her that morning.

She tilted her head suddenly, and her frown deepened as a sudden question crossed her mind. "Exactly how old *are* you?" she whispered.

The face in the portrait was young. Only a few years older than her eighteen years, unless she missed her guess. But she'd assumed the man who'd acted as her host last night was much, much older than that. His hair was white, no longer this luxurious gold, and so wild and unkempt, he looked more like a mad old hermit than a lord's dashing son. But . . . she remembered the arms framing her body as he held the door shut. She'd been startled at the sight of the nilarium encasing his hands, but not startled enough to miss those corded muscles.

He was no emaciated old hermit, that much was certain.

With a sharp huff of breath, Nelle turned away from the portrait. Where exactly had her thoughts wandered off to, anyway? Enough of this! She fairly raced for the stair, taking the treads two at a time. At the landing she turned and hastened up to the second floor, then on without pause until she reached the library again.

The doors stood wide open as she approached. The inside was exactly as she remembered leaving it. There were her piles of books around the base of the sliding ladder. There were the candles in their various stands and sconces, all burned down to puddles of wax. There was the armchair in which she had dozed.

But where was her satchel? Hadn't she dropped it on the floor beside the chair? It wasn't there now.

"Where did I shift it to?" she muttered, searching under the chairs, then turned, a hand pressed to her forehead, to look around at the huge library space. On an impulse she stuck her hand down under the seat cushions, yelped, and whipped it back out. Frowning at the drop of blood, she stuffed her finger into her mouth and pulled the cushion off the seat.

Her little sleeve knife fell out and clattered on the floor. Nelle retrieved it, tucking it back into the sheath still strapped to her wrist under her sleeve. What a relief to be armed again! A knife might not be much use against magic spells and wicked mages, but she felt better for it even so.

Eventually she discovered her satchel high on a bookshelf. Very high, near the top, only three shelves down from the crown molding. Which was . . . odd. She didn't recall searching the books on that particular shelf and could think of no reason to bring the satchel up with her.

Once she'd descended back to the landing, she opened the flap and searched the contents. Everything was there. Including the Sweet Dreams.

She carefully lifted the tiny clay jar, unfastened its lid, and checked the contents. There wasn't much left, only a little residue clinging to the sides and a dollop at the bottom. Without Mother's resources at her disposal, there would be no new supply.

"Must be careful," she whispered. "Need to choose your time . . ."

Her mouth twisted ruefully as she tucked it back into the satchel. A poisoned kiss wouldn't be much use if she couldn't find the man's lips beneath all that hair! Besides, despite Gaspard's insinuations, Mage Silveri hadn't played the part of a desperate lecher last night. He was dignified. For a madman.

Nelle looped the satchel strap over her shoulder as she made her way down the spiral step from the landing to the main library floor. Now that she had her tools back, it was time to determine her next course of action. To make a thorough search of the lighthouse, she would have to find an opportunity when the mage wasn't at home. In the meantime, realistically, she must convince him to let her stay on at Roseward, at least for the next few days.

"That's all very well," she muttered. "But how exactly are you going to manage it?"

As Nelle lugged the sack of stolen larder goods and her satchel out of the library, her mind focused on solidifying a plan. What if she were to tell the mage a little of her true circumstances? A few small lies woven into the truth would make for a compelling story. She could tell him she'd been accused of a crime—let him assume her innocence, of course—and was obliged to flee or face the ax. Play on his sympathies. If she convinced him she needed a place to lie low, just for a few days, and offered to cook in return for his hospitality . . .

"And, if necessary, you can offer *other* things."

She grimaced even as the words left her mouth. The weight of the Sweet Dreams jar at her hip was of little assurance. She shivered and shook her head. Better see what a little food and a little sympathy could do first. She'd worry about the rest later.

Nelle slipped back down through the kitchens and out the side door, as quietly unnoticed as a mouse. Glad to leave Dornrise behind, she picked up her pace and pushed through the briars, back out to the open road. Only once did she indulge the creeping sensation up her spine by looking back over her shoulder.

But the house was merely a house. A pile of stone and brick and glass. No pale figure stood in the window to which her eye immediately fastened. No dead eyes watched her departure.

She shook her head and hurried on. Soon, as she gained the broad path above the cliffs and breathed deeply, letting the sting of salty sea wind purge her lungs of dust and her mind of shadows, her spirits lifted. In truth, she had no memories of clear air or open skies in her past. Such luxuries didn't exist in the winding streets of Wimborne. Even when she'd climbed with

Mother to the highest rooftops of the city, they never could quite climb above the dense smoke rising from the many chimneys below.

With air like this to fortify her and a brilliant sun to warm her skin, she allowed herself to hope that her half-formed plan would work. Only when she came in sight of the lighthouse tower did her spirit sink and her footsteps slow to a standstill. Her sack of stolen goods slipped from her shoulder and landed with a thunk by her feet. Her courage failed her.

"Come on, girl," she growled softly through clenched teeth. "You've made up your mind. No point in dithering the day away." She bent to pick up the sack.

And froze.

A sharp, searing, beautiful, terrible cry echoed across the wind. It wrapped around her soul and pierced her to the core.

It couldn't be real. It couldn't! A sound like that, so pure, so full of light and golden goodness and exquisite sorrow, could melt even the stoniest heart. Her ears reverberated with the echo, and her spirit surged as though to reach out and catch that goodness, to hold onto it with desperate joy.

Then the air split with a chorus of hideous braying chortles. Nelle whipped around, eyes widening. A flock of wyverns formed in the air not far back, along the path she'd just followed. They swarmed just as they had yesterday when Silveri sent them chasing after her. Her heart leapt with terror. Were they coming for her again?

But no . . . they had some other object in focus as they funneled down from the air, striking at something she could not see.

It resounded again—that song, that sound, that agonized and beautiful sensation. Nelle staggered where she stood, and her eyes widened. Whatever it was, the voice came from the same direction as the wyvern swarm.

It was a cry for help.

Leaving the sack where it lay, Nelle whipped her knife from her sleeve and was running before she even realized what she was doing. She had to do something. She had to try.

CHAPTER 15

SORAN WOKE TO A SENSATION OF LONELINESS SO POTENT IT took his breath away.

In the early days of his imprisonment—days he'd not thought about for many years—this sensation of aching, of loss, had been his constant companion. But he had long ago learned to live with it, then to ignore it, and eventually to not feel it at all.

So why did he feel it now? Why should he care?

He blinked once, and his eyes closed again heavily. This wouldn't do, so he blinked again. On the third attempt he managed to keep his lids open and discovered that the sensation of weight on his heart wasn't entirely emotional. A scaly blue lump curled up on his chest, heavier than it had any right to be. It licked its lipless muzzle in its sleep and caught a bit of Soran's beard between its teeth.

"Ugh!" Soran rolled unceremoniously onto his side, upending the wyvern. It uttered a snorting bray as it tumbled onto the floor, then pulled itself upright in a flurry of wings and lashing tail to glare at Soran. He sat up too, hunching to fit in the small alcove space. The picture of offended dignity, the wyvern hissed at him before scuttling up the fireplace stones to perch on the mantel. There it twisted its long neck and began grooming the spines along its back with noisy enthusiasm.

Soran gave his head a shake and ran the cold tips of his fingers through his matted hair, trying to clear the last of the sleep-fog from his brain. He didn't need much sleep; he'd long since trained his body to function on a mere two or three hours. Despite the long nights, despite the bone-wearying exhaustion, he dared not sleep the entire day away. There was always work to be done before sunset.

Still, he couldn't shake the heaviness that weighted his spirit like an iron cloak.

His eyes moved against his will, glancing at the copper pan on the hearth. The wyvern's industrious tongue had scraped it clean, but he'd have to wash it properly before putting it away. And when that was done, all sign of the mortal girl's presence would be gone. For good.

"For good," he repeated and climbed out of the alcove, pulling the folds of his robes straight around his body. He wouldn't let himself picture her crouched over the fire, watching her eggs sizzle. He wouldn't let himself dwell on the image of her seated across from him at the table. He didn't deserve the luxury of company, didn't deserve reprieve from his solitude. He didn't even deserve these memories.

Soon enough the timeless, endless days would close in around him again, and it would be as though this little interlude never happened. As though the small ray of sunlight never pierced the gloom of his eternal prison.

Soran marched to the armoire across the room and flung its doors wide. He groped in the darkness for the small pile of bound books within and pulled one out, an exact replica of the moleskin volume he'd carried with him to Dornrise the evening before. Opening it in his palm, he glanced briefly through the pages. It would have to do.

Leaving the armoire standing open, he tucked the book into the front of his robes and headed for the door. A chortle from the fireplace drew his eye. The wyvern watched him, its one good wing flared, and its head tilted to eye him accusingly.

"Sorry, little friend," Soran said, his hand resting on the doorlatch. "I haven't the strength to attempt repairs on your spell today. We will try again soon. Tomorrow, perhaps." He opened the door, and a breeze gusted into the room, stirring through his hair. "For now, I have other work to attend to."

He pulled the door firmly shut behind him despite the

wyvern's protesting bray. The last thing he needed was for the little creature to try to follow him. Without the proper use of its wings, the wyvern was defenseless. Its teeth were sharp but not exactly lethal, and they obviously had been of little use against whatever monster had chased and savaged it yesterday.

Soran set out down the cliff path to the beach below, moving swiftly and refusing to let his gaze drift out across the waters in search of a little boat or a glimpse of bright red hair. He had a job to do; he refused to be distracted by foolish, forlorn wishes.

He saw few wyverns at the beach. Sometimes they took it into their small brains to flock to other parts of the island as though driven by some faulty migration instinct. No other point on Roseward afforded them proper shelter, however, so they always returned before sunset to tuck away into little caves in the face of the cliff and pull stones in behind them, effectively sealing themselves up against the coming night.

Soran ignored the quiet emptiness while picking his way across the beach to the place where he'd found the wounded wyvern yesterday. There he crouched, his eyes quick and searching. But if the attacker had left behind any trace of its presence that mortal eye could detect, the wind and waves had already washed it from existence.

Reluctantly, Soran drew the little spellbook from the front of his robes. He hated to use more of his precious stock of spells. He'd used three last night, far more than he could spare. But what choice did he have? A faerie beast able to breach the island wards was too powerful for him to face on his own.

He flipped open to a certain spell and read off a series of strange words similar to those of first spell he'd used last night: "*Ilrune petmenor. Mythanar awl sarlino cor . . .*"

His vision shimmered, the effect of the spell playing along the edge of his mind, altering his range of perception. Last night it had sent his gaze deep into the darkness of the Nightmare, piercing into shadows too deep for mortal eyes to perceive.

This time it wasn't darkness but a shimmering, deadly light that became slowly visible to his gaze. The spell pushed his vision through the veils of time, letting him glimpse shadows of the past. Rather, not shadows. More like . . . light-echoes. Outlines of energy that left distinct patterns in the fabric of reality.

He watched movements on the beach, the wheeling of wyverns overhead, their awkward landings and waddlings. He watched the tide roll in and out again.

He watched a slim, upright, light-traced figure approach along the beach, her hair wafting behind her in the wind; and he watched her run away and put out to sea, chased by a swarm of flashing wings so brilliant, he almost had to shut his eyes and break the spell.

Instead, he pushed further back in time until he saw his own silhouette kneel at the stones and pull the little wyvern free. But that wasn't far enough. He pushed on, feeling the limits of his spell close in. It wasn't a particularly powerful spell—an early effort from his student days, one he'd never expected to cast. Back then, his powers had increased almost by the day, and to go back and cast the spells of his youth, his childhood, would have seemed a useless waste of effort and talent.

Now, however, he was grateful for each of these collected and protected scribblings. Without these small spells, he could not have survived this long on Roseward.

The flickering lights suddenly intensified. Soran sucked in a sharp breath. A new image presented itself to his view; a being approached across the beach, moving as lightly as a dancing thought. Its outline was indistinct. He could be certain only of four long legs and what seemed to be a powerful, outstretched neck.

Something small scuttled along the ground before the being: his wyvern, dragging its torn wing behind it as it fled. The large being chased it into the stones, and the wyvern, seeing a crack, tried to squeeze itself down into safety but instead wedged itself fast. It began to scream in terror.

The predator slowed and progressed with more dainty care across the uneven terrain. Soran got an impression of delicate feet sparking against stones. He saw that powerful neck lift high, and a shape like a long blade flashed across his mind's eye.

The next instant, wyverns attacked in swarm. Summoned by their brother's cries, they dived at the strange being, too many and too fast for it to properly defend itself. The being seemed to rise on its hindquarters, tearing the air with its forelegs. But the wyverns were too many, and it soon turned, leapt from the stones in a single arching bound, and raced back along the beach. Half of the swarm pursued it while the other half remained behind, circling their fallen friend for some while as it mewled pitifully for help.

Burning heat seared along the front of Soran's mind, and the spell began to unravel. He'd pushed it beyond its natural range. Hastily he blinked and broke it before it could collapse on its own, which might permanently damage his mortal eyes. For several seconds he stood still, his cold palms pressed over his face, into his eye sockets, waiting for the brilliant afterimages to fade.

When he looked up and gazed around at the silent, empty beach, no sign remained of yesterday's altercation. He turned in the direction the predator had fled. A grimace pulled his mouth into a hard line.

"So," he whispered through the hair of his beard. "One of *them* got through."

Cursing under his breath, he followed the beach until it gave way to sharp, sheer rocks and foamy water. He could see no path up the cliffs; at least, none that he could use. There was no telling with faerie beasts. The creature might have scaled the cliff without a second thought in its bid to escape the wyverns. Or it might have cast itself into the water and fled from Roseward, back to its own shores.

Soran gazed out across the sea, seeking a shoreline through the veiling obscurity. He thought he glimpsed one, terribly distant: a green landscape under a fair and shining sun. But he couldn't count on the faerie beast returning to where it belonged. Now that it had come to Roseward, instinct would bid it remain until it had hunted its fill.

Another curse in his throat, Soran turned back, retraced his steps, and climbed the narrow path. He must find the beast, but direct confrontation would be hopeless. Perhaps he could set a trap for it? One way or another, he would need better, stronger spells than those he'd brought with him.

Reaching the top of the path, he took three steps toward the lighthouse. He'd not taken a fourth before a scream ripped through the air.

Shocked, Soran slowly turned to stare along the cliff path toward Dornrise. There were his wyverns; he saw them up in the sky, the whole flock of them flitting away in all directions.

Was he mistaken? He must have been, must have imagined it. His brain was addled from the use of that old spell.

It couldn't have been the mortal girl's voice he'd heard so clearly.

He waited, balanced on the balls of his feet, waiting for a second scream. But none came. He held his breath until he could hold it no more. Then, a harsh expletive burst from his lungs.

He raced along the cliff's edge, his robes billowing behind him.

The exquisite, pitiful song rang out again and again, battering Nelle's soul with its beauty and urgency.

Some part of her realized there must be a spell at work here. If she were in her right mind, she would never run headlong straight for that deadly swarm of wyverns. What did she think she could do against so many anyway? They might be smallish sorts of dragons, but they had enough teeth and claws among them to make even the most intrepid adventurer nervous, and while she hadn't yet spotted any spurts of fire, that didn't mean they couldn't belch out little infernos if provoked.

Yet against all reason, against all better judgment, she kept charging ahead. She rounded a bend in the path that took her through a thicket of low brush and skidded to a stop.

The wyverns amassed in the sky above and took turns diving down in a stream of merciless attack, striking at a single foe, then careening up and away before returning to the swarm above. The effect created was a funnel of wings and scales and hideous brays. The cloud of colors was brilliant: jewel-colored wings flashing in the sunlight.

But Nelle could hardly see them. Her gaze drew immediately to their target.

It was a unicorn.

She'd heard tell of such beings in stories and songs, glimpsed them in tapestries and murals. But she could never have imagined anything so perfect, so shining, so pure. Nowhere near as large as a horse, it was perhaps more the shape and proportion of a stag, with a little tuft of gossamer beard on its chin. A proud, coiled horn jutted from its forehead, catching the sunlight and refracting it like cut crystal, an iridescent jewel more royal than any queen's diadem. Powerful muscles rippled beneath the velvet-soft coat, but its limbs were so thin, so dainty, Nelle could easily imagine them snapping in two if they came down in a single bad step on that rough terrain.

Blood flowed in precious, silvery streams through the being's white fur. The sight was heart-wrenching and yet so beautiful that it could only enhance the radiant aura pulsing from the unicorn's center. It bugled its tragic and glorious cry even as it rose onto its powerful haunches and lashed out at its attackers with its horn.

But dozens of them came at it from all angles, and even though the unicorn was light on its sharp cloven hooves, the wyverns were too quick to be caught. One ripped at the unicorn's neck, tearing out a gouge of flesh and silken mane. The unicorn turned, thrashing its head, a gesture like poetry even in its wild desperation. Another wyvern attacked its back, hind claws missing their target by only a breath.

For a moment that lasted an eternity, Nelle stood rooted to the spot, mouth gaping, unable to believe what she saw, unable to comprehend the bizarre juxtaposition of beauty and horror, the dance of death and life playing out before her dazzled mortal eyes. Then something inside her snapped.

Forgetting all fear, she caught up a handful of stones and hurled one with all her might straight at the next descending wyvern. Her aim was good; Mother had taught her well. The stone clipped the little monster in the haunch, and it wheeled off to one side, braying in surprise. The next wyvern tore at the unicorn's ear, but Nelle's second stone caught the one after that in the wing, knocking it out of the air. It tumbled to the ground and landed in a heap, shook itself out, and with an awkward flapping run, launched itself back into the sky and sped away from the battle.

After that, time became a blur. Nelle hurled stones as fast as she could find them, all the while closing the distance between her and the unicorn. Soon she stood beside it and brandished her knife. The next wyvern that angled toward her veered off at the last second before her blade could slash its wing.

The unicorn, bolstered by this unexpected aid, lashed out with renewed energy, and its terrified bugle transformed into triumphant song. It knocked a wyvern from the air, sending it careening through the sky down to the water below. It impaled the wing of another with its horn, then shook it off to lie stunned on the stones at its feet.

The wyverns lost heart and pulled back, rising higher into the air, spinning in a dark circle, their brilliant colors obscured by their sheer mass. As though obeying some signal unheard by her ears, they suddenly dispersed every which way, flitting across the island and out over the water.

Nelle panted hard, her knife still gripped in one hand. Blood thundered in her veins, and her muscles jumped with pent-up adrenaline. Pushing hair out of her face, she stared around, still half convinced the attack would renew. Then she faced the unicorn, and her heart turned over in her breast at the sheer beauty of the being standing so close beside her.

It gazed at her from a pair of eyes as luminous as two blue moons. Its sides heaved, and blood ran in trickles from the many cuts along its neck, shoulders, and flanks, streaming down those delicate legs. Its head reached no higher than her shoulder, though the horn made it seem much taller. It shivered and shimmered, so fragile and lovely that Nelle feared merely breathing too hard would cause it to shatter like an illusion.

"I . . . I came as fast as I could," she said. Her voice sounded hard and earthy in her own ears. She felt dirty somehow. Crusted over with her own mortality. Ashamed.

But the unicorn blinked its delicate lashes and continued to gaze at her with an expression of pure sweetness and light. She longed to reach out, to touch that perfectly soft, sweet muzzle, to run her fingers through the silken strands of its mane. But how could she dare? She wasn't worthy of such an honor. No one could be, not even among the glorious fae.

The unicorn took a single step toward her. Slowly, gracefully, it lowered the point of its horn until the tip hovered just over her heart. Nelle's breath caught in her throat. She saw suddenly how very sharp that horn was, how completely deadly. Rivulets of brown and black liquid, like ink, ran along its coils, ugly dark stains that could only emphasize the horn's shining purity. With a single step more, the unicorn could drive that horn through her

216

breast. It would surely break through all bone, muscle, and tissue, straight through her beating heart and out the other side, so clean and so swift that she wouldn't realize she was dead until well after the fact. She might not even feel pain.

Was this, then, how she would die? Her heart surged with sudden agonized longing. Yes! Yes, let this be her death! This moment of exquisite loveliness, this sacrifice of self at the altar of true and perfect beauty!

But the unicorn turned away.

Nelle gasped and looked down, half convinced that it must have stabbed her. She grasped her bosom, searching for a tear in her dress. There was nothing. The unicorn had merely offered her a salute. This was almost too much to bear, too brilliant a moment! Her knees shook, and she nearly collapsed in tears at the pain of such perfection.

The unicorn's dainty feet scarcely touched the ground as it walked, shimmering with inner light, to where the wyvern it had skewered lay snarling and hissing, a flapping bundle of wings and scales and snapping teeth. It was a bright jewel-green thing, but Nelle could hardly see it. Compared to the unicorn, the rest of the world seemed mere shadows.

The unicorn raised its head. Then its lips peeled back, its jaw dropped open, and Nelle saw long sharp fangs protruding from purple gums. One cloven hoof pounded down, pinning the wyvern's spine, and the unicorn dropped its head and ripped the screaming little creature's wing off. A gush of black, inky blood flowed out on the ground as the unicorn threw back its head and, with strange, gulping spasms of its throat muscles, swallowed the wing whole.

Nelle blinked.

In the instant her eyes were closed, blocking out the shining light, she saw a skeletal being, all darkness roiling with a reverberation of red, raw magic. The cloven hooves were sharp as daggers, the pointed horn dripping with gore. A demonic aura emanated from a core as dark and devouring as the night.

She raised her eyelids, and the being was again shining, almost unbearably splendid. It reached down and tore a gash into the still-screaming wyvern's haunch.

"No!" Nelle flung herself at the unicorn. Her knife was still in her hand, and she didn't stop to think what she did before plunging it into the unicorn's shoulder.

A ripple of shock reverberated through the being's body, striking Nelle with such violence that she fell. Only just in time, for the unicorn swung its head, dropping the mouthful from its teeth to lash at her with that lethal horn. Nelle caught herself in time to keep from bashing her head on the rocks, and immediately rolled, narrowly avoiding the skull-crushing stamp of a powerful hoof. Stones cracked, and the whole cliff seemed to tremble at the power of that blow, threatening to crumble away and fall into the sea.

The unicorn stamped again, pounding at her head. Nelle rolled and rolled, vaguely aware of how near she came to the cliff's edge but unable to change direction. A hoof came down on her skirts. She was pinned, trapped. The unicorn's eyes flashed, and the sunlight gleaming on its horn made it burn like a star. It raised its head, ready to strike, preparing to spear her to the ground.

A rattling bray split the air. Trailing inky blood, the one-winged wyvern launched itself at the unicorn's hind legs, its needle-sharp teeth clamping down hard. The unicorn started and reared back, releasing her gown. Nelle rolled again.

And dropped over the edge of the cliff.

CHAPTER 16

SORAN ROUNDED THE BEND JUST IN TIME TO SEE IT ALL: the girl lying on her back at the brink of that drop-off, her hair blowing about her face in a wild storm of sun-glinting red, her fiery blue eyes staring out through the strands. He saw that her skirt was caught, though he could not see by what. He thought he almost perceived a moving shadow, but it might have been cast by a passing cloud.

Then one of his wyverns was suddenly there, a green creature hardly larger than a housecat. Bloodied and one-winged, it launched itself at nothing, savaging empty air with teeth and slashing hind claws. Something shook it wildly, and it lost its grip and flew back through the air to crash on the stones with a heartrending cry.

The mortal girl, jerking her skirt free of whatever invisible force held it in place, went over the brink.

Soran froze. His eyes rounded in shock, and his heart lurched to a stop in his breast. For a moment, the world around him seemed to spin, to tilt.

The shrieks of his wyverns brought him back to himself. He shook his head as though to clear it, then sought one small spell in his book. It wasn't much—a single bolt, a dart of pain. Acting swiftly, he brought it into being, balanced between his fingers, and guessed at his target's location by the wyvern's reactions.

"*Yesrona sarfir!*" He flicked his wrist in a throwing motion.

Reality shuddered in a ripple strong enough to knock Soran back a pace.

His spell hit home.

The next instant would decide everything. Either his enemy would recognize the limits of his paltry magic and attack, pinning him to the ground with a single blow, or—if the gods were still merciful, if any luck remained in the alignment of his sacred stars—it would be shocked by his unexpected attack and retreat. Whatever it chose, Soran could only stand with his arm still outstretched, staring into the empty space where he was nearly certain his enemy still poised over the suffering wyvern.

Something shifted in the air, a darkness flowing away, galloping, vanishing into the trees. He couldn't see it, couldn't really sense it, but he felt it with the kind of certainty that came after years of breathing Hinter air.

So, he would live. For another few moments, at least.

Springing forward, he covered the distance to the fallen wyvern and collapsed on his knees beside the little creature. One wing was torn completely away, and its body was broken, battered, twisted in unnatural angles. It gazed up at him, one baleful red eye blinking and bright, the other crushed to a pulp. Inky blood poured from innumerable wounds.

A sob caught in Soran's throat as he scooped the wyvern up in the palms of his silvery hands. Its head hung limp from its twisted, broken neck, but it managed to give a little vibrating chortle as he held it close to his face.

"I'm sorry," Soran whispered, tears staining his cheeks, running into his beard. "Forgive me. Forgive me, little friend." He brought the scaly head up against his forehead and closed his eyes. He felt the broken creature shudder with a sigh. "I should have released you," he murmured. "I should have set you free."

The next moment, his hands held tattered pieces of parchment. They scattered through his fingers and drifted away on the wind, too fast to follow. He opened his eyes, saw a stain of dark ink running across his hands and dripping onto his knees, and his heart broke.

"*Bullspit!*"

Soran lifted his head and turned where he knelt. The girl! Was it possible . . .? He staggered to his feet, stumbled several paces, then raced to the cliff's edge and stared down.

"By the great gods!" he gasped.

She was there. Clinging to the cliff's sheer wall like a bat, her white face upturned but not seeing him. Her gaze focused intently on her hands and on the stones just above them, the next handhold she must reach. Wind caught and billowed her voluminous skirts, threatening to fling her out over the waves and the rocks waiting to batter her corpse below.

Even as Soran watched, she lunged upward, searching for a grip, and missed. He thought she'd fall, but she reclaimed her former hold and pressed herself hard into the wall, squeezing her eyes tight.

It was impossible. Utterly impossible. Those scrawny limbs of hers should never have been able to catch her body as she fell. Her own momentum should have pulled her arms out of their sockets, and then only if she miraculously managed to grasp a tight enough hold.

Yet he could not deny what his eyes clearly told him.

"Miss Beck!" he cried.

A little shudder ran across her shoulders and through her straining arms. She heard him, but she couldn't lift her head to look up at him.

"Hold on," he said.

He could almost swear he heard her mutter, "Well, that's the idea now, ain't it?"

Hands trembling, he pulled his spellbook free again, turning the pages to find something, anything that might help in this situation. Most of the spells contained in that volume were too minor, foolish little conjurings of the sort practiced by junior students of the Miphates school. But there was one, a levitation spell. Not a strong one; it would last no more than a few seconds. But maybe . . .

Trying not to speak the words too quickly, Soran read off the incantation and felt the pulsing magic drawn from beyond this existence channel through him. He grasped and formed the spell, then threw it even as he had thrown the dart of pain.

It struck the top of the girl's head. She tensed. Her left hand slipped its hold. She scrambled to reclaim her grip, and the stone under her right foot suddenly crumbled and gave way. With a cry, she hung suspended by one arm out over that death-drop.

But the spell took hold. Her hair floated out around her as though she were underwater, and her free arm and leg ceased flailing wildly.

Her eyes widened, and she stared up at Soran, her gaze strangely accusatory. "What have you—?"

"No time!" he barked and crouched, extending his hand. His stomach churned with vertigo, but he would not focus on the drop, only on the girl's pale face several feet below. "Climb now!"

The urgency of his voice cut through her shock. She reached for the cliff wall with her free-floating hand and began to pull herself up, hand over hand, her body floating along behind her, light as a cloud. The wind gusted, threatening to toss her off course. Her eyes widened. She might easily be spun out across the wide Hinter Sea, and when the spell wore off, fall into open ocean.

"Hold on!" Soran might have saved his breath. Her grip was like iron, her knuckles bulging and white as she clung to the stones. Her arms shook, and he feared terror would make her lose hold. But she continued upward with grim determination, her face set, her eyes fixed on him as her goal.

A ripple through the air touched his face, touched his soul. Not wind, but magic.

His spell.

It was beginning to give out.

Her eyes, upturned to his, widened still more, the whites ringing her irises. She felt it too.

Soran flattened himself on his stomach, his arm extended. "Take my hand!" he cried.

For an instant she hesitated. It was almost her undoing.

With a last desperate surge, she heaved her weightless body up the cliff wall. His cold fingers wrapped around her wrist just as the spell gave out, and her body crashed into the wall under the force of renewed gravity.

Soran gritted his teeth; a strangled roar choked from his straining throat. She was a small maid, but the whole of her weight suspended from one arm was almost too much for him. The nilarium encasing his hands clamped down hard, however, ready to break the delicate wrist bones rather than give up his hold.

She scrambled, her feet searching for purchase against the stone. Her free hand caught hold and pulled, relieving him of some of her weight. He braced himself and, summoning power he hadn't known he possessed, hauled her up. Inch by painful inch he pulled her high enough that her other hand could grasp the edge of the cliff.

She took hold and, with more strength than he would have guessed possible in those slender arms, hauled her torso up until she could get an elbow in place. Soran sat upright and dragged her the rest of the way, finally wrapping his arm around her waist and rolling her away from the edge. She collapsed beneath him, flat on her back, her chest rising and falling with rapid breaths. He bowed over her, one elbow supporting his body on the ground. His other hand still held onto her wrist, and it was with conscious effort that he relaxed his hold, noting the terrible red imprint his fingers had left on her skin.

"Miss Beck," he gasped and gripped her shoulder, giving her a not-so-gentle shake. "Miss Beck, are you all right?"

Her gaze was empty, staring straight up into the sky. She blinked heavily. Her eyes turned to focus on his face. Her mouth opened, and her throat moved as though she was trying to speak.

Then her gaze shifted over his shoulder.

She screamed.

Instinct shot through Soran's muscles, driving him to react. He threw himself across the girl and rolled over the stones on her

227

SYLVIA MERCEDES

other side. He saw the impact of something hard and deadly smashing the ground where his body had been but a moment before.

The girl scrambled onto her feet, swaying dangerously but alert. She sprang back, keeping distance between herself and the cliff's edge, her eyes fixed on what appeared to Soran's gaze as empty space.

He knew better.

Pulling up into a crouch, he reached for his spellbook. If only he'd thought to bring along a more advanced book of spells, something that might truly help against such a foe! But with all the monsters he'd anticipated hunting down today, a unicorn hadn't even crossed his mind.

He reached into the spellbook and pulled out another small pain dart. It wasn't much, but he flung the words, flung the spell, hoping his aim wasn't far off the mark. By the way the girl gasped and twitched, he thought perhaps the unicorn had reacted. If nothing else, he had certainly drawn its attention his way.

"Watch out!" the girl cried, her voice piercing.

A faint impression of shadow told him of the impending charge. He dodged to one side . . . but this time he guessed wrong.

Pain lanced through his shoulder, bright as a bolt of lightning, so brilliant his eyes were dazzled. He thought he heard his own voice screaming, but it was distant, so far away. Off in another world beyond this immediate world of pain.

He shuddered, one hand pressed to his shoulder. Blood spilled through his fingers. The tip of a broken white horn protruded through the fabric of his robes.

Two minutes. Two minutes more of consciousness.

If he were lucky.

The ground beneath his feet shifted. Through the sparking, blinding pain, he thought he saw a shadow move, thought he saw the lash of a long serpentine tail, the arch of a muscular neck. He couldn't move, couldn't think.

A scream—inhuman, and so beautiful it could almost tear the heart in two—shattered the air. Soran looked up to see a flurry of darkness and light and then . . . and then . . .

The mortal girl stood beside him. She held a knife in one hand, stained with silvery unicorn blood. "You idiot!" she cried. "What, are you going to stand there and let it skewer you?" She grabbed hold of his arm, disregarding his bleeding wound, and hauled him after her. "Come on! We've got to go!"

He took a step. Staggered. Began to fall. She slipped under his arm, pulling his weight across her shoulders. "I'm stronger than I look," she growled. "Step now. Step, step . . . oh, *bullspit!*"

She stopped. He raised bleary eyes, blinking through the bursts of bright pain. He couldn't see it, couldn't feel it. But he knew the unicorn was there. Blocking their path to the lighthouse.

The girl supporting him trembled and held up her ridiculous little knife. "Get back!" she cried. "Get back, or I'll give you more of this!"

If he'd had the strength, Soran would have laughed. Indeed, he felt a chuckle rumbling in his chest, but it came out as an agonized gurgle. He sank to his knees, pulling her down beside him. She struggled out from under his arm, and he had just awareness enough to see how she braced herself over him, legs in a wide stance, knife clutched tight in her fist. Like a wide-eyed kitten arching its back at a dragon.

A smile tugged at the corner of his mouth.

Then he sank into pain-ridden darkness.

CHAPTER 17

"SIR?" NELLE GASPED AND, HALF TURNING, KICKED AT THE fallen mage with her heel. "Sir? Wake up!"

It was no use. The man was out cold. He might be dead for all the response he gave. There would be no sudden burst of Miphates magic, no enchantment to save the day at the last possible moment.

She was on her own.

Eyes wide, she faced the unicorn, whispering, "Bullspit!" She'd thought if she could just get the two of them back to the lighthouse, maybe the mage would have some magical lock on the door, something that would keep a unicorn out.

It didn't matter now. The unicorn was there, just a few yards ahead of her, blocking her path. And while not so long ago it had seemed small, dainty, delicate, and pure, it had now transformed into a mighty muscular thing with vast shoulders and a thick bull-like neck. Its horn was broken at the tip, ragged and deadly, stained red with Mage Silveri's blood. Two bleeding wounds streamed from its neck—the two places her knife had pricked it. But her blade was much too small to do any real damage.

It had served only to enrage.

Nelle braced herself before the fallen mage, squaring her shoulders. The unicorn blinked its moon-glowing eyes, and for an instant they became two molten suns, their shimmer melting away into red-streaked shadow. It arched its huge neck and lowered its broken horn. Nelle's heart lurched with the realization that she had maybe three breaths left before she died. Before she was gored by that horn and crushed to a pulp beneath those cloven hooves.

The unicorn took a step. Nelle opened her mouth, trying to scream, trying to gasp out a prayer, trying to roar her defiance.

But before she could utter a sound, a strange gulping, braying noise erupted in the air around them.

Nelle recoiled and nearly fell over the mage as she stepped back. The unicorn, distracted from its purpose, turned its massive head to look behind it, and Nelle looked as well.

Her sack of stolen goods from the Dornrise larder lay in the path, spilled out on its side. On top of that sack, upright on its haunches, its one good wing flaring out above its head, perched the blue wyvern. It threw back its head, honking and chortling, and its voice resounded and rebounded against the stones and up to the sky.

The unicorn snorted, flaring its wide nostrils. It tore at the ground, gouging the hard soil, and began to round on the wyvern. It would tear the little creature to pieces, just as it had the green wyvern.

But the fool wyvern didn't flinch. It swelled its chest and chortled louder and louder.

Shadows flicked across the ground. The air filled with the sound of leathery wings.

Nelle looked up, her heart leaping at the sight of the wyvern swarm, so recently scattered, reforming into a dense cloud of scales and teeth and claws. They circled in a wild frenzy above the unicorn.

The unicorn screamed a gorgeous, rippling, wrathful song that drove Nelle to her knees. Then the wyverns attacked—not one at a time, but in pairs, in trios, faster than before. The unicorn lashed out with its horn, its teeth, its hooves. Several times it struck a wyvern and sent it reeling through the air. But the others only swarmed in with more ferocity.

At last the unicorn uttered a shriek so furious that all the beauty of its voice shattered. It reared up, pummeling the air with its hooves, then turned and fled across the island, bounding away from the path through the dense growth of pines and out of sight. The wyverns pursued, streaming after it in a many-colored column, their violent chorus fading away like hunter's horns in the distance.

Nelle, on her knees in the dirt, drew several gasping breaths, her knife still gripped in her hand. She blinked across at the blue wyvern still seated on her sack. It blinked back, showed its teeth, then nosed down into the sack, searching for treats. Its head emerged with half a loaf of fresh bread gripped in its jaws, and its tail twitched happily.

Unable to find the strength either to scold or to thank the little beast, Nelle turned instead to Mage Silveri. His face, what could be seen of it through the mass of beard, was white as death, lying there in the dirt.

"Sir?" Nelle whispered. She quickly dropped her knife and pushed at his shoulder. "Sir, wake up!"

Was the unicorn's blow so deadly? A pool of blood spread beneath him and stained the long strands of his white hair.

Quickly she took hold of his shoulder and heaved him onto his back. Blood soaked through the shoulder of his robes, far too many layers of fabric. Muttering curses, half certain the unicorn would return to finish what it had begun, Nelle set to work unclasping the front of his robes and pulling them open. It took some awkward effort to slide the fabric down over his arms, and from the way he moaned, she knew he felt every jostling of his wound. But she managed at last to get the outer layers off.

A large patch of blood stained the shoulder of his loose white shirt. There were other stains as well . . . many dark brown stains, old stains, all over the soft linen fabric. From previous wounds?

Shaking her head, Nelle worked at the three ties holding the front of his shirt together, her fingers shaking with dread and urgency. She got them loose and pulled the shirt away, easing it over his bloody shoulder. Her eyes widened.

His shoulders and chest were well defined with hard muscle. But it was difficult to notice beneath the dozens and dozens of hideous scars covering every inch of his skin. She'd become somewhat used to the scars ringing the mage's eyes, the only part of his skin visible beneath all that hair. Somehow, she hadn't expected the same scarring to continue down the whole of his body. Many were thick, puckered, ragged. Obviously they had never been properly treated, and the flesh had knit together badly.

Firming her jaw, Nelle leaned over his shoulder to inspect the fresh wound, a single puncture, small but deep. Gingerly she pulled back the raw flesh and thought she saw the tip of the unicorn's horn embedded there.

That couldn't be good. Who knew what magic or poison a unicorn's horn might carry? She had to get it out.

She quickly crawled over to retrieve her knife, finding it covered in silvery unicorn blood and crusted with dirt. Digging around in the mage's shoulder with that would kill him for sure! She wiped the blade off on her skirt, but it didn't seem like enough.

235

A grunting snort caught her ear. Nelle looked up to see the wyvern pull a wedge of cheese out of her sack. Her eyes widened as she remembered: Hadn't she packed a bottle of spirits?

Scrambling to her feet, tripping over her skirts, Nelle lunged at the sack. "Shoo! Shoo!" she snarled, and shoved the blue creature away, little caring how it hissed and snapped at her. She stuck her hand down inside, and her fingers closed around the neck of the little cut-glass bottle. It hadn't broken in all the commotion. That was something, at least.

After a brief struggle with the cork, she finally grabbed a rock and broke the head and neck off the bottle. "Hope it wasn't *too* expensive," she muttered, pouring half its contents onto her knife and hands. It burned a little, but she took that as a good sign.

Returning to the mage's side, she crouched over him again and poured more of the spirits directly onto his wound. An unsettling sizzling and popping followed. She grimaced. That didn't seem natural. But then again, he'd just been gored by a unicorn. *Natural* didn't really fit anywhere in this situation.

Carefully parting the wounded flesh to reveal the top part of the broken horn, she dug her knife down in. He had sunk deeper into unconsciousness and didn't seem to feel her unpracticed and ungentle efforts, which was a mercy! Her stomach churned as blood oozed out. Cursing, shaking hair out of her face, and cursing some more, she finally managed to pry the broken horn up far enough to grasp with her fingers and pull free.

She held it up before her face. Blood dripped down the coils and over her fingers, palm, and wrist, dotting her sleeve. Was it whole? Had it left any shards behind in his shoulder? She didn't *think* so. But how could she know for certain?

The mage's body spasmed. Nelle choked on a yelp and sat back hard, jarring her tailbone. He twitched again, and his head turned to one side. The muscles of his cheek tightened; his eyes squeezed shut.

Then, with a cry he sat bolt upright, drawing his knees up as he came. He cried out again and reached up to touch the gushing wound at his shoulder. Blood poured through his fingers.

"Don't touch it!" Nelle cried. She seized the bundle of his robes lying close by and held it out to him. "Here," she said. "Stop the bleeding with this if you can."

He looked at her, his eyes wide and empty. Then he blinked, and clarity returned. "Miss Beck?"

She pried his hand away from his shoulder and shoved the folds of fabric in its place. She could feel blood soaking right through, and she knew the dirty old robes were not the most sanitary of bandages. But the mage simply sat gaping at her, his eyes blinking through the snarl of his hair.

"What . . . what happened?" he managed thickly.

"You stood there like a great lumpish dolt and let the unicorn stab you through the shoulder, that's what happened," Nelle said. "I thought sure it was going to stab right through your heart, and then where would you be, I'd like to know?"

"The unicorn?" He blinked and looked down at her hands

pressing the robes to his wound. "What . . . what about . . . Where is the horn?"

Nelle jutted her chin to indicate the blood-stained coil of ivory lying in the dirt beside her. His face contorted, and he pulled his legs back as though recoiling from a snake. "Get it away!" he cried.

"Easy! Easy now. It's just—"

"It's poison!" He looked at her urgently, his eyes very round. "It's poison to me!"

Nelle frowned. But he looked as though he might bolt at any moment if she didn't do something, and then she feared he would faint from blood loss, which would be inconvenient. She grabbed his hand, pressed it over his shoulder to hold the robes in place, then plucked up the broken horn. Scrambling to her feet, she carried it to the edge of the cliff.

For a moment, standing beside that sheer drop, she hesitated. It was so beautiful. Even broken like this, even covered in drying blood. Something about the way it spiraled seemed to create a sort of harmonious music in the atmosphere, music she couldn't quite hear with her ears, but which shimmered in her soul as she spun the horn slowly. Would it be so bad to keep it? A talisman of her strange time here on Roseward Isle? She could make it into a necklace or charm, maybe keep it with her to brighten the dark nights, and—

"Miss Beck?"

"No worries, sir!" Nelle tossed the words over her shoulder.

She breathed a sigh, drew back her arm, and hurled the piece of horn as hard as she could.

It spun, caught the light, and shone for an instant like a falling star. Then it plunged into the lapping waves below. She thought she saw a last glint or gleam as it sank. But that may have been her imagination. It was gone, certainly gone.

"Bullspit," she whispered, though she couldn't say why. She turned back to the mage.

To her surprise, he was already on his feet. Was his complexion less sallow than it had been just moments before? He swayed a little but steadied himself and pulled the bundle of fabric away from his shoulder. Wincing, he pressed it back again. Blood still trickled down his torso, ran over the hard muscles of his abdomen, and soaked into the top band of his trousers and the bundle of white shirt hanging about his waist.

"Here, sir," Nelle said, stepping to his side. "Lean on me. Don't want you toppling right over, now do we?"

He looked at her uncertainly, his eyes bright and a little confused. He had the good sense to accept her help, however, draping an arm over her shoulders and leaning on her for support. "Back to the lighthouse?" Nelle said.

He grunted, which she took as a yes. They staggered up the path together. As they passed the wyvern and the sack, Nelle paused to chase the little beast away and reclaim her loot. The wyvern gamboled up the path ahead of them, waddling on its hind feet, dragging its broken wing behind it, flapping the other every few paces, and looking utterly ridiculous. Still, it had undoubtedly saved their lives. She couldn't quite bring herself to laugh at it.

The lighthouse wasn't far off, but their going was slow, and every moment Nelle feared the unicorn's return. To disguise her fear, she demanded, "Why'd you let it stab you like that? You looked a right fool standing there with your mouth hanging open, waiting for it to stick you through."

He grunted, and she thought he wasn't going to answer. But after a few paces, he said, "I could not see it."

Nelle raised an eyebrow. "You couldn't see a fiery beast with a three-foot horn blazing out of its skull standing right in front of you?"

"Unicorns are not visible to mortal eyes."

"Eh?" Nelle tried to look up at him. All she got was an eyeful of beard tangles. "That's daft! I saw it right enough, and I'm mortal as they come."

"Yes, well." The mage took another heavy step or two, clearing his throat. "Unicorns will sometimes choose to reveal themselves to pure young maidens." He hesitated before adding, "Virgins."

A hot flush roared up Nelle's neck and flooded her cheeks. She suddenly noticed how muscular was the back her arm looped around and how hard was the stomach her other hand rested on in support as she aided the mage's footsteps along the path. Her flush deepened.

"Well, I suppose it's a good thing I was around then, ain't it?"

she muttered.

His spine stiffened. Did he blame her for his current condition? It wasn't exactly her fault. She hadn't asked him to come pull her up the cliff; she'd been handling it fine on her own. Or mostly fine. Her gut quivered with the memory of that deadly drop and the sensation of crumbling stones giving way beneath her grasping hands. Heights had never frightened her, at least not for long. Mother had taught her to accept the danger, to accept even the likelihood that she would one day meet her end via a fall. It was a snatcher's fate. It had been Mother's fate.

Still, not even Mother could have predicted the events of this afternoon. Not by a long shot.

They reached the lighthouse, and the wyvern shuffled ahead of them to jump at the closed door. How had the little beast gotten out, anyway? Probably climbed the rafters and slipped out through an upper window. And lucky for them it had!

Nelle led the mage to the doorstep and let go of him long enough to try her hand at the latch. It wouldn't budge, which surprised her. She couldn't see a lock. Could he have somehow bolted it from the inside?

Mage Silveri grunted, shifted his weight, and reached for the latch himself. It gave at once as though answering to some silent command. The door swung inward. More magic.

Nelle shivered, but nevertheless, sidling and ducking, got them both through the narrow opening. She moved to lead him toward the alcove bed, but he shook his head in protest. Instead, he sank into the nearest chair beside the table in the middle of the room.

"Here." Nelle pulled at the bundled robes he still pressed against his shoulder. "Let me see."

He didn't protest, so she peeled it away, wincing along with him as the rough fabric stuck to the drying blood. To her surprise, the wound itself looked much better already. In fact, if she didn't know any better, she could almost swear it had begun to heal.

She felt his eyes on her face and looked up at him quickly. "I-I, um—"

"It's the air," Silveri said, meeting her confused gaze. "The air of Roseward, which flows from Eledria and is tainted with magic. It heals the body swiftly if there is no impediment. Once you removed the poison—the unicorn's horn—the air itself began its work. It will leave a scar, but . . ." He shrugged ruefully.

"What's one more going to hurt?" Nelle finished for him. Impulsively she reached out, touching his shoulder with inquisitive fingers. He flinched but otherwise made no protest, even when she brought her face down close, studying his wound by the dim light coming through the door and high windows. "What about infection?" she asked at last.

"Infection can take no hold here. The air won't support it."

"You mean I wasted a whole bottle of good spirits trying to keep everything clean?"

He frowned. "Which bottle did you use?"

"I don't rightly know. Some fancy liquor I'd never seen before. Couldn't pronounce it, but the label said something like . . . queasy?"

"*Qeise?*" the mage supplied, his voice an anguished sort of bleat. "You mean *qeise?* You used a bottle of the High Lord Sothale's three-hundred-year-old Lunulyrian *qeise?* To what purpose exactly?"

"Well, I poured some of it on my knife, some on my hands, and more on your shoulder."

The mage had hardly looked more ill when lying unconscious with a shard of unicorn horn in his shoulder. He groaned, sank his head into his hand, and leaned an elbow heavily on the table. "To what depths has House Silveri fallen?"

This seemed a bit much. Nelle stood back and crossed her arms. "Excuse me for trying to save your life. Besides, it'll probably just reappear again, like the bread did yesterday. There's plenty of magic to go around the place; and anyway, the stuff I used was on the shelf next to the vinegar, and I'll bet you anything it was gone off and meant for poaching meats and the like. Probably not the good stuff."

He glared at her from between two silvery fingers. "All *qeise* is, as you so eloquently put it, 'the good stuff.'"

"Well, you weren't using it, starving yourself on a seagull-egg diet. What were you saving it for? A special occasion? Got a birthday coming up I should know about? 'Cause otherwise, I'd shut my mouth if I were you, unless it's to say a proper *thank you* like a gentleman ought. That's what I think."

"Oh, is it?" He dropped his hand and sat up straighter, then winced and clutched his shoulder again at the sudden movement. Teeth flashing through his beard, he looked down at the wound, but it was already much improved though obviously tender. While his elbow rested on the table, he let his hand dangle off the edge. He glared up at Nelle. "What were you doing, stealing from the Dornrise kitchens? I told you to leave Roseward. I believe I made myself perfectly clear."

Nelle's mouth went dry and her shoulders stiffened. "You did, sir. But the truth is . . . the truth is . . ."

Her half-formed plans, nearly forgotten during the events of the last hour, came clamoring back to the forefront of her brain. If only she'd had time to come up with a story. One she'd rehearsed, one she could now speak with confidence. She'd just have to hope her improvisations didn't make him more suspicious than he already was.

She drew a long breath. "The truth is I've got nowhere to go."

"You can go straight back to Wimborne," he growled.

She nodded, then shook her head quickly. "I can't go back there. Not yet, anyhow. You see, I . . . I came out this way trying to escape."

"Escape?" His gaze fixed on her face, too intent for comfort. "Escape from what?"

She'd begun now. Might as well push on and see where she ended. "I was caught up in some bad business." She bowed her head, letting her long hair fall in a curtain down one side of her face. Shame warmed her breast, but that was good. Shame would help feed and fuel this tale. "They were going to cut off my hands."

"What?" The question burst so sharply from Silveri's lips that the wyvern, who'd been prowling around his ankles, sat up on its haunches and uttered another tongue-rattling hiss. The mage unconsciously shifted a foot to push the beast behind his chair, then looked at Nelle. "Why would they do that? To you?"

Nelle shrugged one shoulder. "I was accused of something . . . unspeakable."

"But you're just a girl. What could you possibly have done?"

She snorted. This was a little too easy. She needed to be careful she didn't overplay her hand.

Lifting shimmering eyes, she met his gaze again. The tears clinging to her lashes were at least partially genuine, and she knew that helped. "A girl from Draggs Street don't have much but her reputation to shield her. And reputation don't take you far in this world."

He held her gaze. All his anger and frustration seemed to have melted away. She saw belief in his face even through that mess of hair. Belief and, unless she was much mistaken, a trace of sympathy. He certainly wasn't lacking a heart.

He turned away, twisting his wounded shoulder experiment-ally, and looked down at his own hand.

"I tried to get away up the river," she continued. Might as well put as much truth into this story as she could. Just enough truth, but not too much. Let him fill in the blanks however he liked. "None of the ferrymen would take me without payment I couldn't give. Or *wouldn't* give, rather. The only way I could get out of the city was by sea, so I took the boat and made for Roseward. No one ever comes out here, you know. Rumor says it's haunted, so I thought . . . I thought I might hide out a while, maybe a few weeks. Just until they stop looking for me."

"A few weeks?" The mage shook his head. "I'm sorry, but that's impossible."

"Why?" Nelle grabbed the second chair, pulled it around in front of him, and sat so that she could peer up into his face. She hesitated, then, hoping she wasn't pushing too hard, reached out both hands and took hold of his silver-crusted hand. She felt the startled thrill shoot up his arm, and he attempted to pull away, but she held on. "I understand the island ain't exactly safe, but . . . but you've kept me from any real harm. And you've got to admit I helped you out more than a little today. You'd have been skewered and dead by now if not for me! And the unicorn is still out there."

His eyes flashed. He tugged to free his hand, but without much force. Was he weakening? "There are more dangerous things than unicorns here on Roseward, Miss Beck. Things I . . . I cannot always control."

She nodded and spoke softly. "Do you mean the Thorn Maiden?"

He didn't answer, didn't move.

"You kept me safe last night," Nelle persisted. "You didn't let anything happen to me, and I . . . I think I trust you."

"*Trust* me?" The bitterness in his voice was enough to make her pull back a little. She felt unconsciously for the pressure of her knife hidden up her sleeve. But it wasn't there. Had she dropped it outside?

The mage stood, yanked free of her hold, and stalked to the fireplace, staring down into the smoldering embers. His back was to her, his bare shoulders bowed heavily. Beneath the straggling locks of his overlong hair, she saw muscles flex. Another traitorous flush crept up her neck.

Folding her hands in her lap, she stared down at them. "At least let me stay and help you with the unicorn. It's killing your wyverns, and you can't see it to fight it. Let me repay your hospitality by helping you catch it."

He didn't answer for some time. As the moments passed, Nelle listened to his heavy breathing and could almost feel the force of some internal conflict radiating out from him. Pushing further would only drive him to the breaking point, so she shut her mouth and waited, scarcely able to breathe.

At last, the mage's voice rumbled across the shadowy room. "You should not trust me, Miss Beck. But if you choose to do so against my advice, then . . . you may stay. For a few days, at least. Until the danger to you lessens enough that you may safely return to Wimborne and escape your enemies by some other route."

Nelle drew a shaky breath. "Thank you!" she gasped and sprang up from the chair, taking several hasty steps toward him before she stopped herself. She twisted the folds of her skirt gripped in her hands as a huge smile of relief burst across her face. "I won't let you regret it, sir. I'll help. I'll cook and I'll clean. You can use an extra pair of hands around here, that's for sure!"

He turned to look at her so sharply that his pale eyes seemed to ignite. Nelle flung up her arms and laughed outright. "It's a joke! Oi, you don't got much by way of a sense of humor, do you?"

He held her gaze for a terrible moment. Something she couldn't name worked in his expression. Then, much to her surprise—and relief—he chuckled. The sound was warm and strangely sweet coming from the depths of that beard.

"You're right, Miss Beck," he said, holding up both arms with a flashing gleam of nilarium. "I could use an extra pair of hands."

He chuckled again, and Nelle beamed at him, but her gut twisted uneasily. She had him. She knew she had him now. Her plan was going exactly as she'd hoped, and now it was just a matter of time. She would gain his trust. She would make him relax his guard.

Then she would search this whole tower over and find the Rose Book, come what may.

CHAPTER 18

THE GIRL HAD SOMEHOW MANAGED TO STUFF HALF THE
Dornrise larder into her sack.

Soran, with a bit of thin blanket wrapped around his bare
shoulders, watched as she opened the sack and sorted through her
loot. Flour, butter, sugar, packets of spices, and more she laid out
on the table, her movements quick and efficient, muttering to
herself all the while.

"Flapcakes," she said at last, casting him a quick glance.
"Flapcakes, I think. Spiced with cinnamon, warm from the pan,
and lightly dusted with sugar. Can't go wrong there, now can you,
sir?"

He met her gaze with stoic indifference while his stomach

turned over with eager anticipation. He could almost smell the sizzling sugar already, a delectable scent more desirable even than the *qeise* she'd so ruthlessly wasted in her attempts to nurse his wounds. How long had it been since he'd enjoyed even such simple fare? He didn't like to guess. It might well have been a hundred years.

The question burned in his brain as he watched the girl fetch a bowl from among his meager kitchen supplies and begin measuring out handfuls of flour and sugar. She was definitely from Wimborne, but from what era exactly? For all he knew, centuries had passed since Roseward was pulled from his world's flow of time and set adrift on the Hinter currents. Or perhaps it had been mere days.

It didn't matter, of course. He shrugged deeper into the thin blanket and hunched over the table. Once she was gone, all the timeless days would crush in on him, and he would cease to speculate about such things. The mortal world no longer belonged to him.

Which meant he had no right to feel this pool of warmth in his chest as he watched the girl going about her work. He had no right to enjoy her brisk bird-like hands. Or the way she tossed back locks of unruly hair. Or the music of her uncouth voice as she prattled on about gods knew what.

She did not belong to him. She did not belong to Roseward.

She would stay a few days and then it would all be over.

He tore his gaze away and stared down at his silver-crusted

hands. Those visible signs of his own imprisonment, more horrible than any man-made shackles. Hands that would never again feel the softness of a woman's skin, would never again slide through silky strands of hair or soak up human warmth as they glided along the curves of a shapely form—

A furious bray rattled the air, breaking through that dangerous daydream. Startled, Soran looked up and saw the girl with her hand in the basket of seagull eggs. The wyvern, perched in the rafters above her, hung down by its back feet like a bat and hissed at her, snapping its teeth.

"Back off, wormling!" the girl growled. "You're just bound and determined not to like me, ain't you?"

The wyvern hissed and flared its crest at her.

The girl stuck out her tongue and plucked an egg from the basket. Soran watched her test its weight, give it a little toss, and catch it again, her wrist loose and fingers nimble. "We'll see," she said, flashing a grin up at the wyvern. "We'll see what a sugary flapcake can do for *you* as well."

It watched her with unnerving focus as she went about her business. Soran tried to turn his gaze away but, much like the wyvern, found himself drawn back to studying her as she knelt before the fire, heating the pan on the coals. Firelight played on her hair, turning the glossy curls into ribbons of bright lava. She was young and very thin, but her silhouette was softened as she sat in the pool of her skirt, turning the pan so that melting butter slid around and coated it.

Soran's throat thickened. In his day, he had known many beautiful women, experienced women who knew the power of their own voluptuous bodies, who knew how to turn a man's blood to fire with a single look.

But in that moment, he couldn't remember the face of even one of them.

The girl dropped a spoonful of batter into her pan, and the air filled with the aromas of sizzling butter, warm cinnamon, and lightly burned sugar. All other thoughts and sensations fled. Soran's stomach growled so loudly, he feared the girl would hear it. Thankfully, the wyvern let out a little raspy growl of its own. It spiral-crawled down one of the support beams and crept up beside the girl. Its nostrils quivered as it sidled close to the hearth. When a spark flew out and hit its snout, it hissed and withdrew, sitting up on its haunches and wrapping its wings close.

"Oi." The girl cast the wyvern a sidelong look. "Ain't dragons supposed to *like* fire?"

"It's not a dragon."

The girl started. Soran realized he hadn't spoken a word in some time. Had she forgotten he was there? She blinked at him, her wide eyes brightly reflecting the fire's glow. One eyebrow slid slowly upward.

"It's not a dragon," he said again, feeling oddly embarrassed. He ought to reclaim his silence, but somehow the words stumbled out anyway. "It's a wyvern."

"So you say." The girl shook her head and shrugged one

shoulder. Then she turned back to the pan and flipped her cake with expert ease. A loud popping and sizzling followed, but when it subsided, she added, "It looks pretty dragonish to me."

He pressed his lips into a tight line, refusing to be baited. He may have agreed to let her stay for a time, but he would allow himself no indulgences. If she wanted to make a meal, let her. He didn't have to eat it. If she wanted to chatter away, fine. He didn't have to respond. He would maintain every barrier, and when she left, he would feel no pain at her departure. It would be just as though she'd never come.

He turned away from the girl and watched the fading daylight through one of the high windows, watched the sunset-edged clouds trail across the deepening sky. Soon he would have to venture upstairs. He ought to rise even now and escape to the chamber above. Prepare for the night's coming battle . . .

Instead, he sat there listening to the girl as she flipped her cakes, watching from the corner of his eye as she arranged a stack on a wooden plate. One of his hands moved unconsciously to his aching shoulder, rubbing gently at the wound, which had already begun to scar over.

The girl rose, the movement so sudden he could not resist turning sharply to watch her. She stood with a plateful of cakes in her hands, her back to the fire, her head haloed with light. "Hungry, sir?" she said and approached the table.

He sat there, mute. Stupid. Not one of the protests on his tongue managed to get free. She set the plate down on the table and slid it across to him. Six flapcakes filled his gaze, crusted with shining crystals of sugar and just a little burnt around the edges. Though he tried to stop himself, he couldn't resist leaning down and inhaling deeply. His eyes closed as sensations of warmth and goodness seemed to flood his very veins.

Forcing his head up, he looked at the girl. She stood very still, watching him. "What about you?" he asked.

"Oh, there's plenty more to be made," she answered with a dismissive toss of her head. Turning her back to him again, she went about spooning batter into the pan.

He should rise. He should go.

He should steel his soul against such temptations.

But Soran's hands moved against his will, plucking up the topmost flapcake, rolling it with the expertise of childhood memory. He took a bite. Sugar and butter melted across his tongue. He didn't care about the slightly burned aftertaste, didn't care about the undercooked center. He closed his eyes and for a moment was in heaven.

"So, what's the difference anyway?"

Soran swallowed and blinked back into the present. The girl's back was still to him, but her question rang in his ear. "The difference, Miss Beck?" he said.

"Between wyverns and dragons." She sat on her heels and looked down at the wyvern, which was back on its belly, creeping close to the hearth, nostrils quivering. A thin, high-pitched whine squeezed from its throat, nearly beyond range of human hearing but not quite. Despite its fixed reptilian features, it contrived to look both pathetic and hopeful.

The girl pulled a face at it, then flipped the cake. While it cooked, she looked round at the mage, both brows upraised and questioning.

"The wings." Soran set down his half-eaten flapcake and cleared his throat. "A dragon's wings sprout from its shoulders, separate from its forelegs. A wyvern's wings form along the length of the foreleg, rather like a bat's."

The girl dropped one eyebrow and looked down to meet the wyvern's yellow gaze. "A bat, eh? Creepy little spitter."

"Size is another factor," Soran continued. "A wyvern's wingspan never exceeds eight feet, or so I am given to understand. As they do not reach full maturity until approximately one hundred years of age, I cannot vouch for the truth of this statement."

"Eight feet?" The girl gaped at the creature on its belly by her feet. Its wingspan wasn't more than three feet at the most. "Seven gods, what a monster you're gonna be!"

The wyvern showed its teeth at her. "Don't be smug," she snipped and looked up at Soran again. "So, go on. How big do dragons get?"

"The last recorded sighting of a dragon in the mortal world stated an estimated wingspan of forty feet."

Her eyes goggled. For a moment she couldn't seem to move as her mind struggled to process this unnerving information.

Then her teeth flashed, and she grinned down at the wyvern.

"What'cha think of that, little wingling worm? A proper dragon'd snap you up like a flapcake and still be hungry after."

The wyvern rattled its tongue at her and scuttled away toward one of the support beams again. "Oi," the girl called after it. It paused, looked back. She tossed the flapcake through the air in a floppy spin. The wyvern uttered a little gurgle of delight, shot its long body up to full length, and neatly caught the cake, gulping it down in a single instant. Then it scuttled up the beam and scrambled into the rafters, chortling happily to itself.

The girl moved the pan off the fire to cool and, leaving the scraped bowl of batter on one side of the hearth, rose and approached the table. When she took the seat opposite him, Soran paused, another small, folded bit of flapcake pinched delicately between finger and thumb.

"Don't be shy," she said, slumping onto her elbows and resting her chin on her arms. "I'm from Draggs, you know. I've seen table manners that'd make a pimply pig-keeper blush and run for home. What'd you think we use for cutlery down in Draggs, anyway?"

"I . . . dare not venture a guess."

She snorted. "Chicken bone. Yeah, you heard me! I had me a bit of polished chicken drumstick which served rather well in a pinch. Not that there was ever much use for it. Mostly I'd just grab crust or crumb as I could. No call for knives and spoons and the like."

Soran popped his bite of flapcake into his mouth, chewing in contemplative silence. At last he said, "This Draggs of which you speak, it's in lower Wimborne?"

"Yeah." The girl nodded. "Though if I was a maid of more delicate sensibilities, I'd want you to know that I didn't *originate* from that side of town. I might try to make you believe I started out life in Westbend, perfectly respectable. But I'm guessing a fine gentleman such as yourself wouldn't see much difference betwixt the two in any case."

"I . . ." He rested his hand beside the plate and tapped one finger awkwardly. "I have never ventured into either Westbend or Draggs, no."

"Thought not. Fellow like you would have stayed up in Northon with the other Miphates. Did you study at the university then?" He ducked his head, but she quickly pressed on, "Oh, don't be bashful 'bout it! I know you were a Miphato. Everyone knows there's a former Miphato on Roseward Isle, so unless there's some other mysterious spitter wafting about the place in magely robes, it's got to be you. Besides, I just saw you cast a spell or two firsthand. You made me *float*, for spittin' sake!"

His finger froze, mid-tap. Slowly it curled in, and his hand formed a fist—a gnarled fist of silver, the solidified drips standing out like stones. "I am not a Miphato," he said very quietly. "Not anymore."

His words hung sharp and shimmering in the air between them like a dangerous wall.

The girl pulled in both lips, pinching them between her teeth. Then she leaned suddenly across the table and picked up one of the three flapcakes going cold on his plate. "Not much of a one for conversation, are you?" She rolled up the cake and took a bite from one end. "Were you always this charming," she continued around her mouthful, "or'd you just spent too much time with the wyverns these last couple-a years?"

Was she mocking him? Obviously . . . and yet, she didn't seem disrespectful as such. There was a gentle, teasing light in her eye, as though she was trying to get something out of him. Information? Was she here to pry into the secrets of Roseward?

Or did she simply want to make him laugh?

She tilted her head and lifted one shoulder. One lock of her long hair spilled fetchingly across her cheek and neck. What a bewitching picture she made, all artlessness and femininity and undeniable beauty! His stomach knotted around the few mouthfuls of flapcake he'd swallowed.

"Well?" she said, slowly taking another bite and holding his gaze. "You might as well tell me as not. If it's a secret, it's not going anywhere. I've got no one to tell."

His jaw ached with tension. Slowly he nodded. "Yes, Miss Beck."

"Yes, what?"

"Yes, I have spent too much time with the wyverns these last few years."

She blinked. Then she snorted. Then she gulped and laughed outright, shaking her head and rolling her eyes. A chuckle tickled in his throat as well, surprising him, and under the tangles of his beard he felt his mouth twist into what might have been a smile.

She reached across the table suddenly to steal one of his two remaining flapcakes. The front of her gown gaped, exposing rather more fair freckled skin than was entirely becoming to maidenly modesty. Sudden heat burned through his veins, and he looked down at his plate while she sat back in her chair and rolled the cake with no apparent awareness of what her simple act had done to him.

She chewed and swallowed quietly, the silence between them broken only by the wyvern's scuttling among the rafters and the snap of the low fire. When she finished the cake, she briskly brushed sugar from her fingers, leaned her elbow on the table, and rested her chin on her palm.

"So," she said, "what're we going to do about that unicorn then?"

His gazed flicked to her face. "We?"

"Yes, we." She gave him a look. "Ain't that why you're letting me stay on after all? To help you hunt that beast before he sticks you another good one?"

Soran shook his head firmly. "I am allowing you to stay until the danger at Wimborne has passed and you may safely return to your own world. But you will not go near the unicorn again."

"Oh. So, you're just going to hunt it down all on your own." She leaned back in her chair, folded her arms, and narrowed her eyes at him. "Practically blind."

"I won't be entirely blind, Miss Beck. The wyverns, as you must have observed, are able to see it. They will assist me, will serve as my eyes. They are eager enough to be rid of such a ruthless predator."

She looked as though she wanted to argue but instead took a deep breath, swallowing whatever she'd intended to say. After a moment, she shuddered. "I didn't realize unicorns were . . . were like that." She shook her head, half smiling. "Granted, I didn't realize unicorns were entirely *real* either, so I suppose I shouldn't be surprised. I always thought they were something like horses."

"Unicorns are nothing like horses."

"Yes, well, now that I've seen one, I get that." She rolled her eyes again. "But you've got to admit, they look as though they'd eat grass and hay and apples and things. I never expected it would go . . . *ripping* into another creature like that."

"Unicorns are beings of pure magic and, as such, require magical sustenance to survive." Soran frowned as the words slipped out. Why was he bothering to explain? It wasn't as though she needed to know any of this.

But the curiosity in her gaze was too encouraging. He continued despite himself. "My wyverns make for ideal prey, as they are magic-born."

"Magic-born?" She leaned forward on the table, resting both elbows and tilting her head at him, again exposing more skin than she probably realized. It was such an artless and simultaneously alluring pose that he was obliged to look away again at once.

"You said they didn't hatch from eggs," she observed. "Are you saying they're . . . *spelled* into being?"

Soran nodded, focusing his gaze on the blue wyvern perched up in the rafters. "That is exactly the way to put it, Miss Beck," he said. He studied the lines of the wyvern, admiring the graceful proportions of its strange little form. The creature should by all rights be ugly, and yet it wasn't. To his eyes it was exceedingly beautiful, as were they all. *"Spelled,"* he said, unable to disguise the pride in his voice. *"Written."*

He felt the girl's gaze on the side of his face almost as surely as he would feel the tips of her fingers running along his skin. He flushed and wouldn't look her way.

"You made them," she said at last. "They're *your* magic."

"They are the stuff of dreams." His voice softened, dropped to a lower register. "Dreams woven with ink and enchantment and infused with a mere breath of reality. Not a reality that can survive long in the mortal world, however."

"Not in the . . . wait." The girl went silent again. He glanced her way and saw how her brow puckered, how her mouth firmed into a tight, pensive line. She wasn't stupid. She must have guessed at the truth at least in part. She couldn't have passed through the shimmering Veil surrounding Roseward and not felt the change, the moment when her city, her world, suddenly retreated to a distance far greater than before.

But *feeling* the truth was not the same as *knowing*. Or accepting.

"Where are we exactly?" she asked in a breathless whisper.

261

Soran looked down at his hands again. His cursed, helpless, and, for all intents and purposes, useless hands. For a moment he'd allowed pride to seep back in, recalling those heady days of youth when power had been at his fingertips, needing only to be grasped and claimed. All that youthful energy now drained away. He felt old, seated across from the lovely girl. Ancient, even.

"Roseward has drifted too far from its course," he said, the words clear and hard and cold. "Beyond the edges of the mortal map into the unknown. Into that shadowed space behind the moon. That slice of existence where the knife cuts through the veil."

She was silent again for a few breaths before roughly clearing her throat. "So . . . you mean, Faerieland?"

"No." He slowly shook his head. Hanks of hair swung over his eyes. "No, I'm not talking about Eledria. The world of the fae is more like our world than you suppose. Think of it like . . . like a star. A pinpoint of light. A *something* in the *nothing*. And our own world, the mortal world, is another star, another pinpoint. But we are drifting away from our star, away from orbit around that steady light. We are heading for the darkness between the stars. Into the Hinter."

She stared at him, unblinking. He met her gaze and watched the shadow come over her face despite the crackling firelight on one side. She shuddered and placed a hand to her chest. The sun was beginning to set, casting an orange light through one of the high-set windows. The air inside was close and warm and still smelled of cinnamon.

But all around—on the edges of everything—the darkness waited. Slowly, painstakingly gathering its strength. Preparing to overtake all as night fell.

"We are not fully drawn away yet," Soran said. "But year after year the ties binding Roseward to the world you know strain, and their fibers slowly unravel."

"How long do we have?" she whispered. "Until . . . until the ties break?"

"That is not your concern, Miss Beck." He rose abruptly. The thin blanket dropped from his shoulders and landed on the chair behind him. He shivered, though not with cold. He'd not felt cold in years. Possibly in centuries. "You will be gone from Roseward long before then. Now I must bid you goodnight."

He turned and strode to the stair again, fleeing something. Fleeing her? Perhaps. Fleeing all that she seemed to promise with her innocent face and her mortal air and her womanly softness. Enticements he had once held so cheap, and which he could never claim again.

"Mage Silveri."

He stopped, his foot already on the lowest tread of the winding stair. Slowly he looked back at her standing there by the table. What was that expression on her face? Fear? It must be. It couldn't be anything else. What else could a girl like her feel for a monster like him?

"You . . . you . . ." She slipped around the table, picked up the plate and the last remaining flapcake, and carried it across the room to him. "You might get hungry," she said, pressing the plate into his hands.

Surprised, he reached to take it. One of his fingers inadvertently brushed the back of her hand, and he felt the startled chill rush up his arm at that contact. He froze. Poised in perfect stillness as though caught in a spell. She stood there, close enough that he could see the dark centers of her blue eyes dilate. Was she truly as beautiful as she looked to him in that moment? Or was he just . . . starved?

"Thank you, Miss Beck."

She gave a start at the sound of his voice and took a step back. Only then did he fully realize how close she'd drawn to him, close enough that he'd felt the warmth radiating off her body, warmth that had reached out to his shirtless skin like a promise.

"Thank you," he said again, enunciating each word with care in the effort to disguise the tightness in his throat. "I . . ." He paused, uncertain. Every muscle in his body tensed as though readying for battle, and the air between them shimmered with a certain energy. He thought she would back away, would hasten to put distance between them.

But she stood there, eyes round, waiting. For what?

"Rest well," he said and pulled the plate from her grasp. "You are safe tonight."

With those words, he climbed the stairs and disappeared up the tower, away from the firelight, away from her.

Away to the darkness waiting always to claim him.

You lied to me.

Soran focused on the Rose book, reading the spell with slow, deliberate care. He had felt the Thorn Maiden closing in for some time now, but he refused to let her break his concentration. The power of the spell burned out from the page, burned into his eyes. He was sorely tempted to blink, to look away.

But he wouldn't. Not tonight. One false step on his part would mean disaster.

You promised me she would be gone by the time I returned. You promised me, my love!

Thorny briars crept down along the walls, ripping into the stone. They reached the floor and spread like a disease, crawling for his chair, his feet.

But it wasn't real. Not in this world, at least. While he maintained his focus, they could not hurt him. He might feel the pain, but it was an illusion and nothing more.

Lying. Faithless.

The promises of a lover are but sweet poison in the ear!

A shudder quaked through his body. Soran gasped and stooped over the book, his brow almost touching the magic lines scorched across the page. Sweat beaded his brow, and he hastily wiped it away. He dared not let droplets fall and possibly mar the delicate script.

Thorny arms laced his legs, binding them to the chair legs. It didn't matter. He read on. Even when she manifested behind him. Even when he felt her face just at his shoulder, her lips playing at his ear.

I warn you, my love. Break my heart, and I'll break yours.

He turned the page, reading the final powerful lines of spell. Blood marred the yellowed parchment, mottled the text. He blinked in surprise at the sight. He remembered bleeding from his wounds the night before. He remembered that a few drops had escaped. But he'd not realized they caused this level of damage.

Was it too much? Was it too great?

He read on, his silvered hands clenching into fists on either side of the open volume. If only he were still the mage he had once been! If only the power he'd mastered long ago were still there to be grasped! Then he might easily repair this damage, and the Thorn Maiden would remain bound forever. As it was . . .

He reached the end of the spell, read off the last few lines.

With a final hiss and a swipe of thorny fingers across his cheek, the Thorn Maiden vanished, flitting back into the near, dark realm to which she belonged, banished once again. She would not escape into this world tonight.

But tomorrow . . . tomorrow . . .

Soran released a deep tremulous sigh and shut the Rose Book. His awkward fingers fumbled with the straps, but he made certain to secure them. Better to be safe than sorry. Only then did he let his forehead drop to the surface of the desk. He let it rest there for long moments, breathing in, breathing out. Not thinking, not feeling. Merely existing.

The sun rose along the edge of the sea, pouring light across Roseward Isle. A new dawn, a new day.

And thus, his imprisonment continued without end.

CHAPTER 19

COULD SHE TRUST HIM?

Nelle stood for several moments, listening to the mage's footsteps ascending the tower stair. She eyed the opening in the ceiling, half wishing he would return. Somehow, she didn't like to face the rest of the evening and the coming night alone.

An obnoxious chortle drew her eye up to the rafters where the wyvern grinned down at her. All right, so she wasn't *entirely* alone. "But I don't know if you count much as company," she muttered, her lip curling slightly. "I mean, you're just a spell, ain't you? Are you even really *real?*"

It growled and twitched its tail, the picture of offended dignity.

Nelle rolled her eyes at it and set to work, gathering up her cooking utensils. There were water barrels and rags in one corner of the room. She could at least tidy up the mess she'd made. As she worked, she began to notice the aches and pains throughout her body, even in places she didn't know *could* ache. Such as the roots of her hair and the tips of her ears. It wasn't a physical ache exactly, but she didn't know how else to describe it. Everything about her was just so desperately exhausted with the need to let down her guard, even if only for a few moments.

The temptation was strong. The urge to take Mage Silveri at his word.

Finished with the dishes, she decided to arrange the rest of her stolen goods from Dornrise rather than leave them scattered across the table. An armoire stood along one wall. Thinking this the most likely place for storage, she didn't hesitate to open its doors.

At first, she couldn't see anything clearly in the shadows. As her eyes gradually adjusted, however, she discovered multiple shelves and several deep alcoves. A row of shirts hung in one of the alcoves. Beneath and behind them, stacks of books and scrolls had been stuffed with no apparent order or method.

"Books, eh?" she whispered. "Well, that's something."

She cast a glance back over her shoulder at the stair. But there was no sound of Mage Silveri returning. Dared she risk a little snooping?

A chattering voice drew her attention. She looked up to find the wyvern perched on a rafter right above her head. It tilted its head at her, flaring its crest.

"I'm just having a little browse," she said with a casual shrug. "Why don't you go chew your toes like a good little spell-monster?"

It didn't budge from its watchful pose. But, since it didn't seem ready to pounce on her head, Nelle pushed the shirts to one side and pulled books from the armoire, one after another. She looked them over carefully, turning them in her hands.

Almost at once she knew she was closer to finding what she sought than she'd been in the Dornrise library. These volumes tingled her fingers with a sensation much like she'd felt in the Evenspire quillary. They were much smaller books, hardly comparable to the massive grimoires, but the hum of magic they contained was unmistakable.

One volume, a thin red book, intrigued her enough that she opened its cover and skimmed the first page. Immediately, the handwritten words seemed to glow and rise out of the book, straight at her. It was so startling, so unexpected, she dropped the book in her surprise. It snapped shut as it landed.

The wyvern overhead chattered at her. Nelle hunched her shoulders, glaring up at the beast. "I know, I know," she muttered. "I won't be trying that again."

She set the red book aside, half wondering if there was any chance it might be the Rose Book she sought. But no, that would be too easy. Besides, while it was undoubtedly magical, it certainly didn't boast power great enough to make Mage Gaspard so desperately vicious.

None of the other books were as potently magical, so she set them aside without a second glance. When she pulled the last few little volumes from the depths of the armoire, she sighed. The Rose Book wasn't here. Not that she'd really expected it to be. Mage Silveri wouldn't leave something so valuable unguarded.

With a sigh, she pushed the little volumes back inside, refusing to give in to the impulse to stack them neatly. Mage Silveri would certainly notice if she'd gone rearranging his magic stash into an orderly display. One disorderly pile of books was much like another, however, so she trusted he wouldn't notice anything amiss when next he opened the armoire.

This task complete, she rose to inspect the three shelves at the top of the armoire. These were too narrow for books and instead contained loose sheets of paper and scrolls. She stuck her hand deep into one and touched something unexpected: the corner of a box. Curious, she pulled it out and, supporting its weight on her left forearm, fiddled with the little brass latch and popped the lid.

Her eyes lit up. "Interesting," she whispered, her lips pulling to one side in a wry smile. "Very, very interesting."

"*Rrrrlt?*"

Nelle jumped guiltily and glanced to her right, only to find the wyvern's head suspended upside down just over her shoulder. It twisted its neck to right its upside-down head and chirped at her again.

"Never you mind," Nelle said and snapped the box shut. "It's none of your business anyway." She slid the box back onto the shelf, her fingers lingering on its polished lacquer surface for some moments.

Then, with a shrug, she shut the armoire and turned back to her assortment of goods. They couldn't go in the armoire, but another small table and a set of shelves stood against the opposite wall, so she hauled them over to it, one item after another.

Last of all she opened her snatcher's satchel and removed the little jar of Sweet Dreams. It felt so light in her hand. When she lifted the lid and peered inside, her heart sank. There couldn't be more than three applications left. At most.

Well, she certainly wouldn't need to kiss Mage Silveri more than three times. But that was just the problem: Exactly how and when did she think she was going to kiss him at all?

That he was attracted to her she did not doubt. It may be difficult to read his expression behind that thicket of hair, but she hadn't been unaware of how his eyes lingered on her while she prepared the meal. There'd been a certain *interest* in his gaze. She knew that look. She'd been on the receiving end of it often enough.

You shouldn't trust him, you know. Just because he talks posh like a prince and calls you "Miss Beck" doesn't mean he sees you as anything but a Draggs wench. Someone—something—he can use as he likes.

The Miphates were all the same. Arrogant bastards, the lot of them. Secure in their powers, they looked upon the rest of mankind with scorn. It was said the Miphates would bow to no one save higher members of their own order. A Miphato might even stand in the presence of princes and kings.

A Miphato might take any fine lady for his pleasure. But Mage Silveri's options were rather limited. And she had made certain he was well aware of her more feminine attributes this evening.

Still, did she honestly think he would come creeping down those stairs in the dead of night?

Huffing a sigh, Nelle lidded the jar before tucking it onto the shelf behind the little sack of flour. Maybe she was naïve, but she truly didn't believe the scarred mage meant her any harm. He'd tried everything in his power to send her away from Roseward, even risked his life to save her from the unicorn. She could drive herself mad trying to force a healthy distrust, or she could simply accept that he was actually an honorable—albeit very strange, gruff, and taciturn—man.

"Too bad I can't just mix a dose into his flapcakes in the morning," she whispered, her fingers lingering on the jar. It would make things so much simpler. But that wasn't how the Sweet Dreams worked. It required a kiss, an actual kiss, to activate the poison.

"*Fae magic,*" Mother had told her when a squeamish Nelle asked about it years ago. "*Fickle, foolish stuff, but potent.*" Where she'd come by such a concoction, Nelle never learned.

And when this small remnant was gone, there would be no

replenishing the stock.

"Won't waste it then," Nelle said and left the jar where she'd hidden it, innocuous among the stolen larder goods. "I'll wait until I know there's a good chance."

Maybe, if she were lucky, she wouldn't have to kiss the mage at all.

It was a little unnerving to prepare for bed with the wyvern watching from above. The little creature gawked shamelessly as Nelle slipped out of the stained, torn, dirty blue gown and lay down in the alcove wearing only her thin chemise. She'd fetched the threadbare blanket from where Silveri dropped it and now wrapped it around her shoulders, turning away and facing the wall. She closed her eyes firmly.

And waited.

And waited. And waited.

She concentrated on listening for footsteps up above. But none came. Her tensely coiled body began to relax, and her mind slipped into an exhausted haze. She tried to shake it away, to force herself to stay awake. She pictured Papa's face, bloodied and battered as she'd last seen it. She thought about him waiting for her in their attic room, wondering where she was, wondering why she'd abandoned him. She thought about Sam standing on the beach, watching her go and doing nothing to help her. She thought about Gaspard's threat, about Master Shard's ax and chopping block, all the reasons she needed to stay awake, needed to stay ready.

She wouldn't think about sad silver eyes, both youthful and aged at once, gazing down at her from a frame of gold.

Sleep caught her at last. Waking senses dulled, and the unconscious senses of mind and spirit intensified. She felt a strange tugging on her soul, as though the ties anchoring her to her own world were slowly coming undone. She felt the draw of the formless Hinter calling . . . calling . . .

Tip-tap.

Tip-tap.

Tip-tap.

Nelle's breath caught in her throat.

It was dark. So dark. She tried to open her eyes again only to realize they were already open. She rolled over. Slowly her vision adjusted enough to take in the low, reddish glow on the hearth, just visible from her corner alcove. She must have dozed off for several hours, judging by the state of the fire.

Something had awakened her, some instinct of self-preservation that managed to break through her exhaustion. She held very still, listening. Her fingers gripped handfuls of blanket, and her chest rose and fell quickly. The cold air of the room froze along the open neckline of her chemise, but she didn't draw the blanket up. She waited, tense, expectant. Ready.

But there was no sound of footsteps on the stair. No rustle of heavy robes dragging on stone.

Nothing.

She was a fool. She knew it.

But which was more foolish: thinking Mage Silveri meant her harm or thinking he didn't?

One. Two. Three . . . She began the silent count, hardly daring to breathe. When she reached twenty, she kept going. By the time she came to a hundred, there was still no sound.

She swallowed hard, wrapped the blanket up over her shoulders, and turned on her side. Her body grew heavy; her head went fuzzy. Slowly her muscles relaxed, and eventually she slid back into sleep.

Tip-tap.

Tip-tap.

Tip-tap.

CHAPTER 20

SORAN WOKE A FEW HOURS AFTER DAWN, SORE IN BODY and soul from the battle he'd waged. He felt the sting of many cuts, most of which were entirely in his mind, but several had proven too great for his mind to combat and had appeared across his skin, along his back, down his arms. Spatters of dried blood stained his blankets.

He groaned and lifted a cold silvery hand to his face, rubbing at his cheeks and pulling at the skin around his eyes. If he had a choice, he'd remain in his narrow little bed for another twelve hours straight. But the unicorn was still loose somewhere on the island. He had no time to waste.

With another groan, he rolled out of his bed only to realize he was still half dressed. Instead of finding another shirt last evening, he'd immediately sat down at the desk and set to work reinforcing the spell.

He looked down at his pale, mangled torso. At least the puncture wound in his shoulder had scarred over. He was lucky the mortal girl had been there, and with presence of mind enough to dig the shard out right away.

"Not lucky," he growled, stretching his arm and twisting his shoulder tentatively, working out stiffness in the muscles. "Not lucky."

If not for her quick action, he'd be dead by now. Death by unicorn poison would be painful indeed, but unutterably preferable to the embrace of the Thorn Maiden. He should have welcomed his end, the cessation of this torment. Except . . .

Soran bowed his head and, after a moment, shook it softly, his unruly beard trailing across his bare chest. He could reason with himself as much as he liked. He could deny and deflect until the sun set again. The truth remained: His heart was lighter today than it had been yesterday.

The prospect of descending that long stair and being met with a bright lovely face and an outpouring of seemingly endless chatter was pure delight.

Delight he did not deserve.

With a growl, Soran rose. He kept no spare shirts in the tower, and his robes were downstairs as well, bloodstained after their service as a temporary bandage. Oh well. His scarred body hadn't seemed to shock the girl too profoundly yesterday. He raked his fingers through the tangled snarls of his hair, then frowned when he realized what he was doing. A useless gesture. Did he think he could somehow make himself less hideous for his guest?

What did he care what she thought of him anyway?

Growling again, he strode to the stairs and made no effort to disguise his footsteps as he descended. He half expected to hear the bustling sounds of cooking as he approached the opening in the ceiling. All was still, however, and his heart gave a terrible lurch. Had she gone? Had she risen at first light and fled, convinced she was better off risking her neck on the streets of Wimborne?

He took the next several steps in a rush, his gaze flicked to the alcove . . . and his heart settled back into its proper place.

She was there. Fast asleep, lying on her stomach, one hand splayed on the floor, her hair a mass of messy curls around her head. The wyvern lay curled on the small of her back. Their gentle duet of snores was music to his ears.

Soran stood for some moments, gazing on that odd little tableau. Then the girl made a loud snort. The sound brought him back to himself.

With a sharp shake of his head, he pulled his gaze away, continued down the stair, and marched across the room to the armoire. After jerking the doors open, he grabbed the first shirt his hand touched and pulled it over his head. His hands fumbled with the laces as he pretended he wasn't tempted to look around again, to make certain the girl was still there, to assure himself he hadn't imagined her, hadn't dreamed her.

Once he'd managed the shirt ties well enough, he crouched and reached into the back of the armoire, searching for a certain book of spells. Odd. The books didn't seem to be in quite the same order he'd left them in yesterday. Not that he'd ever bothered to properly organize these little volumes of old spells. But he could have sworn the book he sought was in the left-most alcove, and instead he found it in the central one, tucked beneath three other books he didn't remember being there at all.

His brow creased as he pulled the little book out. Was it possible . . .? Had the girl been . . .?

"*Oi!*"

Soran jerked and sprang to his feet, whirling around. In a flurry of scales and flapping wings, the wyvern tumbled out from the alcove. With a raucous bray, the creature gathered itself and waddled to the middle of the room. There it flared its crest and one good wing, puffed out its chest, and rattled its tongue back at the figure struggling out from under the blanket.

"Oi! You spittin' monster, you *impaled me!*" The girl writhed around, twisting her neck and head as though trying to get a look at her own back. One hand clawed over her shoulder, the other reached back up her spine, and Soran got an eyeful of the scanty white underdress she wore and a startling amount of exposed neck and bosom. Before he could so much as blink, she bent double, feeling up her back with both hands. "I'm going to take a paring knife to that hide of yours and peel off a few scales! See how you like that, eh?"

The wyvern swiveled its head to send Soran a persecuted gaze. Soran opened his mouth, tried to speak, tried to squeeze words from his closed-up throat.

Before he could manage more than an inarticulate rumble, the girl sat upright with a little "Oh!" and stared at him, suddenly aware that she was observed by more than a wyvern. He saw the flush of red race across her pale skin.

Then her hands darted out, snagged her blanket, and yanked it across her front up to her throat. She blinked, frowned, seemed to realize what a clichéd show of maidenly embarrassment she was making, and her flush deepened. She released the blanket with one hand and pushed a tangle of hair out of her face before pointing at the wyvern and snarling, "Your rot-winged lizard bloody well attacked me! Little spitter jumped on my back and tried to claw me to bits!"

"That is . . . No." Soran shook his head, glanced down at the wyvern, then returned his gaze to the girl. "As I have already explained, wyverns are protective, not vicious."

"Seems pretty vicious to me!" The girl scrambled to get her feet to the floor and stood, keeping the blanket clutched across her bosom. "Or maybe claws gouged to the spine is a regular sort of 'good morning' in these parts. I'm still new here; I wouldn't know."

Soran opened his mouth, closed it, and blinked. What was that strange sensation bubbling up inside his chest? Was it . . .? It couldn't be laughter, could it?

Hastily he suppressed it, cleared his throat, and held up a placating hand. "I'm sure it isn't as bad as all that, Miss Beck."

"That so? How'd *you* like to be woken up by claws ripping you to pieces?"

The words spoken with thoughtless irritation hung suspended in the air between them. As soon as they were spoken, the girl seemed to regret what she'd said. Her gaze traveled across his scarred face and down to his chest where the badly tied shirt didn't quite hide the scars lacing his skin. Her flush deepened. She ducked her head, and a hank of red hair fell across her forehead.

Soran's throat thickened again, but he swallowed hard. "If you would allow me to see, Miss Beck," he said, trying to keep his voice light though he couldn't fully disguise the roughness around the edges, "I can tell you whether or not you've sustained life-threatening injuries."

Her gaze flashed to him and away again. Then, with a roll of her eyes, feigning a confidence he didn't quite believe, she stepped out of the alcove, turned around, and pulled the lengths of her hair over one shoulder, presenting Soran with a view of her back only just hidden beneath the thin fabric of her chemise. The neckline's deep scoop exposed the sharp protrusion of her shoulder blades and the delicate bones running down her spine.

He stepped closer, scarcely knowing what he did. The draw to be near her was far more intense than he could have anticipated.

A raw, animal-like heat ran through his veins, and it required whatever self-mastery he still possessed to not reach out, slide a hand around her waist, and draw her to him, pressing that narrow back against his chest so that he might breathe in the scent of her hair, her neck, her shoulder.

Was she trembling? Did she know the temptation she stirred in him? He took another step and another, until he stood close enough to see the little hairs on the back of her neck prickle in response to his breath.

He'd been alone so long, so very long . . .

"Well?" Her voice startled him, breaking through the throbbing vibration in his temples. "Am I bleeding to death?" She peered over her shoulder, meeting his gaze.

By the gods, he was not a slave to his own impulses. Not anymore.

He was a man, not a monster.

Soran blinked once and shook his head. "No. No blood, Miss Beck. It would seem the creature has pulled a few threads of your garment, but beyond that I detect no damage."

"Well, that's damage enough, ain't it?" she growled, spinning to face him and shaking her hair to fall across her back. "It's not like I've got garments to spare, have I?"

He had drawn much closer to her than he'd realized. She stood before him, their bodies separated by mere inches, and gazed up at him. He could count the freckles on her nose, could see the dark lashes ringing her deep blue eyes. He watched those eyes

285

SYLVIA MERCEDES

flick back and forth across his face and remembered suddenly what a sight he must be to a young maiden like her—old, torn up, haggard.

He turned away and retreated to the hearth. There he crouched and set to work stoking up the fire. Why he bothered he couldn't say. It was something to do, something to occupy his hands. "You know," he said after what had been a rather long, silent interval, "if you have need of gowns, there are plenty to be had."

"You mean at the great house?" He heard movement behind him and guessed by the sound of rustling fabric that the girl was hastily donning her overdress. "You mean for me to go snatching from the ghosts?"

"There are no ghosts at Dornrise," Soran answered at once. "At least, not in the daytime." He rose from his crouch and, keeping his back to the girl, picked up the battered copper kettle waiting beside the hearth, carried it to the water barrel, and prepared to fill it.

The girl appeared at his side. Her hand shot out and touched his arm. Startled, he froze, and she quickly moved her hand from his arm to the kettle, her fingers closing around the handle next to his. "Here, let me do that," she said, her voice bright and brisk.

Soran cast her a sideward glance. "I've cared for my own needs these many years, Miss Beck."

"Aye, and now you've got me here to help." She tugged, but he didn't let go. She glared up at him then, her brow stern. "Please, sir. You do me a service by letting me stay. Let me repay you as I can."

For a moment he didn't relent. Then, coming to a sudden decision, he released the kettle and stepped back, retreating to the far side of the room. His heart beat a strange rhythm as he moved to the table and awkwardly took a seat. He didn't know what to do with himself, didn't know where to look.

The girl filled the kettle from the water basin and returned to the hearth. Once she had it suspended on the rod over the flames, she fetched something from amid the stash of supplies she'd taken from Dornrise. Through the haze in his brain, Soran realized she was making porridge. For him.

This was ridiculous! He didn't need her cooking for him. Serving him as if he were some high and mighty lord. It was too much.

He rose, casting about the room vaguely. His gaze settled on the folds of his robes draped over the back of the other chair. He swept them up and quickly shrugged into the sleeves, ignoring the stiff patches of blood in the rough fibers. Pulling the hood up over his head, he caught up the little red book of spells, tucked it into the front of his robe, and headed for the door.

"Where are you going?"

Soran stopped, one hand reaching for the latch. He looked around and saw the girl standing with a spoon in her hand, her head tilted to one side, frowning at him. "I have much work that must be seen to today," he said gruffly. "The unicorn is still loose. I cannot rest until it is dealt with."

An eyebrow slid up the girl's pale forehead. "You're going out hunting an invisible monster without even a bit of food in your belly?"

He shifted his gaze uneasily to one side, then back to her again. "Yes."

"In that case, you're a greater fool than I took you for." She lifted the spoon and pointed it at his nose. A little blob of porridge hung from the end. "If you've got half a brain to you, you'll sit and eat your breakfast proper-like and be all the better prepared for the day. But"—She gave a careless shrug and turned back to the fire—"suit yourself! I'm sure the worm and I can make short work of this mess."

The wyvern chirruped cheerful agreement and wound between the girl's feet, scaly nose snuffling eagerly as the aromas of oats, milk, cinnamon, cloves, and a pinch of sugar wafted from the kettle. The girl danced several steps in her effort to avoid it, but one foot came down heavily on the creature's tail. It hissed at her, showing its teeth. "Well, it's your own fool fault for getting underfoot!" she growled and nudged it away. It nipped at her threateningly, and she yelped. "Oi! Little spitter!" She again looked up at Soran, who still stood motionless by the door. "Can you do something about your monster here?"

Soran lifted one hand, beckoning. "Come."

The wyvern uttered a resentful chortle but obediently slinked across the room to its master's feet. Not entirely certain what he did, Soran returned to his seat at the table with the wyvern at his heels. It positioned itself beneath his chair where it could watch the girl and the kettle, its snubby nose resting between its long-fingered, wing-webbed claws. All the while it kept up a steady whine, a whistle through its nostrils so high-pitched it was almost beyond hearing range. But not quite.

"Ugh!" Nelle growled, stirring the pot to test the consistency of the oats. "How does that crawling creeper not drive you completely mad?"

"I . . ." Soran looked down at the beast. "I enjoy their company. It will be much lonelier here when they go."

"When they go? Do they migrate or something?"

"No." He shook his head heavily, and his chest expanded as he breathed a long sigh. "They are prisoners here, Miss Beck. But their term of sentence will end much sooner than mine."

The girl didn't respond to this right away. He watched her from beneath the protective sweep of his hood as she spooned porridge into the wooden bowl. After sprinkling a little cinnamon on top, she set it in front of him. She offered him the spoon, but he didn't move to take it. He simply sat there, breathing in the steam as it rose from the bowl, refusing to meet her gaze.

"So, you're a prisoner," she said.

The sudden flexing of his hands on either side of the bowl was all the confirmation the girl needed. She returned to the fire, wrapped a cloth around the handle, and pulled the kettle away from the flames. There wasn't another bowl, so she simply carried the kettle to the table, sat, and began spooning porridge into her mouth.

Soran sat still, not quite watching her. Then, pretending that his hands did not shake, he lifted the bowl to his lips and sipped from its rim. He had eaten in this manner—and far more messily—for many years. When he had eaten at all. Now, seated across from a fellow mortal, he felt the proper embarrassment of his reduced state.

Gods above, why had he let her talk him into staying?

They finished eating in silence save for the constant, pitchy wine of the wyvern. At last the girl muttered, "Bullspit, you're going to drive me madder than him," and moved the cooled kettle to the floor by her feet. "Go on, worm. Have at it."

The wyvern looked pleadingly up at Soran, who nodded. With a happy burble, it scuttled across the floor and buried its nose in the remaining porridge, which disappeared in moments. The wyvern sat up, its belly bizarrely distended, its winged arms limp, and licked its lipless face again and again to catch any last traces of porridgy goodness.

The girl rolled her eyes. Seeing that Soran had finished his meal, she leaned across the table to grab his bowl, then hefted the kettle from the floor, carried the stack to the cleaning basin, and set about filling the kettle with water, muttering as she did so, "I'll just let these soak a bit before I give 'em a good scrub."

"You don't need to do that," Soran said quickly.

She shrugged and turned his way with a little smile. "I've got to have something to keep me busy while you're off unicorn hunting."

He blinked at her, realizing. "You . . . you will have to leave the tower while I am on the hunt. You cannot stay here alone."

"What?" Her brows drew tightly together. "You're going to kick me out, set me wandering on this unicorn-infested island, with nowhere to go and nothing to do. And we'll just *hope* I don't run into the beastie a second time? It's not that big of an island, you know."

Soran didn't answer. Though he hated to admit it, she had a point. Nowhere beyond the lighthouse door was safe as long as the unicorn was on the prowl.

"Aha!" She smiled suddenly, brilliantly, and crossed the room back to the table, resuming her seat and resting her chin on the backs of her interlaced hands. "Hadn't thought about that, now had you? Tell me, sir, do you have a plan for how you're going to hunt a monster you can't even see?"

He leaned back in his chair. After a moment's hesitation, he pulled the little spellbook out from the front of his robes and set it on the table before him. "I plan to lay a spell trap. If properly baited and sprung, it will hold the unicorn fast. Then I should be able to deal with it. Invisible or otherwise."

She nodded, her lips pursed, her expression keen. "And what're you going to use for bait? One of your wyverns?"

Soran dropped his head, looking down at the wyvern, which was still licking its chops. He had lost too many of them recently and had come close to losing more. But if he didn't do what must be done, the unicorn would soon decimate the entire flock. "There's nothing else to be done," he said.

"What about me?"

Frowning, Soran lifted his gaze to meet the girl's. "Come again, Miss Beck?"

"I was thinking about what you said yesterday. About unicorns showing themselves to mortal girls." She dropped her hands onto the table and leaned forward eagerly. "I may not know much about Faerieland and faerie beasts, but I *have* heard a story or two about unicorns. Granted, most of those stories led me to think they'd be all shiny and beautiful, not bloodthirsty, ravening fiends." She shrugged, her lips quirked in a half-smile. "But if I remember rightly, a unicorn can be lured by the sound of a maiden singing. Am I wrong?"

Soran shook his head. "Are you offering *yourself* as bait?"

"Yes, actually. Sort of. I mean, I'm sure it's not as easy as they make it out to be in the old stories and songs. But we *did* survive yesterday. With a bit of luck and the two of us working together, I think we can manage to survive again. Don't you think a maiden's song will be more effective than a wyvern? It's hunting down wyverns well enough on its own. Why would it take a risk for another one? But if I can lure it—"

"You're mad."

Her smile dropped. She sat back in her chair and crossed her arms again. "You're one to talk."

"A unicorn is one of the deadliest, most ferocious beings to be found in all of Eledria. They hunger for magic above all things. The subtle magic of a maiden's voice will be utterly intoxicating to it. It will want to *feast*, Miss Beck. On you. On your voice. Do you understand me?"

"Can't say that I do. If you were to tell me it'd feast on my heart or something, I might be a bit wary. But if it just wants my voice, then—"

"It's more than that."

Soran stood abruptly and paced across the room. The idea was a good one. The unicorn would certainly be unable to resist a mortal maiden's song. But how could he agree to such a scheme when the girl had no idea what she offered? Sure, if he were quick, if the magic in these old spells were good, then it might be managed easily enough.

He wasn't quick though. Not like he used to be. And these spells . . . He looked down at the slim book clutched in his hand. They were a young man's spells, early efforts. Full of promise and power but unpolished. If he had access to his former abilities, it would be different. If he could be again the mage he was before . . . before everything collapsed . . .

He held up his nilarium-crusted hands, fingers tensed. Curse the one who did this to him! And curse his own fool pride and vanity that had brought him so low.

The girl watched him pace to and fro before the fire. She knew she had caught his interest; he could feel the subtle confidence in her gaze.

Soran rounded on her at last. "Are you certain you want to do this? Certain you are ready to take such a risk?"

She offered another smile, this one smaller than the last. "My life has been nothing but risk since I got here. I'd rather face any risk head-on than hide. Besides, it's a good idea, ain't it?"

"Yes, Miss Beck." He grimaced, speaking the words through clenched teeth. "It is a good idea. And if we are incredibly lucky, it might just work."

CHAPTER 21

NELLE HAD THOUGHT THEY WOULD SET OUT RIGHT AWAY. Instead, to her surprise, Mage Silveri took a seat at the table and began paging through his spellbook. Not another word or even a glance her way. He just sat there, slowly turning page after page.

It was unnerving, to say the least.

With nothing else to do, Nelle set to work scrubbing the breakfast dishes, occasionally casting a quick look back at the mage to see if anything had changed. But he was determined in his silence, and eventually Nelle gave up. She concentrated on the immediate task before her but couldn't stop her mind from spinning.

Why in all the bullspitting blazes did you go and do that? she wondered, scraping at a particularly sticky side of the cooking pot. *You've got one job to do here, girl. You can't very well save Papa if you go and get yourself skewered by a unicorn!*

It was stupidity itself. But then again . . . She closed her eyes a moment, remembering how the little green wyvern, having already lost a wing, threw itself at the unicorn's hind leg yesterday and saved her life. It was no doubt brutally dismembered shortly after this final display of courage, yet it had saved her.

You owe it to the little beasts, she told herself firmly. *Besides, if you do this job right, Mage Silveri will be bound to trust you afterward. The more trust you gain, the better your chances.*

She finished up the dishes, stacked them to one side of the hearth, then moved quietly back to the table to resume her seat.

Offering no acknowledgement of her presence, Silveri turned another page.

"What are you doing?" she demanded at last.

He glanced at her over the edge of the book. "I am making certain this volume contains all the spells I will need for our venture. I don't intend to be caught unprepared if I can help it."

"So, it *is* a book of spells," Nelle said and instantly wished she'd kept her mouth shut when he shot her a suspicious glance. Did he know she'd been rooting around in his armoire last night? Did he guess? The books had been in such a hodge-podge of a mess, she didn't think he'd be able to tell the difference. Hastily, she covered her tracks. "I thought it might be, you know. You being a Miphato, after all."

"I'm not a Miphato. I have told you this."

"All right, well, a *former* Miphato. I figured you probably had spellbooks lying around." She leaned forward in her chair to rest her elbows on the table, tilting her head and blinking innocently. "I've never seen one before. A spellbook, that is." The lie slid all too glibly from her tongue, and she hurried on to disguise the flush threatening to rise. "May I see it?"

He answered with another one of those looks. "You wouldn't be able to make anything of it, Miss Beck."

She frowned and sat back in the chair. "I like that! I can *read*, you know."

"Perhaps. But I think it highly unlikely you were ever taught to read Old Araneli, the language of magic."

She opened her mouth, paused, and shut it again. After all, she couldn't exactly argue the point. She shrugged instead and let a huff of breath blow between her lips. "Well, if I can't read it, then I can't inadvertently cast any spells, can I? So, you might as well let me have a look."

"Inadvertently . . .? How exactly do you think . . .?" The mage shook his head and closed the book with a loud snap. "Power such as this is not for the uninitiated. You could neither cast a spell nor wield one, but you certainly *can* be harmed by the magic contained herein. Do I make myself clear? You are *not* to touch my spellbooks. You are certainly not to *open* any of them."

"Fine, fine," Nelle held up both hands in a gesture of surrender.

The mage continued to fix that look on her for an uncomfortable span of time, but at last he reopened the book and continued paging through slowly, even more slowly than before.

Nelle sighed and rolled her eyes up to the wyvern crawling around in the rafters. It gave her a friendly crest-flutter, and she returned a half smile. It probably only wanted more oatmeal, but she'd take whatever sympathy she could get.

At long last the mage shut the book again and tucked it into the front of his robes. Rising from his place at the table, he moved for the door. "Wait!" Nelle cried, springing up from her place and hastening after him. "Is that all you're taking with you? On the hunt?"

He looked round, peering at her from under his hood. "What else would you suggest I bring on such a venture?"

"I don't know. Maybe some rope. Or a sword."

"Do you honestly think mortal steel would have an effect on the being you glimpsed yesterday?"

"My knife did."

The mage seemed taken aback. "Yes," he admitted slowly. "That was . . . unexpected." He paused in the lighthouse doorway, his large frame silhouetted by morning light. "Do you have that knife on you now, Miss Beck?"

She frowned and glanced around the room uncertainly, fingering her empty sleeve sheath. She'd last used the knife to dig the shard of unicorn horn from the mage's shoulder. After that, she couldn't recall. "It's probably outside. Near whatever's left of that bottle of queasy."

"*Qeise*," Silveri growled. She could almost hear his teeth grinding. He stepped outside and motioned for Nelle to follow him. She obeyed, walking into a morning that was a little too bright after the shadowy dimness of the lighthouse. "We'll look for it," the mage said. "Your knife that is. I suspect it is of Eledrian make and therefore might be of some use to us."

Nelle gaped at him as he turned to shut the door. The wyvern waddled to the threshold, hissing and chortling, but the mage pushed it back inside with a firm hand. "Not today, my friend. I don't want you risking your fool life again. You stay here until the danger is past."

The wyvern uttered a last hiss before the door shut. The mage turned to face Nelle again.

"Did you say *Eledrian* make?" she demanded.

She could see a glitter of eyes beneath his shadowed hood, but she caught no sense of his expression. "Yes, Miss Beck. I did."

"As in . . . as in *Faerieland?* As in, my knife is from *Faerieland?*"

"If you insist on the colloquialism, yes."

"Oh."

He moved past her, away from the door, and took long strides down the path she had helped him along the day before. Nelle turned and fell mutely into place behind him, her mind spinning.

But really, why should she be so surprised? It made perfect sense that her little secret knife was faerie made. Mother had apparently possessed any number of fae treasures—the nilarium claws, of course, but also the Sweet Dreams. Why not the knife as well?

But how in heaven's name had she come by them? As a child, Nelle had easily accepted Mother's glib explanations. *"They're gifts,"* she'd say with a tinkling laugh. Part of Nelle had believed it while another part suspected it was Mother's way of getting out of an explanation she preferred not to make. After a while Nelle had simply stopped bothering to ask or even to think about it.

But wasn't it odd that one mortal snatcher-girl from the lower districts of Wimborne City would have in her possession *quite* so many faerie artifacts?

These thoughts occupied Nelle's mind until they reached the little stretch of path along the cliff's edge where they'd encountered the unicorn the day before. Mage Silveri marched purposefully to the exact spot where he'd lain near death. The bottle of spirits was still there, its top smashed off and half the contents gone. He picked it up, and though his hood was pulled too far forward to allow Nelle any impression of his expression, she could almost feel the disappointment radiating from him.

"Go on," she said, standing at his elbow and crossing her arms. "Give it a whiff. I'd bet anything it's gone off."

"Qeise never goes off, Miss Beck," Silveri said, raising the broken bottle to his nose. The words had scarcely left his mouth before he gasped, choked, bent nearly double, and dropped the bottle to smash and spill the rest of its precious liquid on the stony soil. There was a sizzling, a popping, and then a pungent

stink of fermentation rose in waves, making Nelle's eyes water.

She threw back her head and laughed outright, dancing several paces back to get away from the stench. The mage staggered after her. His hood had fallen back over his shoulders, and he shook his head, looking for all the world like a big shaggy sheepdog, which only made her laugh harder. He glared at her, his eyes pale and sharp through the mask of scars, and she quickly slapped a hand over her mouth. But it couldn't suppress the laughter clogging her throat, so she turned away, wrapped her arms around her belly, and let it out completely. It wasn't a sensible laugh, she knew. Completely out of proportion with the situation. But releasing it was a great relief after all the tension, all the uncertainty, all the fear that had suffocated her for the last many days.

Ever since Cloven showed up on Mistress Dirgin's doorstep to collect Papa's debt. Ever since all this wretched business began.

A pang passed through Nelle's heart, snapping her back to herself. She let out a few more half-hysterical bursts, then closed her mouth tight and turned back to the mage. He was the picture of offended dignity. "Are you quite through, Miss Beck?"

"For now," she replied with a sniff.

He held something out to her. It was her knife—her sleeve knife, crusted with dried blood. "I was right," the mage said as Nelle accepted the little blade and wiped it on the skirt of her already foul overdress. "That blade is wrought of pure *virmaer* and is almost certainly of Solirian origin."

"Oh?" Nelle lifted an eyebrow. "I thought you said it was from . . . what's that name you keep throwing around? *Eledria,* was it?"

"Solira is one of the Great Courts of Eledria, the capital of Raphyr. The Daylight Kingdom, as you might know it."

Nelle's other eyebrow rose slowly. "I don't know it. It's all Faerieland to me."

He gave her a disapproving look. "Yes. Well." Dismissing both her and her ignorance, he turned away, took the little spellbook from the front of his robes, and began paging. He stopped a quarter of the way through the book and began to read, his lips forming strange words and occasionally muttering even stranger sounds that Nelle couldn't interpret at all.

The air just above the open book began to shiver. Her interest piqued, Nelle took a step nearer, angling her head to try to catch a glimpse of the page itself. She thought she saw the words inscribed there pulse faintly, causing a ripple effect in the atmosphere. It seemed to radiate up into Silveri's eyes, forming a column of weird, shimmering connection that she couldn't quite define with words, but which she *felt* with a clarity that defied definition.

When her own eyes started to burn, Nelle blinked and looked away. The world, which had been bright before, now seemed weirdly dim, though there wasn't a cloud in the sky. She rubbed her eyes with the heel of one hand, first one eye, then the other. When she pulled her hand away, her vision had cleared somewhat, and with a few more blinks it was nearly normal.

She scanned the ocean view before her, unconsciously seeking and finding the point of the Evenspire in the distance. Half a dozen wyverns sported in the breeze out over the waves, but otherwise all was desolate. A cold wind bit through both her gown and her chemise, nipping at her skin.

Nelle shivered. Her gaze traveled to the very place where she had, yesterday, gone over the edge of the cliff. Her stomach jolted all over again, as though experiencing that first breath-stealing plunge anew.

"Ah!" Silveri's voice reclaimed her attention. He took several long-legged strides to one side and crouched. Happy to have her attention diverted, Nelle hurried after him, peering around his broad shoulder. At first, she saw nothing. Then, narrowing her eyes and peering more closely, she thought she glimpsed . . . a little shimmer . . .

"Is that unicorn blood?" she asked.

He turned sharply where he crouched, looking up at her over his shoulder. "You can see that?" His voice came out in a sharp bark of surprise.

Nelle glanced at him and nodded, suddenly uneasy. "What? I stuck the beastie several times, you know, and it was bleeding a fair bit when the wyverns chased it off. Bound to have left a little gore behind. Are we going to track it?"

Silveri slowly stood, towering over her. His gaze fixed intently on her face. She thought she caught a telltale trace of the rippling spell in the centers of his dark pupils.

"You shouldn't be able to see any blood," he said. "Not without . . . magic."

"Oh?" She frowned up at him. The way he studied her was unnerving. She wished she could back away, put more distance between them. But she hated to show any weakness. "Ain't it part of the whole *mortal maidens* bit?"

"It is not." The mage's eyes narrowed slightly. "If the unicorn *chooses* to reveal itself to a mortal maid, then and only then will she see it. But this blood . . . this is nearly a day old now. It should have faded from your perception hours ago."

"Well, you can see it, can't you?"

"I called up a spell to reveal it to me."

"Yeah? Well, I guess the spell is working for me too."

He didn't answer. He held her gaze so fixedly, it almost hurt. Did he expect her to confess something? Some secret, some sin? She couldn't begin to fathom it.

Folding her arms, she assumed a defensive stance. "I don't know much about it, and I don't care to, neither. All I know is that it looks like unicorn blood to me, and if we're bound and determined to catch ourselves a unicorn today, following that trail seems a likely place to start. Don't you agree, Mage Silveri?"

He pressed his lips together in a thin line until they disappeared in the bush of his beard. Then, with a grunt, he turned on his heel and set off, making his way into the trees, the same direction the wyverns had chased the unicorn the day before. Nelle hurried after.

That spell of his must have been some sort of tracking or seeing spell, for he followed the splatters of unicorn blood without hesitation. He continued even after the splatters faded to occasional drops and kept on going after Nelle could see no blood at all.

They cut across overgrown stretches of the island into dense piney forests full of shadows and through meadows of tall grasses whispering in the breeze. Roseward felt much larger, while crossing it on foot, than Nelle had expected.

She directed her gaze at Silveri's back, wondering again and again why she'd gone and offered to help him with this crazy venture. Was it too late to back out, to tell the mage she'd changed her mind about being bait for his trap and beg his leave to slip away? She didn't think he'd argue. He didn't want her along with him anyway.

"Ah. This looks likely."

Nelle nearly collided with the mage from behind. She stumbled back a few paces, grunting in annoyance, then stepped to one side to peer around him.

They must have reached the far side of the island, the side opposite Wimborne and the mortal world. The ocean spread before them, but in the distance, along the hazy horizon, a strip of purplish land was just visible. A shore that certainly wasn't part of the mortal world. Nelle's throat went dry. Despite the mage's explanations, despite everything she had witnessed with her own eyes, it was unnerving to be faced with still more evidence of how far she'd traveled beyond her own comfortable reality.

The mage diverted her attention by raising an arm to point, not out to that distant land, but along the shore. This curving northern edge of the island was less steep and sharp than the lighthouse side, but the sea lapped up against a rock-strewn shore. A person could easily fall from one of those jagged boulders and end up trapped in a deep tidepool.

"Look there. Among the rocks," said the mage, still pointing.

Nelle peered in the direction he indicated. Not many yards away, a sea cave lay almost hidden among the great rocks. When the tide was high, it would be nearly flooded out, but just now it was open. It looked dark, dank, and utterly foreboding.

"Bet your life, Miss Beck—that is where the unicorn has chosen to conceal itself."

"My *life*, eh?"

He gave her a sidelong look. "A figure of speech."

"I know." She lifted a brow and met his eye. "A poorly chosen one given the circumstances." Squaring her shoulders, she lifted her chin and scrutinized the forbidding cave mouth. "Do you think it knows we're here?"

"Unlikely."

"Why's that?"

"If it did, we would probably be dead by now."

"Oh. Well, that's a comfort anyway."

Silveri turned abruptly and set off back up the way they'd

come. Nelle hastened after him, calling as loudly as she dared, "Oi! Where're you going? Didn't you say the unicorn was that way?"

"Indeed," he tossed back over his shoulder. "But I spied an alder tree some little way back, standing on its own in a clearing. That will be the place to lay our trap, Miss Beck."

"Oh, really?"

"Yes."

She tossed her hands up, puffing as she lengthened her stride in the effort to keep up with him. "All right, I'll bite: *Why* is that the best place, exactly?"

"Because," he answered, in a tone that indicated he had better things to do than inform her of such simple matters, "the alder tree originated in Eledria. The first alder saplings were brought to the mortal world as a gift from the King of Solira to the High Priestess of Seryth some thousand years ago. Its peculiar scent will be calming to the unicorn, which must otherwise be overwhelmed by the abundance of overtly *mortal* smells clinging to Roseward Isle. The scent will soothe it into a more placid frame of mind, making it far less likely to notice a latent spell."

Nelle couldn't pretend she understood more than half of what he said, partly because he mumbled, the words clipped and fast and distracted. He seemed to have forgotten she was there by the time he ended the speech. It probably wouldn't make a difference anyway. Nelle didn't bother to question him further.

When they reached a solitary tree growing on a little rise off by itself, Nelle guessed it must be the alder by the way the mage circled it, looking it up and down and muttering to himself. "Yes, this will do," he declared at last and, turning abruptly to Nelle, gestured with his arm. "If you would, Miss Beck?"

She lowered her chin and narrowed her eyes. "If I would *what* now?"

"Have a seat." He gestured again. "We shall begin at once to lay the trap. And then you must sing."

"Oh. Right." She moved to obey, sitting on a mossy root and smoothing her stained and torn skirts around her. "I feel a bit of a fool," she muttered, not really expecting the mage to hear or care.

To her surprise, he crouched in front of her, bringing his unsightly face level with hers. "Why is that?"

"Oh, well." She shrugged and looked down at her lap. She still held her knife—her *faerie* knife—in one hand and twirled it between her fingers, taking care not to cut herself. "You know, I never fancied myself the sort of girl who goes around *luring* unicorns, as it were. I mean, in the stories, those girls are all golden-haired and fair as the dawn and all that nonsense, you know."

She jumped a little when cold nilarium fingers closed over her hand, stopping her nervous fiddling with the knife. She looked up and met his pale eyes. They studied her again in that intent and completely nerve-wracking manner she never would get used to. He opened his mouth, seemed as though he would speak, and shut it again.

Then he squeezed her hand, a little too hard to be encouraging. "Stop fooling with the knife," he said. "Hide it up your sleeve or give it to me. Otherwise, the unicorn will smell its own blood, and all this will be for nothing."

Nelle grimaced ruefully as she slid the dagger into its accustomed place up her sleeve. "Very well, Mage Silveri," she said, folding her hands on her knees. "Set your trap then."

He stood, sliding the spellbook out from his robes, and paged to somewhere in the middle. Without another glance her way, he began to pace around her and the alder tree, muttering, presumably reading off the spell. She twisted in her seat to watch him.

And felt another start of surprise when she saw streams of shimmering energy flow out from the book, from the mage's mouth. It wasn't truly visible . . . more of a feeling than anything. Like a creeping certainty, a frisson in the gut.

Magic. Magic winding its way from the mage's lips, from the book he held, and planting itself in the ground around her. She half thought she glimpsed something like iron bars stretching up as tall as the alder tree, but they sank out of sight. By the time the mage had completed a single circuit of her and the tree, by the time he'd come to the end of his reading, she couldn't feel or see any magic.

"Is that it?" she asked, looking up at him. Her chest felt tight; her heart constricted. She was more nervous than she liked to admit.

Mage Silveri nodded. "The trap is set. Latent, but set." He stamped his feet several times in the moss in front of her. "Here," he said. "You must get the unicorn to approach you as far as this spot. When it steps just *here*, the trap will activate."

Nelle looked down at the mage's feet. Her stomach twisted uneasily. She didn't like the idea of the creature she'd seen yesterday standing as close to her as he now stood. "Are you sure it will work?"

"Yes. If you do your part well, Miss Beck, the spell will do the rest. Now!" He shut the book with a snap and tucked it out of sight in his robes. "I must take care to conceal myself, or the unicorn will certainly suspect something. Remember, Miss Beck, I cannot see this monster. I will do what I can to protect you, but you *must* stay within the confines of the trap itself until the last possible moment. Then, when the unicorn sets foot on this very spot, you *must* remove yourself quickly."

"Um!" Nelle frowned and looked around the space. "What do you mean, *remove* myself? How far do I got to get so I won't be trapped in here too?"

"The boundary is where I walked. Here." The mage nudged a fallen branch into place a good three feet to the right from where she sat. "That should serve as a marker. Get beyond that point and you'll be safe. But be certain you don't move until the unicorn reaches the point of triggering the spell. Otherwise it will remain at large and will surely kill you."

"This is all a great deal more complicated than I'd imagined,"

Nelle muttered, glancing uneasily back the way they had just come, toward that rocky shore and the dark cave. For all she knew, the unicorn might even now approach, creeping through that stand of trees, invisible to her mortal eyes, ready to slaughter with savage efficiency.

Silveri gave her a look. Even with her face turned away from him, she felt it. "You can back out," he said. "I'll use a wyvern instead. It will mean sacrificing the creature, for there is no chance that it will be able to escape the snare in time, but—"

"No, no," Nelle said quickly. She remembered again the poor wyvern who had bravely leapt at the unicorn yesterday, saving her life at the cost of its own. Perhaps it was silly to think she owed a spell-beast anything. But there it was. "I'll do it. I said I would, and I will."

She grinned then, fixing the mage with a determined stare. "Let's catch ourselves a spittin' unicorn."

.

CHAPTER 22

SORAN REMOVED TO A LITTLE DISTANCE, FAR ENOUGH that he hoped the alder tree's soothing scent would disguise his presence from the unicorn. The spark of the sight-spell he'd set back on the cliff's edge still lit his eyes, and though it wouldn't be enough to reveal the unicorn to him with any clarity, it should give him an impression of magical aura.

He'd have to hope it was enough to go on.

He crouched behind a little clump of gorse bushes to watch and to wait. His nilarium-covered hands felt none of the prickles as he carefully parted the branches to peer into the clearing at the girl. She sat with her hands in her lap, looking as demure as a princess from any of the old tales. Sure, her gown was stained, her hair disorderly, her whole demeanor the worse for wear. But she possessed undeniable dignity—a dignity that stemmed from somewhere deep inside, not from any outward molding or training.

She was brave. Very brave. Too brave for her own good.

Soran ground his teeth, stifling a curse. How many times had he nearly convinced himself to turn her away after all, to change the plan and not put her through this ordeal? Why should she risk her life so needlessly? He ought to put a stop to it. Even now he could. He should.

After all, what did it matter ultimately if the unicorn slaughtered his wyverns one after another and then turned on him? What did it matter if he were put out of his misery at long last?

He knew the answer all too well. He had to live. He had to keep a hold, however tentative, on his sanity, and he had to live. Everything depended on it. On him.

If that meant using this innocent maiden like a tool, so be it.

"Why isn't she singing?" he muttered, narrowing his eyes as he watched her. She'd sat for some moments now without uttering a single note. Had she forgotten?

Soran rose partway from his crouch and tossed a pinecone, which struck her in the leg. She flinched, her eyes rounding in a flash of undisguised fear as she turned to him. On seeing his face around the gorse, her expression relaxed into an irritable glare. "*What?*" she mouthed.

"*Sing!*" he mouthed back, motioning at his throat with one finger.

She scowled, nodded, and turned to face toward the shore, which was hidden by the stand of young trees. Her hands twisted folds of skirt in her lap, and for several breaths she didn't make a sound. But at last she opened her mouth, and . . .

> "*Oi'm tellin' ye tary, Oi'm tellin' ye true,*
> *My life be'in merry when Oi'm inna brew!*"

Soran choked. "What in the gods' seven secret names!"

This was *not* what he'd expected. She sang the tuneless alehouse ditty with a brash, rolling sort of lilt, the words all slumped together so as to be hardly recognizable as any language he knew.

> "*We toil on six-en—aitch day may be t'last*
> *We shifted and shirked an' now we's on fast!*
> *We lives 'pon chick bones, when chickens be had*
> *An water-in pottage, th'taint n'ere so bad!*"

He pressed his hands to his ears. Then, springing to his feet, Soran hurled a second pinecone, which struck the back of her head.

"Oi!" She broke off mid-verse and glared back at him. "What's that for?"

SYLVIA MERCEDES

"No," he answered and spun a finger in the air by his ear. "What's *that* for?"

"What do you mean?"

"That sound you're making! I thought you said you could sing."

Her expression darkened. "I *am* singing."

"That is *not* singing. That is possibly the farthest thing from singing I've encountered in all my life."

"Well, I never claimed to sing *pretty*, now did I?" She tossed up her hands and started to form what he suspected was a crude gesture but changed her mind at the last moment and simply crossed her arms. "I'm a maiden. I'm singing. Is it enough to call a unicorn or ain't it?"

He ground his teeth, suppressing the first several words that sprang to his lips. After all, she had a point. Would the unicorn care about the actual quality of song or voice? The magic ought to be the same regardless.

"Fine," he growled, pulling his hood back up over his head. "Sing on, Miss Beck. But for the love of all that is holy, pick a different key. Something a little lower, if you please."

She pointedly rolled her eyes before turning away from him. He sank back behind the gorse, and she began to sing again. This time, with her voice pitched deeper, the melody was less jarring, and she was better able to find some clarity within each note. It wasn't exactly pretty. But a kind of rawness in the combination of her voice and the song she'd chosen had its own rude sort of appeal.

"Owd Perrigan's sent to the axman ter-day
For-ee clobbered his man, e'now he mun pay
We'll sing fer'm at the old chop block fer shore
As affer we'll drink to his good health na'more."

Soran buried his head in his hands and ran his fingers through his hair, pushing the hood back as he did so. What had he expected? The girl was lovely, to be sure, but it didn't follow that she'd mastered the womanly graces of the highborn ladies in whose sphere he had once moved.

She wasn't . . . she wasn't Helenia . . .

The song came to an end. The girl coughed and cleared her throat. Through the gorse branches, Soran watched her settle herself a little more comfortably on that mossy root, then start singing again. Her throat was tired already. She certainly wasn't used to singing for prolonged periods. Would it be enough? There was magic in her voice, subtle though it may be. The spark of spell in his eyes revealed a faint aura radiating out from the girl—so faint he would miss it if he didn't know what he was looking for. Would it be sufficient to attract the unicorn? To distract it from the far more potent, powerful spell laid in the ground around the girl? Would it—

Something plucked at his senses. Something he could neither define nor ignore. A powerful shift in the atmosphere reverberated in the depths of his bones.

Soran sat up straighter. Moving with utmost caution, he parted the gorse branches just enough to clarify his view.

It was coming. The unicorn was coming.

A powerful wave of magic rolled up through the trees. Song—unicorn song, sung in response to the maiden's voice. Soran couldn't hear it. It wasn't meant for him. But he felt its churning power flow up into the grassy dell. His senses clouded around the edges, and when he blinked, he saw flashes of mighty vistas, star-studded, twisted with clouds and light and depths and beauty.

He shook his head, opened his eyes. He couldn't let himself be drawn into even the fringes of the unicorn's spell. The beast must have feasted again since their encounter yesterday, for its magic had increased to a deadly degree. Its voice was like poison in the air.

The girl stood up in the center of the spell-trap beneath the alder tree. By the way her gaze was fixed, Soran guessed she could see the unicorn approaching. She could also hear that song—that entrancing, enthralling song. She was rapt, wonderstruck. A sort of glory glowed from her skin, a response to the magic reaching out to her.

Was she aware? Did she remember who she was, what she was here to do?

Soran rose slowly. In one hand he held his little spellbook open to a certain page. He dared not read it off until the last possible moment, for the burst of a spell coming to life would certainly draw the unicorn's attention his way.

"Come on," he whispered. "Come on, Miss Beck. Bring it to

you."

As though in response to his urging, the girl redoubled her singing, raising her voice louder than before. The charm of the unicorn was affecting her, melding with her song, transforming her mortal voice into something beautiful, something astounding. The lyrics themselves melted away to nothing, leaving behind only pure sound, a golden harmony that struck the heart to the core.

She wasn't going to move.

Soran stared, aghast, momentarily paralyzed by the realizetion. The girl was thoroughly caught in the unicorn's spell. She was going to let it come right to her, and she wouldn't spring free at the last moment. The unicorn would trigger the trap, and they would both be caught.

Then it would tear her to pieces.

How close was it now? He couldn't tell for sure, could only gauge by the intensity of song pouring from her mouth, by the ripple of power seeping from the empty air. It had to be near. He had moments, maybe only a single moment left in which to decide, in which to risk everything.

Soran sprang upright and waved his arms. "Hey! Here, over here! This way, you one-horned monstrosity!"

The girl's song broke.

She choked, gasped, staggered back a step. Her hair fell in her face, but she tossed it back, turning to look at him, her eyes still dazzled with the glow of enchantment. Then she blinked, shook herself, and her expression clarified.

Her eyes widened.

"Run!" she screamed.

It was so beautiful. More beautiful than she'd remembered, more beautiful than she'd imagined.

The unicorn emerged from the trees into the alder clearing, and Nelle's entire soul swelled at the sight. It was so great, so glorious! This time it didn't seem small and delicate as it had the day before. It was huge, the size of a warhorse. Yet its every movement was perfectly graceful, poised, and lovely. Its luxurious mane glinted, the white strands iridescent as they wafted in the gentle breeze, and the blood-stained scars on its pure white hide reflected sunlight like strands of polished silver set with diamonds.

Nelle took one look at that being, and her mind exploded with a deep, agonizing *why?* Why would anyone want to harm such perfect beauty? Why would anyone be unwilling to give life, limb, soul, *everything* to offer this exquisite, ethereal creature whatever it wanted?

Somewhere in the back of her mind something writhed, wriggled, and screamed: *You fool! You fool, it's enchanting you! It's caught you in a spell, and you're just standing there, letting it march up and kill you!*

But that voice wasn't worth listening to. That was the old Nelle, the old self who did not understand the power and majesty of the unicorn.

Nelle lifted one hand, reaching out, beckoning the unicorn closer. It took a step, a single step, and the world around it seemed to fade behind fluttering curtains of shadow, unreal compared to the shining aura of light emanating from that soul. Hardly knowing what she did, Nelle lifted her voice, singing louder. It was just another little alehouse song, something she'd picked up one dark night in a back alley off Draggs. But it transformed as it left her tongue, blending into the unicorn's song in a sublime harmony that made her heart leap and try to fly from her breast.

The unicorn's eyes blazed like two brilliant water-moons, liquid and endless, full of promises and doom. It drew nearer and lowered its head, its horn flashing. Nelle saw the lethal sharp point and half wondered that it had already grown back after snapping off yesterday. But it wasn't a real thought. Just another irritating buzz from that voice in the back of her head.

Another step. A mighty cloven hoof came down, crushing leaves and twigs beneath it, shaking the corporeal world all around.

Just another few paces and that horn point would pierce Nelle's breast, and she would pour out the last gasps of this glorious song. In death, her voice would become a true perfection of beauty like the unicorn itself, and—

"*Hey! Here, over here! This way, you one-horned monstrosity!*"

That voice . . . It was part of this world.

It cracked through the shimmering reality around her, breaking the harmony of song, lancing her soul with its harsh humanity.

Nelle choked on her own voice, and her connection with the unicorn shattered. The loss of that connection lacerated her spirit, and she nearly doubled over with pain. The unicorn swung its head, turning its horn away from her, and Nelle turned as well, searching for whoever would dare to interrupt her communion with perfection.

A wild, hairy man stood behind a gorse bush not many yards off, leaping up and down and swinging his arms. A madman, a lunatic, a . . . a . . .

No, wait. She knew him. She knew that wild bush of face; she knew those flashing, panic-stricken eyes.

It was the mage. It was Soran Silveri. She'd come here with him, hadn't she? She'd come . . . to . . .

The unicorn surged. Nelle's eyes widened as her mind snapped back into place, the enchantment at least temporarily broken. She no longer saw the great, glorious, shining being. It was skeletal, burning, with lips peeled back from enormous, bloodstained fangs. It charged straight for Silveri, its horn down and ready to drive straight through his chest.

And he couldn't see it coming.

"*Run!*" Nelle screamed.

The mage turned and plunged to one side, throwing himself headlong into a thicket of trees. The unicorn thundered past, its cloven hooves tearing up the ground where he had stood a moment before. It veered and turned about, and its eyes blazed like balls of fire.

Silveri appeared between two trees a little to Nelle's left, and she saw him open his spellbook, hold it in place. She saw his mouth move. Great bullspitting boggarts, was he going to stand there reading off a spell, waiting for the unicorn to run him through?

She snapped her wrist, and her little knife slid down into her palm. Flipping it in the air, she caught the point in her fingers.

The unicorn, its gaze fixed on the mage, took two great steps, preparing to charge again.

"*Oi!*" Nelle yelled.

It swung its head toward her, a ripple of flame running down its neck and across its shoulders. Its wide nostrils flared, spouting dark fumes.

Nelle drew back her arm and threw. The dagger—her Mother's little fae blade—spun in the air, end over end, flashing like a comet.

It planted, blade first, in the center of the unicorn's right eye.

A roaring scream sent a shockwave through the air, knocking Nelle clean off her feet. The world spun overhead, flicking between darkness and light. Was she losing consciousness? No! She couldn't! She pushed up onto her elbows, shaking her head.

The unicorn bore down upon her, death raging in its eyes. She drew a tight breath. In a flash, her father's face appeared before her mind's eye. She had just time enough to think, *I'm sorry, Papa. I've failed you.* Another breath, and—

A broad back covered in rough-fibered robes blocked her view. The mage stood before her with a huge flaming sword gripped in his upraised hand. It filled her whole vision, so bright, so hot, as though he'd called down a star from the heavens and shaped it according to his will.

The unicorn skidded, churning up the soil, and nearly sat down on its haunches. With a bugling bellow that was somehow, impossibly, a wondrous string of music so beautiful it could break a heart, it tossed its head, angled its horn.

The mage couldn't see it. He was looking the wrong way, still standing on guard between her and it, but blind.

"To your right!" Nelle shrieked. "*Now!*"

He pivoted on his heel, stepped back, and brought the sword swinging down just as the unicorn lunged. There was a flash, a brilliant clap of light and magic. Nelle fell back, throwing her arms over her face to keep her eyes from being seared from their sockets. She curled on her side, trying to tuck into herself, to shrink her very existence into a small, invisible ball.

The wave of magic rolled past. She had to move. She couldn't just quiver here and wait for the unicorn to finish her off. With a sob in her throat she wrenched her arms away and pushed up, looking around.

A bundle of limbs and robes caught her eye. Mage Silveri . . . stunned? Or dead? The flaming sword, still burning bright, had landed point down in the dirt close to her. Flames licked right up to the hilt, but it did not burn.

The unicorn lay on its side beneath the splintered trunk of a young pine tree off to her right. Even as Nelle's eyes found it, a spasm of light and magic rippled across its hideous, skeletal body. It thrashed one hoof, then another. Then it hauled its head up, teeth clashing, horn slashing. One eye was a mass of gory silver blood, the hilt of her dagger still protruding. The other eye flickered, darkened, then flamed bright like an oil-soaked torch igniting.

With an ungainly scramble of limbs, the unicorn pulled itself to its feet. The long, coiled horn no longer gleamed; it was broken in half, the edges of the break ragged and dangerous. It let out another agonized cry that rippled through the air and grazed Nelle like the near miss of a death blow. She felt the power in that sound, felt the terrible enchantment that surely would have overwhelmed her had it struck home. But it was badly aimed, if aimed at all, and she was still master of herself.

She had a moment to decide her next act. Only a moment.

She lunged to her feet and sprang for that flaming sword. The flames licked at her hands, but she clenched her teeth and clasped the hilt, yanking the blade out of the ground. It responded at once to her touch, and though she felt their heat, the flames did not burn her hands. It was a large weapon, too large for her, but she braced her legs, raised it over her head, and faced the unicorn.

It looked at her. Its fanged, horse-like head turned to one side to fix her with its single eye. Rearing onto its hindquarters, it slashed the air with its forelegs and sent a blast of song straight at her.

Nelle saw the ripple of magic approaching. There could be no ducking, no avoiding that blast, so she did the only thing she could think to do: She swung the sword. Its red, glowing edge cut through the enchantment, breaking it to pieces.

The song broke into a discordant screech and scattered on either side of her, leaving her unscathed.

"Bullspit!" she breathed. "That actually worked!"

The unicorn flared its nostrils and tossed its head. It took a step as though ready to launch at her, but hesitated.

Nelle, aware of the alder tree behind her, backed up. She dared to cast a swift glance, searching for the place Soran had marked, the trigger point. Could she get the unicorn that far? Could she lure it still?

"Come on," she said, taking another careful step, the blade of her sword swaying, its flames dancing in her vision. "Come on, you ugly spitter. You know you want me!"

It tossed its head again and took several quick paces, snarling like a wildcat, a long purplish tongue protruding between its enormous teeth.

"Yeah, I know you're mad," Nelle said. "Come on! Come finish me off. Or . . ." She stepped into the ring. Was the trap still set? Was the mage's magic still good? It'd better be. "Or do you need something to sweeten you up?"

The unicorn eyed her weapon, and her hands tightened their grip on its hilt. It would not approach while she held the sword, not after what it had done first to its horn, then to its enchantment.

"All right," she whispered and flung the sword from her. It didn't fly far, for it was much too heavy, but it landed beyond the ring of the spell-trap, beyond her reach. She stood exposed, her arms at her sides. "All right," she said. "Come get me."

The unicorn tossed its head and pawed at the soil, churning up chunks of earth. It took a step but hesitated again, its ears twitching, its tail lashing.

Nelle swallowed with difficulty. Her throat was dry. But she had to try. She opened her mouth and sang the first song that sprang to her mind:

> "Red blooms the rose in my heart tonight,
> Fair as the dawn, new as the spring
> Dark flows the tide, but the stars they shine bright
> And summon my soul now to sing."

Where had she heard those lyrics, that lilting melody? It was like something from a dream, a faraway dream. She knew she didn't sing it right, not the way it was meant to be sung. Her voice was too sharp, too thin, too high.

This song was meant for a deep-throated, husky voice full of warmth and depth and passion. A voice she'd heard before, though she could not recall where or when.

> *"Come down to the water, my love, my love,*
> *Come down to the banks of the sea.*
> *Come down to the boat, set sail in the night*
> *And your true love forever I'll be."*

The unicorn lifted its muzzle. Sharp, hair-tipped ears cupped. Its tail stopped thrashing, and its whole body went perfectly still.

Then a shiver of flame ran up its spine, like eagerness, like hunger ready to be satisfied. It took one step, then another. With the third step, it began to sing. Nelle watched the enchantment ripple toward her, mingling with her own voice.

The words of the song vanished. But the song itself grew, the beauty and the majesty of it swelling far beyond her poor vocal range, far beyond her poor mortal ideals. This time, when the voice in the back of her head screamed that she was falling for the spell, that she was caught, she didn't try to argue it away. It was true. She knew it was true. But there was no point in fighting.

The unicorn paced closer, closer, its one good eye burning. It needed only a few more steps to set off the trap. Three more . . . two more . . . one . . .

A burst of pain shot through her arm as hard fingers clamped around it. Shocked, Nelle broke off singing as a wrench in her shoulder made her stagger.

The walls of the spell-trap shot up from the ground. For an instant, the air split with the unicorn's shriek as it realized what it had stepped into. But the next instant the spell solidified, and all sound was blocked off.

Nelle rolled into the moss and leaves and dirt, her mouth open in a soundless scream, her mind seared with the pain of that broken enchantment. When her body came to rest, she found herself lying with her head on a broad heaving chest, her face smothered in a tangle of snarled beard.

CHAPTER 23

SORAN LAY PERFECTLY STILL, HIS ARMS WRAPPED TIGHT around the girl. The sky high above spun wildly, framed by interlacing branches, and darkness closed in, tunneling his vision. He feared he might lose consciousness.

Was the girl alive? For that matter, was he? Maybe he'd died. Maybe the clash of magic when his spell-sword met the unicorn's horn had been catastrophic enough to tear his mortal body apart, and he now lingered only in ghost form.

Maybe that would explain why he'd thought he heard Helenia's song ring through the trees, calling to him . . .

No, that couldn't have been Helenia's voice. He must have

imagined it in that terrifying moment when he believed he stood on the brink of death.

Soran blinked hard, trying to clear his vision by sheer force of will. He lifted his head a few inches and tilted his chin down to see the tumbled red hair across his chest. "Miss Beck?" he said, his voice tight. Gently he shifted one of his hands from her shoulder to pull hair away from her cheek, trying to catch sight of her face. "Miss Beck, are you—"

A spasm jolted through her body, and she sat upright, both hands planted on his chest. Wide blue eyes stared down at him, half wild, half stunned. Dirt smeared one side of her face, and her hair was full of leaves and gorse stickers.

"You're alive!" she gasped. Her fingers tightened on the front of his shirt.

"Yes. So I am." He pushed up onto his elbows, blinking hard to drive back the last of the fading darkness. Shifting his weight onto one arm, he lifted the other. Carefully, hesitantly, he rested his cold fingers on her hand. "It's all right, Miss Beck. The danger is now past."

She shuddered, hunching her shoulders up to her ears. Slowly she uncurled her fingers, released her hold on his shirt, and slipped her hand out from under his. He felt a strange sense of loss but quickly suppressed it.

They rose to their feet and stepped away from each other, straightening their garments and not quite meeting each other's eyes. The girl looked back over her shoulder. Soran followed her gaze to the spell-trap beneath the alder tree. The shimmering spell held fast despite the unicorn's raging as it tore about the periphery of its small prison. Those walls wouldn't last much longer, however. He needed to act quickly.

"Where is my sword?" he muttered, casting about. He soon located it, but not where he'd expected it to be. Nowhere near where he and the unicorn had clashed. Frowning, he took a step to retrieve his weapon.

Not quite fast enough.

"Oh!" the girl exclaimed. "I tossed it over here, sir." Moving quickly, she stepped closer to the alder tree where the sword lay just beyond the circumference of the trap. She knelt, took hold of the hilt in both her small hands, and lifted it.

Soran stared at her. He closed his eyes, twisted his head sharply to one side, then looked again. But the image didn't change. She stood there, holding that spell, offering it to him in the same matter-of-fact way she would offer a plate of flapcakes.

It was impossible.

"How . . . how are you *doing* that?" he gasped at last.

Startled by the brusqueness of his voice, Nelle frowned. "It ain't that heavy, sir, for all it's a hulking big thing. I'm not sure it's entirely real, as it were."

"Not entirely . . .?" Soran took a ragged breath and passed a hand over his face. "It *isn't* real, Miss Beck. It isn't . . . isn't made of physical substance and does not exist!"

She glanced down at the sword in her hands, its firelight

reflected in her eyes. When she looked up again, one eyebrow slid uncertainly up her forehead. "Exactly how hard did you hit your head, sir?"

"No, you don't underst— Never mind!" He covered the space between them in a few strides and deftly snatched the weapon out of her hands. He half expected it to disintegrate at once, the power of the spell compromised by her interference. To his astonishment, however, it held perfectly true, truer than he could have hoped following that blow from the unicorn's horn. In fact, it might even be strengthened.

"Impossible!" he whispered again, his eyes widening.

"So," the girl said, hovering at his elbow, "exactly *how* don't it exist? I mean to say, it looks pretty real to me."

"It shouldn't look like anything at all to you," Soran retorted, casting her a half glance. "It shouldn't . . . You shouldn't . . ."

She shouldn't be able to see the spell. At most, she might perceive the effects of the magic he'd cast, but the spell itself existed on a different plane—in the *quinsatra*, the magic dimension, beyond mortal perception. She shouldn't be able to see it, she certainly shouldn't be able to touch it, and above all, she shouldn't be able to wield it. It wasn't possible.

And yet . . .

Such raw natural ability with magic did not happen by chance among mortals. Something else was going on here, something he hardly dared contemplate. But if these suspicions churning in the back of his brain proved accurate, then . . . what else might she be able to do?

You've witnessed what else. The thought whispered through his mind before he could stop it. *She walked outside her body into the Nightmare and survived. She survived the Thorn Maiden.*

It was possible, then. Possible that she could be taught to do much more.

Soran felt the girl's gaze on his face, studying him closely. He couldn't bring himself to look at her again, afraid of what his eyes might betray. Hope. Fear. Longing.

No, no. It was too much to put on her. Besides, all of this might be caused by the combined influence of Hinter air and the unicorn's potent magic. To assume anything else would be dangerous, and she didn't deserve to be put in more danger, not after she'd risked so much already.

"Never mind," he growled. Turning away from her, he approached the edge of the spell-trap and peered through the shimmering magic bars. Even with the sight-spell still in his eyes, he could not see the physical form of the unicorn inside. But the rippling effect of magic emanating from its enraged soul created a sort of relief in shadow, a silhouette he could *almost* see.

The unicorn, aware of his presence, threw itself at the wall directly in front of him. The spell shuddered in response. It couldn't withstand many more blows like that. He must end this. Now.

Soran readied his sword. It still held plenty of power, enough to deal the final deathblow. He must do it in a single stroke, for the impact of that blow would certainly shatter the spell-trap. If his blow wasn't fatal, if he only wounded the beast, all would be lost.

He adjusted the set of his shoulders, watching the rippling patterns of magic, watching for the silhouetted shape to draw near once more. The unicorn seemed to be turning, seemed to be eyeing him. He took a step.

"Wait!"

The girl appeared at his side, staring into the trap. He glanced down at her, surprised at how cold and pale her face had gone, her eyes wide and hollow in their sockets. Something moved in her pupils, a remnant trace of enchantment. The unicorn's hold over her wasn't completely broken despite the barrier his spell created.

"What are you going to do?" she said softly, her gaze fixed on the beast in its cage.

"What I must do, Miss Beck," Soran answered. "I cannot allow the unicorn to live."

"Can't you . . . I don't know. Can't you send it away?" Her lip quivered, and tears gathered on her lashes. The sight was enough to twist his heart.

But Soran shook his head firmly. "Impossible. Even if I could somehow manage it, the beast would only return and possibly bring more of its kind with it. There's only one way to deal with a monster of this nature. It must be ended."

She blinked. Tears escaped to roll down each cheek, leaving

delicate trails on her pale skin. "It's so beautiful."

It wasn't. It was a devil, a devourer. A fiend of the cruelest, most savage nature. But the effect of its song was so great that, despite all she had seen and experienced, the girl could only perceive a being of perfect beauty here in its final, terrible moments. Perhaps it was the unicorn's own doing, a purposeful manipulation, an attempt to save its life. Perhaps it hoped to turn the girl to its side, convince her to attack its captor.

Soran set his jaw and drew his shoulders back. "I'm sorry, Miss Beck," he said, his voice grim. "It is the only way."

She shuddered and, when he reached out to take hold of her shoulder, to turn her away, she resisted. Her lips formed a soundless, "No." He pressed, and her resistance crumbled. Even in her half-enchanted state she must realize that the unicorn was influencing her. She turned her back to the beast and the cage and, at a firm push from him, took several steps away. With a hastily choked-back sob, she wrapped her arms around her middle, bowed her head, and squeezed her eyes tightly shut.

Soran faced the trap and the malicious magic thrumming within. The unicorn knew it was defeated. He felt despair mingled with rage ripple from between the spell-strands. It wouldn't go quietly to its death.

"Come on," Soran said, stepping closer and readying the sword. "You know you want one last go at me." He bared his teeth, sneering. "Take my heart, rip it from my body. Take it!"

Another step took him right into the line of the spell. The

unicorn lunged.

He could neither see how it lowered its horn nor perceive how the powerful muscles of its haunches bunched, how its nostrils flared. But he felt all this and more as the roiling magic bore down upon him. He gripped his spell-sword hard, forced himself to wait a second longer than he liked, then brought the blade arcing upward in a single, brutal stroke.

The end was much less violent than he'd expected. His blade sliced through its throat, cleaving through bone, muscle, and sinew, and severed the unicorn's head from its body. There was a burst of light as the spell-sword dissolved in Soran's hand, as the bars of the cage broke and dispersed into the air, the magic returning to the *quinsatra* where it belonged.

But the unicorn itself . . . One moment it was there. The next, it was gone. Soran stood in poised stillness, his empty hands closed around nothing. He blinked, shook his head, and blinked again. Could it truly be over? Could it be so easy? Perhaps he was fooling himself, and the unicorn had broken through the cage, avoided his stroke, and even now prepared to pierce him from behind. He turned on his heel, searching with wide, disbelieving eyes.

There was no unicorn. Only the girl collapsed on her knees, her hands pressed to her heart as she sobbed and sobbed.

"Miss Beck?" The words grated from his thickened throat. He hastily dropped to his knees beside her, hesitated a moment, then slipped an arm around her shoulders and drew her toward him. She turned her face to his chest, and her tears fell on his beard, dampened his shirt. He wrapped his other arm around her, cradling her close as she wept.

"I'm sorry," he whispered softly, hardly knowing what he said. "I'm so sorry. It's the unicorn's voice. It leaves its mark on any soul that hears it. It will pass though, Miss Beck. I promise it will pass."

She shook her head, seemed to try to speak. But the words broke into more sobs, and she could only press closer. Her arms slid around his neck, and Soran held her as the pain of fading enchantment racked her soul.

How small and delicate she felt! And yet how strong she was at the same time. The incongruity was tremendous, almost overwhelming.

Soran grimaced as a strange uncertainty crawled through his limbs, deep down in his veins. With a sudden shake of his head, he pushed the girl from him with more force than necessary and got to his feet. Her weeping had calmed by now, but she still could not raise her head. She knelt, her hair falling in a long curtain, her face buried in her hands.

He turned away, unable to bear the sight, and looked to the alder tree and the place where the unicorn died. Something gleamed on the ground amid the blackened moss and gnarled roots. Eager for something to distract his mind, Soran moved to investigate.

Kneeling, he discovered the hilt of the little knife. The

unicorn's death had been too much for even a virmaeri blade. The bright metal was blackened, and when he plucked it up, it crumbled to dust.

Soran hefted the blood-stained hilt in his palm. Its workmanship was simple enough, something that might be carried by an upper-class Solirian lady, secreted up her sleeve. Like a wasp's sting hidden behind delicate butterfly wings.

How had a mortal girl come to possess something like this?

He looked back over his shoulder at her. The impossible girl with her impossible abilities. His brows pulled into a contemplative knot. Rising quickly, he strode back to stand over her where she knelt.

"Miss Beck," he said, his voice sharper than it needed to be.

She raised her heavy head. Tears and dirt streaked her face, and bits of hair clung to her cheeks. Yet the sight was so lovely, it wrung his heart.

His frown deepened, and he held out the hilt. "I'm afraid your weapon was destroyed. But it served you well to the last. Would you like to keep this? As a . . . as a reminder?"

She gazed wordlessly at the offering. Then, with a little shrug, she took it and slipped it away into some hidden pocket. When he kept his empty hand extended, she slid her fingers into it and allowed him to help her to her feet. But she tripped on her long skirts, staggered—her grip on his hand tightening—and fell toward him. He hurriedly stepped back, putting distance between them. Her shimmering eyes lifted to his face, questioning.

"Come," he said and turned away, pulling his hood up to cover his face. "Let us go from this place."

CHAPTER 24

THERE WAS AN ACHE IN HER HEART. AN AGONIZING ACHE, as though the unicorn's horn had driven through her chest, piercing to a place deeper than blood and bone.

She could still hear the last note of its death song, that final exquisite moment of pure beauty, pure rage, and pure sorrow. Just before the spell-sword swung and ended the song forever. She had thought she would die herself at the sundering. Who could bear to go on living, having heard a song so beautiful brought to its end?

The rational part of her mind, buried deep beneath her despair, tried to warn her that it was just enchantment working in her head. But reason seemed a pathetic waste compared to the wracking sorrow reverberating through her soul.

However, as she staggered across the island behind the tall mage, the first shock of pain subsided. Aftershocks threatened but did not yet strike, and she was able to center her mind on those broad shoulders and the back of that hooded head. Part of her hated him for killing the unicorn. Part of her feared him for having the power to bring about such an end.

Part of her wished he would stop, turn around, and fold her into his arms. Wished he would let her rest her head against his heart and remain there for a long, long while. She wanted to hear that deep voice of his rumble gentle encouragements that somehow reached through the shattering in her mind and touched her heart, making her realize it wasn't wholly broken.

Nelle ground her teeth hard enough to make her jaw ache and forcibly shook away these thoughts. They had reached the cliff path leading to the lighthouse now, and the crooked tower itself loomed before them. She shifted her gaze from the mage's back to the lighthouse as her new point of focus. Her feet were heavy, and though the distance was no longer great, it suddenly felt insurmountable.

One more step, she silently urged, her inner voice strict and unyielding. *Just one more step. Then one more . . .*

Somehow she made it to the door. The mage opened it wide, and she stumbled into the dark, square chamber and all but collapsed into a chair by the table. The thudding of her heart filled her head, and she was scarcely aware of the movement around her, of Mage Silveri stoking the fire and filling the copper kettle, of the wyvern twining around her feet, chortling and chirping in curiosity. She simply sat staring at nothing, thinking of nothing, hearing only that dull throb in her temples and, in perfect rhythm with that throb, the last notes of the unicorn's song.

Cold fingers suddenly closed around her wrist. Startled, she looked up and found Mage Silveri standing before her. He lifted her hand and pressed something warm into it.

"Here, Miss Beck. Drink this. It will help."

Did she want help? Once the pain went, the song would go with it. What if she never heard such a song again?

But the mage didn't move. His eyes held a force not to be gainsaid.

Nelle lifted the cup to her lips. She took a sip, and something bitter coursed across her tongue and stung down her throat. She choked, pressed a hand to her mouth, and forced the rest down. It settled in her gut, churning unpleasantly.

"Another," the mage urged. "Come, Miss Beck. One more sip should do it."

She shuddered and flashed a glare up at him. But already the song had faded. Hands trembling, she downed a great gulp of the brew, then set the cup down with a clatter, spilling the last drops.

The mage crouched beside her and tilted his face up, presenting her with a view of snarled beard and awful scars. She focused on his eyes, surprised to see concern shining there.

SYLVIA MERCEDES

"Bloody awful stuff," she growled, wiping her mouth with the back of her hand. "If I didn't know better, I'd think you was trying to poison me!"

Relief flashed through his gaze. "How do you feel?" he asked.

She thought a moment before answering truthfully, "Hungry."

"That's a good sign."

"Is it? Well, it can't be too good since there's nothing decent to eat in this house that I don't make myself. Let me up, and I'll whip together a few flapcakes—"

"No, no. Don't get up yet." He rose and, stepping away from her, moved to the tall armoire. He must have stoked the fire on the hearth; between its glow and the light still streaming through the upper windows, Nelle could see clearly enough when he opened the doors and rummaged along the upper shelves. He moved aside a box, and she saw a flash of light glint off the brass latch. It was the same box she had found and peered into the night before.

Once again, an idea struck. She pressed her lips together, considering.

"Ah!" The mage pulled something from the back of the armoire. Leaving the doors open, he brought back a little tin decorated with crowns and prancing deer. Taking his seat opposite Nelle, he popped the lid.

A delicious, buttery aroma filled the room.

"What . . . are those Queen's Cakes?" Nelle gasped. All other thoughts fled as she sat upright in her chair.

346

In answer, he simply extended the tin to her. She looked inside. Sure enough, it held a dozen or more delicate crown-shaped biscuits decorated with jewel-like candied fruits. Mother had occasionally brought home tins of Queen's Cakes as a special treat, but they were hard to come by even for a talented snatcher.

Nelle's mouth watered, and her hand moved almost against her will, ready to claim the topmost biscuit. She recalled herself just in time and hesitated, glancing up at the mage.

He nodded. "Help yourself. Please."

Trying not to be too obvious in her eagerness, Nelle plucked up a cake and brought it to her lips. For a moment she simply held it there, closing her eyes and breathing in the sweetness. Her first bite was slow, delicate. But the taste was too good and her hunger too great. Before she knew it, she'd devoured the whole thing.

The wyvern, smelling sweets, whined piteously and twined around the table legs. "Don't even think about it, wormling!" Nelle hissed, carefully using the tip of one finger to collect the last of the crumbs. She glanced up at the mage. "Where'd you come by treats like those? I thought you weren't a man for comforts."

"I'm not," he replied, setting the tin down in the middle of the table. With a wave of his hand, he indicated that she should take another. Nelle didn't wait to be urged. While she ate a second and even a third, Silveri rose, returned to the fireplace, and set about brewing tea.

Taking advantage of its master's turned back, the wyvern stuck its head up on Nelle's lap and fixed her with a hopeful stare. She shooed it off and determinedly finished the last bite. Then, avowing she would *not* make a pig of herself by eating a fourth biscuit, she turned away from the tin, trying not to look at it. The wyvern growled and sank dejectedly to the ground, muttering to itself.

The mage returned to the table to set a steaming wooden cup before her. Nelle took a sip. It tasted particularly bitter after the sweetness of the cakes yet was still soothing, so she drank it down. The mage neither ate nor drank but sat across from her at the table, his arms folded into the deep sleeves of his robe, his long legs stretched out before him and crossed at the ankle. He'd pulled his hood low again, shielding his face so that all she could see was the foam of beard spilling out over his chest.

She toyed with her mostly empty cup, studying him closely. At last she reached for that fourth biscuit and, nibbling it with more delicacy than she had the first three, asked, "So, what now, sir?"

"Eh?" He started as though he'd forgotten she was there. When he lifted his head, she caught a glimpse of flashing eyes. "Come again?"

"What now?" she repeated. "The island is safe again. What do you do with yourself all day, alone out here? I would imagine you've got various magely duties. Eldritch arts to practice and whatnot."

He blinked slowly, then turned back to the fire. "The island is never safe," he said after a long silence. "It never will be. And there is nothing I can do about that."

"Nothing?" Nelle picked a candied cherry off one of the crown points and popped it into her mouth. "Seems like you handled the unicorn handily enough. I wouldn't call that nothing."

He didn't answer for some while. At last he shrugged and nodded her way without quite looking at her. "I must thank you for your assistance, Miss Beck. I doubt I would have been as successful without your aid. You were . . . you were very brave."

A foolish warmth crept up Nelle's cheeks. She ducked her head, hiding a smile that had no right to be there. What did she care for the scarred mage's praise? Yet the warmth remained for some time, long after she swallowed the last bite of biscuit.

She reached out to close the tin before temptation drove her to eat four more. It was amazing what a few baked sweets and a little cup of tea could do for a battered soul. If she let herself think of it, the unicorn's song was still there, deep down inside. But now she heard it as though through many thick curtains of existence. It may yet return to haunt her in the darkness of a sleepless winter night, but she no longer feared it would pursue her at every waking moment, poisoning all other thoughts with exquisite sorrow.

"We ought to celebrate," she said, pushing the tin away. He cast her another look, and she laughed outright. "Don't be such a gloomy goose! We fought hard today, and we won. That's worth a little celebration, don't you think?"

He seemed to reflect for some moments before finally clearing his throat. "I hardly think—"

"Don't think! Celebrating ain't the time for thinking. It's the time for eating Queen's Cakes and drinking queasy and toasting our success. Or . . . I know."

She rose suddenly. Moving quickly before the mage could stop or question her, she stepped up to the armoire, which was still wide open. She stood on her toes to reach the box—a pretty box of red wood inlaid with ebony bands—at the front of the topmost shelf, slid it down into her arms, and carefully carried it back to the table. Feeling Silveri's gaze hard upon her, she popped the latch and began to lay out the contents: a small bowl and brush, two ornate lidded jars, a set of combs, and a hard-bristled brush. Last of all, a razor and strop. One by one, she arranged them in a row on the table.

The mage was silent. Painfully silent. So silent that she could hear the wyvern's breathy snores as it snoozed in a ball of scales and wings under the table.

Nelle took a seat and leaned her elbows on the table. "Well?" she said at last.

He looked up. His hood fell back softly from his face, revealing the great bush of hair and beard. One eyebrow lifted slowly, and those bright pale eyes flashed. "Well, Miss Beck?"

"What do you think?" She waved a hand to indicate the shaving box and barber's instruments. "I saw them in your cupboard just now, and I figured why not?"

Another long silence followed. Nelle resolved she wouldn't be the one to break it, but before long she began to think that would mean sitting there with her mouth firmly shut until darkness fell. At last she shook her head and leaned back in her chair. "All right, you can say it."

"Say what?"

"It was stupid."

He didn't answer. His other eyebrow rose slowly.

"I just thought maybe . . ." Her voice trailed off, and she ducked her head, another telltale flush staining her cheeks. She lifted her lashes and peered at him again. "It's just, you're so posh in the way you talk and move and are. I thought maybe you might not actually *like* looking like a hairy beast all the time."

"A hairy beast?"

"Yes. A wild, crazed, ridiculously hairy beast." Nelle quirked a smile his way. Then she sobered. "I used to shave my Papa. Still do, that is. When I'm home. When I get back home." Her throat went tight, and she had to clear it before continuing. "You've been good to me, Mage Silveri, letting me stay here. I can do more than cook and clean, you know. You're a kind man, and—"

He stood. It was so abrupt that Nelle gave a little yelp and shrank back in her seat. His head was bowed, his face again completely hidden by the deep hood, but his voice growled so deep, it seemed to rumble in her gut.

"I am not a kind man, Miss Beck. Nor a good one. I do not need your help. Nor do I desire your sympathy."

Before she could recover herself enough to even begin to think of an answer, he had already climbed the stairs and vanished through the hole in the ceiling.

Nelle sat on the doorstep, watching the sun sink slowly to the far horizon. The wyvern joined her, dragging its broken wing across the floor to sit beside her, upright on its haunches. They were silent together. The wyvern, when Nelle looked down at it, seemed to be watching the sky for some glimpse of its brethren soaring high among the clouds.

Her own gaze was drawn across the water to the Evenspire, the only visible sign of her own world. A world that felt distant both in miles and in memory. Was it only two days since she'd set out from that misty shore? Two days since she'd passed through the veil and entered this Hinter Realm? It felt so much longer.

The wyvern gave a sudden enormous yawn and turned to slink back into the room. She heard it crawl up into the rafters. After some scurrying, muttering, chortling, and a tediously prolonged grooming session, it finally fell asleep, leaving Nelle in peace. She dropped her chin to her updrawn knees, turned her head a little to one side, and watched the way the water moved, the way the clouds drifted.

In her mind she kept seeing the flash of the unicorn's horn, and traces of its song echoed in her ears. She also saw the blazing brightness of the mage's sword, a sword that had fit so comfortably in her hands. And the look in Silveri's eye when he saw her holding it.

How strange the world had become! Strange, and yet so full of possibilities. Her heart throbbed over unformed thoughts, unformed wishes, half ideas that would never have occurred to her mere days ago but now lingered on the brink of understanding.

A little smile pulled at the corner of her mouth.

"Oh Mother!" she sighed at last, breaking her long silence. "What would you think of me now?"

The words had scarcely left her mouth when she heard footsteps on the stair behind her. Nelle sucked in both lips and bit down. She kept her back to the room, her eyes fixed on that distant haze of horizon, and waited until she heard him reach the bottom step, until she knew he stood on ground level.

Then, lifting her chin from her knees and stretching her legs out in front of her, she said loudly enough to be heard over her shoulder, "Are you all through sulking yet?"

Silence answered her. Then more footsteps crossing the room, the sweep of long robes on the floor, the scrape of a chair being pulled back. Nelle turned just in time to see Mage Silveri take his seat. He'd dragged the chair away from the table and sat facing the fireplace.

Nelle got up, arms wrapped around her middle. Leaving the door open behind her, she approached the mage slowly until she stood directly in front of him. His hands rested on his knees, and she saw the gnarled fingers tense slightly as she drew near. The last of the daylight falling through the upper window illuminated his unhooded, shaggy face, revealing every snarl and mat, emphasizing the scars. His eyes held a gleam that, if she didn't know better, she might interpret as fear.

Which was nonsense, of course. What did he have to fear?

She planted her fists on her hips. "It'll probably take a couple hours, you know. You look like a sheepdog."

"I am well aware, Miss Beck."

"A sheepdog what ran through the briar and then had a roll in a mud hole."

"Yes, Miss Beck."

She reached out and hated herself a little when her fingers flinched before touching the straggling locks falling across his shoulder. Did he notice her faltering? Probably. That quick gaze of his noticed everything. She lifted a hank of hair, holding it up for inspection. "Shall I get to work?"

One nilarium-crusted hand came up and almost, but not quite, touched hers. His eyes flashed again, and this time she had no doubt about the fear in them.

"Before you begin," he said, "you need to know . . ." His voice trailed away.

"What? That you're all scarred up underneath this mess?" Nelle shrugged. "There's no one here to be bothered by it. Just me."

His eyelids dropped, momentarily shielding his gaze. "It's worse than you think."

"Bullspit." Nelle reached for the razor lying beside the strop, already sharpened to a dangerous edge. "I don't give a scatting dragon about scars. Now hold still, will you?"

He obeyed. He held so still, in fact, she could easily have believed his whole body had been coated in nilarium, not just his hands.

She set to work with a will, first slicing away at hanks of hair, cutting through thick matted patches, and pulling snarls. She was relentless, and soon his shoulders and the ground around his chair looked like a sheep-shearer's shed. His hair was so thick, she was half tempted to cut it down to the scalp. But, remembering the young man in the gold-framed portrait, she decided to preserve as much of the length as she could by working out the tangles with her fingers where necessary and then moving to the comb and brush.

"Ouch," he said at one point, very softly through his teeth.

"Sorry, did I hurt you?" she asked, pausing with the comb partway yanked through a particularly unruly snarl.

"Not at all, Miss Beck," he answered at once, despite evidence to the contrary. "Not at all."

She snorted and continued working, noting every time she saw him wince. "You know," she said after a little silence, "I wish you wouldn't call me that."

"Call you what?"

"Miss Beck. It makes me sound like I'm a fine lady or something. I'm not, you know. I'm just a Draggs Street girl."

"What would you have me call you then?"

355

"Nelle, if you like. That's what most folks call me."

The mage cleared his throat. "I would never presume to address any young woman so informally. It is simply not done."

"Not done?" She yanked at another knot, pulling his head awkwardly to one side in her efforts. "Bullspit, sir!"

"Such informality is only appropriate within the family circle."

"Within *your* family circle?" She took a step back, meeting his eye and shaking the end of her comb at his nose. "If I was anywhere near *your* family circle, I'd be nothing more than your lowest scullery maid. If you called me anything, it'd be 'Here, girl!' or 'Fetch, wench!' That's if you ever noticed me to begin with."

He blinked up at her. Though his hair was beginning to look more gentlemanly, his beard was still a mass of tangles. Nevertheless, she thought she saw the pull of his lips in a sideways smile. "I don't imagine you are a creature who often escapes notice."

She quickly darted around behind him again and applied the comb with more vigor before he could see the heat rising in her face. "You mean 'cuz of the hair, I suppose. Right flaming torch-head, I know. Boggarts, I keep it tied up under a cap most times! I'm really quite demure, sir, though you mightn't believe it."

"Demure. Yes. I'm sure you are, Miss Beck."

She sniffed and set the comb aside. It was time to tackle the beard now. She set to work at first with a pair of trimming scissors, though hedge shears may have been more useful. When she'd got it cut down as close as she could, she applied soap with a brush and carefully set about scraping with the razor. As she worked, her eyes widened. Each stroke of the blade, each clump of hair that fell away revealed more and more of the scars covering his cheeks, his jaw, and down his neck.

It was, as he had said, much worse than she'd realized. His skin was a spider web of interlacing cuts, most of them years old and faded, but many of them still red and purple, puckered against his ghostly pale flesh. The scars pulled oddly at the corners of his lips and twisted the shape of his nose, his ears, his brow. She could still see the ghost of the man from the portrait, but it was like looking at him through a warped glass. Perhaps she ought to have left some of the beard for covering.

But no. No, it had to go. All of it.

When she tilted his chin up for better access to the stretch of his neck and throat, he cringed. "You be sure you hold still now, sir," she said. "I wouldn't want to add to all these cuts of yours. Though one good thing: You'd never notice!" She snickered, then held the razor away and flicked his ear with her forefinger. "It's a joke. If you can't laugh at yourself a bit, what's the point? Or do you want me to pretend your face doesn't look like you sleep on a bed of thorns each night?"

His eyes flashed to meet hers. And now that the hair was out of his face, now that the bush was scraped away from his mouth and chin, she could see his expression—and he wasn't angry or irked, sardonic or sad. He was startled. Shocked, even.

"Oi, another joke is all," Nelle said, rolling her eyes. She

357

finished up, then stepped back and closed the razor with a snap. "There, sir. You're finished. Now, was that so terrible?"

The muscles of his throat moved as though he found it difficult to swallow. One silvery hand lifted and tentatively felt along his jaw and throat, though more out of almost-forgotten habit than anything. She was sure he couldn't feel anything with those fingers. The scars around his mouth pulled as he grimaced.

"It's . . . uh." He coughed and tried again. "It's a little . . . uh . . ."

"Raw?" Nelle supplied. "No worries, sir! I've got just the thing." She sprang to the table, dropped the razor back in its box, and selected one of the bottles of lotion. When she opened it, the scent of rosewood filled her nostrils, almost intoxicating in its intensity. She pulled back, blinking, then quickly poured some of the ointment into her palm.

Rubbing her hands together, she approached the mage and stood in front of him again. "Hands down," she said, and he dropped both hands back to his knees. "Hold still."

She didn't hesitate this time. She rubbed the lotion into his skin, her fingers trailing across those brutal ridges and crevices without a pause. He kept his eyes lowered during her ministrations, fixed on his own lap. But she saw his nostrils flare with an indrawn breath.

As realization struck, she slowed and almost pulled back. This was probably the first time he'd been touched by another person in fifteen years.

How old was Mage Silveri anyway? Gaspard had said they

studied together, and Gaspard was in his late thirties at least. Silveri was presumably the same age, but his white hair had made him seem much older. Now that the hair was tamed, however, and now that she could see his face clearly . . . Nelle frowned, her fingers rubbing gently along the ridge of his cheekbones. It was impossible to say through the scars, but he didn't look to her much older than the young man in the portrait.

She realized her hands had stopped. Standing there, holding his face between her palms, she thought, *Bullspit, girl! How short-sighted can you get?*

Hardly any space separated her from him. He couldn't have stopped her from stealing a quick kiss. If she'd had the foresight to apply the Sweet Dreams before he came back down from the tower, she could have used this opportunity. He would be startled, yes. He would react, possibly with violence—memory of Gaspard's savage blows flashed through her brain—but he would be down on the floor and helpless within a minute. And she could climb the stairs, search his room, find the book . . .

It would be so simple.

Her gaze had been fixed on his mouth for the last several seconds. She looked up and found his eyes locked on hers. Heat flared up her neck.

She dropped her hold and backed away quickly, hiding her embarrassment behind a saucy smile. "All done! And you're as pretty as mortal hands can make you, if I do say it myself."

He stood. His rough robes fell in deep folds, the long sleeves slipping to cover his hands. The hood was back, and his combed hair hung down across his broad shoulders. He was tall, and in that closed-in space seemed taller still. Taller and stranger, suddenly. Nelle had become accustomed to the wild-haired host of the last two nights. That man had been merely unsettling. This man was difficult to look at. The sight of those scars made her feel phantom pain across her own skin.

But the flickering glow from the fire and the shadows of deepening evening softened the harsher lines, making him look more human. Almost gentle, somehow.

"Miss Beck." The words rumbled low in his chest. "I—"

"You don't have to thank me, you know." Her voice was bright. A little too bright. Could he hear the underscoring tension? "Really. It was no trouble."

He lifted his gaze to her. She again saw the man from the portrait peering out through that mask of ragged lines. The gentleness was gone, and Nelle suddenly felt her extreme vulnerability. She had spent two nights under this man's roof, and he had not harmed her, just as he'd promised. But could she truly trust him after so short an acquaintance?

She held his gaze, made certain her eyes didn't drift to one side. To the jar of Sweet Dreams sitting unobtrusively among the kitchen ingredients.

He moved. Nelle tensed, and her hands formed fists. But he didn't move toward her. Instead, he made a deep and graceful bow. It was a courtly gesture, completely out of place in this world, in those robes, and with that face. Yet he made it look utterly natural.

"I bid you good night, Miss Beck," he said. "Sleep well."

With those words and nothing more, he retreated up the stairs, leaving her alone with the flickering fire.

CHAPTER 25

SORAN STUMBLED UP THE STAIRS, HALF BLIND, HARDLY aware of what he did. Though the weight of the coming battle bowed his shoulders, his mind was elsewhere. Dangerously distracted.

What a fool he was! He should have stayed away from her, never let her touch him with those sweet callused hands of hers. Never let her get close, her face mere inches from his own.

It was one thing to let her stay a few days, to give her shelter. But this . . . this was dangerous.

If Helenia found out . . . if she even suspected . . .

Soran reached the doorway at the top of the stair and sagged heavily against the frame, his cold fingers gripping the wood hard enough to leave a dent. With his other hand, he touched the smooth skin of his face. His fingers felt nothing, but his cheeks reacted to the nilarium fingertips, shivering. How cold and bare he felt! Exposed.

What had she felt when she stood so close to him, peering through the hideous scars, the warped and puckered features rendered nearly inhuman? What had she thought when she met his gaze? He'd seen her sudden uncertainty, noted each subtle fluctuation of color across her fair skin. Had the fire suddenly flaring to life inside him blazed out through his eyes? Had she realized what the nearness of her did to him, the intoxicating smell of her? And her touch, her gentle touch, her slender fingers caressing his face . . .

He bowed his head, growling deep in his throat. He was a fool. A damned, dangerous fool. The girl was a true innocent, fresh and pure enough to see unicorns with her own mortal eyes. And he was nothing but an old broken monster. He would not indulge these feelings. These instincts.

He would not allow himself to remember how her eyes had drifted down to his lips, fixing there with such intensity.

"Enough!" he snarled and pulled his hand away from the door. Staggering into the upper chamber, he crossed to his desk and took his seat. The sun was already mostly set; he had no time to waste.

Soran closed his eyes and drew three long breaths, holding

each one for as long as possible, waiting until his heart rate slowed before releasing it. He could not take this fiery distraction into the battle ahead of him. He could not let these thoughts, these sensations linger anywhere in his mind. He had to be firm, centered. Hard as stone.

When he next opened his eyes, his vision was steady. The Rose Book lay before him, bound tightly shut. He felt the power humming within it. He found a candle, struck a light, and set it in a bowl where its glow would shine upon the pages.

The time was come. The work must begin.

His fingers did not shake as he unbound the straps and opened the book to its first page. A waft of dense rose perfume clouded his senses. He fiercely shook it away and concentrated. His eye was steady as he began to read the first lines. The words forming in his mind, in his soul, were clear and bright. He felt the power of the spell come to life, felt his own mastery and control. Tonight would not be the night of his undoing.

He read slowly and with great care, turning pages one after another. The words burned bright as he read them, rising in response to his call as pulsing strands of energy that he caught and manipulated with masterful care. Only one part of his mind was unfocused now . . . the part waiting for the Thorn Maiden's approach.

Surely, she would come. She was not unaware of all that had taken place in her realm during daylight hours. She would crawl through the window, slither across the floor, and tear into him. Or she would stand out in the moonlight and moan in a voice of pure heartbreak that would cause him to stumble over the spell, to falter.

But there was nothing. No sign of her either in voice or in deed.

Soran read on uninterrupted. The power of the spell grew, and he congratulated himself on his command over it and over his own emotions. He was stronger than he thought. Perhaps the encounter with the unicorn had done him good.

He reached the end of the spell much sooner than he'd expected. Just as his candle guttered out, he closed the book. For some moments he sat there in the dark, his eyes slowly adjusting from candlelight to the pale gleam of moonlight pouring through the windows behind him. A certain uneasiness twisted in his gut.

That had been too easy. Far too easy.

Had he missed something? Had he somehow, in his over-confidence, missed whole pages and left the spell incomplete? Had he read a word wrong or a line out of order without realizing what he did?

No. He hastily fastened the book's straps and pushed it away. He'd done what he set out to do. The spell was wrought, the binding reaffirmed. What use lay in second-guessing himself now?

He was tired. So tired after the events of the day. He needed rest.

Rising from the desk, Soran slipped out of his heavy robes and left them draped across the chair. He kicked the sandals from his feet and loosened the laces of his shirt while staggering over to his bed. For a moment he paused and ran his cold fingers across the bare, puckered skin of his cheeks.

A smile pulled at his mouth, but he suppressed it.

Crawling into his bed, he pulled the blanket up to his chest, rested his head back on the pillow, and stared at the ceiling rafters above him. All was dark and still. Dawn would come soon, however, and the new day it heralded. But not a silent day. Not a cold, lonely, endless day with nothing but wyverns for company. No, tomorrow there would be smiles and eye-rolls and snorts of disbelief. There might even be laughter, real laughter . . .

Soran closed his eyes, rolled onto his side, and let sleep claim him, drifting gently off into deeper shadows and a place of unconscious stillness. There he rested for he could not say how long, not fully asleep but not awake either. He felt the cold air against his bare skin. He felt the warmth of his blanket, the roughness of the fibers across his chest. He felt the ache in his bones, the slow uncoiling of his muscles.

And he felt a sudden quickening in the air. A tension. A presence.

The Thorn Maiden? No, that couldn't be. The spell was read, the binding complete. She could not come again, not until the following sunset. He couldn't be mistaken about that. Could he?

He tried to wake up, but his eyes were like lead weights, heavy in his skull. He only managed to roll onto his back. When he tried to move his arms, they were paralyzed. His soul hovered in that strange place between waking and sleeping, helpless.

Then something touched him. Soft, warm. A pressure against his lips.

Feather-light at first. Then deeper, more insistent.

Fire flared in his gut, roared through his limbs.

Soran opened his eyes.

Nelle lay down in the alcove, fully clothed and still wearing her thin slippers. She curled up under the blanket, her shoulders hunched to her ears, and watched the fire as it slowly died on the hearth.

And she waited.

This is a stupid idea, you know.

Maybe it was. Maybe she ought to listen to her own over-cautious council.

What if she were to confess everything to the mage, tell him the truth? The whole truth this time, not the partial story she'd spun for him yesterday. Tell him about Gaspard and his threats, about Papa and his debts.

Tell him about her need for the spellbook.

Would he be willing to hear her? To listen? To hand the book over?

Nelle scowled into the deepening darkness and tucked her body tighter beneath the blanket. If the book was so important to Gaspard, it was probably of equal importance to Silveri. To trust the mage with her secret would be idiotic.

If only she knew how time was passing in the outer world! She might be able to wait a bit then, think of some other angle to try. But she couldn't risk it. She needed to act. Tonight.

An hour passed. Possibly two. The sun had set long since, and night spread dark and deep across the sky.

Still she waited.

Another hour passed before she realized that her whole body was tensed with listening. Listening for a gentle *tip-tap, tip-tap, tip-tap* outside the door. But all was still. Quiet. Peaceful. Her pricked ears heard the distant murmur and groan of the ocean far below. Now and then, a wyvern's chortling cry sounded in the darkness. The wounded wyvern snorted in its sleep, unseen in the rafters overhead. The world was at rest.

Nelle closed her eyes.

Then suddenly, she opened them again. How long had she slept? The fire had gone out completely, and the room was pitch black save for a stream of moonlight pouring through one high window. The air felt dense—the air of a world that had wandered into the far side of midnight.

It's time.

Nelle pushed back her blanket and rose from the bed. She ought to be blind and fumbling in this darkness, but she moved with deft confidence. Mother had taught her well how to manage in minimal light. She stepped to the shelves displaying the kitchen goods and pulled the jar of Sweet Dreams from its in-plain-sight hiding place. She lifted the lid. Pungent vapors burned her nostrils. She pulled back, grimacing, then carefully put one finger in, scraping up the traces around the base of the jar. Only three doses left. At most. She couldn't waste them.

Her lips stung as she applied the ointment, but she ignored it. She secured the lid and set the jar carefully back in its place, then turned to the stair. Her heart hammered in her throat as she crossed the room and began the climb, keeping one hand firmly on the wall.

Within a few steps she felt the lack of a rail, the open fall waiting to claim her. The ascent seemed endless. By the time she passed above the ceiling into the tower proper, she was practically blind. But she continued doggedly, one step after another, sliding her hand along the wall.

Why was she so nervous? She'd pulled off far more dangerous stunts more times than she could count, her recent climb up the Evenspire not least among them.

She half expected to see a gleam of candlelight from the doorway high above. But rather than the warm glow of fire, there was only the silvery glow of moonlight pouring through the big windows. Still, it was light. She quickened her pace, eager to leave the hungry shadows behind.

Something moved. *Slithered.* Brushed along the edge of her hand.

Nelle jerked it back. Her heart stopped, then jumped hard enough to choke her. Nothing was there. She strained her ears, but there was no sound. She forced her fingers to feel up and down the stone wall. Nothing. Absolutely nothing. It was just her mind playing with her.

Come on, girl. You've got to do this. No stalling.

Papa needs you.

She set her jaw and kept going, racing up the last eight steps to the door above. Clutching the doorframe with one hand, she peered into the upper chamber.

Moonlight fell in a perfect, clear stream, illuminating the little bed along one wall, shining on strands of long, pale hair that covered the back and shoulder turned Nelle's way.

Silveri was asleep then. Good. That was good.

Nelle turned and looked at the mage's desk on the far side of the room. It was cast in shadow, too dark for her to properly see the books and quills and parchments. But she felt them there, an indistinct mound. The Rose Book was among them. It must be.

She took a step and stopped at once when a creak and a sound of shifting broke the stillness. She was almost too afraid to look but turned her head anyway.

The mage had rolled over in his sleep. He lay on his back now. His eyes were closed, and he breathed deeply, steadily.

Could she risk it? Could she try to find the book in this darkness and hope she didn't wake him? She was stealthy and nimble-fingered. She might just manage it.

But if he were to wake, all would be lost.

Don't be stupid, girl.

She ground her teeth. The Sweet Dreams burned on her lips, ready. She came up here to deliver the dose. To make certain of her mark. Then to find the book and hurry across the island to her boat before dawn. If she were quick, if she were careful, she could be back to Wimborne by sunrise.

She moved silently toward the mage's bed but stopped within two steps and looked down, frowning. Why was she wearing only her chemise? She'd not undressed for the night, she was sure. Not when she planned to make a hasty getaway. And where were her shoes? Had she not been wearing them for the climb up the tower stair?

Something was wrong here. Something was . . .

No. No, she must be misremembering. Besides, once the dose was given, she'd have plenty of time to dress properly. The Sweet Dreams would leave her victim in a paralyzed slumber for hours. The amount she'd applied to her lips might well knock him out for the whole of the next day.

One . . . two . . . three . . . She steadied herself, counting slowly. When she reached twenty, she moved again, creeping to the mage's bed. Her hair fell over her shoulder as she bent over, and she feared it would tickle his face and wake him. Hastily she pulled it back, tied it in a knot. Then she looked again.

Strange how the moonlight played with the eyes. Strange how the otherworldly glow smoothed out his skin, melting away the ugly scars so that he looked more and more like the young man in the portrait. The long hair spread across his pillow might almost be golden rather than white. And his hands—one lying across his breast, the other at his side—in this light, she couldn't even see the rough coating of nilarium.

Why not?

This wasn't right. This wasn't . . .

Was it real?

It had to be. She could feel her heart thudding, could hear her own uneasy breathing. The skin on the back of her neck prickled as each fine hair rose. It had to be real. And she had to act. Now, before she missed her moment.

Nelle leaned over the sleeping mage. Her lips found his in the darkness, softly at first. They were full and soft, not puckered with scars as she'd expected. She pressed a little harder, forcing his mouth open. She had to be certain the dose got through.

He stirred. His eyelids fluttered. His lashes rose. His gaze was muddled, foggy.

Then he zeroed in on her, his eyes sharp as two blades in the moonlight.

Nelle drew back a few inches. For a moment she gazed down at him, every muscle braced. *Let him think it's a dream. Let him think it's a dream long enough for the poison to—*

Hands caught her upper arms. Warm, living hands, fingers pinching to the bone. He pulled her down to him and captured her mouth in a burning, eager kiss that shocked her to the core. One hand let go of her arm and grabbed the back of her head, fingers tangling in her hair, and held on so hard she couldn't draw back.

A thrill of fear shot up her spine. Or perhaps not fear. She got her hands under her, trying to push against his chest, to put some distance between them. He wore only a loose shirt, and her palms met with bare skin and muscle. He shivered at her touch.

And suddenly she was pulled off her feet. He rolled her onto the bed beside him, her back flat, her lungs heaving. His head and shoulders above her blocked out the moonlight. The curtain of his hair fell along his shoulder, shimmering and pale. One arm supported his torso, his fist and elbow pressed into the thin mattress. His other hand caressed her cheek, and she noticed again, behind the wild pounding of her heart, that his fingers were warm, not cold dead silver. Heat blazed in his eyes, and within that heat, a single urgent question.

She needed to get free. She needed to bring a sharp knee up between his legs, scramble out from underneath him, get beyond his reach until the poison took effect. Every nerve in her body sparked with fire, with the need to act.

So why did she reach to cup his cheeks between her hands? Why did she push a strand of pale hair behind his ear?

Why did she close her eyes, tilt her chin, and lift her mouth to be claimed?

His lips were hungry yet gentle. There was nothing harsh or demanding about the sweetness with which he kissed her. One kiss led to another, and then to more kisses from the corner of her mouth along her cheek to her ear. His breath tickled the delicate skin of her neck, and she drew a sharp, quick gasp, which she knew he heard. She felt excitement racing through him, felt his heart drumming in a rhythm that matched her own.

Wait. *Wait.* A desperate part of her mind screamed in protest. He ought to collapse. Any moment now. The poison should have overcome him already. He should be lying in a helpless heap of limbs while she found the spellbook and made her escape.

But there was nothing helpless about him. He was strong, confident. His arm wrapped around her waist, pulling her into a deeper kiss. Any resistance remaining to her melted away. Her hands slid around his neck, her fingers pulled at his hair, and her body pressed against his, heartbeat to heartbeat. She broke away at last, gasping for air, her head falling back on the pillow.

But he didn't stop, couldn't stop. His lips searched along her jawline, down her neck, every touch soft and warm and fervent. He continued trailing kisses to her collarbone, and his hand slid up along her arm to her shoulder, gently pulling back the fabric of her gown to expose more skin. His mouth moved to explore along the curves of her neck and shoulder, and her whole being responded to his touch in thrilling bursts. He slid the sleeve down farther still, his fingertips playing dangerously along the loose neckline, tracing across the uppermost curve of her breasts.

Nelle shivered, and he lifted his head at once, the question again in his eyes. She stared up at him, and blood pounded in her temples.

Then she reached and pulled the laces of his loose shirt open.

Though her fingers trembled, she untied each one and slid the garment open so that it fell away from his broad shoulders. He sat up to shrug out of the sleeves, letting the shirt fall around his waist. Moonlight gleamed on the hard muscles of his chest and abdomen, the effect exaggerated by contrasting light and shadow.

Her throat was dry, and a pulse of heat thrummed through her body. He must have seen the look in her eye, for he smiled suddenly, a knowing, dangerous smile. Once more his hand slid behind her neck, cupped her head, and pulled her lips up to his in another long, lingering kiss.

Something creaked. Something groaned.

Rock tearing under tremendous force.

Nelle's eyes flared open. "Sir!" she gasped against his mouth. "Mage Silveri!"

He pulled back, blinking, his gaze muddled, bemused. "Miss Beck?" His brows drew together in a knot. He looked surprised, and a moment later horrified. The bemusement melted from his gaze, replaced by pure shock. "Miss Beck, what are you—"

Movement behind him.

Nelle screamed.

Dark, writhing briars poured through the window and climbed the walls, stretched up to the ceiling overhead and swarmed over the oil basin. Black as living shadows, they ripped into stone, like crushing pinchers grinding the rocks to dust. They wound up the legs of the bed, tore into the mattress, tore into Nelle's arms. Thin canes wrapped around her neck, her waist, her arms, and their thorns bit like knives into her flesh. She screamed again, tried to thrash against those bindings. But she was caught, helpless.

Distantly she thought she heard Silveri's voice crying out, "Miss Beck! Miss Beck, wake up! *Peronelle!*"

CHAPTER 26

SORAN'S HEAD SHOT UP FROM THE DESK SO FAST, HE nearly fell out of his chair. He stared around in the darkness, unblinking, almost blinded by the bizarre images playing out inside his head. Images of thorns . . . briars . . .

"No!" he growled and looked down at what lay before him. It was the Rose Book, open to the middle. An intoxicating perfume emanated from its pages, from the shining words, a stink like burning roses. It filled his nostrils, filled his head.

Oh gods, no! He'd fallen asleep. Slipped into the Nightmare without realizing what he'd done.

Traitorous.

Her voice whispered in his ear.

She stood at his back, poised and ready.

I know what is in your mind. I saw you with the mortal girl. Faithless! Heartless! Cruel!

Soran bowed over the spellbook. The magic still throbbed in the air around him, not yet broken. He'd nodded off for only a moment, but even a moment was too long. But perhaps he could still somehow reclaim his hold on the spell. He found the place near the top of the second page where it began going wrong and began to read, speaking the words aloud in a strong, clear voice.

It doesn't matter, she hissed. An arm twined around his shoulders, across his chest, fingers toying with the open laces of his shirt, reaching for skin. The gentle caress turned malicious, thorns biting deep.

Soran gasped and clutched the edges of the desk to support himself. Blood welled, soaked into his shirt, poured down his front. Grinding his teeth, he hunched over the book and read on, slow and steady despite the pain. By some miracle he managed to catch the threads of the spell and tie them back together.

It would hold. It must hold. Please the gods, let it hold!

It doesn't matter, the Thorn Maiden whispered again, toying with his ear. Cutting hands trailed up and down the back of his neck. *I saw the truth. I saw where your desire lies. You may bind me back tonight, but what about tomorrow? What about the day after and the day after that?*

Her teeth sank deep into his shoulder. He cried out, hunching over the desk and the book. The spell shuddered, compromised. With an effort of will, he pulled himself together and forced the words to flow in a continuous stream.

The magic strengthened once more, solidified.

I'll reach her in the end. The Thorn Maiden spat out each word, spraying blood. *I'll draw her into my realm, draw her into my embrace. You can fight, my love, but you cannot win. You cannot win . . . You cannot . . . win . . .*

Her voice faded as the power of the spell intensified and the bindings drove her away. Soran pulled his shoulders back, wincing at the fiery cuts and punctures. But there was no time to deal with them, not yet. He had to finish the work, truly finish it this time. What a fool he'd been, so easily duped, so easily taken in by a sensual fantasy!

An image appeared in his head—the girl beside him on his narrow bed, her face upturned to his, her body warm and willing.

Her lips parted, beckoning, soft.

A dream. Nothing but a dream. He shook his head, driving the image away. He'd come into this battle distracted and exhausted, and it had taken its toll. The Thorn Maiden was a subtle one, sly as a snake in the shadows, and she'd played with his mind, played with his imagination, his vanity, his weakness.

And the girl? What had happened to her while his defenses were down? There was no way of knowing how long the dream had lasted. Judging by the state of the spell when he awoke, he had nodded off for a few moments at most. Was it time enough for the Thorn Maiden to get through, to attack the young woman while she slept?

With an effort of sheer will, Soran drove these thoughts back and locked them down hard. He must focus. After such a deadly slip, he dared not make another mistake. The spell must be completed, the binding firmly established. He aimed everything he had at the words before him, at the power emanating between the page and his mind. He wove and threaded and knotted and spun, the words slipping from his tongue with practiced precision.

Hours slipped past. His candle burned down.

At last he reached the end of the final page. The moment the final word was read, he slammed the book and fastened it tight. Power throbbed beneath his hands, but the spell was well wrought. This time for real.

Heaving a great sigh, Soran leaned back in his chair and rubbed his hands down his face. The touch of silver on his skin startled him. Memory of the girl standing before him filled his head, her hands wielding that razor as she carefully scraped away his beard.

Gods, how he'd nearly repaid her for her kindness! How close he had come to letting the monster through and . . . and . . .

His eyes widened. His hands dropped away from his face. The girl! Did she still sleep?

He sprang to his feet and, leaving his heavy robes draped over the back of the chair, raced from the chamber and down the long stairwell. His pace was too fast for safety, but he couldn't bring himself to slow. Taking three steps at a time, he almost fell the last several turns.

He emerged through the opening in the ceiling, peered through the rafters to the alcove bed. There she was—lying under the blanket.

Afraid of what he would find, Soran sprang to the ground floor and strode across the room. He collapsed on his knees beside the girl, struggling to see her face by the light of the low fire on the hearth. "Miss Beck!" he said, his voice growling in his thickened throat. He grabbed her by the shoulder and shook her roughly. "Miss Beck, wake up! *Peronelle!*"

Nelle opened her eyes.

She lay in the alcove on the bed of fur rugs. A gleam of firelight illuminated the stone wall arching over her and lit up the scarred face hovering just above her own.

With a choking cry, Nelle sat up, scrabbling at the blankets and the tangle of her skirts. Her heart raced, panic thrilling through every vein. She looked frantically at her arms, her wrists, her torso, still certain she felt the constricting pressure of lithe canes, the tearing of thorns in her flesh. It was so real, so excruciating . . .

But there was nothing.

"Easy, Miss Beck. Easy." Hands gripped her shoulders. Nelle looked up into that ugly mask of scars and whimpered. She tried to shrug his hands away, but he held on. "Look at me. Look into my eyes."

Something in his voice compelled her, something she couldn't resist. She looked. Her fear-fogged brain cleared somewhat, and those frightening features coalesced into a face she recognized.

"Mage Silveri!" she gasped.

It wasn't the moonlit vision who, just moments ago, had held her in his embrace. It wasn't the perfected dream of a man, all scars melted away into a haze of unreal beauty. Every last raw pucker and ragged indentation was prominent on his newly shaved face, dark and ridged in that fire glow. But there were fresh cuts too. Many of them. Slicing across his forehead, his cheeks, down along his neck, his ears. Blood soaked in stark lines through the light fabric of his loose shirt.

What was this? What had happened? Visions of briars and thorns filled her head. But why was she not bleeding too? And why was she *here,* in her alcove bed?

"It's all right, Miss Beck. You're safe now." Silveri's voice broke through the wild panic rising inside her and brought her focus back to his eyes. She held his gaze, almost hypnotized. His grasp moved from her shoulders to her face, holding her head steady. Cold, hard fingers crusted with nilarium touched her skin. She shuddered.

"You had a dream," he said. "I'm so sorry. I fell asleep. I didn't mean to. It was only for a moment, but she got through while I slept. Are you hurt?"

A dream? It was . . . it was just a . . .

"I'm not hurt," she breathed. When she pushed his hands away this time, he relented. He drew back, still crouched beside her bed, his elbows resting on his knees, his eyes fixed intently on her. She rubbed a hand down her face and pushed her hair back from her forehead. Her gaze shifted again to his bleeding face and torso; the cruel cuts were exactly like those she still felt slicing her own skin.

"What happened?" she demanded, her voice breathy and tight. "What . . .? You're . . ." A cold fist gripped her heart, and her eyes widened. "Was that the Thorn Maiden?"

He nodded, his eyes downcast.

"It's a dream?"

"Not a dream." He shook his head. His long hair wafted across his shoulders, the white strands soaked with blood. "A nightmare." His jaw worked as if he struggled to find the right words. When none came to him, he gathered himself to rise.

Nelle's hand darted out quicker than thought and caught hold of his arm. "Tell me what's going on."

His eyes fixed on her fingers. "It's best you don't know. You're safe now, and—"

"Bullspit." Nelle bit the word through clenched teeth. "If you think you're gonna get all mysterious and terse with me, you'd better scatting think again! What *is* the Thorn Maiden? What just happened to me? And why are you . . . are you . . ." She waved her free hand, indicating his many wounds in a single sweep. "Why are you carved up like a holiday roast?"

His arm muscles tensed under her fingers. She felt the strength of him, felt how easily he could break her hold. She tightened her grip, though she knew it was useless, and stared at him with such ferocity that she knew he felt it even though he wouldn't meet her gaze.

At last his chest expanded, and he breathed a heavy sigh. He lowered one knee, then sank into a seated position beside her bed. "The Thorn Maiden is a Noswraith."

Nelle blinked. "Say again?"

He closed his eyes and ran a hand down his bleeding face, smearing blood. "A Noswraith. A . . . a creature of the Hinter."

A shiver prickled the skin up her spine. Nelle let go of the mage's arm and instead gripped the threadbare blanket draped over her lap like a flimsy shield. She waited, unable to think what to ask but knowing there must be more. Much more.

Mage Silveri drew a long breath and let it out slowly. "It's a bit of a story, Miss Beck. Not a good story; not one I like to tell."

"I'm listening."

His gaze flicked to hers, then down again. "You know something of the war between mortals and the fae, do you not?"

Nelle shrugged but nodded. Everyone knew about the Great Fae War, though details had been lost with time. Some said the fae tried to invade the mortal world and take humans as their slaves. Others claimed that mortals infiltrated Faerieland, seeking to plunder the many treasures there. Both versions probably included some truth. And a great many lies as well.

"The War came to a head three centuries ago," Mage Silveri said, "and mortalkind was losing. It was then that the Miphates delved deep into dark arts, searching for a weapon that might be used against the seemingly unstoppable fae. Mortal magic had proven ineffective up until then; their skill with pens and parchment and written spells was no match for the natural enchantments that burned through every vein of a fae's body and soul.

"But the Miphates knew there was more; they knew there existed shadowy places as yet unexplored. They channeled their magic through their pens and wrote to life the first of the Noswraiths—a nightmare made flesh."

Nelle hunched her shoulders and tucked her head. The shadows on the edge of the room seemed darker than before, seemed almost to creep in toward her and the mage.

"It did not manifest in physical form in the mortal world," Silveri continued, "so at first the Miphates didn't realize what it was they had created. They were unaware that this being, sprung from the most vile and deranged depths of their minds, took life and shape in Eledria, the fae realm. It stepped out of thin air, powerful beyond imagining, and destroyed an entire city in an onslaught of horror such as cannot be fathomed by those who have not seen the like.

"But the Miphates, drunk on the wine of victory, did not stop at one. They fashioned more terrible creations and sent them hurtling into Eledria. The fae were powerless. The Noswraith were beings born of mortal minds, given life through mortal pens. As such, they could only be bound via pen and paper. But the fae do not understand written magic. They have no form of writing of their own, cannot conceive how figures and scratches can be made to contain words, worlds, and ideas. So they threw themselves at the nightmares. And they died.

"The Pledge was signed not long after. As part of the lasting peace between fae and mortalkind, the Miphates agreed to turn over the books in which the Noswraith spells were written, and all practice of nightmare-creation was banned. The theories of Chozarsk and Morningtree—famous mages of the Miphates order, leaders in the development of the Noswraith spells—were banned and destroyed."

A sick feeling pooled in Nelle's stomach. She realized, at least in part, where this story was going.

The mage's voice dropped to a lower register. "I was . . . young. Ambitious." He swallowed hard. "Arrogant."

"You made the Thorn Maiden. You wrote her to life." The words slipped from her lips in a whisper.

"I was accepted into the Miphates Order when I was still a child," he said. "I showed an *unusual* aptitude for magic, they said. My masters and mistresses petted and praised me and fed me on the most complicated theories and spells. I devoured them, always eager for more, always keen to expand my abilities, the range and breadth of my burgeoning powers.

"But it seemed there was always this *wall.* I would get so far, and they would stop me. Redirect me, send me down a new course of study. I would charge ahead, only to be thwarted again and again. I knew there must be secrets they weren't telling me . . . secrets they themselves possibly did not know.

"There was a fellow student: Dusaro Gaspard."

Nelle shivered at the name but quickly disguised it with a little cough and a nod.

Silveri continued, apparently without noticing. "Though he was not my equal in skill, we were alike in our ambition and spent time enough together that one might call us friends. Fellows, at the least. He, too, chafed at the restraints our superiors placed upon us. And when we uncovered the secret histories of the War and learned of the Miphates' role in bringing about its end, we were intrigued."

His words seemed to weigh him down until his head hung heavily from his shoulders. Blood dripped from his cuts, spattering his already stained shirt, and falling to the stone floor. Nelle cringed at the sight. "So, you and . . . and this Gaspard. You figured out how to make a Noswraith, did you?"

"Er, to put it bluntly, yes." He lifted a hand, catching a little rivulet of blood on the edge of his finger. It stood out bright and crimson in contrast with the silver. "It was illegal, of course, and we dared not pursue the task within the Evenspire itself. So, we contrived to smuggle a Miphates quill out of the university. We could not so easily smuggle a spellbook, however, so I bound and prepared one myself for the intended spell."

The Rose Book. He was talking about the Rose Book. He must be.

Mage Silveri's eyes swiveled away from her, gazing up at the ceiling and away to some distant place. "I'll never forget that night. That long, long night. Gaspard tried to stop me. He had been so keen to try, but when the moment came . . . he knew the spell was beyond him. So, he stood by, and I worked. For hours I worked, pouring everything I had into that creation. Delving into the darkest parts of my spirit and drawing up what I found there. I was so . . ." He closed his eyes, and the muscle in his torn cheek twitched. "I was so confident. I *knew* I could create something even the Miphates of old would fear. I *knew* I could prove myself superior to all those who thought to contain and control my power. A true Master of my craft."

Shame scored lines into his face deeper than any of the cuts and scars. He suddenly looked much older. Not the illusion of youth and silvery beauty from her dream. This was a man who had seen things he should not see, done things he should never do. A man who had leapt for the stars only to discover how far he could fall.

A fierce urge coursed through her arms, through her soul—an urge to reach out, to take that lined and bloodied face between her hands. To draw his head down to her heart and give him a place to rest.

What the bullspitting boggarts was wrong with her?

Nelle shook herself and twisted the folds of fabric in her lap, staring down at her hands. "I'm guessing it worked," she said, her voice a growl. "You wrote this . . . this Thorn Maiden into being. And she . . . what? Appeared in Faerieland?"

He nodded. "She destroyed the City of Darunia. Laid it waste and left it in ruins. She had already moved on and was making her way to Aurelis when King Lodírhal of the Dawn Court found me." He bowed his head and dug his silver-crusted hands into his long hair, pulling it at the roots as though he would like to pull his head from his shoulders and dash it to the ground. "I am responsible for the deaths of hundreds. Thousands, perhaps. They never told me the full extent of what I'd done.

"They came with swords and violence, expecting to meet with a warlord's mage, thinking that the Pledge was broken. They didn't expect to find me. Only me, for I had told Gaspard to flee by then, knowing as I did what must be in store. I thought they would kill me, but they had need of my powers. They needed someone to bind the Thorn Maiden. And no other mages left alive possessed the skill."

"Bind her?" Nelle pulled in both lips and bit down hard, uncertain of what she was about to say next. Then she blurted out, "Why would you *bind* her? You created her. Couldn't you just *un-create* her again?"

Silveri shook his head slowly. "In a sense, I'm not certain I *did* create her. At least, not from nothing, and not in the way you or I think of creation. It's as though she existed already—as though she's always existed in the darkness just beyond perception and understanding. When I wrote her into being, I merely gave life and flesh to something lifeless and fleshless but already fully real. Such beings cannot be unmade. A dream never truly dies.

"Instead, I bound her with words, writing her imprisonment into the same spellbook in which I wrote her liberation. It was far more difficult, more dangerous than calling her to life had been. I barely survived the process. But I didn't care. Once I knew what I had done, what I had brought into the worlds, I would gladly have died to atone for my sin. But the fae king of the Dawn Court had other ideas."

He held up his nilarium-crusted hands. "King Lodírhal saw to it that I should never endanger the worlds again."

Nelle looked at those hands. Clumsy and stiff, barely suited to basic human tasks.

A Miphato's power came from his ability to write. An ability no longer within Silveri's grasp.

For a long moment the mage was silent, and Nelle could think of nothing to say. She could only stare at those hands and think how agonizing it must have been to have them covered in liquid nilarium, to watch the alloy harden. To be crippled forever. All that power, gone. Everything that made him who and what he was. It was like cutting the legs off a racehorse.

Silveri dropped his hands into his lap and shrugged. "The Thorn Maiden is contained for the time being in the Rose Book," he said. "I have been able—*just* able—to maintain her bindings over the turning of the Hinter cycles. But it cannot last."

And what would happen when the nightmare woman escaped? Nelle shuddered, and her skin flinched at the memory of those cuts, which had occurred only in her dream.

But wait. That dream . . .

"Did the Thorn Maiden plant the dream in my head?" she asked quietly. "Tonight, I mean."

"Yes. Ordinarily I remain at my post throughout the night while she's hunting. I keep her at bay. Tonight, I . . . I must have nodded off over my work. She got through and went after you." He looked at her, his expression painful to behold. "I'm sorry. I'm so sorry, Miss Beck. I've done what I could to protect you from her. But she is vicious beyond imagining. And she . . . she is not pleased by your presence here on Roseward."

How much did he know about what she had dreamed? And how much of that dream had been planted by the Thorn Maiden?

Had the nightmare creature made her experience the intensity of those stolen kisses so vividly that she felt them even now, burning against her lips, along her jaw, her neck . . .

Nelle hid her face in her hands, pressing her fingers hard against her cheeks as though she could force the blush away. It was only a dream. Nothing more. And dreams could not be shared, so there was no reason to believe Silveri knew the details.

Oh, seven gods above, let him not know the details!

Pulling her shoulders back, Nelle pushed hair out of her face and shook her head. "So," she said, her voice a little too loud, a little too firm. "So you're telling me you've kept her contained all these years. How exactly?"

"Magic," Silveri said. "Years ago, I wrote the spell of her binding. Now, each night I read it in its entirety, reaffirming the spell."

"That doesn't sound too hard." The look he gave her made her scowl. "All right, all right! I know I don't know much about your magical arts and the like. I'm just saying it doesn't *sound* too hard. And as long as you've got the spellbook, as long as you . . . How did you say it? . . . *reaffirm* the spell, she can't get free, right?"

Silveri shook his head slowly. "Magic always takes a toll, especially on the physical world. The spellbook cannot survive nightly surges of magic forever. It will eventually disintegrate."

"Couldn't you, maybe . . . I don't know. Couldn't you transfer the spell to another spellbook?"

He held up his hands again. "Not with these, I can't."

"What happens when the book disintegrates? What happens when she breaks free?"

Silveri looked at her. "Then she will manifest in full physical form. And she will kill me."

"Kill you?"

"Yes." He blinked slowly. There was no fear in his face, only resignation and absolute certainty. "But once Roseward has pulled free of the final ties binding it to the mortal world, my death will not matter. She will kill me, and she will remain here, trapped forever. Floating through the Hinter ever deeper into the void."

Something in his face unsettled her. Nelle drew a careful

breath before saying, "But if the ties are not broken? If Roseward remains connected?"

"Then she will escape from here into the world of mortals. She will take root and spread, slowly but surely, from mind to mind. And eventually, Miss Beck, she will destroy everything you know and love."

CHAPTER 27

SILVERI LEFT HER SITTING ON THE BED WHILE HE MOVED to the fire, stoked up the flames, added a log, and put the kettle on to boil. Nelle watched him through a mental haze as he went about fetching tea leaves from among their dwindling supplies. She didn't quite follow what he did, simply watched without comprehension.

Her mind churned with new thoughts, new terrible ideas.

His story was thorough and humiliating, and she did not doubt anything he'd told her. He could not possibly lie with such incriminating thoroughness.

But she knew a thing or two about story-spinning. About how

to tell a truthful tale without telling the whole of the tale. Something was missing from this little history he'd related, something she could not place but felt with absolute certainty.

She closed her eyes . . . and felt again the warmth of his hands sliding across her skin, exploratory and tender and thrilling. She felt the heat of his lips pressed against the curve of her shoulder, felt the thudding pulse of his desire matched to her own wild heartbeat. A shiver raced down her spine.

Nelle's eyes flew open. As though reading her thoughts, the mage looked up from the fire. She didn't meet his gaze but studied her hands in her lap. It was only a dream, she reminded herself. Even if the thorns hadn't broken through, even if . . . even if passion had continued its breakneck course . . . it wasn't real.

But why did it feel so real?

Images played in the back of her mind. Images of her first night in Roseward. That first dreadful night and that first dreadful dream. Choking thorns . . . flaming roses . . . and something else. Something she'd almost forgotten.

Her lips moved, silently forming the words of a song: "*Red blooms the rose in my heart tonight. Fair as the dawn, new as the spring . . .*"

The clack of a wooden spoon drew her attention back to Silveri at the hearth. He stirred something into the wooden mug, then rose from his crouch and approached her, offering the brew. She took it, held it up to her face, and breathed deeply of the steam. It wasn't the most aromatic tea, but something about its earthy bitterness was grounding.

Silveri did not partake but sat again on the floor in front of her, his legs crossed, his elbows on his knees. Nelle took a sip, regarding him over the rim of the cup. It was a harsher flavor than she'd expected and rather too hot. She swallowed, and it burned all the way to her gut.

Licking her lips, she lowered the cup again. "Your cuts," she said. "They're mending."

He lifted a hand, touching the ugly gash above his eye, then fingering another, more savage wound at his ear. If she wasn't much mistaken, that one looked like a bite mark. But maybe it was just a trick of the light.

"The Hinter air," he said with a shrug, lowering his hand. "It repairs quickly. Just not . . . accurately."

Nelle nodded. Her gaze traveled over his many facial scars now prominently displayed thanks to her barbering efforts. She would hardly recognize him as the same man whose dream kisses she had reveled in such a short time ago.

Ducking her head, she quickly took another scalding sip of tea.

"When the sun comes up," the mage said after an uncomfortable silence, "you should go."

"Go?" She sputtered into the cup, speaking too fast. Hastily she wiped her mouth with the back of her hand. "What do you mean?"

"Now that you've seen what the Thorn Maiden can do." He

shrugged and shook his head. "You must see that it is impossible for you to remain here in safety."

"Oh." Nelle frowned, took another absent-minded sip, and stared into the contents of her cup. Should she argue? Did she want to?

She pressed two fingers to her temple, rubbing hard. If only she could rub some sense back into her head! She couldn't leave, of course. Not yet, not until the job was done. But how could she possibly think of an excuse to make, one that would convince him without giving too much away?

There was an added concern as well—the Rose Book. Now that she knew what it was, could she truly bear to fulfill this mission? To take the powerful spell and carry it back into her own world? If all that Mage Silveri said was true, a more dangerous weapon could hardly exist in all the worlds.

And she was going to . . . what? Simply pass it into the hands of a man like Gaspard?

She must think. She had to somehow pull her mind together and come to a decision. But with Silveri's gaze fixed upon her, so bright and silver in the firelight, she couldn't seem to force any coherency into her head. She kept flashing back to that dream. The heat, the excitement . . . the terror . . .

With a little moan, she set the cup down hard on the edge of the rug-stacked bed. It nearly overturned, but Silveri's quick hand reached out and caught it.

"Miss Beck," he said, leaning toward her, concern lacing his voice, "you are exhausted. Sleep now. You should be safe for whatever remains of this night. The binding is complete, and the Thorn Maiden will not attempt a return until after sundown tomorrow. Please, Miss Beck. There will be plenty of time for you to leave Roseward before her return, I assure you. But you mustn't attempt a removal until you've rested."

Nelle nodded mutely, letting his words roll over her, allowing herself to be comforted. She lay down on the rugs, her eyes staring and unfocused, and was vaguely aware of him as he draped the blanket over her body, vaguely aware when he rose and slowly backed away. Perhaps she ought to say something, but she couldn't think what. Part of her wanted to reach out, to beg him to stay. She didn't like the idea of remaining alone in the dark after all she had seen, all she had learned.

But she couldn't quite bring herself to say the words.

Silveri looked down at her. He appeared tall and ominous in the shadows; she couldn't see his face, only the glint of his eyes. "Rest," he said again. "You are safe. For now."

With those words he turned for the stair, and within a few breaths he had climbed up through the ceiling and vanished.

The weight of loneliness closed in around her. Nelle tucked herself down under the blanket, pulling her legs up to her chest. Sleep was impossible. Dire prospects loomed on the horizon of her mind no matter which way she turned.

Would she return to Wimborne and face Gaspard? Or would she attempt to elude him, to find her father and escape the city according to her original plan? Could she and Papa make a life of some kind for themselves out in the wide, terrible world beyond Wimborne's walls? They'd starve in a ditch soon enough, unless she returned to her Mother's training. Her nimble fingers could keep Papa alive for a little while at least.

Until Cloven and his crew hunted them down and dragged them back to Gaspard on their knees.

She squeezed her eyes tightly shut. Then, suddenly, she sat up. Her brow knotted in a curious frown. Perhaps those questions couldn't be answered; perhaps she couldn't fathom even the next few hours of her future. But one thing she could know, here and now . . .

Flinging back the blanket, she slid out of the alcove bed. Her feet, still slippered, made no sound as she crossed the cold floor to the little stash of kitchen supplies on the side table. She reached among them and withdrew the jar of Sweet Dreams. Carrying it with her back to the hearth, she knelt down to where the fire's remaining light could shine on the jar's contents. She lifted the lid, looked inside. When last she'd checked, there were three doses left of Mother's fae concoction.

Now there were only two.

Nelle drew a long breath and let it out slowly, her breath frosting in the air. She replaced the lid and sat there on the hearth for some time, her gaze on the flames but her vision far away.

"It was only a dream," she whispered. Then again, more

firmly, "It was only a dream."

But this wasn't true. At least, not entirely.

Soran stood at the south window of the lighthouse tower, watching the sunrise.

The Evenspire was clearer this time of day, more visible through the boundary haze. He watched how the sun played on its brilliant white surface, almost too blinding to look at. Proof that the connection between Roseward and the mortal world was still strong. Proof that he must go on living and striving.

Yes. He must go on. Alone.

He couldn't have said how long he stood there. Nor could he consciously admit what he watched for. But when suddenly a bright head of red hair appeared down below, walking to the edge of the cliff, his heart lurched in his chest.

So. She was going.

Without waiting for him to come down, without saying goodbye.

She was making good her escape. Just as she ought to do. Whatever she'd experienced at the Thorn Maiden's hands last night, it must have finally been enough to convince her. Better to face the wolves on the streets of Wimborne than the nightmares haunting Roseward.

Turning away from the window, Soran stalked across the chamber and sank down on the edge of his bed. He rested his elbows on his knees and buried his face in his hands. He wouldn't watch her go, wouldn't watch her walk away along the cliff path, making for the harbor where her boat waited. It would do no good to prolong the pain. He must accept it now, endure it.

And then forget.

Forget the events of these last few days. The wonder, the surprise. The pleasure.

Forget that fevered dream.

His hands were cold against his skin, yet he remembered how warm they'd been in those unreal stolen moments. The sensation of her soft form beneath his fingers had been sheer delight. He had felt himself whole again, full of power and passion. Everything he had once been, everything he'd thought lost forever.

And her. Peronelle Beck.

Nelle.

Odd, funny, brave. Foolish and aggravating and lovely.

She was pure beauty come to life.

His fingers tightened against his scalp, digging into his skull. Soon enough, his hair and beard would grow back, covering his hideous face. Soon enough, his memories of these last brief days would be long gone. Other memories would fade as well—his name, his family—all those pieces of himself that were too heartrending to remember, but which her presence had brought back and somehow made bearable.

Roseward would drift on its endless cycle through the Hinter. The ties to the mortal world would loosen. One day they would pull apart altogether. And on that day, he would make a decision: Continue to fight or simply . . . stop.

It wouldn't be a hard decision to make.

How long he sat there, he could not say. But eventually he must rise, must face the emptiness of the room down below. Not total emptiness, anyway. There was still the wyvern with its broken wing he must try to repair. There were still the various small tasks that must be seen to, the wards to protect Roseward's shores from future invasions from the Eledrian realms. He would fill his day, fill his hours. And when night fell, he would go to battle again. He would save the world.

Shrugging into his outer robe, Soran descended the stair, his pace heavy and slow. No smell of cooking porridge or buttery flapcakes rose to meet him. Only the wyvern greeted him as he appeared through the hole in the ceiling. It lay curled up at the door and lifted its long neck, flaring its crest. Then it sprang up onto its hind legs and scrabbled at the door with the claws of its wing-arms. It brayed and chattered eagerly.

"I'm sorry, my friend," Soran said, his voice dull and strangely echoing in that dim chamber. "She's gone. And you must not mourn her going. She deserves to be free."

The fire had burned down to almost nothing on the hearth, and he stood a while, looking at it dully, trying to work up the energy to stoke it back to life. The wyvern crawled over to him and twined around his feet, growling irritably. Probably hoping he could be prevailed upon to attempt a pot of porridge.

Soran curled his lip and turned away. He had no appetite. The wyvern could help itself to raw seagull eggs for all he cared. He needed air, he needed action. He needed to get out of this room. Marching to the door, he took hold of the latch and flung it open.

He froze on the threshold.

She was there. Standing on the edge of the cliff, her arms wrapped around her small frame. Wind billowed through her hair and her skirts, an icy blast that she did not seem to feel.

Soran stared. It couldn't be true. It must be another dream. With a quick shake of his head, he closed his eyes and pinched the bridge of his nose. But when he looked again, she hadn't vanished. She'd only turned slightly to look back at him over her shoulder.

"Morning, sir," she said.

"Miss Beck." The words slipped from his lips, almost soundless. "Miss Beck, what are you . . . Why are you . . .?"

She turned to face him fully, her arms still folded tight. The wind blew her hair across her face, but she shook the stray locks from her eyes and fixed him with the full force of her gaze.

"I've decided I ain't leaving," she said.

The blood drained from his face. Were his knees not locked fast, he would have grabbed the doorway for support.

The girl waited, allowing him a chance to respond. But though his mouth dropped open, no response would come.

She drew a deep breath and exhaled it in a loud gust. "Look here," she said, stepping toward him, her face upturned to his. "I've faced the Thorn Maiden twice now and survived. You can call it luck or fate or chance or whatever you like. But you can't deny I *have* survived."

She was close now. Close enough that he could have counted every one of the freckles dusting her nose and cheeks. Close enough that, if he dared, he could reach out and take hold of her. Just to make certain she was still real. Just to assure himself he was not actually alone.

She tipped her head to one side, fixing him with a studying gaze as though trying to read his expression. "You won't talk me out of it," she said at last. "I feel I have a chance against her, because . . . well, because I have *you* with me."

"Miss Beck—"

One of her hands flashed up sharply, palm out as though to block his words. "No, listen. Back home, I . . . There's no one on my side. I'm alone. All alone against all the monsters. And don't tell me there are no monsters in our world. You lived in it long enough to know better. I'm not saying there are unicorns rampaging up and down the streets, but truth is, I'd face another unicorn any day rather than what waits for me back there. Here, I have a fighting chance. But if I go back to Wimborne, I'm alone. And I'm done for."

Her eyes were bright and round, fixed on him with mingled entreaty and resolve. He hardly knew which was stronger. All he knew for certain was that he could not, in that moment at least, utter any of the protests crowding in the back of his mind. He could only look at her, could only drink in the mere fact of her presence.

Later he would regret it. But later had not yet come.

"Miss Beck," he said at long last, each word as carefully spoken as though he read a spell into being, "you may stay in Roseward as long as you need. And I will do whatever lies within my power to protect you."

"Yes. I know." Pure relief flooded her face, and her mouth curved into a brilliant smile, brighter than the rising sun. Her arms unwrapped from around her middle as though she no longer needed to hold herself together, and she pushed unruly tendrils of hair back out of her eyes. "I know you'll do what you can. But," she added, "I've a few thoughts on that score as well. I think it's time you stopped doing all of the protecting, sir."

He blinked slowly, uncertain he'd heard her right. "I'm sorry? What exactly do you mean?"

"I mean," she said, flashing another of those devastating smiles up at him, "I want you to teach me magic."

ABOUT THE AUTHOR

Sylvia Mercedes makes her home in the idyllic North Carolina countryside with her Handsome Husband, sweet Young Lady, the Tiny Gentleman, and Gummy Bear, the Toothless Wonder Cat. When she's not writing she's . . . okay, let's be honest. When she's not writing, she's running around after her little girl, cleaning up glitter, trying to plan healthy-ish meals, and wondering where she left her phone. In between, she reads a steady diet of fantasy novels.

But mostly she's writing.

After a short career in Traditional Publishing (under a different name), Sylvia decided to take the plunge into the Indie Publishing World and is enjoying every minute of it.

Don't miss the next thrilling installment in

THE SCARRED MAGE OF ROSEWARD
BOOK 2: PRISONER

Meanwhile be sure to read The Rose of Dornrise
And learn the secrets of Soran Silveri's dark past.

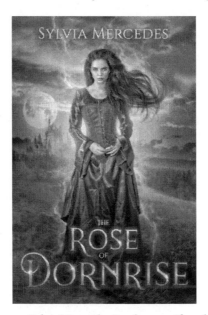

Visit www.SylviaMercedesBooks.com/free-book2
to get your free copy.

Made in the USA
Middletown, DE
13 December 2023

45379834R00243